Peter Watt has spent time as a soldi
trawler deckhand, builder's laboure
salesman, private investigator, pol
chainman and advisor to the Royal Papua New Guinea
Constabulary. He speaks, reads and writes Vietnamese and
Pidgin. He now lives at Maclean on the Clarence River
in northern New South Wales. He has volunteered with
the Volunteer Rescue Association, Queensland Ambulance
Service and currently with the Rural Fire Service. Fishing
and the vast open spaces of outback Queensland are his
main interests in life.

Peter Watt can be contacted at www.peterwatt.com.

Author Photo: Shawn Peene

Also by Peter Watt

The Duffy/Macintosh Series
Cry of the Curlew
Shadow of the Osprey
Flight of the Eagle
To Chase the Storm
To Touch the Clouds
To Ride the Wind
Beyond the Horizon
War Clouds Gather
And Fire Falls
Beneath a Rising Sun
While the Moon Burns
From the Stars Above

The Papua Series
Papua
Eden
The Pacific

The Silent Frontier
The Stone Dragon
The Frozen Circle

The Colonial Series
The Queen's Colonial
The Queen's Tiger
The Queen's Captain
The Colonial's Son
Call of Empire

Excerpts from emails sent to Peter Watt

'Had to drop a quick note. Reading *Cry of the Curlew* again and just had to tell you it's evidence that you are a superb writer/author. You are still at the top of my list. Again thanks for how you weave and blend love, hate, mysticism, tension and other emotions into an addictive work!'

'G'day Peter, I have just finished your book *Call of Empire*. Reading your book was an excellent way to relax. Thanks for the excellent read.'

'Hi Cobber, I have never been so hooked on a book as with your books so please keep the Australian stories going.'

'G'day Peter, I have just about finished reading *Call of Empire* and I felt inspired to write to you. I don't normally read fiction! As an (amateur) historian, I prefer to deal with facts and therefore generally read non-fiction, but I have to say, I am enthralled! Great work, Peter, and all the best for your future efforts.'

'Love all your books, what's next? I've run out!'

'Peter, reading the Frontier series again, I fully realise just how superb an author you are. Everyone I've loaned, described or recommended your books to agrees and does so with enthusiasm and excitement. Alas the poor unfortunate who loves to read and has missed your books!'

'Really enjoyed this [Colonial] series. I am just wondering if you intend to write another one. Hopefully so!'

The Ghosts of AUGUST

PETER WATT

MACMILLAN
Pan Macmillan Australia

Pan Macmillan acknowledges the Traditional Custodians of Country throughout Australia and their connections to lands, waters and communities. We pay our respect to Elders past and present and extend that respect to all Aboriginal and Torres Strait Islander peoples today. We honour more than sixty thousand years of storytelling, art and culture.

This is a work of fiction. Characters, institutions and organisations mentioned in this novel are either the product of the author's imagination or, if real, used fictitiously without any intent to describe actual conduct.

First published 2024 in Macmillan by Pan Macmillan Australia Pty Ltd
1 Market Street, Sydney, New South Wales, Australia, 2000

Copyright © Peter Watt 2024

The moral right of the author to be identified as the author of this work has been asserted.

All rights reserved. No part of this book may be reproduced or transmitted by any person or entity (including Google, Amazon or similar organisations), in any form or by any means, electronic or mechanical, including photocopying, recording, scanning or by any information storage and retrieval system, without prior permission in writing from the publisher.

A catalogue record for this book is available from the National Library of Australia

Typeset in 13/16 pt Bembo MT Pro Regular by Post Pre-press Group

Printed by IVE

The maps featured on pages viii, ix and x are by Laurie Whiddon at Map Illustrations.

The author and the publisher have made every effort to contact copyright holders for material used in this book. Any person or organisation that may have been overlooked should contact the publisher.

Aboriginal and Torres Strait Islander people should be aware that this book may contain images or names of people now deceased.

MIX
Paper | Supporting responsible forestry
FSC
www.fsc.org   FSC® C018183

For my beloved wife, Naomi

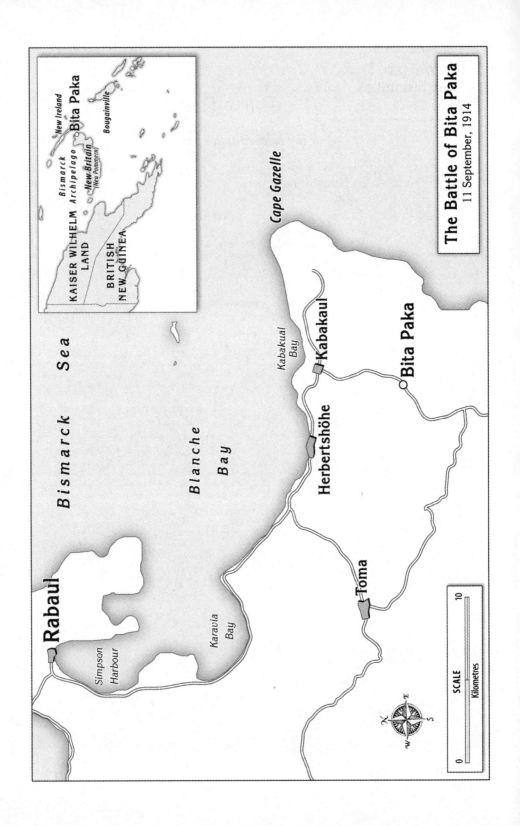

The Battle of Bita Paka
11 September, 1914

Bita Paka

New Ireland
Bismarck Archipelago
New Britain (Neu Pommern)
Bougainville
KAISER WILHELM LAND
BRITISH NEW GUINEA

Bismarck Sea

Cape Gazelle

Kabakaul

Kabakaul Bay

Herbertshöhe

Bita Paka

Blanche Bay

Toma

Rabaul

Simpson Harbour

Karavia Bay

SCALE
Kilometres
0   10

N
S
E
W

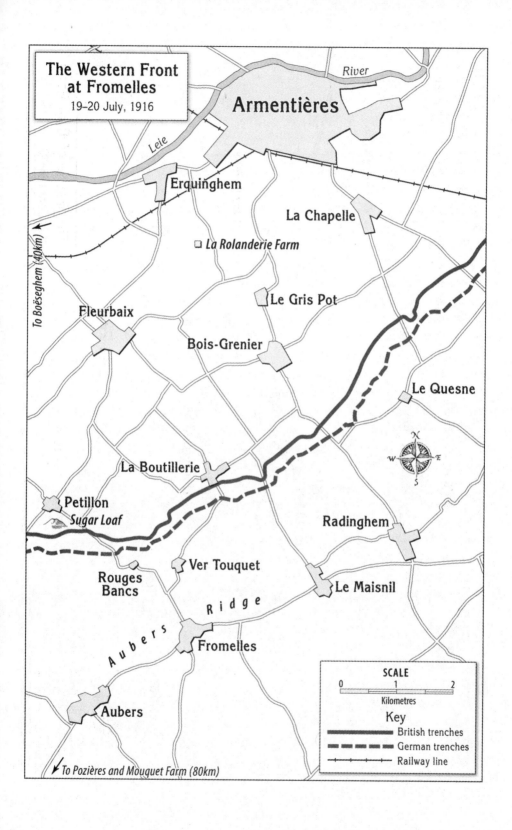

The Western Front at Fromelles
19–20 July, 1916

River

Armentières

Leie

To Boëseghem (40km)

Erquinghem

La Chapelle

◻ *La Rolanderie Farm*

Le Gris Pot

Fleurbaix

Bois-Grenier

Le Quesne

La Boutillerie

N
W E
S

Petillon
Sugar Loaf

Radinghem

Ver Touquet

Rouges
Bancs

Le Maisnil

R i d g e

A u b e r s

Fromelles

SCALE
0   1   2
Kilometres

Aubers

Key

British trenches
German trenches
Railway line

To Pozières and Mouquet Farm (80km)

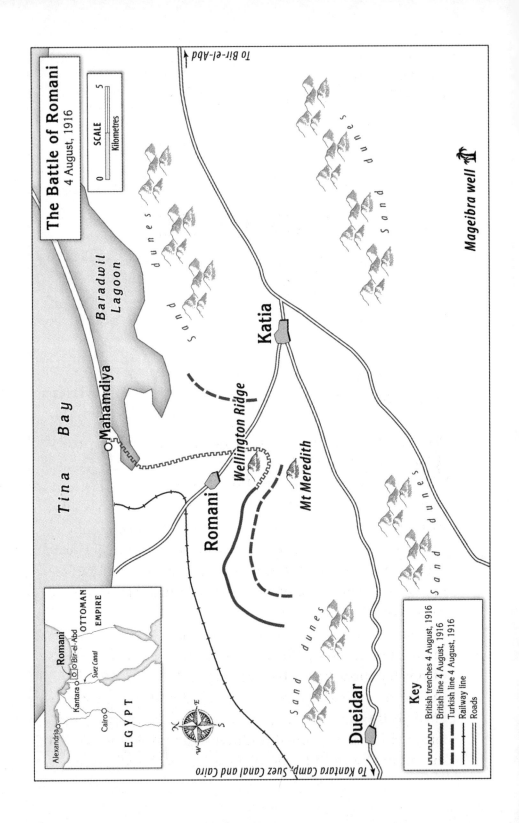

The Battle of Romani
4 August, 1916

SCALE

0   5
Kilometres

To Bir-el-Abd ↑

Tina Bay

Baradwil Lagoon

Mahamdiya

Sand dunes

Sand dunes

Katia

Wellington Ridge

Mt Meredith

Romani

Sand dunes

Sand dunes

Mageibra well

Dueidar

To Kantara Camp, Suez Canal and Cairo ↑

Key
— British trenches 4 August, 1916
– – British line 4 August, 1916
▬ ▬ Turkish line 4 August, 1916
+ + Railway line
═ Roads

OTTOMAN EMPIRE

Romani
Kantara ○ ○Bir-el-Abd
Suez Canal

Alexandria ○

Cairo ○

EGYPT

N
W E
S

PROLOGUE

New Year's Eve, 1913

Josiah Steele sat alone in the library of his mansion over-looking Sydney Harbour.

By his hand was a glass of single malt Scotch. The dim light of the electric chandelier illuminated the face of a man in his mid-fifties, a man who had seen much of life in military campaigns from Afghanistan to Africa many years earlier in service to the Queen. The creases at the edges of his eyes were those of someone who had stared into the vastness of those arid lands.

Outside his great double-storeyed house with its manicured gardens, Josiah could hear the distant sounds of revelry: boat horns bleated on the harbour below and the cheers of drunken revellers drifted up from the streets of his leafy suburb. He glanced at the face of the grand-father clock as it chimed midnight and raised his glass to the night sky outside the open window. Josiah fervently hoped that 1914 would prove a better year than those just past.

Tragedy had dogged his family in recent months, with the death of his beloved sister-in-law, Rosemary, wife of his younger brother, Samuel, in early 1913. She had been such a vibrant and beautiful woman, so active in furthering the social causes of women, that she had seemed invulnerable. What had appeared to be a summer cold had quickly developed into pneumonia and she had died in Samuel's arms. Josiah saw that the death of Rosemary had ripped the heart and soul out of his younger brother. Completely devastated and still grieving, Sam had set sail in the family schooner, the *Ella*, for ports in the South Pacific on Steele company business, leaving behind his children, ten-year-old Georgette and nine-year-old Saul. Both children were in the care of a nanny Josiah had employed.

Josiah knew his younger brother loved his children, but the death of Rosemary had broken him, and Josiah understood that Sam needed time to mourn in his own way. The *Ella* had been a possession that had provided so many wonderful memories for Sam and Rosemary as they had sailed the Pacific in their first couple of years of marriage. Both of Sam's children had been conceived on the schooner. Josiah knew that his brother needed time to accept the loss of his wife and that he would eventually return home to his family and children.

The family was scattered; Josiah's beloved sister, Rebecca, was married to a German aristocrat, Duke Maximillian von Kellermann, and lived on their vast estate in Bavaria where Josiah's son, David, a young man in his late twenties, was currently visiting his best friend, Hermann – von Kellermann's son by his first marriage.

Josiah's other son, Benjamin, still lived in Sydney.

However, to Josiah's consternation, despite being only a year younger than David, Ben lived a rootless life. He had attempted to take on a job with the family enterprises but was obviously bored with the clerical position. Josiah anguished over his younger son's future.

Josiah's daughters, Judith and Rose, were now in their mid-twenties. Both were happily married with children and living in Sydney. Josiah reflected on the fact that all his family members had drawn closer to the practice of their Jewish religion – except his sons who, although they dutifully attended their synagogue, tended to stray on matters of a kosher diet and did not always observe the Sabbath. But his daughters were more spiritual, and both had married successful Jewish men and adhered to the traditional ways of their strong faith.

Josiah felt guilty that he was not a stricter observer of the old ways himself, but he had through his life found himself with a foot in the two worlds of Judaism and Christianity. His own father had been a Catholic, although in name more than in deed. Such was the nature of Australian culture, Josiah mused. His wife, Marian, was also a Christian, but had always encouraged her children to practise their Jewish faith.

Josiah raised his glass to the open window once again and muttered, 'To 1914 – may it bring peace and happiness to my family.' He took a long sip of his Scotch and sighed.

★

Samuel Steele moaned and sweated on his bunk under a mosquito net erected inside his tent. Malaria had him in its grip once again. Although Sam's camp was deep in the rainforest on the western-most edge of the range of rugged hills of the Markham Valley of German New Guinea, the hiss of a lantern was the only sound he could hear. Malaria meant his gold prospecting venture was on a temporary hold.

'Sam, we need to pack it in and return to the coast.' The voice of Sam's friend Nate Welsh broke through the gentle noise of the dim lantern sitting on a wooden crate beside Sam's field cot. 'We haven't had any luck up here and our natives are sure the Kukukuku have a raiding party nearby.'

Sam was in his late forties and the man kneeling beside him was of a similar age. Nate, a native of New Zealand, had served alongside Sam in the Transvaal during the Boer War fourteen years earlier, which was where Sam had lost his leg at the battle of Elands River. The bonds forged in war had united them as brothers. Nate's own brother, Brendan, was on the *Ella* anchored off the mouth of the Markham River east of the valley. Brendan had also fought at Elands River. The three men were a well-known trio in the waters of German New Guinea.

'They sure the Kukus are skulking around?' Sam asked in a hoarse voice as Nate raised a canvas water bag to his friend's lips.

'Pretty bloody sure,' Nate answered, knowing the well-earned fierce reputation of the small but stocky warriors of the inland tribes. 'By the way, happy new year.'

'Might explain the silence around us,' Sam said, struggling to sit up while reaching for the Lee Enfield .303 rifle by his bed. 'I think you're right; it might be time to head for the coast, but we will wait for first light before we make a move.'

'You sure you're okay to trek out of the hills?' Nate asked, his concern apparent. 'I notice your leg has been playing up a bit lately.' Nate nodded towards Sam's artificial leg which connected below the knee.

'I'll be okay,' Sam replied, placing the rifle over his shoulder, fully loaded and ready for use.

Nate nodded and rose to his feet, leaving the water bag beside Sam. 'I will be keeping watch with our head boy. The sun should be up in about three hours, and then we will break camp.'

Sam fell back against the damp pillow. His whole body was bathed in sweat, but the fever appeared to be dissipating – along with the fevered dreams of death that had accompanied it.

But when the sun rose over the rainforest giants that shadowed the world beneath, the vast canopy was suddenly rent by the war cries of the dreaded native warriors, who unleashed a shower of arrows down on the tiny camp in the clearing. Sam and Nate were once again fighting for their lives, pouring a volley of high-velocity rifle rounds into the surrounding forest. Aside from his rifle, Sam was also armed with an American Browning semi-automatic pistol on his hip as a last resort in case he had no time to reload the rifle.

This was not the first time that Nate and Sam had faced the Kukukuku warriors. In a previous clash a few weeks earlier they had killed three of them for the loss of two of their own native porters. These were savage lands, but they were also a frontier made attractive by the promise of gold, even though the source was yet to be discovered. German and Australian prospectors vied with each other over an unmapped territorial boundary across the centre of the island, with its raging rivers and rugged, almost impenetrable tropical rainforests. Once they had retreated out of the mountains, Sam knew they would reach the broad Markham Valley with its tall kunai grass plains, and beyond that the mouth of the river and the relative safety of their schooner.

Then, as suddenly as it had started, the rain of arrows ceased and the warriors surrounding them fell back under the cover of the thick rainforest foliage. Taking a quick head count, Sam saw that none of the five native porters had been injured, but he and Nate knew it was time to retreat to the *Ella* and reassess their gold prospecting expedition into this wild, mysterious land that was under the control of the German government.

Part One

January–August 1914

The Storm Gathers Over
the Pacific

ONE

Archibald Stokes was a civil servant working for the Australian Department of Defence, and at twenty-five years of age he was already prematurely balding. Always clean-shaven and humourless, he made no secret of the fact that he harboured dreams of climbing the civil service ladder as a career public servant, which was why he was now wondering why he had been delegated the task of examining a cabinet full of files left by Sir Douglas Wade, who had died peacefully in his sleep a fortnight earlier.

Archibald knew that Sir Douglas had been a shadowy high-ranking civil servant in the new federal government. There had been rumours in the stuffy offices of the federal bureaucracy that Wade, who had never married, had had little time for a social life, so dedicated was he to shielding the new nation from any possible foreign enemies. Sadly, many of Wade's colleagues had dismissed his warnings that one day Australians might face a war, given the tense conditions in Europe over the past year. Perhaps the worsening situation was the reason a directive had been made for a civil servant from the department to retrieve a file sent to the Australian government some short time after Federation.

Archibald retrieved the file in question from the wooden cabinet, aware of its title: *An Outline of Possible Imperial German Threat in the Indian and Pacific Oceans.* The public servant sat down at a desk, opened the folder and adjusted his spectacles. It was midmorning, and he could hear others of the small staff chatting as they took morning tea in the adjoining office, which had a single window overlooking the streets of Sydney. Beyond their chatter, he could just make out the sounds of horse-drawn wagons and flimsy automobiles moving along the narrow streets below.

Inside the folder were a jumble of papers. The top sheet contained typed copy by Sir Douglas, along with his signature. The report summarised his concern that the Pacific German fleet operating out of China and also Rabaul might pose a serious threat to Australia in the event that war became a reality between the British and German empires. Archibald scanned the document and nodded his head in agreement with the former head of the obscure information-gathering department. He shared the belief that the close proximity of the Germans in the Pacific might pose a problem if war broke out in Europe.

Archibald turned to the next sheet of paper, which appeared to be a covering letter attached to a thick pile of documents. He raised his eyebrows when he saw the signature at the bottom of the covering sheet. It was simply a single letter in green ink: *C.*

Archibald took a breath when he recognised that the covering report was a recommendation from the head of the British Secret Service Bureau of the Admiralty War Office in London. It was the signature of the eccentric naval captain Mansfield Smith-Cumming, whose reputation was well known to the Australian government. He was a driven man who collected information to be converted to intelligence. Archibald had heard rumours that the British naval intelligence officer and Sir Douglas Wade had become personal friends after the late knight's numerous visits to London.

Archibald turned his attention to the thick pile of papers beneath this letter. They comprised a translation of a strategic German report that had fallen into British hands years earlier outlining that, in the event of war between Britain and Germany, the German navy should attack and bombard Australia's eastern coastal cities, and land troops at Gladstone to seize its highly graded coal supplies. There was a similar strategy for neighboring New Zealand. No doubt an attack along these lines would be devastating to the coastal towns – major centres of population – located along Australia's east coast. Archibald also knew that such an attack would force a significant part of the British navy to steam from European waters, thus weakening its ability to defend Britain as well as stymie any known strategy to blockade German ports.

Archibald leaned back in his chair and considered the international state of affairs. He knew trouble was brewing in the Balkans and that Turkey had been involved in fighting in Bulgaria. There had been a military coup in Turkey by what the newspapers called the 'young Turks' the previous year, but Archibald did not consider the Turks to be any threat to British interests. It had also been reported that Serbians were slaughtering unarmed Moslems in the Balkans. The year 1913 had even seen strife on the border between the United States of America and Mexico, where American troops had clashed with and killed Mexican army troops. The dawn of 1914 had seen Ulster in Ireland on the brink of civil war in Britain's backyard. Reports from London were troubling; most European nations appeared to be arming for what was considered a coming war on the continent.

It was no wonder Sir Douglas Wade's report had suddenly raised interest in the Department of Defence, Archibald mused as he closed the file. But for now, it was time to join his staff and indulge in a cup of tea in the staffroom.

★

Josiah's second-eldest boy was a problem. Like his uncle Sam, who he worshipped, Benjamin was big and strong and had a restless nature. Josiah was fortunate to have friends in the police who were able to keep Ben out of prison for his brawling ways in seedy hotels, a habit Josiah had hoped would wane as Ben neared the age of thirty, but which had stubbornly remained a feature of his son's life. However, it was not the brawls that worried him most but the fact Josiah knew his son was attractive to the ladies who mixed in those establishments. As a father, Josiah feared his impulsive son would one day bring one home as a prospective wife.

Ben now stood in Josiah's library at his harbourside home sporting a large bruise on his cheek and appearing remorseful.

'There were two of them, Father, and I was forced to defend myself when they started taunting me as a Jew Boy.'

Also in the library was Ben's beloved uncle Sam, recently arrived back from German New Guinea, and, still weakened from his latest bout of malaria, leaning on a cane.

'Did you win?' Sam asked.

'I used some of that Chinese stuff you taught me, Uncle Sam.' Ben beamed. 'They both had to be taken to hospital.'

'God almighty!' Josiah exploded. 'What if you had killed them?'

'I made sure that their injuries were not fatal,' Ben replied sheepishly, and Josiah glared at his brother for a moment.

'Ben is more like you every day,' Josiah said, rubbing his forehead in despair and turning back to his son. 'What am I going to do with you?'

Ben did not reply. He knew that his father had attempted several times to incorporate him into the family business, but, despite achieving good marks at school when he'd put his mind to it, Ben had failed to prove himself competent. Josiah had even sent Ben west to one of their sheep stations, but there, too, he had proved himself inept at management. He was uncomfortably aware he was the black sheep in the family.

For his part, Josiah despaired. Both his sons were unmarried, and Ben was such a contrast to his elder brother, David, who had proved to be a model son, stable, conscientious and good. It was interesting that David had not inherited the large frame that Ben had; Josiah suspected his younger son took after their Russian ancestors on Josiah's mother's side. Not that either of his sons had much interest in their heritage. Oh, if only he had four daughters and not just two, Josiah thought, but then felt a touch of guilt, remembering that David was still in Germany attempting to develop business interests for their numerous products being produced in Australia.

Josiah also knew that within the week Sam would be returning with the *Ella* to the waters of German New Guinea, where he had established a good rapport with many German officials. It helped that he spoke reasonable

German – as did David. This was because Josiah's sister, Rebecca – or Becky to her family – had lived in German society for fifteen years as a lady of high rank. Thinking about Ben's latest fight, Josiah recalled a suggestion Sam had put to him earlier in the week, and made a decision.

'Ben, I want you to go with your uncle Sam when he sails back to New Guinea,' he said, and noticed Ben's face light up.

'Truly, Father?' Ben exclaimed.

'I discussed the matter with your father when I got back,' Sam said. 'I think you need to get away from the vices that Sydney offers, and experience real work. We could use you on the *Ella*, and in New Guinea.'

Ben turned to Sam. 'Thank you, Uncle Sam. I am more than prepared to work hard.'

Sam grinned. 'You might be begging me to come home after a few weeks in the jungle of the mountains we trek in search of gold,' he replied. 'But we will see. I suggest you get your kit together, because we sail tomorrow morning.'

'You are dismissed,' Josiah said. He found it hard to break with his military past as an officer for the Queen and then for Australia; he often still resorted to military language.

When Ben had left the library, Josiah turned to his brother. 'Your children will miss you very much,' Josiah said, unstopping a bottle of single malt Scotch, pouring two crystal glasses and handing one to Sam, who sat down in a leather chair opposite his brother.

'I miss Georgette and Saul all the time I am away from them, but I need to finish what I have started,' Sam said with a note of sadness. 'When I have done so, I will always be with them. In the meantime, I know they are being well cared for.'

'You know that what I am asking you is more important

than finding the elusive mother lode of gold,' Josiah said. 'When I was approached by the man from the Defence Department, he told me that in his research into the late Sir Douglas Wade's papers, our family name came up on top-secret missions our father, you and I conducted in German New Guinean waters all that time past. He also knew our intimate connection to General Maximillian von Kellermann's family. In these troubling times in Europe, he said our government has a desperate need to know what the Imperial German Navy is planning in our part of the world.'

'I remember so well those sad days when we lost our father.' Sam sighed. 'We have a blood connection to New Guinea, and I raise a toast to one of the most remarkable men this country has ever known. To Colonel Ian Steele, our beloved father.'

Josiah raised his glass to meet Sam's.

'So, your man in the Defence Department wants us to travel to Rabaul and observe any signs that the Germans have a plan for us in the event of war,' confirmed Sam. 'I know one or two military officers there from my days drinking in the German Club when we were purchasing copra.'

'You would not be viewed as a threat; I have heard reports from contacts that you are seen as a simple gold prospector and occasional merchant, and there is some respect for your war service in South Africa. The Germans – particularly the Prussians – hold a man's military service in war in high regard. That it cost you your leg is almost akin to the pride some Prussian officers hold for receiving a duelling scar. Plus, it helps that your sister is married to a German general.'

'The perfect cover,' Sam said with a facetious note in his voice. 'But I will need to keep your son in line around any *Fräuleins* we may encounter up there.'

'I am sure you will be able to do that,' Josiah said with a smile. 'I sometimes think Ben would rather have been your son.'

'That is not true,' Sam replied. 'It is just that he does not understand that my life has not been all good. When I look back on it, the best thing that happened to me was meeting Rosemary and having my children with her. I see Rosemary in my beloved daughter Georgie's face every time she smiles. It breaks my heart.'

Josiah could see tears welling in his big and tough brother's eyes and stood to walk over to him, placing his hand on Sam's shoulder.

No further words were needed, and Sam rose to walk away, aware that he was now once again in the military service of his country.

★

Archibald Stokes hurried to the office of his head of department. It was confirmed that the Steele family would assist with a covert operation to Rabaul, where Archibald felt most intelligence could be gleaned on German intentions in the Pacific. The Kaiser held sway over islands from Samoa to the Micronesian spread, as well as the northern section of the big strategic island of New Guinea, while Australia occupied the southern section.

It had occurred to Archibald that it would be a good idea to suggest that the New Zealand government be informed of the Australian government's plans to collect intelligence for any future joint operations in the Pacific region as they, too, would be under armed threat should war erupt between Germany and Britain. This would have to be discussed with the department head, though, which was why Archibald was making his way to the head's office. Reaching the door, he knocked and held his breath. Although Australia was not at war, he knew it was a certainty that the Australian government would declare its military support for Britain if the powder keg of nationalist sentiment that was Europe in the present day were to ignite. Australia was a proud member of the British empire, and it would be loyal to its roots. Archibald was an intelligent man and had a feeling in his gut that if Australia went to war with Germany, the first shots would be fired in their own backyard – the Pacific Islands.

'Enter,' a voice boomed, and Archibald stepped inside his superior's office armed with his ideas on strategies that might – most probably would – be needed to counter the Imperial German Navy stationed in China and Rabaul. But he was not sure that his thoughts on the subject would be paid any attention, because Archibald knew the man he was about to speak to was a pompous, self-important and ignorant fool.

TWO

David Steele did not have his younger brother's physique. He was shorter, although still just above average height for a man growing up in Australia. But he had a handsome countenance attractive to women who were aware that he was an intelligent and charming man, and the bearing of a military man who had once held a commission in his grandfather's militia regiment based in Sydney. However, David had been forced to resign his commission some years prior due to the demands of his work managing the vast commercial enterprises of the Steele industries and the family's farming concerns.

David knew that the seeds of their family fortune could be found in his own grandfather's military campaign in the Crimean War, where he had been involved in the looting of a Russian baggage train. But that was just a vague old family story long dismissed by his descendants.

It was early spring in Bavaria, where David was taking time off to catch up with his dear friend, Hermann von Kellermann, and also his aunt, Rebecca von Kellermann, sister of his father and wife of Prussian general and duke, Maximillian von Kellermann. It wasn't his first visit to his friend's castle, the capital of the dukedom, as he had visited with his brother, Ben, five years earlier. However, Ben had not been very impressed by the culture, despite the beauty of the Bavarian countryside with its medieval houses and beautiful forests bordered by rolling fields of grazing cattle and dairy cows.

On this trip David had been on a tour of England, France and now Germany, working in the interests of his family to investigate and establish future trade connections, so he was enjoying the respite from work afforded him by the visit to his close friend and his aunt Becky.

He had now spent two weeks as a guest at the castle, and in that time had found himself wined and dined by his German family. It had been at one of the lavish dinners that David had glanced across the candlelit table lined with German aristocrats to see a beautiful young woman sitting opposite him. She had raven-black hair, elegantly arranged, and striking green eyes. David took a breath. She was a beauty in any language. As she spooned soup from her bowl, she looked up at David. A faint smile crossed her face, and it was then that David knew he must be introduced to her.

He leaned towards Hermann, who was wearing his dark army dress uniform with its ornate display of colour and rank.

'Who is that remarkable lady sitting opposite us?' David whispered as Hermann lifted his goblet of wine.

'Oh, you mean my cousin, Caroline. She is the daughter of Count von Neumann, and his only child. Her mother passed away some years ago and the old man dotes on her,' Hermann replied, smiling at Caroline, who returned his gesture with a tilt of her head. 'As a matter of fact, her father has commercial interests in copra plantations in your part of the world – along with factories in the Ruhr – and other business interests with the Krupp family. I'm afraid my cousin has a reputation for being a bit wild and I imagine her father fears he may never marry her off to a respectable family. She prefers to use his money to travel the world seeking adventure, and, I suspect, takes the odd lover or two.' Hermann turned to David. 'I would give you some advice, old friend, and that is not to fall for her charms, as you will only be hurt. Better find a village girl while you are here and have some amorous fun before you return home. Actually, I was planning to spend an evening in the village tavern tomorrow night, if you'd like to join me. I go there from time to time to let off steam.'

David turned back to his dinner, but despite Hermann's warning, he could not take his eyes off Caroline. He was confident she wasn't aware of his attentions, though, as she spent the evening laughing and smiling at the conversation of a young and handsome German naval officer sitting beside her, who Hermann confirmed had escorted Caroline to the dinner that night. David experienced an irrational surge of jealousy towards the man, despite the fact that he knew nothing about Caroline – except what Hermann had told him.

Eventually the dinner finished and David and Hermann made their way to the ballroom where the guests gathered to drink French champagne while the men smoked cigars. Laughter and loud voices filled the room as the aristocratic guests mingled to gossip and discuss the problems Europe was facing.

Looking around, David noticed that the German naval officer had left Caroline alone for a moment while he spoke with other senior German officers present. David gripped the sleeve of his friend's uniform. 'Hermann, will you introduce me to your cousin?' he said, and Hermann frowned.

'If it is your wish to get your fingers burned, I will do so, but remember I warned you, she will only toy with you.'

But true to his word, Hermann set off across the room, David in his wake.

'My dear cousin, Caroline, I would like to introduce my very good friend and guest of the family, Mr David Steele. His aunt is my stepmother.'

Caroline turned to David. 'I already know about you, Mr Steele,' she said sweetly in German. 'You are from Australia and a successful businessman. I heard you speaking earlier, and I must compliment you on your German – it is very good. I also speak French and English and hope to learn Russian.'

'That is very impressive,' David answered in English.

'Thank you, Mr Steele,' Caroline replied, also in English. 'I hope my grasp of your language is adequate.'

'I am even more impressed,' David answered. 'You speak English with little trace of an accent.'

'I was able to live in London for a few years and I have always had an interest in foreign languages.'

'It was fortunate you did not live in Scotland,' said David with a grin. 'Otherwise, you may have developed their accent, which even many English speakers find hard to understand.'

Caroline broke into a broad smile. 'I can see that you have a sense of humour, which is something we Germans are not renowned for,' she said.

Hermann shook his head. 'I can see that you and my

cousin have plenty to talk about,' he said. 'I think I might join a friend from my regiment to discuss more important subjects than a grasp of foreign languages.' With this parting statement Hermann made his way to a young German officer a short distance away.

'Ah, here we were, almost alone,' Caroline said as her German escort returned.

'Caroline, I see you have company,' the young naval officer said in German with a note of aggression in his voice.

Caroline replied in English. 'Kurt, I would like to introduce Hermann's friend from Australia, Mr David Steele, who is a guest of Duke von Kellermann. Our duchess Rebecca is David's aunt.'

With the mention of the general's connection to David, the naval officer lost some of his antagonism – presumably, David thought, because the highly respected Bavarian family had strong links to the Kaiser himself. But he did not extend his hand in friendship.

'Pleased to make your acquaintance, *Oberleutnant zur See*,' David said, using the low rank of the navy officer's designation in a way David knew would irritate him.

'You have not served?' the German officer asked in a subtle war of words.

'I have held an infantry commission in our army at home,' David replied. 'But I can presume neither you nor I have seen active service – so we are even.'

The German officer stiffened, as though David's remark were a slap in the face. 'With the tense situation in Europe, that situation may change,' Kurt muttered, scowling.

'Gentlemen,' Caroline interrupted serenely, 'I am sure that neither the Kaiser nor the Russian Czar, or the French president or King of England, for that matter, desires that we ever go to war, and as I will be departing shortly for

Rabaul to inspect the management of our copra plantations in that part of the world, I too hope peace prevails.'

David glanced at Caroline in surprise. 'When do you leave?' he asked.

'My father has organised that I depart next week from Hamburg,' Caroline answered. 'I am looking forward to visiting that part of the world as I have read many stories from our administration there of cannibals and headhunters. It sounds like an exciting adventure.'

'My grandfather died in that part of the world as a result of a native arrow,' David cautioned. 'It is dangerous country for any man – let alone a woman.'

Caroline appeared bemused at David's declaration of danger. 'I was not born to be a *Hausfrau*, Mr Steele. Life is an adventure and sometimes dangerous, I know. I have always wanted to visit the lands of headhunters and canni- bals. Germany is a land of docile agrarian people living a safe and boring life, so it is only in its colonies of Africa and the Pacific that one can face real excitement. They are still frontiers we know so little about.'

David could see that Hermann was right in his observa- tions concerning his cousin; she was no ordinary woman. He could also see that her beauty would allow her to have her pick of any eligible man anywhere in the world. Hermann had informed David that she was just twenty-five years of age but had travelled more widely in that quarter of a century, and been exposed to many more diverse cultures, than most people would experience in their lifetimes. David found himself both fascinated and smitten by the beautiful woman, but he also realised that it would take a very special man to win her heart. He hoped that would be him.

★

Ben Steele prayed for death to take him out of his absolute misery. As tough as he was – or had thought he was – this sickness went beyond all that a human could bear.

'Tea helps,' Nate Welsh said cheerfully while Ben leaned over the railings of the schooner as she rose on the big waves then slid gracefully into the following troughs of the tropical seas off the coast of Queensland.

'Just let me die,' Ben groaned, lifting his head before the next bout of nausea struck him.

'Not what you expected?' Nate chuckled, sipping on his own enamel mug of unsweetened black tea. 'If it is any consolation, I was the same way on my first trip on the *Ella*, but I got used to it and now I very rarely get seasick.'

The former New Zealander's words did not help but at least Ben knew he would probably survive despite the agony he was currently suffering. The last week of sailing north had been a living hell, and he had lost some weight as a result. But there had been times when the seas had been calmer and his stomach settled, and he had actually enjoyed a few moments of his first seagoing voyage under blue skies.

'I hate to interrupt you feeding the fish but your uncle Sam needs us all below for a meeting,' Nate said.

Ben wiped his mouth with the back of his sleeve and pushed himself away from the railing. When he straightened up the world spun around him, but he forced himself not to be sick again, and on unsteady legs he followed Nate below where they were met by Sam and the schooner's captain, Keith Ward. Ward was in his fifties, tall and with the tanned face of a man who had spent a lot of time in tropical waters. He was very experienced with island trading and knew the waters as well as he knew his family back in Sydney.

'You look like you could do with a good meal of fried eggs and bacon.' Sam grinned at his nephew.

'Hold the bacon,' Ben groaned. 'It's not kosher.'

Sam shook his head. 'Since when have you ever complied with our dietary laws?' He knew his nephew was not a strict adherent to his Jewish religion and suspected that it was really the thought of the greasy bacon that had prompted the comment. 'Anyway, I asked you down here for this meeting, Ben, because I am about to tell you what the real mission of our expedition is. Our primary role is to collect information about the German navy in this part of the world. The task has been sanctioned by your father, who hopes that he can trust you to be discreet in anything you learn from our less-than-innocent activities in German territory.'

Ben nodded even though he was stunned by the announcement – although not entirely surprised. He had heard whispers over the years of a similar mission undertaken by his father long ago in German New Guinean waters.

'Our best source for any intelligence will be Rabaul,' Sam said, pointing to the northern tip of the large island a few hundred miles off the eastern coast of New Guinea. The chart was labelled *Neu-Pommern*. 'The Germans have established a naval port there as it has a deep harbour. Rabaul will be our base for as much time as we need to find out all that we can. We have also been tasked with learning as much as possible about a vital German radio station we know is located near this place, Bita Paka, a short distance from Rabaul. Do you have any questions at this stage?'

The three other men shook their heads.

'And now for some good news,' Sam continued. 'We are not far from Townsville, and we will be docking to take on supplies. I think that we have all earned a day's shore leave.'

To be on a surface that did not rise, fall and roll was something Ben thought had to be the next best thing in his life to bedding a beautiful woman. He made his way back to the deck, where the four Islander deckhands were carrying out their tasks of maintaining the schooner's equipment. Ben hoped to sight land. Even now he thought he could feel the seasickness abating as he imagined sitting down with a cold beer in one of the town's hotels.

THREE

An opportunity arose two days after the dinner at which David had met Caroline for David to be in her company again. Hermann suggested that he and David participate in a boar hunt in the castle estate forests, and mentioned that his cousin and the naval officer would be accompanying them, along with a couple of his regimental officer friends and the mayor of the nearby village.

It was a beautiful spring morning and the rolling pastures were already sprouting wildflowers with a backdrop of snowcapped mountaintops on the horizon. Despite spring arriving there was still a chill in the air and steam on the snorting muzzles of their mounts. David was presented with a superb handcrafted German hunting rifle similar to the one Hermann carried.

Servants packed a horse-drawn cart with picnic delicacies to follow the hunting party into the forest, where they would set up a pavilion. A bet was made between the two close friends as to who would make the first kill, and Hermann added that any deer also counted, as venison would help stock the castle's larder.

David swung himself into the saddle of his mount just as Caroline arrived on her horse, which David admiringly appraised as a large and expensive black thoroughbred gelding. Caroline wore a long dress split to allow her to ride as a man would, and atop her head she had piled her shiny black hair into a bun which supported a small and elegant hat. Beside her rode the German naval officer, who gave David a frosty reception. He was wearing a civilian suit and hat.

'Mr Steele,' Caroline greeted David when she rode up to him. 'I see that you must also enjoy the thrills of the hunt.'

'It will be an experience,' David answered. 'We do not have the variety of game that you have here in Germany. We hunt our pigs because they have proved a nuisance to farmers, but I am afraid my experience with hunting has been mostly as a young boy shooting the many rabbits that infest the pastures on our sheep farms.'

'Well, I hope that we bag at least a deer as I rather enjoy venison,' Caroline replied as Hermann rode over to them.

'Time to commence the hunt,' Hermann said, and the small party set out for the forest ahead of them.

It was eerily silent when they entered the forest. The hunting party spread out in a skirmish line. David rode holding the reins in one hand and his rifle in the other. After they had gone a short distance, Hermann turned to him.

'You ride like a cavalryman,' he noted.

'My old regiment is a mounted infantry unit that saw action in the South African war when my uncle Sam was a member. Sadly, he lost his leg in the Transvaal fighting at the siege of Elands River.'

'Ah, our Kaiser was more inclined to support the Boers in that war,' said Hermann. 'We were able to supply our Dutch brothers with Mauser rifles to resist the English, and also some artillery.'

'My uncle Sam said he had a very healthy respect for the Mauser rifles,' David replied, just as Caroline rode up to join them.

'I notice that you are both talking about war, which I find boring,' she said. 'It seems that my cousin is obsessed with military matters, but I suspect, Mr Steele, you are not of a similar mind.'

'My family has a strong military tradition, but it's true, I prefer the challenge of the financial world.'

'Then you are a man I think I could have a conversation with away from military matters, which seems to be the only subject among the menfolk at most social functions I attend lately. Even my escort, Kurt, is gripped by the subject. Maybe it will be different when I visit my father's copra plantations in New Guinea. After all, they are literally on the other side of the world, so perhaps European matters do not truly interest people there as they do here.'

'I think that now we have modern radio and telegraphic communications the distances have been made smaller in the world,' David said. 'I have been informed that you will be travelling with *Oberleutnant zur See* Jäger, and I am sure that he will be eager to discuss with his brother officers in Rabaul the current tense state of politics in Europe.' David couldn't help glancing at Kurt some distance away through the trees. He had not been pleased to hear the pair would be travelling together.

'I will just be forced to find a more interesting man if that occurs,' Caroline said with a wicked smile, and with that she wheeled her mount around and trotted down the advancing line of hunters to take up her position in the hunt.

'Boar!' someone yelled, and the crack of a rifle shot echoed in the forest, followed by a German curse.

David caught a split-second movement on the forest floor in the brush only yards away and spurred his horse forward while raising the rifle to his shoulder, using his legs to guide his horse. The big, tusked boar was running away from him, but David made his calculation quickly as the mount settled into a steady canter. Behind him he could hear Hermann gaining on him.

David aimed and fired, knowing that when he had served in the militia regiment he had been recognised as a skilled marksman, but this shot was from a moving horse at a moving target. However, the big beast squealed as David's bullet struck its spine behind the pig's head. It immediately fell to its knees and skidded a few feet on the damp earth.

'You got it!' Hermann exclaimed loudly in English. 'Damned fine shooting, old chap.'

'A little lucky, perhaps,' David replied.

Both men swung out of the saddle and cautiously approached the boar, which was lying on its side. They knew if it had only been wounded it could still be extremely dangerous to a man on foot. But the shot had hit true; the boar was dead.

The other members of the hunting party rode over to examine the first kill of the day. 'It will make a fine trophy mounted in the castle hunting hall,' one of Hermann's fellow officers commented.

'It is the biggest beast I have ever seen,' Hermann agreed. 'I am sure my father will be pleased that his favourite guest has done so well. Mr Steele felled the boar with one shot while his horse was at a canter. I have never seen that done before.'

Hermann's description brought further praise from the others in the party just as two servants on foot caught up with them. Hermann gave orders for the animal's head to be removed and the usable meat cut from the carcass.

Caroline sat astride her mount a few yards away. 'I did not think that a businessman had the talent to carry out such an excellent kill,' she said. 'You are a man of many talents, Mr Steele.'

David could see the expression of respect in her slight smile and felt a surge of hope that he might get to know this enigmatic woman better. But then he remembered that she was departing on a supply steamer to German New Guinea within the week. All David knew was that they were destined to meet again. But how?

★

The *Ella* anchored in the bay off Townsville and Sam organised a three-day stopover to resupply and carry out minor repairs before setting a direct course to Rabaul. Ben asked to go ashore to visit the family supply depot and look around the township. Sam granted his request, and Ben was rowed ashore by a crew member to the sprawling frontier town on Queensland's far north coast.

A few hours later Sam was able to secure the schooner at a wharf and wait for the supplies to arrive from their depot, which was used as a point of entry for goods transported from the Pacific Islands – such as the highly valued copra that was in great demand around the globe.

But that night Ben did not return, and when Sam awoke early the next morning he was told by his captain, Keith Ward, that Ben was still absent. Sam shrugged as he sipped his morning coffee on the bridge of the schooner; he imagined Ben had simply stayed up late carousing and making the best of his shore time. But as he was thinking this, he noticed a uniformed police officer strolling down the wharf. Sam felt his stomach churn. He stepped out onto the deck as the burly policeman stopped by the *Ella*.

'Can I help you, Constable?' Sam asked.

'You Mr Samuel Steele?' the police officer asked gruffly.

'I am,' Sam replied.

'A Mr Benjamin Steele is currently a guest of ours in the lockup and said you would vouch for him.'

Inwardly Sam groaned but at least Ben was not laid out in some dismal alleyway in the town. 'What's he done?' Sam asked.

'He was arrested in one of our pubs for brawling. He caused a bit of mischief to some of our local boys,' the officer replied. 'But he might need a doctor for a head injury.'

'What will happen to him?' Sam asked, silently cursing his nephew for causing so much trouble but admitting Ben was very much like himself at the same age.

'He will go before the court, and the magistrate will decide whether he goes to gaol or pays a fine. You can visit him at the station if you like.'

Sam nodded and thanked the burly policeman who turned on his heel, striding away.

'Captain Ward,' Sam called to Keith who was standing a distance away on the deck, watching the contact between the uniformed police officer and Sam curiously.

Keith approached Sam. 'What was all that about?' he asked.

'Ben has got himself into a spot of bother with the traps for fighting. I have to go to the police station and see what I can do to get him out before we sail.'

'I kind of thought the lad was a bit like you – more so than his father.' Keith grinned. 'You go, I will look after things here.'

Sam went below to shave and put on his cleanest shirt and trousers as he wanted to make a good impression when he reached the police station.

★

Before midday, having walked back under a hot sun, Ben stood in the cabin of the schooner, his head heavily bandaged. Sam had taken him to a local doctor and for a hefty fee had had the deep laceration stitched.

'One bloody night in town and you get yourself into trouble,' Sam said in a cold voice.

'But I was defending the honour of a young lady . . .' Ben said sheepishly.

'I don't bloody care if you were speaking up for the King. It cost me a lot of money to get you freed, and I had to promise that you will never step ashore in Townsville ever again. That payment will be coming out of your wages. You know the vital importance of our mission and all you can think about is bedding some sheila you met in the pub. By rights I should find you a berth on a ship returning to Sydney and let you explain your reckless behaviour to your father. As it is we sail in the morning, and I do not have the time to organise to get rid of you.'

Ben hung his head, appalled at his beloved uncle's words, but he understood that Sam was right. 'I swear that what happened last night will never happen again, Uncle Sam,' he said.

'It probably will happen again, knowing the Steele blood in your veins, but not on this trip.' Sam sighed. 'Because of your head injury I am ordering you to go to your cabin and

33

get some rest, but I expect you to resume your duties the moment we sail. Understood?'

'Understood.' Ben felt he had got off lightly as he knew his uncle meant every word of what he had threatened. Ben greatly feared that if he had been sent home, the disgrace and shame of letting down his father would have been more than he could have borne.

When Ben left Sam's company, he passed Keith on the deck. Unbeknown to Ben, Keith had heard the story of the pub brawl from an old ship mate living in Townsville who had been in the pub when the violent incident occurred.

'Hope she was worth it.' Keith grinned. 'I heard that you took on six of the local lads and fought like a demon before they cracked the bottle over your head.'

Ben glanced at the *Ella*'s captain. 'The fight was,' he said. 'I laid out four of the bastards before they got me from behind.'

Keith nodded. Young Ben was definitely a chip off his uncle's block.

★

The German cargo steamer had reached the choppy waters off the east African coast after passing through the Suez Canal, but *Oberleutnant zur See* Kurt Jäger was used to such conditions. He sat at a small desk in his rather dingy cabin, some papers from a leather satchel he guarded closely at all times spread out before him. He read carefully the words of *Kapitänleutnant* Willy Hermann written four years earlier:

The stretch from the Torres Strait westwards to Cape Leeuwin is the least advantageous for cruiser warfare. The stretch between Cape Leeuwin and Adelaide is used by most transoceanic trading vessels and thus far more advantageous. The stretch from

Adelaide to Brisbane via Bass Strait is the Australian trading centre, which includes Melbourne, Sydney and Brisbane, the principal overseas trading ports of the three most profitable provinces, Victoria, New South Wales and Queensland. This is the obvious target for our operations. The remaining stretch from Brisbane to the Torres Strait is also busy, but used almost entirely by coastal traffic and therefore not suitable for our purposes.

Kurt turned to another report of an even more highly sensitive nature compiled by *Kapitän zur See* Otto Kranzbühler and revised after his voyage to Sydney Harbour four years earlier on the German warship, the *Condor*. He outlined that auxiliary cruisers should operate out of ports in the Solomon Islands to raid the British–held islands of Fiji and the former British colonies of New Zealand and Australia.

Kurt rubbed his forehead. As a secretive member of the Imperial German naval bureau the *Kriegnachrichtenwesen* – the War Intelligence Section – his mission to Rabaul was vital to assess the preparedness of imperial outposts in the event of war. Like Germany, Britain had an empire, and it was taken for granted that the Australians and New Zealanders would side with their Mother Country. Kurt sensed that any future war would span the globe and impact both empires.

The German naval intelligence officer had been concerned about the poor state of military preparedness when he had visited Rabaul two years earlier. He had learned that this part of the Pacific had seen the withdrawal of most of its gunboat cruisers elsewhere, and there were very few army troops available. Germany would have to rely on its native troops, which were under the command of German officers. Most vital was to defend the scattered radio stations from Rabaul to Samoa, as without this means of contact with naval forces, Germany would be blind in the

Pacific and unable to carry out their operational strategic plan to attack British imperial interests in the region.

Kurt sighed, not looking forward to reporting back to Berlin what he knew would be the real situation when he arrived: a lack of resources with which to defend their Pacific empire. His government was more interested in watching the British navy in the Atlantic; the imperial territory in the Pacific was a mere backwater to German naval interests. But Kurt appreciated that Australia and New Zealand were potentially storehouses of supplies for the island of Britain and he had read reports of the ferocity of Australian and New Zealand troops in South Africa during the Boer War fourteen years earlier. Their involvement could prove to be a problem in any future conflict if they were not contained by Germany's modern navy.

Kurt slipped the reports back into the satchel, locked it and secured it in a safe specially supplied aboard ship by his intelligence section. For now, it was time to dine with the ship's captain and the Countess Caroline von Neumann, who was to visit her father's copra plantations near Rabaul. He smiled as he considered the delights that awaited him in her cabin in the early hours of the morning. At least her company made the journey worthwhile.

FOUR

Josiah Steele stood up from his desk to welcome the Commonwealth civil servant, Archibald Stokes, into his city office. He had already met the young man earlier when Stokes had proposed that Sam take the company-owned schooner north to Rabaul in an attempt to gather intelligence on German armed forces in the Pacific region. The purchase of copra was their excuse to visit the deepwater harbour of Rabaul, which lay in the shadow of the very active volcano that overlooked the town and shipping port. They would not be viewed suspiciously, as the schooner was well known to the German administration from its previous visits loading copra cargoes from the German plantations. It was the perfect cover for the crew of the *Ella*.

'Good morning, Colonel,' said Archibald, using Josiah's military title for his current command of his father's old militia regiment.

'Mr Stokes, please take a seat,' Josiah said, shaking the man's hand and gesturing to a comfortable leather chair in his office with its view of the harbour and city skyline.

Archibald removed his hat and placed it in his lap. He also carried a leather satchel which he set down beside his chair.

'Would you like a cup of tea?' Josiah asked, sitting back down behind his desk.

'Thank you, Colonel, but I will decline your kind offer as I have already had morning tea at my office.'

'I have read that progress is being made in establishing our new national government west of Sydney at a place called Yarralumla, and that the impressive homestead will be the residence of the Governor-General. Before you know it, you and the rest of our federal administration will be housed out there, too.'

Archibald squirmed a little in his chair. 'I think many of us would prefer to remain in Sydney. I suppose it's fortunate we won't be sent to Melbourne, but I have been informed that the region chosen by Sydney and Melbourne as a halfway point endures unbearably cold winters and wretchedly hot summers. At least Sydney has all its cultural attractions and milder weather. But the matter of the future capital's name has been settled after some discussion. The minister for Home Affairs wanted to call the new city "Shakespeare", but was overruled by Lady Denman, who preferred the local regional name of "Canberra". But that is not why I am here – I am hoping that you may have had word from your brother.'

'Ah, yes. Samuel telegraphed me from Townsville last week that they were to set sail directly and, all going well, they will have reached Rabaul. Now all we have to do is wait until he is able to provide a report of their findings.'

'I have faith in his success,' Archibald commented. 'His war record – being decorated with the Distinguished Conduct Medal – speaks for itself, and your own war record exemplifies the loyalty of your family to His Majesty and the empire.'

'In this case the mission has more relevance to the defence of our own young country,' Josiah said. 'But I pray that the mission becomes redundant and peace continues in our part of the world. Do you feel that war clouds are gathering in Europe, Mr Stokes?'

Archibald frowned. 'It is my opinion that Europe is a powder keg, and if the fuse is lit we will be drawn into a conflagration such as we have never experienced before. No one in Europe will be immune; even the Russian empire might be mobilised in the event of a war over there.'

'I have similar fears,' Josiah said gloomily. 'I know most of our countrymen are oblivious of international politics, but I have experienced them at first hand in my past.'

'We are of similar minds, Colonel, but many of my colleagues have their heads up their . . . in the sand. But as you have said, our first priority in the event of a European war breaking out is our own homeland and its protection as, from what I know, the German navy has a strong contingent based in China to cover what the German naval administration calls "the Australia Station". Their warships with their big naval guns could easily ravage our east coast.'

Josiah rose from his chair and walked across the office to gaze out at the busy harbour below. For a moment he imagined German cruiser gunboats steaming into it and blasting the city while the Australian navy might be elsewhere and the German navy able to slip past them.

'Well, Colonel, I should return to my office and complete my report to our Defence Department on the plausible threat to our shores, which it seems at the moment holds little interest for our elected politicians.'

'Good luck on that, Mr Stokes,' Josiah replied, holding out his hand to the young civil servant. Stokes had impressed him with his willingness to make unpopular suggestions to his political masters, who it seemed were more interested in their pursuit of popularity with the voters than addressing the future threat to Australian waters.

When Archibald had departed, Josiah slumped back in his chair and pondered the future. He still prayed that peace would reign in a world where technology was making weapons more lethal all the time. Better-designed artillery and the invention of the machine gun had changed tactics on the battlefield. At sea the navies of the opposing empires comprised deadly dreadnoughts and battleships equipped with huge naval rifles.

Josiah sighed. He would prefer to be aboard the *Ella*, standing beside his son and brother. But he also accepted that his financial empire might one day be supporting a war effort, and Josiah knew that was just as important as the soldier or sailor physically engaged on a battlefield or at sea. Economic power was instrumental in winning wars.

★

Caroline had been absent for almost three weeks now, but David could not get her out of his thoughts. Hermann noticed that David was distracted and guessed it was due to the impression his cousin had made on the young Australian.

The two men were now in Berlin, as Hermann was due to return to his barracks in the city within forty-eight hours, and currently stood on one of the wide streets watching a military parade passing by. It was late spring, and a hint of summer warmed the clear skies of the beautiful city. The street was packed with civilian spectators cheering the squadrons of dashing lancers on horseback and the solid infantry columns marching with the unique 'goosestep' David had heard was the term used by English observers. The high, stiff raising of the legs on the march was in contrast to how David had been drilled in Australia. But what struck David most of all was the greater than usual enthusiasm of the civilian crowds gathered to see the might of their army parading before them.

'My friend, forget Caroline,' Hermann said unexpectedly. He was wearing his dress uniform and many pretty young ladies were casting him admiring glances. 'You can see that you and I have the pick of Berlin's girls today.'

'I was not thinking about Caroline,' David lied. 'I am impressed by the way the Berliners support your soldiers.'

'In these difficult times they have a greater respect for what we do in the defence of our Fatherland,' Hermann replied.

'It is as if the people were sending them off to war,' David said.

'I would disagree,' Hermann replied. 'I think the people are fearful of politicians losing control of matters in Europe, and it does not hurt to let the people see they have an army that is invincible and able to protect their homes and families. I read that recently the United States sent its marines to seize the Mexican port of Vera Cruz because their president, Wilson, accuses Germany of sending arms to the Mexican federal president, Huerta, who Wilson dislikes. I'm afraid such intervention is a sad sign of our times. The Americans are showing the world they openly hold us in contempt.'

'But the Americans have a rigid policy of remaining

neutral in the event of any European war,' David stated. 'As far as I know, they are not a current military threat to Germany.'

Hermann broke from the topic of military matters when he saw two young ladies watching them. 'My friend, it is time that we introduce ourselves to those ladies, who obviously have an interest in meeting us,' he said cheerfully, and David followed in his wake as Hermann pushed through the throng towards the two girls, who he guessed were in their late teens. They blushed prettily when Hermann introduced himself and David.

'I can see that you young ladies are impressed by gallant soldiers,' Hermann said, and they nodded, seeming overwhelmed that this handsome young officer would deign to make their acquaintance. They told the men they were shop assistants and as such had only known the company of enlisted soldiers – never an officer in the Kaiser's army.

'Well, I feel that such lovely ladies should be treated to something special today to mark this glorious weather we are experiencing. Shall we take a stroll in the park by the river?'

Both the young women were obviously vying to be Hermann's escort. Hermann offered his arm to the girl with the raven hair, so the blonde reluctantly attached herself to David as if he was the runner-up prize.

The four made their way to a park dotted with copses of evergreen trees, where they strolled amid the families of those who had broken away from the parade. The soldiers were now dispersing to their barracks. The blonde girl had introduced herself as Helga, and after she questioned David about his accent, she asked him where his country of origin was. When he said Australia, she admitted that she did not know where his country was, and it was obvious to David that the pretty young lady was from a working-class background. It was not that David was a snob, but he realised they had little in common.

But there was laughter, and as they sat on the lawn watching the river glide serenely past, David let Hermann lead the conversation until the sun began to sink over the city. Then the ladies excused themselves, but Hermann promised to rediscover their acquaintance in the future. Heads together, they giggled as they walked away, casting coy glances back at the uniformed officer and the foreigner.

'I think that I have someone to spend the night with when I return to Berlin,' Hermann commented smugly as they departed the park. 'But, as this is your last night in Berlin before you leave our shores, I think that we should find a cozy beer hall such as we have in Bavaria and see the night out, my dear friend.'

David agreed, but his mind was wandering to Caroline once again. He was already plotting to find an excuse to visit Rabaul after he returned home to Sydney. After all, the Steele enterprises did business with the copra plantations of German New Guinea, and it was high time that he personally went to see how things were done in the Pacific islands of Melanesia.

★

The *Ella* entered the harbour at Rabaul midmorning under full sail as Sam stood by his captain, Keith Ward, who manned the helm. The skies were blue with just a few clouds scudding over the surrounding mountain range.

'I can't see any cruiser gunboats in port,' Sam observed.

'But we do have company,' Keith replied. 'Looks like an official launch approaching.'

Sam saw the open boat and the white uniforms of German

administrators who hailed them just off the bow with a megaphone.

'What is your business here?' a voice asked in German. Sam's own knowledge of German was very basic, so he replied in English, 'We are with Steele Enterprises, and we are here to purchase copra.'

There was a moment of silence before the German official replied in broken English, 'Go to wharf. We will board you.'

Keith followed the motorised launch to a wharf and secured the schooner before the sweating German in the white suit scrambled aboard, escorted by two German native police who carried Mauser rifles on their shoulders. Sam recognised the police from his previous visits as members of the Tolai tribe.

Keith already had their papers ready for inspection and passed them to the German, a man in his fifties who obviously had not yet acclimatised to the hot and humid conditions of Rabaul. He glanced at the papers written in English but concentrated on a paper in German granted from previous dockings in Simpson Harbour – known to the Germans as Simpsonhafen. Satisfied, he handed back the papers. Sam thanked him in German and with a nod, the official departed. When the man was out of earshot, Sam turned to Keith. 'We have never been boarded like this before when visiting Rabaul,' he said. 'The Germans are a bit edgy.'

Ben joined the two men in the wheelhouse, gazing out at the coast lined with tall coconut palms and the many timber houses designed in a German style yet with tropical architecture in mind. They were all built off the ground with wide verandahs to catch any breeze, and Ben could also see some substantial two-storeyed buildings that were obviously government offices. Rabaul had been chosen as the headquarters for the German administration even though it was dubiously located in the shadow of two still active volcanoes. Despite the ominous threat posed by the volcanoes, Rabaul's drawcard was a deepwater port suitable for commerce and naval ships.

Behind the township the jungle rose up the slopes of high hills crowned by billowing white clouds.

'What do we do now?' Ben asked, still taking in the panorama of the tropical German version of European civilisation.

'We change into those white suits I purchased in Townsville and go ashore so that I can make contact with an old cobber,' Sam answered. 'He owns a building in the town with premises upstairs called the Coconut Tea Room, where the German Club is also located. That is where the who's who of the German administration relax away from the sun and heat, and it will be there that we begin to find out what is happening in this part of the Pacific.' Sam turned to his nephew. 'Ben, I expect you to be discreet.'

Ben nodded his understanding and the two went below to change out of their work clothes. Keith would remain aboard with the crew to ensure their security – not that this was essential, as the German authorities had swift and severe methods of enforcing public safety with the whip and hangman's noose.

When they were ready, Sam led the way into the town, taking note of the uniforms of police, army and navy personnel they passed as they walked the hard-packed earthen streets lined with houses decorated with ornate fretwork. He also observed that there were not a lot of women and children to be seen, which was understandable given that this was the frontier of the Kaiser's Pacific empire.

Those he did see strolling on the street with sun parasols he guessed were the wives of the government employees or civilian planters.

Finally, they reached a two-storeyed building advertising that it was also an emporium of goods and trade. It had an upper veranda and both men could see a couple of German naval officers in uniform standing and chatting with cups in their hands.

They entered the large shop on the ground floor, where big fans rotated slowly overhead to disperse some of the midday heat. The shelves were packed with a variety of commercial goods, and most of the floor space was taken up with crates of trade goods.

'Ah, Herr Steele,' a voice greeted them in English. 'It has been some time since I last saw you.'

A portly, balding man wearing spectacles and sweating profusely stepped out from behind a counter, wiping his flour-covered hands on an apron he wore around his waist.

'Herr Gottfried, it has been too long,' Sam replied, gripping the outstretched hand.

'Who is this young man?' the German businessman asked, glancing at Ben.

'My nephew, Benjamin Steele, who has chosen to go to sea and learn the ropes of copra transportation, and that is why we are here,' Sam answered.

'The prices are high now for you.' Gottfried sighed. 'A lot of international demand for copra.'

'We can pay,' Sam said. 'But I promised Ben that we would partake of refreshments in your tea shop upstairs before we return to our ship.'

'I can arrange that,' Gottfried said. 'You have come at the right time if you are looking to buy copra, despite its high price. There is a party upstairs for plantation owners who have just had their meeting and are now having lunch. Maybe you could introduce yourselves and do some business.'

'I guess we are in the right place at the right time, then,' said Sam.

Sam and Ben made their way up the stairs and entered a spacious room full of tables and chairs occupied by many civilian businessmen in their white suits. The walls were adorned with the heads of deer and pictures of the Kaiser. Hardly anyone took any notice of them when they entered. They approached a bar where an elderly native man wearing a smart white uniform jacket stood awaiting orders.

Sam ordered two lime juices in soda water and turned to locate somewhere to sit. Moving to follow him, Ben noticed one woman sitting among the men at a table, and was stunned by her great beauty. He stopped still, almost gawking at her. He did not expect to see such a beauty so far from European civilisation. She was laughing, but for a second caught him staring at her and smiled directly at him. Ben experienced a chill, as if she was reading his mind, and looked away lest she think he was ogling her. But he was smitten, and when he thought it was safe to turn his attention back to her, he noticed a large name placard on the table. He could discern in the Gothic script that her name was Countess Caroline von Neumann.

FIVE

A month earlier, brass bands had played popular tunes on the wharf at Hamburg alongside the majestic ocean liner. People cheered, wept or laughed as the passengers prepared to board.

Near a gangway onto the ship bound for England and then on to India, David stood beside his best friend.

'Well, old chap,' Hermann said. 'This is not goodbye, because I know that you will be visiting us once again in a couple of years for your father's business interests.'

'I hope so,' David replied, gazing up at the passengers already lining the railings of the big steamship. 'I will plan to visit when spring arrives in Europe. By then you might have given up your bachelor ways and found the lady who will be the mother of your children.'

Hermann laughed. 'I do not intend to wed until I have bedded every last beautiful woman I can. It may be you who marries first, and I will be able to bounce a child of David Steele's on my knee.'

'If that ever happened, my children would know you as "uncle".'

Hermann's expression changed. He had that serious look David knew from when they were young teens together. 'I hope that will be, as I consider you closer than a brother,' said Hermann.

The German officer's statement took David by surprise, as his friend had always been playful and less than sincere. 'The feeling is reciprocated,' he said, clasping Hermann's hand firmly. 'We will meet again in 1916, my dear friend.'

Both men stood stiffly facing each other as a great horn blasted its warning for all remaining passengers to embark. David gripped the small briefcase containing his papers – his luggage had already been stowed – and with a last nod to his friend, turned to walk to the gangway where the crew were welcoming passengers aboard.

David did not go directly to his cabin but joined many at the railings to gaze down on the uplifted faces on the wharf below. He saw Hermann waiting to see the ship slip its moorings and drift into Hamburg Harbour. David waved and Hermann returned the wave with a salute before the Australian turned away to be escorted to his cabin in the first-class accommodation.

The big liner blew its horns as it began steaming away from Germany.

As David sat in his cabin, his thoughts returned to Caroline, already so far away in the German islands of the Pacific.

★

A month after Ben's brother boarded at Hamburg, Ben was fast becoming infatuated as he glanced furtively at

49

the woman sitting at the table of plantation owners. Sam noticed his nephew's acute interest.

'Remember why we are here,' he said quietly. 'For all you know she might be married, and a jealous husband is the last thing we want interfering with our dealings.'

Ben felt a twinge of embarrassment that his interest in the woman was so obvious.

'Uncle Sam, you have to admit that she is a bonzer-looking sheila.'

'That she is,' Sam grudgingly conceded. 'But remember, we need to single out people who might unwittingly assist us with answers as to how prepared the Germans are in this part of the world.'

The two men returned their attention to observing who was in the room, and Sam was disappointed to note it was mainly white-suited civilians, albeit people he would be dealing with in his cover operation of buying copra.

Eventually the luncheon meeting broke up and Ben watched the woman depart with the grace of an aristocrat. He was smitten, but he reluctantly heeded his uncle's advice – he appreciated that his impulsive nature could jeopardise the aims of their strategic mission. He did not want a repeat of the events that had occurred in Townsville.

In the late afternoon Sam and Ben returned to the *Ella* to review the little they had gleaned on their first day in Rabaul. It was hot and humid, but dark clouds billowed on the horizon, heralding a heavy electrical storm that drenched the port that evening. By morning it was gone, and clear, blue skies once again dominated the drought-stricken island.

Keith, Sam and Ben were sipping tea in the wheelhouse as the crew went about their morning tasks when one of the Chinese crew members poked his head through the doorway.

'Cap'n, a white woman like see you. She on deck.'

The three men glanced at each other, and Sam shrugged. 'Guess I will see who she is and what she wants.'

Sam hauled himself onto the deck and was utterly surprised to see the woman Ben had been so fascinated with the day before standing on the wharf.

'Good morning, madam. My name is Samuel Steele and I have to admit that I remember you from our visit to the German Club yesterday. I don't think any man in the room would have forgotten your presence.'

'I am the Countess Caroline von Neumann, and I thank you for your flattering observation, Mr Steele,' said the woman in lightly accented English.

Caroline was wearing a long dress and carried a sun parasol. Behind her was a tall Tolai man wearing a kilt-like skirt and a clean, white shirt. At his waist was a machete.

'I am pleasantly surprised to have you as a guest. I presume that you are a plantation owner from yesterday's meeting, representing your husband?'

'I am a *Fräulein*, Mr Steele, and the plantation I have come to inspect belongs to my father who is currently in Bavaria,' Caroline replied. 'I believe from what I have heard that you are in port to purchase copra.'

'That is correct. I must congratulate you on your perfect grasp of English.'

Caroline acknowledged his compliment with a nod. 'I have lived for some time in London and also Paris,' she replied. She looked beyond Sam's shoulder as Ben came out onto the deck. 'Ah, the young man I noticed with you yesterday,' she added with a smile.

'My nephew, Mr Benjamin Steele,' said Sam. 'I think he

considers you one of the most beautiful *Fräuleins* he has ever seen.' Ben blushed under his heavy tan. 'And now he has been formally introduced to you, Countess,' Sam continued with a grin.

'Pleased to meet you, Countess,' Ben mumbled.

'But we have not spoken of why we have the pleasure of your company, and it would be rude of me not to offer refreshments,' Sam offered.

'The refreshments will not be necessary, Mr Steele, as I am to return to the Coconut Tea Room shortly to meet with my colleagues once again. I am here to ascertain if I might prevail upon your visit to Rabaul for some urgently needed assistance. I will "get to the point", as you English say.

'The overseer of my family's plantation, a wonderful German man, was taken by fever and died yesterday while I was in town, and I am urgently in need of someone to replace him until another can be sent out from Germany. As you are a copra merchant, I hoped I might prevail upon you, or a trusted member of your crew, to assist me to manage my plantation until my new overseer arrives. That also means that when you depart, I will be able to ensure that you receive a very generous purchase price for my copra, a price much better than any of the other plantation owners can provide.' Caroline mentioned a figure and Sam raised his eyebrows. It was a very generous offer and would make them a great profit upon resale.

'Are you not able to hire another European to act as an overseer?' Sam countered, feigning caution but in reality considering that this would provide a good excuse to linger in port, which suited his needs well.

'The men here are either military, police, or work for the German Company,' Caroline answered. 'It would take too much of their time. Your visit to our harbour is very opportune, and as the price of copra is so high at the moment, I felt it might be an attractive offer. It is only a temporary assignment, in any case. The work requires a European.'

Sam thought over the situation and silently decided it had advantages. 'I can spare my nephew,' he answered. 'But I must warn you, he has little knowledge of copra production.'

'That does not matter. What matters is that he has an air of confidence and can impress my Tolai workers,' Caroline said. 'If possible, I would like him to accompany me to my plantation at Bita Paka later this afternoon.'

'I am honoured to assist, Countess,' Ben said, and she beamed a broad smile at him.

'I am grateful to you, Mr Steele.' She paused, then added, 'I am not sure if your family name is common in your country of Australia, but I had the pleasure of spending some time in the company of a Mr David Steele whilst he was visiting his friend, my cousin Hermann von Kellermann, in Bavaria. He mentioned that he was an Australian.'

Both men were stunned. There could only be one David Steele from Australia in Bavaria. The world was definitely shrinking!

*

Ben was supplied with a horse and given a .303 Lee Enfield rifle for his journey to Caroline's plantation outside of Rabaul. Sam explained that it was the same rifle he had carried in South Africa, which he had been able to purchase through family contacts, and Ben understood that his uncle was hoping it would ensure his nephew's safety.

Ben was guided to the plantation by one of the countess's Tolai workers, who easily strode out ahead of Ben on foot even though Ben was on horseback. Ben admired the man's stamina under the blazing sun, and remembered that his uncle had told him the Tolai had proved themselves fierce warriors when pitted against the German troops and police sent to subdue them years earlier.

The two men followed a rough, winding road through the hills until they reached a sprawling bungalow with sweeping, trellised verandas built up from the ground to catch the tropical breezes. Off to one side Ben could see the jungle bordering the main house and huts he presumed belonged to the workers' families. The lawns surrounding the main house were manicured with flowering frangipani and acacia trees, and on the far side were masses of coconut palms, where he could see men working with the help of their families. It seemed a peaceful oasis in the tropical rainforest.

A tall, fine-looking young Tolai man took Ben's horse to stable it, whilst Ben flung his kitbag over one shoulder and his rifle over the other.

Caroline came onto the veranda and looked down at him. 'Welcome to my father's plantation, Mr Steele,' she said.

Ben tipped his broad-brimmed hat to acknowledge her greeting.

'Come upstairs. I have refreshments for you after your long ride. My residence also has a bath and I have had a spare room prepared for your stay.'

The mention of a bath and refreshments appealed very much to Ben, whose shirt and trousers were both wet with sweat and caked in dust. He was ushered into the house up a broad set of wooden steps, where Caroline met him.

'I have had a bath drawn for you as I am sure you would like to freshen up before joining me on the veranda for a drink.'

Ben thanked her and was led to a spartan room with a single bed, desk and one tall wardrobe. It had a large window overlooking the front lawns and also a mosquito net over the bed. A young native girl shyly showed him the bathroom and closed the door as Ben stripped to wash away the remnants of his journey.

After bathing he pulled a second set of clothes from his kitbag, changing into the clean shirt and trousers. He gave his dust-covered riding boots a quick rub-down, but it did not make them shine. Satisfied, he made his way to the veranda where he found Caroline sitting in a high-backed cane chair with a small table next to her and a second cane chair alongside.

'Please take a seat, Mr Steele,' Caroline said, gesturing to the empty chair. Ben did so, taking in the impressive view before him. He noticed that the coconut plantation was now deserted as the sun began to set.

'You have a wonderful estate here, Countess,' Ben remarked.

'Please, call me Caroline,' she answered. 'The David Steele I mentioned earlier – a friend at the German Club tells me you are his brother. David is a truly charming and extraordinary man, and I can see the likeness between you.'

'It is remarkable that I should be working for a lady who also knows my brother,' said Ben. 'Especially in this part of the world. The biblical Paradise must have been like this.'

Caroline turned to the same Tolai man hovering nearby who had greeted Ben when he arrived. 'Solomon, please fetch two gin and tonics and the savories,' she commanded, and he ducked away.

'You commence your duties early in the morning. All you have to do is be on your horse and be in the presence of the workers. You will need your rifle to reassure them that they are protected from any marauding tribesmen. We dine at midday at the house, which is when I stand down my workers for an hour. If you have any questions, I hope that I can answer them.'

Two frosted glasses arrived on a silver tray and Ben took one.

'What is it you say? Chin-chin,' Caroline toasted, raising her glass, and Ben raised his own, taking a sip of the chilled spirit. As far as he could remember no drink had ever tasted better as he sat in the golden light of the setting sun in the presence of a beautiful woman, looking out at paradise and covertly undertaking his task of infiltrating German society in Rabaul.

★

At that moment Sam was sipping on a glass of rum, poring over a chart of the waters around Rabaul. It had been a stroke of luck that the countess had appeared and made her request when she had, not only because it gave them an excuse to linger in Rabaul for longer, but because Sam had heard the name of the location of her plantation – Bita Paka. He knew from his notes that it was suspected the Germans had a radio station in the area, from which they communicated with their naval cruiser gunboats.

Ben had been briefed on the intelligence and given instructions to find and fix the station's location, thereby verifying if it was active. From what Ben had been told, the Germans relied on this vital system of modern communications to alert their naval squadrons to British naval dispositions. Knocking out the radio station would be like blinding an opponent.

'Do you think the young fella will be safe?' Keith asked when he joined Sam in the cabin.

'Maybe not safe from the countess,' Sam answered with a twisted grin. 'I have known ladies like her before who enjoy the chase, capture and inevitable destruction of men. I could see it in her eyes when we met.'

'Ah, a terrible fate awaits our young Ben,' Keith said, pouring himself a generous tot of rum.

As if by design, a moth flew into the cabin, flew towards the kerosene lantern and fell away when it was struck by the heat of the flame inside. Sam couldn't help but wonder if Ben would suffer the same fate.

SIX

Winter 1914

Ben quickly settled into a routine, and his easy manner with the workers on the copra plantation earned him their liking and respect. In the evenings he would sit on the veranda sipping a gin and tonic and talking to the countess. Their conversations ranged over many subjects, and between the serenity of the tropical night and Caroline's infectious laughter, Ben could feel his attraction to her go beyond simple lust – although that was there too.

One evening in the third week of his employ on her plantation, Ben bid Caroline a good night and retired to bed. He lay naked under the mosquito net to try to stay cool in the lingering intense heat of the day, glad nonetheless that he was not enduring the cold and wet of a Sydney winter. Suddenly he became aware that he was not alone in the room. The closed door had opened, and when he gazed across to the silhouette outlined by the hallway lanterns his heart felt as if it had suddenly ceased to beat. He could see the shapely form of a naked woman, and knew immediately who it was as the figure glided towards him in the dark. He felt the mosquito net lift as Caroline slid into his single bed.

Ben was wordless as he felt her soft, warm hand brush his face. 'You do not need to say anything, my beautiful man,' Caroline whispered. 'Just accept what I have to offer.'

Ben was only too happy to oblige, and the explosive power of their lovemaking was beyond anything he had ever experienced in the past. No words were required, and Ben had a fleeting thought that this was truly paradise.

In the early hours of the morning, they lay side by side, facing each other, and Ben could not help himself. 'Why?' he whispered.

Caroline touched his lips with her fingertips. 'I did not think I would ever find a man like you,' she said. 'You are so different from all the others I have ever known. You are strong, gentle and intelligent. I love your eyes and smile and the way you accept life, seeking the best in all men. You are unique in my world of stuffy aristocrats and military men.'

Ben was afraid to ask the question that now played on his mind: *What does the future hold for us?* He knew that Caroline was due to return to Germany in the next couple of weeks and felt a twinge of guilt about his mission to spy on her people. Ben also knew that he would eventually have to return to the *Ella* and sail home to Sydney. The situation seemed hopeless, and when Caroline slipped from his cramped bed to oversee the breakfast preparations, Ben lay back, frowning. He was sure that he was in love, but the tyranny of distance between Germany and Australia seemed a major factor and one that would destroy his future happiness.

When he later joined Caroline on the veranda for a

breakfast of coffee and tropical fruits, she briefly took his hand across the table. No words were spoken, but Ben thought he saw her eyes glisten and saw the sad smile.

'No matter what happens, we will be together,' Ben blurted, knowing they were just mere words.

'I am a realist,' Caroline said. 'All we really have is this short time here and now. I know our worlds are very far apart.'

'It is possible that when I return to Sydney my father will be convinced that I am capable of being sent to Europe on missions for trade,' Ben said. 'That way we could meet again.'

Caroline shook her head gently. 'When you have left here you will forget me, as you must. Any plans to meet again are simply dreams – no more than that.'

Ben was about to protest when Solomon joined them on the veranda.

'Missus, a man here.'

Ben rose and peered out into the soft tropical morning to see Sam astride his mount in the yard below.

'Uncle Sam, come join us on the veranda for breakfast,' Ben called down, and Sam dismounted and made his way to the veranda.

He slapped his dusty broad-brimmed hat on his thigh as he greeted them.

'What has brought you here today, Mr Steele?' Caroline asked as she sipped from her fine china cup. 'I hope it is not to take your nephew away.'

'No, Countess,' Sam said as a servant brought him a cup of coffee and he sat down in a spare chair near the table. 'I have come to finalise our agreement on the shipment of copra you have stored at the wharf for the price we agreed to.'

'Certainly, Mr Steele. My agent in Rabaul has the contract drawn up for you. I hope you will be satisfied.'

'I am, Countess,' Sam answered, observing his nephew closely. He thought he could detect a subtle change in him. Sam had known Ben from the day he was born and was very aware of the changes in his demeanour. He was also confident he knew the cause. 'But it will mean Ben must return within five days – regardless of whether your replacement overseer has arrived – as we will sail as soon as the copra is loaded. We have government clearances from customs.' Sam's suspicions were confirmed when Ben spoke.

'I was hoping to remain longer to learn more about copra farming,' Ben almost pleaded.

'I'm sorry, Ben, but you know how important it is that we return home. I am sure you have done a good job here, but I am afraid the countess must release you.' Sam saw Ben cast Caroline a helpless, despairing look – which she returned. 'If you would please grant me a moment, I need to speak with my nephew privately before I return to my schooner,' Sam added.

'Certainly,' Caroline replied. 'I will fetch the papers concerning our agreement.'

When Caroline went inside the house, Sam led Ben downstairs out of earshot of Caroline and any staff.

'What have you learned of the radio station supposedly near the plantation?' Sam asked.

'Nothing,' Ben replied guiltily, knowing that it had not been a priority for him in the last few weeks. 'I have been too busy managing the plantation to leave without raising suspicion.'

'No matter,' Sam said, but with a hint of annoyance. 'I found it.'

Ben looked surprised. 'When?' he asked.

'I have been in the area for a couple of days and stumbled on it,' he said. 'I have mapped its location and ascertained that it appears to be in working order. I think there is little else we can do here.'

'Have we achieved anything by coming here?' Ben countered.

'I strongly suspect that you have won the favours of the countess,' Sam said disapprovingly.

'How do you know that?' Ben asked, although he was well aware that his uncle was a perceptive man – more perceptive about him than his own father.

'I just know,' Sam replied. 'Now, you will have to understand that anything you feel for the countess was doomed from the start, and just leave with the good memories you will have of this time.' He placed his hand sympathetically on his nephew's shoulder. 'I know it is going to hurt like hell when you lose what you consider love.'

Ben guessed his uncle was reflecting on the loss of his own wife, and changed the subject that was already weighing on him more than he wanted to admit to himself. 'Did we learn anything else in Rabaul?' he asked.

'A bit of importance to our government,' Sam said. 'It seems most of the cruiser gunboats have been withdrawn from around Rabaul, and the major base of the Imperial German Navy is now at the Chinese port of Tsingtao. At the moment the only threat would be from the cruiser *Kormoran* which is suspected of being nearby. The threat at Rabaul itself would be the native police and the native troops under the command of the very few German officers barracked here.'

'Then we have succeeded in gathering facts that may be of interest to our Defence Department.' Ben sighed. 'Our mission might be considered of importance.'

'If we were ever to go to war with Germany, it would be vital,' said Sam. 'But we are at peace, albeit an uneasy one. I just learned that the successor to the throne of the Austro-Hungarian Empire was assassinated last week in some Balkan city. It has Europe talking about repercussions if the Austrians retaliate against some place called Serbia, who are strongly bound to the Russian Czar. With that in mind, it is time for us to get out of Rabaul while the going is good.'

Ben thought about this. He knew from conversations with his father that Europe was like a set of dominoes. The logical conclusion was that the Germans would side with the Austrian Emperor if Russia sided with the Balkan state of Serbia in the event the Austrians chose to go to war with them. That would mean the French would side with the Russians against Germany, which had been their traditional enemy ever since the Franco-Prussian War of 1870–71, when Bismarck's armies had captured Paris. The French had not forgotten the humiliation. But where would Britain stand? Ben asked himself. He hoped they would remain neutral in any continental conflict.

'I will join you next week,' Ben said reluctantly, glancing back at the house. 'I am sure the little we have learned here might be of importance to our navy.'

'Good,' Sam said, returning to his horse. 'We will see you next week.'

Sam rode away, leaving Ben in turmoil. Matters so far away from the Pacific seemed to be causing dark clouds to gather over paradise. He walked slowly back to the house.

★

Archibald Stokes completed the handwritten draft of his assessment report to be typed and submitted to the highest echelons of government. Its conclusions were gloomy: that the two pistol shots fired in some obscure Balkan city on the other side of the world, which had taken the lives of the future Austrian emperor and his wife, could be the catalyst for a massive mobilisation of armed forces by the major powers on the European continent, and potentially lead to imminent hostilities. The question at the back of Archibald's mind was about the position Britain might take if war broke out on the continent. If Germany and France went to war, Belgium might be entangled, and Britain had a longstanding treaty with the country that had chosen to be neutral in any future conflict between the two major powers on its doorstep. Surely the French and Germans would respect Belgium's neutrality?

When the report had been typed, Archibald had it sent to his immediate supervisor, a dull man facing retirement and a generous pension, and it was not long before Archibald was summoned to the man's office with its smell of leather and wax polish for the expensive panelled walls and floor.

'Stokes, I read your ridiculous report and I have chosen not to forward it to our political masters. It is bad enough that our prime minister, Mr Cook, has dissolved parliament for a new election. The last thing they need to hear is a preposterous alarmist report of a possible impending war on the other side of the world which is of no concern to the British empire. No, it will not do. I suggest that you find something else to report, as all I saw in this document was overblown speculation.'

Archibald was well aware of the double dissolution brought on by a prime minister dissatisfied with the Senate opposing all that the Lower House attempted to achieve. Now, standing before the desk of his department head, he felt like he was back in his exclusive public school facing the principal for a breach of the rules. His face reddened but he knew better than to challenge his superior. 'With all due –' Archibald was cut short.

'Damn it, man!' the dull-witted public servant exploded. 'I have been a loyal servant of governments that have come and gone since Federation, and my years in civil service have provided me with the wisdom to know what our political masters wish to hear – and what they don't. Go back to your duties before I make a report on your obvious incompetence.'

Humiliated, Archibald meekly left the office to return to his own. It was rumoured that his boss was about to receive a knighthood from the King for his service to public administration. What a terrible joke, Archibald mused as he slumped down in the chair behind his desk. He stared at the copy of the report. He knew the information it contained was important and wondered if he should discreetly forward it to the Defence Department. Maybe there was someone in an influential position over there who was not due for a knighthood and was prepared to rock the boat of political decision-making.

*

Little did the Australian civil servant know that far north in Rabaul, a junior German naval officer had come to the same conclusions. *Oberleutnant zur See* Kurt Jäger had requested a meeting with the staff of the senior German administrators in Rabaul to voice his concerns. Four men sat at a table with Kurt in a large room as fans whirred overhead, moving the humid air that was filled with tobacco smoke.

'Gentlemen, I am sure you are well aware of the recent incident in Europe with the assassination in Sarajevo. I am almost sure the Austrian government will retaliate, and this will mean a confrontation with Serbia's ally, Russia. I strongly believe this will drag the French into support of Russia, and hence the Austrians will call on us to provide armed support. At this stage we do not know if the English will remain neutral, but if they do not, it is probable they will side with the French despite their historical animosity. If that occurs, the greater British empire will support their Mother Country and we will be at war with the Australians in our own Pacific backyard. I feel it is time to take steps to look to our defence.'

There was a moment of silence as the four government officials took in the gravity of the information coming from a man they knew was a naval intelligence officer for the Kaiser's Imperial Navy.

'We are not really in a position to defend ourselves,' the leader of the delegation of senior German administrators protested. 'Most of our grand navy is elsewhere, and our land forces are not great enough in number to defend the islands. We would have to rely on our native troops and police under the few German officers we have stationed here.'

'We have a duty to our Fatherland to resist with all we have if the English come to attack us,' Kurt said, leaning forward to emphasise his patriotism and causing the protesting speaker to look uncomfortable.

'What do you suggest we do in the meantime?' the man countered.

Kurt already had a plan. 'The first thing we can do is account for all non-German citizens currently in Rabaul and surrounding districts. We cannot afford to have spies living among us.'

'That can be achieved,' the delegation leader replied. 'But what do we do then?'

Kurt knew that his plan could not contain any possible suggestion of undue harassment – lest the situation developing in Europe fizzle out and peace reigned. Good relations needed to exist between Britain and Germany for the purposes of trade and stability in the Pacific German empire.

'The only foreign ships in the harbour are two from China and one registered to an Australian trading company, Steele Enterprises,' replied the chief of police. 'I happen to know its captain, Mr Ward, a good fellow.'

One of the other members of the delegation piped up. 'I doubt that they are spying on us as they have been here before to purchase copra.'

The name Steele had immediately sparked Kurt's interest. He had heard a rumour that Caroline had employed a man by the name of Ben Steele as temporary manager of her father's plantation near their vital radio station needed to communicate with German naval vessels in the Pacific. That made him suspicious, as only an intelligence officer could be of such a coincidence.

'Are any of you aware of a man by the name of Benjamin Steele working for the countess at her plantation?' Kurt asked.

'Herr Ward informed me that the schooner owner's nephew was sent there at her request for assistance after her previous manager died from the fever,' said the delegation leader. 'It seems they have an arrangement to purchase her copra.'

Kurt was an ambitious man and the strategic placement of this Australian sounded deeply suspicious to him. He did not suspect Caroline of complicity to commit treason but simply of naivety in her selection of the man. His first act would be to send police to Caroline's plantation to bring back the man to be immediately deported.

Steele, Kurt mused. This was the same family name as the obnoxious Australian he had met in Germany in the company of the countess months ago. A coincidence? Kurt did not believe in coincidences.

SEVEN

The early-morning peace aboard the *Ella* was rudely disturbed when a contingent of armed native police scrambled aboard. The native police were also considered soldiers by the Germans and their uniform of khaki peaked cap, sailors' shirts and red-banded shorts gave them the respectability of colonial servants.

They were led by a young, uniformed German naval officer who demanded in relatively good English that the captain present himself. Both Sam and Keith did so as the rest of the crew assembled on deck, flushed out from their quarters by the police who went downstairs and forced the crew members at gunpoint to join their captain.

'What is the meaning of this uninvited boarding of my schooner?' Keith demanded of the German officer.

'I have orders to search your vessel for any contraband goods,' Kurt answered. 'Do you have a wireless radio?'

'No,' Sam answered, stepping forward. 'I wish we did, but we won't be able to get one fitted until we return to Sydney. But why do you ask? Would a radio be considered contraband?'

'It would depend on how it is used,' Kurt said, scanning the masts for any sign of an aerial. 'I also need to know why your nephew is working on a plantation owned by Count von Neumann near Bita Paka.'

'It is no secret that my nephew is on temporary loan to the Countess von Neumann as her manager. He will be returning to my schooner next week before we depart with a cargo of copra from her plantation.'

'I have come to learn that you have another nephew, David Steele, who was recently in Bavaria,' Kurt said. 'Do you know where he is now?'

'Lieutenant,' Sam said, using the closest English rank he could equate to the naval officer facing him. 'I cannot see what concern it is of yours where my nephew is.' Sam's voice was cold. 'I also strongly object to you boarding my ship without invitation as I sail under the flag of my country, Australia. Your unwanted intrusion will be reported to my government.'

'But you are in German waters and thus fall under our jurisdiction,' Kurt countered. 'In these troubled times I have the authority of my government to take all security measures to protect the Kaiser's territory.'

'We are not at war,' Sam protested. 'And even if we were, your boarding of a commercial trader might be considered piracy.' Sam knew this argument was tenuous as it was an accepted practice to seize all shipping of a foreign declared enemy.

'I must reluctantly accept your argument, Mr Steele – as you say, we are not at war – but you must understand that the situation in Europe is strained. I am only doing my duty for the Kaiser in the current troubled times.'

'I can see your point, Lieutenant,' Sam conceded diplomatically. 'But I hope you can also see mine. I can assure you we are only in Rabaul to purchase copra which is currently fetching a high price on the international market.'

Kurt glanced down at Sam's leg. 'I was informed that you were once a soldier and fought in South Africa where you lost your leg to our Dutch kin,' he said. 'We Germans admire men of war who are prepared to give their lives for their Fatherland.'

Sam was surprised that the naval officer knew about his war record, and it dawned on him that this young man was not just a simple naval officer sent to the far reaches of the German Pacific Empire and must be part of German naval intelligence.

'Yes, at a place called Elands River,' Sam replied. 'But I had no intention of sacrificing my life for my country. On the battlefield your cobbers come first – not your King or Kaiser.'

Kurt glanced at his contingent of police and ordered them to shoulder arms in a language that neither Sam nor Keith understood but presumed was the local Tolai dialect.

'If you do not mind, my men will carry out a search of your vessel,' the officer said. 'I am sure we will not find anything that might prove to be incriminating.'

'You will not find anything to concern you,' Sam said with a shrug. 'In the meantime, Captain Ward and I would like to have our morning cup of tea, and our crew their breakfast, if you do not object.'

'I do not object, Mr Steele,' Kurt said in a less aggressive tone.

Sam and Keith went below decks where a couple of

police were making a very rudimentary search of cupboards. They made their tea and went back up to the deck to sit on a cargo hold and watch the search. It did not take long and eventually Kurt approached the two men.

'We have finished with our business here,' he said. 'I apologise for the intrusion, but I have a duty to check all foreign shipping in our harbour.'

'Apology accepted,' Sam said. 'I would have preferred to have met on more social terms at the German Club.'

'It might be possible that we can, Mr Steele. I will bid you a good day so that you can get on with your duties.'

Sam and Keith watched the naval officer and the contingent of native police depart the *Ella*. When they were gone Sam turned to Keith.

'Don't ask me why, but I wager that German is going to go looking for Ben at the countess's plantation,' Sam said. 'I just have this gut feeling.'

Sam's gut was right.

★

David stood in his father's office. He had disembarked the previous day only to find that Josiah was away in the Blue Mountains west of Sydney, but Josiah had returned to the city early that morning to greet his son.

'It is wonderful having you finally home,' Josiah said, extending his hand to David. 'I have so many questions for you as regards your venture into the markets of Europe.'

'It is good to be home, Father, but I miss spring in Germany.'

'I have a good single malt in my cabinet,' Josiah said, opening the glass door displaying a small range of spirits. He poured two tumblers and added ice from a refrigeration system he had installed.

David walked to the window with his Scotch and gazed down on the peaceful waters of the harbour, where the ships of many countries lay at anchor whilst ferries plied their way between the north and south shores. Josiah moved to stand beside him.

'I have already heard from your sisters how pleased they are to have you home,' Josiah said. 'Not a lot has changed here since you left. I read with interest your correspondence from London and the continent. I also read that your aunt is now a true Bavarian.'

'Things were changing in Europe just before I took the voyage home,' David said, taking a sip of the fine Scotch. 'There seems to be a shift in the mood of the German people, and I noticed the same thing when we docked at Southampton among the English. There is a kind of tension, even though no one I spoke to believed war really would break out on the continent. But since I have returned, I have read that the Austrians are demanding revenge against the Serbians. It's strange, though – when I look down on the people on the streets below, they seem to have no idea how unstable Europe is at the moment.'

'I would hope that Britain remains neutral in the event of conflict between the Austrians and Serbians,' Josiah said.

David walked over to one of the big leather chairs in his father's office and slumped into it. 'Rose told me last night that Ben and Uncle Sam sailed to Rabaul some weeks ago.'

'Your sister is correct,' Josiah replied. 'They are up there to load a cargo of copra for our Pacific enterprises.'

'Why would Ben go to sea?' David asked.

'To keep him under the watchful eye of my brother, and out of trouble back here,' Josiah answered dryly. 'As it was, he got himself into a bit of bother with the police when they sailed into Townsville, and Sam had to extract him.

I have heard nothing from them since, but presume they are in Rabaul.'

David immediately thought of Caroline. No doubt she would already be there by now. He secretly cursed that the family schooner was not readily available to take a trip to the German Pacific territory. But it would return, and then David would find an excuse to travel to Rabaul. Even now that the distance between him and the woman who had stolen his heart had been reduced, all that he could focus on was finding her again.

'There is something else I should tell you about your uncle Sam's journey to Rabaul,' Josiah said. 'While he is there on behalf of our company buying copra to trade, he is undertaking a covert mission for our government.'

David looked sharply at his father. 'What do you mean by a covert mission? Is Uncle Sam a spy now?'

'There are a handful of people in the Defence Department who fear that if war comes to Europe, it just might draw Britain in, and the presumption is that we would provide military support to the Mother Country. The real threat to us is that we might find ourselves at war with the German empire on our doorstep in the Pacific Islands.'

David's blood ran cold. That would mean Caroline would be considered an enemy. He felt a renewed and pressing desperation to find her.

★

It was late afternoon. Ben was on horseback deep in the groves of coconut trees with the workers when Kurt arrived at the von Neumann estate with his contingent of armed native police. Kurt dismounted from his horse and was met by Solomon.

'I am here to speak with Countess von Neumann,'

74

Kurt said, removing his riding gloves. 'Inform her that *Oberleutnant zur See* Jäger requests a meeting of great importance concerning a matter of national security.'

Solomon entered the sprawling residence and located Caroline at her desk perusing company documents. He passed on the German officer's message, and Caroline placed her fountain pen on the desk, wondering what could possibly concern the empire's security. For a moment she was confused, but then she realised the matter must be related to Ben, as he was a foreigner. Caroline knew that Kurt, her former escort, worked for the German naval intelligence service. She felt a chill of apprehension run through her.

'Solomon, please warn Master Ben discreetly that he must find a place to hide himself until the police have departed. Be quick,' she said quietly.

'I know a place,' Solomon answered. He had no love for the native police and German troops as the Tolai had resisted occupation of their lands and had paid a high price in blood.

Caroline brushed herself down and appeared on the balcony overlooking the grassy yard.

'*Oberleutnant zur See* Jäger, I believe you wish to speak with me? You are welcome to join me in the house,' she called down to him.

Kurt detected a coldness in her tone he did not expect. After all, he had been her lover on the sea voyage to Rabaul, and now she spoke to him as if he were a total stranger. Had she taken this Australian he had heard about as a new lover? Kurt felt a surge of jealousy mixed with anger. He had hoped the trek to her plantation to carry out his official duties would also provide a good excuse to reestablish the relationship they had enjoyed on the journey to Rabaul. He had presumed she would invite him to her bedroom, and yet her change in attitude towards him suggested otherwise. Kurt surmised this must be because of the foreigner she had employed.

Kurt left his mount with one of the police and strode up the wide steps leading to the first floor, where he was greeted by a young serving girl in a clean dress. She shyly escorted Kurt to the dining room with a view over the estate where a silver pot of coffee had already been prepared alongside small, iced cakes.

Caroline sat in a chair on one side of the table but did not stand to greet him. 'I daresay you will welcome fresh coffee after your journey. Or would you prefer something stronger?' she asked.

Kurt took a seat in the chair opposite her. 'It is a pleasure to see you again, Caroline,' he said as she poured him a cup of coffee.

'I was informed by my manservant that you are here on official business,' Caroline said, cutting short any attempt on his part to make small talk.

Kurt stiffened, realising from her frosty reception that she had no interest in him as a man she had once shared a bed with. Well, two could play at that game.

'I have been informed that you are currently employing a foreigner, a Mr Benjamin Steele, from the schooner the *Ella*,' he stated in a cold and official voice. A rage was rising in Kurt, and he knew he was no longer thinking with the calmness of a good intelligence officer. He would kill the man he strongly considered to be the new man in her life. His pride was seriously wounded by Caroline's obvious rebuff to his reappearance. 'I require that you hand him over to me now.'

'Mr Steele is with the workers in the coconut groves, but he could be anywhere. He occasionally rides out to scout for any possible threats to the workers from bandit raiders. I am sure you are aware of the threats we face so far from the protection of the police in Rabaul.'

'The man must be captured and interrogated,' Kurt said, the coffee souring in his stomach. 'I am sure you are aware that we have a radio station not far from your plantation and its security is of the utmost importance.'

'We are not at war,' Caroline countered. 'Don't you think that your concerns are a bit paranoid?'

Kurt's face flushed with anger. 'I presume that you are ignorant of political matters currently in Europe,' he said tightly.

'Politics is not of much interest to me,' Caroline retorted. 'My mission to Rabaul was to inspect my father's copra interests here before I return to Germany next week.'

'Oh, you do not know? The steamer that was to arrive has been held back in Hamburg. You will not be leaving here for the foreseeable future. I am sorry for the inconvenience.' Kurt's voice held a note of bitter pleasure.

Caroline was taken aback by the announcement and irritated that she had not heard this latest news. She admitted to herself that she had been preoccupied with sharing her bed with a man for whom, to her surprise, she had come to feel that most elusive of emotions – love. Now she sensed his life would be in dire peril if Kurt caught up with him. No doubt a report following Ben's death would state he had resisted arrest and been shot in the process. She hoped that Solomon had delivered the message to Ben to hide himself.

'I thank you for the coffee, Countess,' Kurt said, rising from his chair and striding to the door. 'I will be ordering my men to make a thorough search of your plantation, and your house.'

'You can be sure your unauthorised search of my estate will be reported back to my father,' Caroline snapped.

'But my search *is* authorised,' Kurt replied, 'and we will not be leaving until Mr Steele is found and interrogated as to his real reasons for being on your plantation. I bid you a good afternoon.' With that he left Caroline to march downstairs and issue orders for the search.

Caroline made her way to the balcony and watched the party of fifteen police break away in small groups. Five headed into her house while the rest went directly to where her workers were labouring among the tall coconut palms. She could hear the shouted, raised voices of the police when they reached the workers, and the heavy footsteps of the search party entering her house. Her serving girl's voice cried out in protest but was silenced with a sickening thud, as if she had been clubbed with the butt of a rifle.

Caroline felt real fear – not for herself, but for Ben should he be captured.

EIGHT

Sitting astride his horse, Ben was lifting his hat and wiping the sweat from his face with a colourful bandana Caroline had given him as a gift when he saw Solomon running towards him. The Tolai man waved, and when he reached Ben he informed him in a mix of English, German and his own language that Ben must immediately find a place to hide. Ben gathered from the garbled warning that the police had arrived at the plantation to take him away. For a moment he was confused, but the expression on Solomon's face convinced him the situation was serious.

Solomon was able to indicate he knew a place deep in the thick undergrowth of the rainforest, a place they could go to hide. The Tolai man pointed to a narrow track leading into the bordering forest, and not long after they'd set out along it, Ben could hear the shouts of the police threatening the workers not far away.

After a while the track petered out and Ben dismounted. With Solomon in the lead, hacking at undergrowth with a machete he always carried in his belt, they were soon deep in the humid confines of the forest. It felt to Ben as though the jungle had swallowed them, as if it were a living organism sympathetic to the two men.

After an hour of struggle through the thick scrub, Solomon led Ben into a small clearing where Ben saw two crudely constructed thatch huts. A group of wizened old men and women stared with curiosity at the intruders. Solomon walked over to a toothless elderly man sitting cross-legged on a thatch platform and the man greeted him with obvious happiness. Ben could see that they knew each other, and the old man rose to his feet, following Solomon back to Ben.

'Safe here,' Solomon said in English. 'My father's father help us.'

The old man was short and looked up at Ben's face with the glimmer of a smile. Suddenly he took Ben's hand to guide him to a hut while Solomon tethered the horse at the edge of the clearing. Ben became aware of the silence around him, punctuated only by the occasional call of tropical birds high in the canopy. The forest floor felt dim and cool.

'I go back to Missus,' Solomon said. 'You stay. I come back.'

Ben did not question the Tolai man, knowing that his life was in his hands.

*

Night fell quickly on the plantation as it always did in the tropics.

Kurt had called his police officers in to camp on the

80

lawns of Caroline's grassy front yard, where he had erected his own small tent. Now he sat outside this temporary residence before a small fire, sipping coffee and brooding once more over the likelihood that the missing foreigner was Caroline's latest lover.

The senior native policeman approached Kurt to report in.

'Do you have any idea where the man we are looking for is?' Kurt asked.

'He has gone bush,' the man replied. 'We see horse tracks and follow, but my men fearful. The country he has gone is very hard to track in and there are people living there who have bad sickness that makes them the walking dead.'

Kurt could hear the genuine fear in his man's statement and guessed that he was referring to the disease of leprosy commonly found across the Pacific Islands. As far as Kurt knew, there was no cure for the hideous, disfiguring illness.

He grudgingly accepted the reluctance of the police to possibly expose themselves to the 'walking dead', but nonetheless knew it was time to make a decision. Dismissing the policeman, Kurt spent the rest of the evening weighing up his options.

The following morning he packed his tent and departed for Rabaul township without bidding farewell to Caroline. He knew that Benjamin Steele would have to reappear if he wished to leave Rabaul, and at that point he would be detained.

★

Solomon came back two days later to inform Ben it was safe to return.

When Ben arrived at the house he was greeted by Caroline, and he could clearly see the concern in her expression as she ran down the stairs, flinging herself into his arms.

'My darling Ben, I was afraid that they might have found you.'

'Thanks to Solomon,' Ben said, 'I was well hidden, and his grandfather looked after me.'

'I have been informed that I will not be leaving Rabaul for at least a month,' Caroline said, knowing that her statement changed the course of their relationship. 'But I also know that you must find a way to get away before the authorities find you.'

Ben wanted to say that her delayed departure was great news, but he also realised that it was impossible for him to stay. Solomon had already warned him that word from the native police was that he was not to be taken alive, and this confused Ben, as to kill him would surely be considered murder under any nation's law.

'I am afraid the man leading the police is someone I am acquainted with, and I think he has a personal grudge against you because he and I knew each other in the past,' Caroline said, stroking his unshaven face. Ben did not want to know what Caroline meant by *knew each other*.

'Who is he?' Ben asked, and Caroline told him of Kurt and his role as an intelligence officer for the Imperial German Navy.

'But we are not at war with Germany,' Ben said. 'Nor will we be, God willing.'

It was mid-July, and unbeknownst to Ben and Caroline, matters in Europe had reached the point of no return. Neither Ben nor Caroline were aware that the storm clouds of war were about to amass even in this paradise so far from Europe.

★

Keith Ward paced the deck of the *Ella* waiting for Sam to return, and when he did, Keith immediately saw the look of concern in the schooner owner's face.

'They sent police to the countess's plantation to arrest Ben,' Sam said when he boarded the schooner. 'Apparently they failed to do so, but the German officer in charge has sworn to find and arrest him.'

'What do we do under the circumstances?' Keith asked.

Sam rubbed his face with his hand as if attempting to rid himself of the critical decision he knew he must make. 'We have little choice,' he sighed. 'If we stay in port waiting for him, he risks being caught in any attempt to board the *Ella*. I know that they are watching us, and I think that the authorities are concerned because Ben has been located close to their radio station. With the political atmosphere at the moment, they might attempt to accuse him of spying, and that would not bode well for Ben or for us. So, I say we sail on the outgoing tide this afternoon. I have faith that Ben can take care of himself until all this concern about a coming war dies down, and we all get back to business trading in the Pacific with the Germans. I am pretty sure Ben is safe in the hands of the countess, judging by the last time I saw him with her.'

Keith nodded. He liked the young man and prayed that Sam was right. But Keith had also heard rumours around the German Club that the countess was having an affair with Ben, and that the officer who had led the police to the plantation at Bita Paka, one Kurt Jäger, had also once been a lover of the enchanting woman. Maybe jealousy was playing a part in the naval officer's obsession to find Ben? Human emotion so easily overrode logic, in the sea captain's experience. He hoped the rumours were wrong, but he worried that the young German officer was out for revenge.

★

It was the end of July and Archibald Stokes pored over the latest communiqués from London, which had been delivered by the magic of modern telegraphic transmission via undersea cables to Australia.

He had long ago learned to read between the lines, and thought that the French president's visit to St Petersburg in Russia for a state meeting with the Czar was ominous under the current tense circumstances.

The next item he read was that a conference concerning the future of occupied Ireland had failed to find resolution at a meeting in Buckingham Palace. Archibald pondered this item but set it aside as a domestic matter between the English and the Irish.

But the next message caused the civil servant a real chill of fear: the Austrians had commenced their invasion of Serbia!

He sat up straight at his desk and scoured the sheet of paper for further details. As far as he was concerned, the French president's visit to meet the Czar and the move by Austria were linked. The Russians would not allow an invasion of Serbia and would mobilise for war against the Austro-Hungarian Empire. In turn, France would declare its support of Russia and three mighty empires would clash in a bloody war. Archibald also considered that if this occurred the Austrians would call on their ally, the Germans, to support them, thus dragging in a fourth empire – and empires meant interests across the world. This would be a conflict on a global scale.

But what would be Britain's response?

Britain also had an empire, but stood outside the current political entanglements on the European continent. Rifling through the other communiqués, Archibald found the deciphered copy of a coded telegram from London. Three words turned the liquid in his stomach to acid . . . *War is imminent.*

Archibald made a hasty note on the item concerning the Austrian invasion, which at this stage had been conducted without a declaration of war against the Serbs by the Austrians. What Archibald did not know was that precisely this news was already being transmitted through the cables under the sea to Australia.

He pushed his chair aside and hurried to his supervisor with his calculated opinion. But, not entirely surprisingly, he was dismissed with the scornful comment, 'It is just another European skirmish and will fizzle out by Christmas. England has no military links to the French and Russians. After all, the Kaiser is a cousin to Czar Nicholas. I am sure the royal families will work it out between themselves and that the telegram sent to us is simply some overenthusiastic civil servant – not unlike you and your pessimistic concerns. I would forget about it.'

The King of Great Britain was also a cousin to the rulers of Germany and Russia, Archibald thought gloomily.

'However, I can see that you are not a happy servant of His Majesty, so I will pass on your conclusions to our defence committee,' Archibald's superior grudgingly added. 'I just hope your alarmist views are not held against you in my next review of your performance.'

Archibald did not respond to the veiled threat, but he couldn't help but imagine doing violence to the arrogant and ignorant man sitting before him. But that was not the way of civil servants, so he thanked the man he would have liked to sock in the mouth for his reluctant support before leaving the office.

The report was duly forwarded to the defence committee, which included a couple of former serving army and naval officers with distinguished service as well as government officials. One of those men was Josiah Steele, who closely read the comments made by the civil servant who he had previously met and respected for his perceptive intelligence. But the committee also included a man named Sir Horace Anderson, who was the most despised person in Josiah's life. Their mutual animosity ran as far back as their schooldays when they'd both attended a prestigious boys' college in Sydney. A member of the Federal Senate, just over a decade and a half earlier Horace Anderson had been behind the attempted election of his nephew, who had been disgraced as a coward in the Boer War. The nephew had taken his own life, but rumours persisted that he had been murdered by a member of the Steele family.

Sir Horace was a new inclusion on the committee, and unfortunately was seated directly opposite Josiah when the group sat down to discuss the situation in Europe. Anderson glared at Josiah when their eyes met across the table and Josiah forced himself to try to ignore his old enemy.

After the preliminaries were dealt with and the current state of affairs clarified, a fresh news report was tabled at the meeting: Austria had made a formal declaration of war against Serbia.

Josiah shuddered as the tobacco smoke drifted across the meeting room where the committee sat smoking pipes, cigars and cigarettes. He knew there was a high chance that his brother Sam and son Ben were in German waters. As far as he knew, the heavy German cruisers *Scharnhorst*, *Gneisenau* and the light cruiser *Emden* might be in the vicinity of Rabaul. If Britain entered the war on the side of France and Russia, the *Ella* would be an easy target for the big guns of the German navy. Sam and Ben's safety now hinged on Britain staying out of the European conflict.

Despite being a less than frequent worshipper at his local synagogue, Josiah made an entreaty to God that the *Ella* had already sailed for Australian waters.

The meeting concluded and the committee members drifted from the meeting room to the hallway beyond, where Josiah found to his dismay that he was alone with Anderson.

'I have heard a rumour that your brother is on some secret mission to New Guinea,' Anderson said. 'It is the type of thing one comes to expect of the people you belong to.'

Josiah wanted to strike the man before him but remained calm. 'I presume you mean Australians, Anderson?' he replied.

'It is Sir Horace to you, Steele,' Anderson flared, 'and you know that I meant the Jews.' His lip curled.

'Sadly, I'm not a devout member of my religion, but I am a devout Australian who served in the army while you were grovelling in society to make money and achieve your unwarranted royal recognition. I am afraid that I could never recognise your knighthood knowing the despicable man that you really are.'

Anderson's face reddened at the rebuke. 'I have never really believed that my nephew shot himself,' he spat. 'I believe he was murdered by your brother.'

'Well, the police and the coroner were convinced that your nephew died by his own hand. I believe they call the incident suicide – the coward's way out – and we know he was one. If there is nothing else, I am a busy man and I will leave you to wallow in your bitterness.'

Josiah turned on his heel and strode down the hallway, leaving the federal senator spluttering in his fury but determined to have the last word. 'You will rue the day you were born, Steele,' he called to Josiah's departing back. 'Mark my words, my nephew will get his eventual revenge against you and your brother.'

Josiah ignored the threat. He was more concerned by the international events that might impact his family – especially his beloved brother and youngest son somewhere on the seas of the Pacific Ocean.

★

Ben was always on the alert when he stayed in Caroline's house – in case the police should suddenly return – but his nights shared with Caroline were worth the risk.

When the sun rose each morning, life went on as usual for Ben as a plantation supervisor working alongside the Tolai employees, and by night he and Caroline lay under the mosquito net, limbs entwined after their lovemaking, not wanting to consider the grim news of the burgeoning European crisis that was trickling through to the plantation.

Ben hoped it would all blow over and cool heads would realise that a European conflict was not in anyone's interest.

But he was wrong.

On one such night, in the darkened bedroom, Ben and Caroline slept peacefully, unaware that Kaiser Wilhelm II had sent a message to his cousin Nicholas II of Russia, stating that if he did not withdraw his support of Serbia and demobilise his army within twenty-four hours, Germany would fully mobilise its armed forces to counteract the Russian and French alliance.

Europe was on the brink of calamity.

★

Archibald groaned when he read the report from London that the Germans had rejected offers from Britain to mediate the dispute between them and the Russians. The German Kaiser had described the offer as English arrogance, and despite being neutral, the British navy had been placed on a cautious war footing. The question of Irish home rule was now forgotten with war looming in Europe.

But Archibald still hoped Britain would remain neutral in the event of full-scale fighting on the continent. He knew well that developing technology had changed the way any war would be fought. Archibald was a keen observer of military technology and knew that the days of dashing cavalry charges with swords and lances were over, as the Boer War had proved only a decade and a bit earlier.

But still there was no real sense of urgency among his peers, who preferred to discuss the sports results and scandals of high society and dismissed the ominous signs from half a world away. Archibald had long accepted that he was viewed as an outsider at best and an irrational alarmist at worst, but he was reassured to know that he was not alone after a private conversation with Josiah Steele at the Australia Club one evening. He had been invited as Josiah's guest on the premise that it was an opportunity for Josiah to brief Archibald on the situation in Rabaul, but Josiah admitted he had heard nothing since the family schooner left Townsville weeks earlier.

★

Bad news travels fast, and a trader at Caroline's plantation informed her that as of three days earlier, on the first day of August, the first shots had been fired between the Germans and Russians. Caroline met Ben with the news on the steps to her house when he rode back from the plantation to meet with her for dinner.

'Did the man mention anything about the situation

between Germany and Britain?' Ben asked, noticing the concern in her expression.

'No,' Caroline answered. 'All going well, England will stay out of any war and you will be safe here.'

Ben hoped against all hope that this was true, as he had learned the day before that Caroline thought she was pregnant. Ben was overjoyed at the news and had immediately gone down on one knee in the traditional method of proposal.

'I will marry you, Benjamin Steele,' she had replied with tears in her eyes. But they both knew a terrible cloud hung over their future together. Everything depended on Britain remaining neutral while the European empires savaged each other on the continent, however neither knew of the old treaty Britain, France and Germany had signed with the tiny Belgian nation to the north of France, which dated back to 1839 and guaranteed Belgium's independence and neutrality. It would change their lives forever.

On the fourth day of August, 1914, Britain declared that it was at war with the German and Austro-Hungarian empires. Caroline and Ben did not know it, but as they held hands at the dining table lit by candles under a beautiful starlit tropical night sky, sharing a bottle of expensive champagne to celebrate Caroline's pregnancy and their plans to wed, they were considered enemies by their respective nations.

The following day another trader stopped by the plantation with news that Britain was at war with Germany and that the Australian schooner, the *Ella*, had been lucky to leave the harbour when it did. Ben was now alone in enemy territory.

Part Two

August 1914

The Storm

NINE

It was at noon on the fifth of August that the German merchant ship, *Pfalz*, was granted permission to steam from the Melbourne port docks. Word had not yet reached Australian shores that Britain was at war with Germany, but by 12.10 pm the news reached the gunners at the Melbourne coastal artillery defences manning Point Nepean.

The German steamer was still within the coastal guns' range. A warning shot was fired about fifty yards astern of the unlucky German merchantman and a signal transmitted demanding it return to port.

By 5.15 pm the ship was in Australian hands, anchored at Williamstown. It was only then that the German crew understood why they were now prisoners of war, detained by the Australian government.

A shot had been fired in a war that most in the British empire believed would be well and truly over by Christmas 1914.

★

News reached Sydney that crowds were celebrating in the streets of London, Paris and Berlin at the announcement of war. Mobilised troops paraded to cries of fanatical encouragement from the cities' civilian populations, who showered the proud young uniformed men with flowers.

Josiah Steele shook his head as he stood in his office by the big window overlooking the harbour. The people in those crowds were fools who had never experienced the conditions of bloody combat, he thought bitterly. They were cheering for the lives that might be taken from their husbands, sons, brothers and lovers. He guessed that it was fixed in the minds of people who had never served that the war would comprise gallant cavalry charges across open fields with the cavalrymen shouting *Hurrah!* as they faced their opposites, and infantrymen closing with their counterparts with bayonets and bravery. No, war was personal terror, the mangled bodies of close friends, the deafening noise of shell and shot as young men were struck down and screamed for their mothers in hopeless despair as they died agonising deaths. Josiah knew all this as he had experienced it in colonial wars; and he knew that people would soon learn the hard way that war was a bestial experience.

A knock at his office door broke into Josiah's dark reflections.

'Mr Steele, your son is here.'

'Send him in and please fetch a pot of tea for us,' Josiah replied, stepping away from the window to greet David, who appeared wearing an army uniform with the two pips denoting he was a commissioned officer with the rank of lieutenant. Josiah was not surprised to see that David had resumed his commission.

'Good morning, Father,' David said, removing his peaked cap and taking a seat.

'I don't know how you resumed your commission so fast,' Josiah commented.

'It helps when your father happens to be a member of a committee advising on military matters,' David replied, crossing his legs and appearing smug and relaxed. 'I was able to convince a few chaps that experienced men were needed immediately for service.'

'You have yet to experience actual active service,' Josiah cautioned. 'Peace-time soldiering does not prepare you for the sight of your first friend dying before your eyes.'

David shifted slightly at the subtle rebuke but knew the outbreak of war had provided him with the chance to prove himself worthy to uphold the military tradition of the Steele family. This dated back to his legendary grandfather, Captain Ian Steele, who had fought from one end of the British empire to the other for Queen Victoria – and even his own father, Josiah, who had served in Afghanistan, and Africa in the first Boer War.

'Has any word arrived from Uncle Sam and Ben?' David asked.

A tray was placed on a small side table by Josiah's personal secretary – a young man with aspirations of rising in the company ranks. Josiah poured two cups of tea but did not reply until the man was out of the room.

'Your uncle sent a telegram from Townsville yesterday,' he said finally. 'Alarmingly, Ben is not with him. Sam was forced to leave Rabaul without him, due to circumstances I am yet to discover. A full report has been posted to us which will explain everything concerning the mission and why Ben is still in German territory.'

'Damn!' David swore. 'I pray that my brother is safe and wonder how in hell he could have found himself trapped in German-controlled territory.'

Josiah frowned and rubbed his forehead. He was even now bitterly regretting letting his younger son join the expedition to Rabaul. But he half-heartedly consoled himself that no one could foresee the future.

'Thankfully Ben is a civilian. If he is captured by the Germans, he should be treated as such,' Josiah attempted to reassure his son. 'I am sure that a system of prisoner exchange will be put in place by both sides.' Josiah knew all this was true, but he also grimly realised that his younger son had a reputation for being hot-headed and impulsive. He was his own worst enemy.

★

Sam Steele found a bar in Townsville where he could simply drown his guilt. He couldn't get past the fact that he had chosen the mission over his beloved nephew's safety.

He ordered a beer and listened to the hum of conversation among the men around him. The main subject of discussion was naturally the war, although most men thought that it would be swiftly brought to a close once the British Expeditionary Force landed in France to fight side by side with their French allies against the brutal Huns. Stories of the killing of innocent men, women and children were filtering out of Belgium as refugees fled from the unstoppable advance of the Imperial German Army south towards Paris itself.

But word was that the professional British army – albeit small – was more than a match for the Germans. It would all be over by Christmas, denying Australian armed forces an opportunity to join the fight in Europe. One or two patrons who were Boer War veterans told of their experiences in Africa. Sam could see that the idea of seeing the world and participating in a grand adventure swirled in the thoughts of many young men listening, who had likely never travelled more than a few miles from their homes.

Sam glanced down at the place where his leg should have been, the leg he had left behind somewhere in Africa.

'We should let the bloody English fight their own war.' An Irish-accented voice spoke up in defiance of the general mood of support.

'Shut up, Paddy,' another voice yelled, but Sam could see that a handful of tough-looking men appeared to agree with the Irishman's resistance to fighting alongside the English in France.

Sam noticed that the mood was turning ugly in the confined space of the hotel and turned away from the bar.

'I wouldn't be in any hurry to sign up, if I were you fellas,' he said, attracting the interest of the crowded bar.

'That's fightin' talk,' one belligerent young man countered. 'I'd knock yer block off if you weren't so old and crippled,' he added.

'How do you think I lost my leg?' Sam asked with a faint smile. 'I'll tell you. It was during a battle in some bloody obscure place in Africa called Elands River, and it left me the old and useless cripple you think I am.'

A hush descended in the bar as Sam spoke, and a few of the men shifted their feet in embarrassment. Sam went on, 'The army gave me the Distinguished Conduct Medal, but it does not replace my leg, and the medal means very little to anyone else. So, be thankful some Pommy will lose his leg or his life while you get the chance to come here every day and have a cold beer, then walk home to your families on two good legs.'

Finished with his speech, Sam turned back to the bar to see a fresh glass of beer in front of him.

'My shout,' the publican said, meeting Sam's gaze.

'I served with the Queensland mounted infantry in the Transvaal and I know what happened at Elands River.'

The conversation in the bar was far more muted after Sam spoke, and a couple of the patrons came up to Sam to slap him on the shoulder, one paying for another beer for him. Sam made his way back to the schooner as the sun was going down over the distant hills of Townsville, weaving his way unsteadily along the broad streets until he reached the wharf and was helped by the crew to board.

Once aboard, Sam stumbled to his cabin and collapsed into sleep, but it was a sleep disturbed by the nightmarish sounds of exploding artillery shells and the screams of dying and wounded men. It was all happening again to a younger generation.

★

Even as Sam slipped into his nightmares of war, Ben prepared to be taken by Solomon to a safe place. Standing in his room, Ben shouldered his rifle and had the fleeting thought that his uncle's military-issue .303 might now be used in war against the declared enemies of Australia. It was surreal; that felt like a world away from this paradise of exotic flowers, butterflies and the love of a beautiful woman who had accepted his marriage proposal. Now he knew that he would be hunted until he was captured – or more likely killed – if what Caroline had told him of the young German officer was true. Caroline thought Kurt's true motivation was to remove the person who stood between him and his former lover, and now he had the perfect excuse to legally do so.

'Please be careful, my love,' Caroline said from the doorway. 'Kurt will not give up until he finds you.'

Ben turned to her and she came to him, throwing her

arms around his neck and kissing him passionately on the lips. Ben wanted the kiss to linger but he pulled away gently, gazing into her eyes.

'It's all a bloody mess,' Ben said. 'But wars cannot go on forever and I promise you that afterwards we will be together for the rest of our lives.' He placed his hand on her still-flat stomach. 'Besides, we have a third party to consider.'

Caroline touched his face with her fingers. 'And hopefully more children in the future. The trader told me that people back in Germany are saying the war will be over by Christmas.'

Ben hoped so, but could not express that his hopes were for a victory by the allied forces of Russia, France and England.

'We go now.' Solomon's voice cut in as he appeared in the doorway. Ben could see the concerned expression on the Tolai man's dark face. 'Some in our village are loyal to the Germans in Rabaul and would report you to the police, so we must hurry.'

Ben nodded and hugged Caroline once more before breaking away to scoop up a kitbag containing canned food and ammunition. It was time to go.

★

Oberleutnant zur See Kurt Jäger left the briefing held in a large sandbagged tent set up outside Rabaul in case of a sudden naval bombardment. The briefing had been pessimistic. All naval and army officers knew they had few resources to fend off a determined attack. As far as the Kaiser's government was concerned, the defence of Germany's Pacific territories was just a side show to the grand operation to capture Paris and Moscow. There were no cruiser gunboats in the immediate vicinity to oppose a naval assault nor enough German troops. They would have to rely on their trained native auxiliaries, which were considered loyal and competent as they had received thorough German training.

Kurt had been able to mention to the meeting that he was aware of a possible spy for the British currently located in the vicinity of their vital radio station who needed to be detained before he could communicate with the enemy about its current operational state. Kurt knew he would be automatically granted his wish to hunt the man down before he could possibly sabotage the radio station, and he was given the command of thirty armed native police to carry out his mission.

Satisfied, Kurt stood outside the tent headquarters and lit a cigar, blowing smoke into the tranquil tropical night. It was possible that the Countess von Neumann was in league with the man he knew as Benjamin Steele and as such, she would be considered to be committing treachery against the Fatherland – if she was actually aiding and abetting him.

Kurt smiled grimly. Her fate was also in his hands.

He set out the next morning to carry out his search for the Australian lurking somewhere around Bita Paka. *How the mighty have fallen*, he mused. Caroline had little choice but to acknowledge his important role if she was to remain a free woman and not bring disgrace on her father and family in Germany.

It was only a matter of time.

TEN

Solomon led Ben on foot to the small village deep in the forest where he had taken shelter when Kurt Jäger first came looking for him. Ben had decided to leave his horse because its tracks would be easy for any search party to follow. They arrived as the sun was descending behind the rugged hills, and Solomon told Ben that from here he would be guided deeper into the hills by one of the younger men of the village.

Ben knew the man from his previous visit and cursed himself for shuddering at the thought. The young man was disfigured by the disease of leprosy but was still able to function. The ancient condition still remained throughout the Pacific Islands where leper colonies had been established by missionaries such as Father Damian.

The man known as Abengo gestured to Ben to follow him which Ben did for over an hour, pushing through scrub until they reached a cave just below the ridge of a string of high hills. Abengo carried an animal fur bag which he placed at Ben's feet when they reached their destination.

Abengo spoke no English, but Ben thanked him before entering the small dark cave, which did not stretch far into the side of the ridge, but at least provided shelter from the elements.

Abengo disappeared, leaving Ben alone with his kitbag, rifle and the animal fur bag, which Ben now opened to find cold cooked pork pieces, porridge-like sago in a small gourd and a form of cooked tuber. For a moment Ben hesitated to eat the food, then decided it would be best warmed over a small fire he was able to light at the entrance of the cave. He felt guilty about his aversion to the man who had helped him, but also hoped that the flames of the fire might burn away any traces of the dreaded disease he knew Abengo had. Even so, his hunger after the long trek forced Ben to put aside his dread of contracting leprosy and eat the food.

As he ate, the clear skies and strange sounds of the jungle around him fell silent as dark, ominous clouds dimmed the starry night sky and rain began to fall as if dropped out of a giant bucket.

Ben was grateful that his new home kept him dry and safe for the moment, but nevertheless he fell asleep with the rifle by his side, hoping that the cave would only be a temporary residence until the situation changed.

★

They came in the early morning.

Caroline was alerted to the presence of the native police by the startled cries of her workers. She rolled onto her side and stared for a moment at the empty space where Ben had laid with her for so long, touching the pillow his head had once rested on. Then Caroline pushed aside the mosquito net and quickly clothed herself in time to hear the banging on her front door.

'Countess,' Kurt said, his expression grim when she let him in. Behind him were two native police with rifles in their hands. 'I am sure that you know why we are here.'

'Mr Steele has left my plantation and I do not know where he is,' Caroline answered defiantly.

'When did he leave?' Kurt asked belligerently.

'A day past,' Caroline replied. 'He left because we have learned of war between Britain and Germany and we realised that you would consider him an enemy alien. I think that you would do the same if you were in his situation.'

'He is a spy, and as such I have the authority to execute him but, if he surrenders himself, my superiors will take this as a sign of goodwill and simply detain him,' Kurt said. 'I am sure that you have the means of getting that message to him. We are civilised people; we do not shoot fellow Europeans on sight.'

'I am not in a position to make contact with Mr Steele as I do not know where he has fled,' Caroline replied. 'Your guess is as good as mine.'

Caroline could see in Kurt's expression that he did not believe her. She hoped that Solomon had been successful in finding a safe place for Ben to hide. As if reading her mind, Kurt said, 'I do not see your head man around the plantation. Where is he?'

The question caught Caroline off guard. It was obvious that Solomon had not returned from taking Ben to sanctuary. 'Solomon was given the evening off to visit his family in the forest,' Caroline blurted, and immediately regretted her words.

Kurt turned to the two police standing behind him and

issued an order for them to locate the head man. Then he turned back to Caroline. 'You are ordered to remain in your residence until I allow you to leave, Countess,' he said. 'At the moment you are under suspicion for aiding and abetting an enemy alien. I have the authority to forcibly remove you to Rabaul to face a military enquiry as to your relationship with the Australian spy.'

'Relationship!' Caroline flared. 'Mr Steele was managing my plantation, which was perfectly above board until this war began, at which point he left my employ. What you really mean is that you are jealous of my feelings for Mr Steele.'

'I have no feelings for you, Caroline,' said Kurt coldly. 'I am just doing my duty to capture a dangerous spy who we suspect has a mission to gather intelligence on our radio station not far from your plantation. I further suspect that he has used you to do that.' Kurt sneered at her. 'You are a foolish woman, but that might go in your favour if I am forced to escort you back to Rabaul.'

Caroline was acutely aware that as Germany was now at war, the military had great powers over the civilian population and Kurt might well carry out his threat. Never before had she felt so vulnerable and confused. She loved her country as a true patriot, but she also loved a declared enemy of her nation. Loyalty to Germany or her love for Ben? The question haunted her.

Caroline glanced over Kurt's shoulder to the yard below and saw that the two police had Solomon between them as they approached their commander. Caroline could see that one of Solomon's eyes was swollen and guessed that he had been arrested using physical force.

Kurt turned to his men with a satisfied smile.

'I am sure that Solomon is a true supporter of our

administration and might cooperate with us to help find Mr Steele.'

Caroline felt a chill of fear. It was all too easy to imagine how Kurt would get Solomon to talk as they dragged him away.

★

At least Archibald Stokes had the satisfaction of knowing that he was right all along about the war that had now come. The senior department head who had dismissed his concerns had been duly promoted for his diligence, and despite his annoyance Archibald understood that this was how things worked in the civil service – incompetence was often rewarded, and initiative stifled.

But he knew he always had an ally in the highly regarded Josiah Steele, who had been able to hand on the intelligence report compiled by his brother, Samuel Steele, on the situation in Rabaul. This meant Archibald could incorporate the latest information into a briefing for the heads of the army and navy, who all agreed that they could strike a blow for the British empire by targeting German territory nearer to the Australian mainland. As many considered that the war would be over by Christmas, this was an opportunity to demonstrate the might of Australian and New Zealand arms to the Mother Country.

The main target selected for Australia was the radio station at Rabaul, while the Kiwis would target a radio post in German-occupied Samoa. By neutralising the radio stations, they would deny any German warships in the region vital intelligence as to their enemy's positions.

Archibald leaned back in his office chair and stared at the portrait of the King on the wall opposite, satisfied that he had been responsible for the mission to collect intelligence on the vital radio station at Rabaul that had been integrated in the plan to send a fleet there.

★

Ben spent a week in the cave, at which point his supply of rations was exhausted. More disturbing was that Solomon had not visited him to deliver more food as he'd said he would, so Ben knew that something was wrong.

Ben had not been idle, leaving the cave by day to find water and cautiously carry out a reconnaissance of his surroundings. Climbing higher on the ridge he was disappointed to discover that the tall trees and thick foliage concealed any real view of the world below his cave, which made it feel to him that he was the only man left on the planet. Alone in the cave at night, he began to formulate a plan to trek to the coast where he might be able to find a way of escaping the German territory by sea, but Ben knew that this plan was desperate and fraught with danger. But it appeared from the absence of Solomon that the situation at the plantation had dramatically changed, and this worried him more than his plan to escape the island. Had something happened to Caroline?

Before he sought escape, he knew that he must find his way back to the plantation and find the woman he had come to love more than his own life. On the eighth day, Ben hoisted his rifle and kitbag over his shoulder and made his way cautiously down the ridge.

By nightfall, after trekking through the dank and often dark rainforest, he finally found Solomon's grandfather's small village, where all appeared normal. But the villagers shrank away from his appearance, and the old grandfather hobbled towards Ben wielding a stick and yelling angry words.

Ben was startled. Obviously something had occurred to upset the old man. Ben thought it prudent to keep his distance, and backed away into the forest before taking a course he hoped would lead him to the plantation. The night was as dark as pitch, so he made a rough camp, dozing with the rifle in his lap and his back against a forest giant. The mosquitoes plagued him with their bites and buzzing, and he had little sleep as the starry sky rotated slowly overhead. In the dim light of dawn Ben drank the last drops of water from his canteen before setting off again, trudging almost like a sleepwalker until just after midday the forest surroundings became more familiar, and he knew he was close to the house and the tall rows of coconut groves. He could even hear the now-familiar voices of the Tolai people who worked there.

Ben gripped his rifle and edged forward until he could see the village adjacent to the plantation. Men, women and children appeared to be going about their lives, but Ben also noted that no one appeared to be harvesting the valuable nut for copra production. He hoped that he would see Solomon, and from his concealed position in the forest he carefully scanned the villagers for the familiar face, but with no success. Ben waited for a couple of hours, fighting off insects, and then muttered to himself, 'Damn it!'

He rose and walked cautiously towards a group of children playing with sticks. As soon as they saw him, they immediately broke away from their game and ran back to the adults. Ben approached them, holding up his hands in a non-threatening gesture.

Despite knowing who he was, the villagers shrank from him. Ben could see that he was being observed with a mixture of curiosity and fear by the men and women, which confirmed for him that the situation had radically changed.

Ben called in a loud voice, 'Solomon, Solomon?'

One young man stepped forward. Ben knew him as intelligent and hardworking. He also spoke some English, and had often come to Ben to learn more. Ben remembered that his name was Jacob.

'Masta, Solomon . . . he sick,' Jacob said when he approached.

'Where is he?' Ben asked, and Jacob gestured to one of the thatch houses. Ben followed Jacob to the hut and stepped inside. At first his vision was impacted from moving from the bright sunlight into the darkness of the windowless hut. When his sight finally adjusted, he saw an old woman crouching by a prone body lying on a woven mat. Ben felt his heart skip a beat when he saw that Solomon's back was almost raw. It was obvious that he had been severely whipped almost to the point of death.

Ben knelt by the old woman and Solomon turned his head to acknowledge Ben's presence.

'God almighty! What have they done to you!'

'Missus gone,' Solomon replied in a pain-racked whisper. 'Police take her to Rabaul. They beat me but I do not tell them where you hide.'

'I am so sorry that you had to suffer,' Ben said gently. 'If I was not here you might still be all right.'

'Bloody Germans,' Solomon said hoarsely and with passion. 'I kill them all. They say you are dangerous man.'

'If I get the chance, the Germans will find out that I am,' Ben replied with conviction. Already he knew that he was well and truly at war with the German empire. But he also realised that he was just one man with limited resources to wreak any vengeance on the people who had so cruelly whipped Solomon and left him to die.

'You must hide,' Solomon said. 'They kill you.'

It was then that Ben finally recognised the hopeless situation he was in. Alone, deep in German territory without local support he would not survive for long. He would likely die either from a Mauser bullet or simply of hunger or malaria.

As if sensing Ben's despair Solomon said, 'Jacob will help you. He a good man and hate Germans who took our land.' Ben turned to see Jacob hovering in the doorway of the hut. He was grateful for this lifeline, but his concern now was for Caroline's fate; had she been arrested for aiding him – or worse?

No matter the odds against him, it was time for Ben to wage war on the German island of Neu-Pommern.

ELEVEN

Ben and Jacob retreated to the inland hills to seek sanctuary. As a Tolai man, Jacob was more easily able to
move about and seek supplies from sympathetic villagers.

With little other than his rifle and a limited supply
of bullets, Ben knew he was not in a position to engage
in a firefight with the armed native police if they came in
strength for him, and his only forlorn hope was that his
government might have a plan to attack Rabaul. Ben
would spend his nights gazing at the starry sky, wondering
where Caroline was at that very moment. His greatest
desire was to survive and find her.

The days passed. Ben had grown a small beard which
itched, but shaving was not an option as he had run out of
razor blades. His whole body was covered in tropical sores
and insect bites, and he had lost weight.

One night, after they'd eaten a meal of sticky sago

porridge that Jacob had prepared, Ben noticed that Jacob was squatting by the fire, gazing at the small flames. Ben could see that he was concerned about something.

'What worries you, old chap?' Ben asked, returning the bolt to his rifle after lightly oiling it.

'I think I bugger up,' Jacob replied. 'There was a chief who warned me that a man in the village has a brother in the native police. He tells me that there is a reward for your capture.'

Ben experienced a chill, but he was not surprised. Betrayal was something he knew might occur. 'What do you think?' Ben asked, and Jacob shrugged his shoulders. He was only armed with a machete and no match against the German Mauser rifles. Ben hoped that if they had been betrayed, the police would have difficulty finding them in the rugged terrain.

Ben was wrong.

★

Josiah, Marian and David were invited to a Sunday lunch with their eldest daughter and sister, Judith, and her husband, Dr Maurice Cohen, a well-respected surgeon who practised in the prestigious surgeries of Macquarie Street. Judith's children were staying with her sister, Rose, and her husband for the day.

Josiah always felt a twinge of guilt when he was with his devout daughter, as he was not a frequent visitor to their synagogue. He had at least ensured his two boys had their *bar mitzvah* when they were younger. The pressure of managing the family enterprises kept him busy but he kept his conscience free with generous donations to the local Jewish community.

David was wearing his army uniform. Josiah knew he had

been assigned to a newly formed unit, the Australian Naval and Expeditionary Force. But the talk at the lunch focused on Ben, as nothing had been heard of him since Sam had been forced to sail from Rabaul many weeks earlier. Josiah attempted to reassure his family that he thought Ben would be safe and unharmed; at worst, he might be a prisoner of the Germans, but as a civilian, he should be in no danger. The Germans appeared to respect the rules governing war.

'But what of the stories we are hearing of the German atrocities in Belgium?' Judith asked.

'I am sure the stories are exaggerated,' Josiah replied. 'It is the way of war to demonise our opponents.' His explanation did not seem to reassure his daughter, who frowned.

It was Maurice who changed the subject. He was a balding man in his mid-thirties who wore spectacles. Maurice was always known to Josiah as his quieter son-in-law, but Josiah knew this had much to do with his studious nature. Josiah always thought that Maurice would have made a good rabbi. 'What is this new unit you are with?' Maurice asked David.

'I am afraid it is all a bit hush-hush,' David replied, pausing in lifting his spoon of delicious soup.

'I understand,' Maurice replied. 'I suppose I will know more when I get my uniform.'

A stunned silence followed, and all eyes went to Maurice at the end of the table.

'Maurice, what are you talking about?' Judith exploded. 'What uniform?'

Without looking at his wife Maurice replied, 'I have been accepted as a surgeon in the Australian army, and I will be reporting to Victoria Barracks next week.'

An expression of horror crossed Judith's face. 'But you

have a thriving practice and a family,' she said. 'You did not discuss this with me. You would desert us?'

'I knew that it would be useless to attempt to convince you why I feel it is my duty to enlist for King and Country. I have organised for my partner in the practice to continue while I am away. It was not an easy decision – I am fully aware of my responsibilities to you and our children – but it appears the war will be over soon, and then I will return to you all.'

Josiah was stunned by his shy son-in-law's decision but understood why he had taken it. The army would need every medical practitioner they could get hold of in the event of a modern war, and surgeons most of all. He also knew that Maurice had been correct in not discussing the decision with Judith, as she was a very strong woman and the real ruler of her family. Maybe Maurice had taken a giant step in asserting himself, Josiah mused.

Judith immediately pushed her chair away from the table and stormed out of their dining room, leaving a silence behind. Marian put down her napkin, excused herself and hurried after her daughter.

It was David who spoke first. 'Morrie, welcome to the army. We truly appreciate your sacrifice.'

Maurice nodded his head, but Josiah could see he was a troubled man. Josiah knew that when they all departed, Maurice would have to face his wife, and Josiah was glad that they would not be there for the confrontation.

When Marian returned, she addressed Maurice sitting forlornly at the end of the table. 'I think that we should depart, as I suspect you will need to sort things out in the family before you report for duty.' Her declaration was issued in a cold voice. It was obvious whose side she was on.

Maurice nodded grimly as the others stood, and David

walked over to him, placing his hand on his shoulder. 'The army will look after you and you will be back home before you know it.'

Josiah knew this was a feeble promise, but hoped it would comfort Maurice. Then Josiah glanced at David, who he alone knew would likely be involved in the action being planned to defend Australian interests in the Pacific in the coming weeks.

It was a gloomy, silent drive in Josiah's automobile back to the Steele mansion. Josiah suspected that he was about to be given a very stern talking to by Marian.

★

The jungle had become a green hell for Ben. Day in and day out all he knew was the forest and scrub around him. He greatly appreciated the company of Jacob when he returned from his forays to fetch food. But being separated from Caroline was agony, and not knowing where she was – or what fate may have befallen her – was worse still. At times he would climb to the top of a ridge or climb a tree to give him a view of the sea just a relatively short distance from his hide-out, only to view a blue emptiness. Despair was a creeping disease that sapped the body and soul, and it grew ever worse when after the five weeks he had counted since the outbreak of war it appeared no one was coming to his rescue.

In the sixth week Ben's despair hit its lowest point. Jacob was two days overdue to return to their camp. Ben could only conclude that something had happened and that he would probably never see the young man again. He looked at his rifle leaning against a tree, and for a fleeting moment he had a dark thought that he quickly shook off. No, if he was going to die, he would leave the shelter of the hills and return to the plantation where, if the police came again, he would stand and fight until he was taken down by a bullet.

Ben gathered his meagre kit, slung his rifle over his shoulder and took a deep breath to reassure himself. He was going down to confront the Germans and go out fighting. After all, it was the sacrifice any soldier knew he could face on the battlefield. In the shadow of the great trees, Ben set out on his final mission, fully aware that the odds were stacked against him.

★

It was a beautiful late spring day when Lieutenant David Steele stood at the front of his platoon at the Moore Park showgrounds. Military bands stood ready with their drums and trumpets, and the contingent of approximately six thousand soldiers and sailors of the Australian Naval and Military Expeditionary Force prepared to step off to the cheers of the civilian population who had gathered to farewell them for overseas service in the name of King and Country. They were not bound for Europe but for the Pacific, in defence of Australia's east coast and Pacific interests.

The order was issued and the men, arms sloped with gleaming, long bayonets attached to their rifles, stepped off with heads held high under slouch hats. They swung into leafy Randwick Road and marched until they reached Oxford Street, which was lined with shops and two-storeyed office buildings. People crowded the footpaths, cheering and sometimes dashing into the parade to place miniature Union Jack and Australian flags in the barrels of the soldiers' rifles. Men wearing straw boater hats and ladies in long dresses roared their acknowledgement to the proud young men who had been selected for active service overseas. They would show the people of Australia and England that they were more than a match for the dastardly Germans, who some now referred to as Huns after the invasion of Belgium.

From Oxford Street they marched down College Street, passing St Mary's Cathedral, and then along Macquarie Street, where David made a point of glancing up at his brother-in-law's medical suite. He was cheered to see Maurice and Judith peering down at the parade.

David could hear the crowd singing 'Advance Australia Fair' and also 'God Save the King' with enthusiasm, and felt a surge of pride. As the echo of six thousand pairs of hobnailed boots striking the hard surface of the city streets rang out, David looked ahead to their final destination at Fort Macquarie, where he knew his family planned to be.

★

Marian and Josiah stood side by side as the parade passed by them. When they saw David at the head of his men, Marian gasped. He looked so dashing, and yet she knew that he was marching to war. For Josiah, the sight of the military parade brought a rush of memories from the time when he too had marched along the same streets to embark for the Sudan. Only the uniforms and rifles had changed since then; the faces were the same, those of young men anticipating an adventure and confident in their ability to fight. The idea of being maimed or killed was far from their thoughts.

'Will we have the opportunity to personally farewell our dear boy?' Marian asked.

Josiah shook his head. 'We made our farewells yesterday at Moore Park,' he replied as more columns of soldiers and sailors marched past them to the beat of the military bands. 'They will begin embarking from Circular Quay to travel to Cockatoo Island, where their troop transport, the *Berrima,* will take them aboard. If we go home now, we will be able to view the ship from our garden as she steams for the Heads. I am sure David will be at the railings to seek out his home.'

Marian agreed, and with some difficulty they extracted themselves from the packed crowds and made their way back to Josiah's automobile.

★

Aboard the troop ship David ensured that his men were allocated their assigned accommodation before granting them leave to go to the ship's railings. Within minutes he could see his home overlooking the harbour and the two tiny specks he knew were his parents. He waved, but most of the soldiers manning the rails were also waving to the little boats and yachts following in the ship's wake, so David knew it was doubtful that his parents would be able to pick him out. He felt glad that he had seen them, though, and waved anyway.

Then, as the sun began to descend behind the Blue Mountains to the west of Sydney, the ship passed between the twin headlands and steered north into the rough swell of the Tasman Sea. Soon they would be joined by the mighty battle cruisers *HMAS Australia* and *HMAS Melbourne*, as well as other smaller warships and even a submarine, *AE1*, to provide protection against any German warships stationed in the Pacific Islands. David had been briefed that they would rendezvous just off New Guinea.

That evening David mingled with the naval and army officers in their designated mess area where the atmosphere was jovial, with just the slightest undercurrent of unexpressed fear for what might greet them when they landed on the German island of Neu-Pommern.

TWELVE

It was obvious that Caroline's plantation was no longer functioning as a commercial interest when Ben arrived in the early morning. The once-manicured lawns were overgrown and the workers seemed to have disappeared.

With the rifle in his hands, Ben moved cautiously as he approached the main house and walked up the stairs. Once inside he could see that the house had been looted and guessed that the departing workers had helped themselves to cooking utensils, bedding and anything that might fetch a price at their local markets. But the looters had not attempted to destroy any property, and even a paper calendar remained on the wall in the kitchen. Needless to say, all foodstuffs were gone from the kitchen.

Ben examined the calendar, and from his careful recording of the days and weeks that had passed he could see that it was most probably around the 11th or 12th of

September in the year 1914. He reflected that if he was right, it was his sister Rose's birthday. She would be around twenty-five, he thought.

A movement in the house alerted Ben to the fact that he was not alone, and he brought the rifle up to his waist. The hair on the back of his neck stood up as he strained to locate where he had heard what he thought were muffled footsteps.

Ben moved silently to the kitchen door to peer down the hallway.

'God almighty!' Ben swore when he saw Jacob walking towards him. Startled at the sight of Ben and his rifle, the young man froze.

'Don't shoot, masta!' he exclaimed, throwing his hands in the air.

Ben lowered the rifle and walked towards the frightened man.

'Sorry, Jacob,' he said. 'What has happened here?'

'Government take the mistress away and tell workers a German man will come to take over managing them soon.'

'Where did they take the mistress?' Ben asked.

'To Rabaul, and put her on a boat to go to a place called Samoa. That is all I know.'

Samoa. Ben knew that was also part of the German empire in the Pacific and was relieved to at least have some idea where Caroline might be. But this knowledge did not help his present situation. He was starving and relatively weak from his weeks hiding in the jungle. When he glanced in a broken mirror left by the looters, he saw a wild man looking back, with a scraggly beard and long hair. He hardly recognised himself.

'You did not return,' Ben said gently. 'I thought something might have happened to you.'

'Police came and it was too dangerous. I was told by a man of the village they were watching me and would follow me. I am sorry, masta,' Jacob replied. 'But I have food for us.'

'Good man,' Ben said, slapping the Tolai man on the shoulder.

'I will fetch, and we eat.' Jacob smiled.

He hurried away, leaving Ben to roam the house, where he found a bath with water in it, as well as a bar of soap that had been overlooked by the looters. So, a German manager was to take over, Ben mused as he used his hunting knife to cut away his beard and then rummaged through his kitbag for his cutthroat razor. With water and soap he shaved away the stubble, using the broken mirror he had found to guide his hand. There was little he could do about his long hair for the moment. Stripping off his tattered shirt and long trousers, Ben immersed himself in the tub of tepid water, washing himself with the recovered soap, and for a moment he let himself relax.

'Masta!'

Ben sat bolt upright in the bathtub. The urgency in Jacob's cry from the yard was obvious. Ben quickly dried himself and dressed in his well-worn trousers and shirt, and snatched up his battered broad-brimmed hat and rifle. Joining him, Jacob said breathlessly, 'German man and five police come. They are almost here.'

Ben grabbed his kitbag, which contained his spare rifle rounds, and cautiously stepped onto the veranda, facing the track from Rabaul. Sure enough, he spotted a portly man on a horse escorted by five native police break into the open about two hundred yards away. The men appeared relaxed and blithely unaware of Ben's presence.

Ducking back inside the house, Ben knew he must make

a quick decision. The German on the horse was dressed in civilian clothes and Ben guessed he must be the new administrator that Jacob had mentioned. But the native police were armed and in uniform. Ben now felt better for his attempts to clean himself but he was still ravenous.

So: fight or flee? Ben remembered his desperate oath to himself back on the ridge, that he would fight to the death, hoping his stand might eventually be known to his family. He now knew that Caroline was relatively safe. What he could not know was that the New Zealand army and navy had peacefully captured the German territory of Samoa almost two weeks earlier, when the German governor, realising that his meagre defence force was no match for the overwhelming force of New Zealanders, had surrendered without resistance.

Jacob was staring at Ben with the unspoken question: *What do we do?*

The instinct to survive overrode the idea of a glorious death.

'We have to get out of here,' Ben hissed, and saw the relieved expression on the Tolai man's face.

Ben knew the best means of escape was by the back door and across a clearing to the adjoining rainforest, in which they could conceal themselves.

Quickly they made their way to the rear of the house and down the steps. The jungle was only about a hundred yards away, and Jacob followed Ben at a sprint.

But their escape was detected by one of the policemen, who had stopped outside to urinate and saw the fleeing figures from the corner of his eye. He yelled a warning to the other men of his detachment. Ben and Jacob were only about halfway across the clearing when the first shot cracked, shattering the bright, sunny day.

'Run!' Ben screamed to Jacob unnecessarily, because the Tolai man was already ahead of Ben.

More shots followed, but the presence of the fugitives had taken the police by surprise, and they hardly had time to take proper aim at the running men before they'd reached the relative safety of the forest.

Ben and Jacob crashed with relief through the low scrub, but when Ben glanced back, he could see that they were being pursued.

Ben knew his only hope of escaping was to deter the armed police, and quickly went down on one knee to take aim at the leader of the police detachment. Ben was breathing hard from the run and had to force himself to calm down. Propping the rifle barrel against a small tree he took a sight picture on the man bearing down on him. The rifle's recoil bit into Ben's shoulder but the man fell, causing his companions to immediately stop, turn and retreat from the lifeless body of their leader. The shot had been fatal.

Ben did not wait to see if the police would attempt to follow him and Jacob into the forest – or call up reinforcements. He and Jacob moved quickly away from the plantation under the cover of the leafy canopy until Ben figured that they were at least a mile away, when he called a rest. Both men were exhausted from hacking their way through the thick undergrowth in the oppressively humid air. They collapsed under a rainforest giant, and Jacob handed Ben a piece of cooked pork which Ben wolfed down. After gulping water from his canteen, the men fell into a deep sleep. Ben cared little that the mosquitoes feasted on his blood that night.

When morning came, Ben was awoken by distant voices calling to each other in the language of the Tolai. He guessed the native police had sent for reinforcements and that he and Jacob were now being hunted. No doubt the death of one of their brothers meant that no quarter would be given if he or Jacob were found.

'C'mon, Jacob,' Ben said, rising unsteadily. 'We have to get out of here.'

Jacob gripped the only weapon he had, a machete, and followed Ben on a course that would see them reach the coast. From there, Ben did not know where he would go and grimly acknowledged that his self-imposed oath to die fighting might be realised whether he liked it or not.

★

From the deck of the troopship *Berrima*, David gazed out at the naval force of battle cruisers and destroyers now escorting them on the final leg to Neu-Pommern.

News of the successful New Zealand operation to attack German Samoa had reached the fleet, and David hoped the Australians would have the same result at Rabaul. But at the forefront of his thoughts was Caroline. David had made a discreet enquiry as to where her family's plantation was located, and discovered to his concern that it was not far from their target, the radio station at Bita Paka. But intelligence gleaned from many sources, including the report from his uncle Samuel, indicated that the island did not have a strong military force to resist them. All German military interests had now been drawn to the Western Front in Europe, and the chances that Rabaul had been reinforced were very slim – as demonstrated by the New Zealand conquest of Samoa.

Whatever the situation, it was now time to face the enemy, and as the Australian squadron of naval warships steamed towards Rabaul Harbour, they faced no resistance from the shore.

Destroyers broke off from the naval squadron to steam into the harbour, and reported that there was no sign of any shipping. Then it was the turn of the destroyer, *Parramatta*, to sweep for sea mines and check the long wharf for any demolition charges in the harbour. They too reported back that they did not encounter any such devices. So far, all was going well for the capture of the island.

The call went out for naval reservists from the *Sydney* and the destroyer *Warrego* to man longboats and row ashore at the nearby settlements of Kabakaul and Herbertshöhe, as the latter town was the gubernatorial capital of Neu-Pommern. After they landed, signals from shore to ship indicated no armed resistance had been encountered and that it was safe for further reinforcements of naval sailors to be landed from the *Warrego*.

David was annoyed – as were his brother infantry officers – that the navy was getting all the glory for being the first ashore, but was pleased to hear that the army would now land its infantry while a small naval force landed at Kabakaul Bay to proceed inland to capture the radio station at Bita Paka.

Thus far, the operation had proceeded without any confrontation with the German forces stationed on the island, and David hoped it would remain so for the duration of the landings. He had been trained to fight on land and felt that was where he and his platoon of infantrymen should be. He also knew that the majority of his hastily recruited soldiers had never faced combat, but was reassured that he had a couple of non-commissioned officers with experience fighting in the Boer War to steady his men should they come under fire.

However, everything changed when the sailors ashore were finally resisted by a mixed force of German reservist soldiers and native police. The first Australians to fall in this new war would die fighting in the rugged jungle-clad country in the Pacific.

★

The situation was desperate for Ben and Jacob as the skirmish line of native police closed on their location in the forest. Ben was weakened by the onset of malaria; he had recognised the symptoms of chills and fevers for what they were and hoped they would be able to find safety before he was too incapacitated by the illness. Jacob was aware of how precarious their situation was but refused to leave Ben, even when the latter insisted he should. Instead, he took the rifle from Ben's hands and prepared to fight for the life of the man he had come to like and respect, as well as his own.

Then he heard something strange. The enemy were so close that he could hear them calling out to one another, but then he made out the urgent command of their German officer recalling the police to the plantation. Something had diverted their focus, and Jacob knew that it had to be something very important for the search for Ben and himself to be called off.

Whatever it was, it had come just in time to give them temporary respite from what would have been almost certain death if the police had closed in.

Kneeling beside Ben, Jacob could see that he was already in the grip of delirium, and Jacob knew from experience that the chances of him dying were very high. There was no way he could help. Jacob knew enough to know that the disease had to run its course – and a man either got better or died. It was usually the latter.

THIRTEEN

Although frustrating, the army could only bide its time until their military leaders deemed it appropriate for them to go ashore. Even as David stood at the rails gazing at the island, a letter of demand written in both German and English was taken to Herbertshöhe, south of Rabaul. It was supposed to be delivered to the German governor there, but he could not be found, so it was handed to a German civilian who assured the messenger that it would be delivered to the absent acting governor.

Just after dawn the following morning an advance party of twenty-five naval reservists under the command of one Lieutenant Bowen, a former Victorian public servant, struck out inland to seize the radio station at Bita Paka. Bowen was joined by an Army Medical Corps surgeon, Captain Brian Pockley, who had volunteered to travel with the advance party. He brought with him a medical orderly and telegraphist operator. Another ten troops joined Bowen's party from the *Warrego* and *Yarra*.

From the rubble breakwater at the beach, Bowen led his men along a track fringed with bush and coconut palms. They passed a plantation before coming across a trading post owned by a Chinese merchant, who was able to tell Bowen that the narrow road at the crossroads was the one that led to the radio station, and showed them the way.

Bowen realised that any advance along the clearly defined road cutting through the dense rainforest was suicidal. An ambush would catch them in the open, so he gave orders to his sailors to take up a skirmish line on either side of the road. But this was not easy, as the thick undergrowth and tall trees forced the forward scouts to break back onto the white sandy track from time to time, exposing them to any enemy defending the radio station. Bowen appreciated that the almost impassable jungle meant his line-of-sight communications with his men were thwarting his advance. By nine in the morning they had only travelled half a mile from their starting point at the crossroads. What Bowen could not have known, however, was that his decision to avoid the road was the right one. It had been heavily mined with explosives that would have torn his advance party apart.

Petty Officer Palmer's section was on the right-hand side of the track, and his men were held up by a patch of scrub much thicker than they had encountered so far, forcing them to move away from the line of advance. Two men became separated from the rest of the section, and from their position were able to spot around twenty armed native police under the command of a German non-commissioned officer, about thirty yards ahead of them.

Contact with the enemy had been made.

They also observed near the road two more Germans and a native policeman watching the advance of the main party under Bowen's command. It was an ambush. One of the sailors who'd become separated from the group fired at the German NCO to alert the advancing Australians, which resulted in return fire from the native police, who scattered into the jungle. The German NCO dropped his rifle and was attempting to draw his revolver when the sailor who had fired the shot called on him to surrender. The German responded in English that he was wounded, and the sailor realised that his shot had found its target – it had shattered the German's right hand.

The wounded German turned to the dense scrub where his men had scattered and ordered them to cease fire. When questioned, he gave his name as Sergeant Major Mauderer. His wound was bound before he was taken to Lieutenant Bowen, who quickly assessed that he could use the wounded man to defuse the ambush ahead of the advance. Bowen ordered the German to walk up the road under threat of being shot, calling out to his German comrades that a force of over eight hundred soldiers was advancing behind him and that resistance was futile.

The bluff worked.

The remaining two German officers and a native stepped out and were taken prisoner by Bowen's men.

Captain Pockley saw that the wounded German was losing a lot of blood and would bleed to death unless he received immediate medical attention. With Bowen's permission, the army doctor took the wounded German to the side of the road and amputated his hand. The German, who remained stoic, gained the respect of those who observed the essential but gruesome medical procedure. Once this was done, the wounded German NCO was accompanied back to the beach for further medical care. When the escorting sailors reached the shoreline, a message was signalled to the destroyers offshore for more reinforcements to be landed.

The second German officer to be captured by Bowen was also a commander of a defensive force of native police. Without knowing it, Bowen had destroyed the command structure set up to protect the radio station. The captured German officer admitted that he thought the Australians would rush down the road, but they had instead chosen to move through the jungle, which had foiled the German plans to ambush them.

★

Jacob knelt by Ben as the Australian fought the dreaded disease. For a moment he thought he could hear the sound of distant gunfire, and strained to listen. More muffled sounds drifted to him, but he couldn't work out what any of it meant. The only thing he could do was try to assist the fevered Australian. Jacob was aware of the treatment the German population on the island used to fight the disease. It was called quinine, and knew he must obtain the drug if he was to save Ben.

Jacob would have to leave Ben unattended if he was to seek help, but he had no other choice and time was running out. Jacob had so often seen his fellow villagers die from the terrible fever that shook its victim with bouts of hot and cold delirium, and knew that it was the real enemy for now.

Jacob stood and set out with Ben's rifle, knowing that he might need it if he bumped into any of the police who had mysteriously given up searching for them. He hoped that if he was successful, Ben would still be alive when he returned.

★

The intensity of the fighting in the dense forest increased as the Australians advanced while being shot at by well-concealed native troops. Bowen's men could not see where the firing was coming from but so far, none of them had been killed or wounded. But their luck ran out as they continued through the low undergrowth.

In the early midmorning, Able Seaman Williams observed a group of Tolai in a plantation hoeing between the palms. He turned to direct Stoker Kember to approach the workers, and the sailor had not advanced far when a shot rang out from the direction of the nearby scrub and Williams fell. Without hesitating, Kember ran to his badly wounded comrade, hoisted him on his shoulders to carry him half a mile for medical aid. But the shot was fatal and Williams, a former council worker from Northcote, Victoria, was the first battle death that day. He would not be the last.

★

Captain Pockley found Kember kneeling beside Williams, who had been shot in the stomach. The army doctor could see that the wound had proved fatal. He removed his Red Cross brassard to tie around Kember's hat. This universal sign was respected by all combatants and was mostly understood to indicate an unarmed medical man. The doctor directed Kember and another sailor to take Williams' body back to the beach.

The army doctor then attempted to move forward in case others had been wounded in Bowen's party, but he had only gone about ten paces along the road when he was hit and seriously wounded by a Mauser round. He lay bleeding where he fell until a hospital cart could retrieve him and convey him to the troop ship, *Berrima,* where he later died from his wound. Had he kept his medical brassard it was thought that he may not have been shot, and his selfless act in handing over his red cross insignia to Kember was recognised by those around him.

The death count of Australian troops would continue as they fought their way to the radio station using maps taken from captured German officers. Then the forward scouts of Bowen's detachment stumbled on a formidable rifle trench, which extended out on either side of the road and was manned by a force of native troops. Their sniping pinned Bowen's troops down.

At around 10 am, the arrival of the reinforcements requested from the destroyers improved the situation for the advancing troops. But while they were engaging the trench in battle, a sniper's bullet found Bowen and he fell, seriously wounded. Bowen was carried to the shade beside the road and first aid was rendered. Nonetheless, the attack against the trench continued, with steady progress. Further reinforcements were called for, and around noon the request was granted for troops to be sent from the *Berrima*.

★

It was a hot day with no sign of a cooling breeze as Jacob stumbled into a clearing, Ben's rifle slung over his shoulder.

'Don't move! Hands up!' came a command from about fifty yards away.

Jacob froze. He understood the order and stood with his hands in the air.

'The bugger's got a rifle,' he heard as three khaki-uniformed men approached with their own weapons levelled at him. 'Got to be one of them native troops. Do we shoot him?'

Jacob could see from the corner of his eye that the three soldiers were not wearing German uniforms and could only presume that they were British troops invading the island.

'Me friend,' Jacob replied carefully, hoping his limited English would be understood. 'Need help for wounded Australian man.'

The three men were now face to face with Jacob, who remained frozen, fearing the last sound he might ever hear was a rifle shot.

One of the men removed the rifle from Jacob's shoulder. 'Bloody hell!' he swore. 'It's one of ours – not a Mauser. Where did you get it?'

'Belong to man, Ben Steele. He back in bush very sick. He need help. Maybe quinine.'

Puzzled, the three soldiers glanced back into the bush Jacob had emerged from. The leader, an army corporal, examined the rifle. 'I had one of these in South Africa, when I was with the mounted infantry. Not all our troops over there were issued the Mark 1 Lee Enfield,' he said. He turned his attention back to Jacob. 'If you tell the truth and lead us to your friend, we will not shoot you.'

Jacob felt a surge of relief. He would take them back to Ben and the Australian would be provided with medical help. All he could do was hope that Ben was still alive.

At the point of a bayonet Jacob led the way back to Ben, who was lying absolutely still in the shade of a forest giant. Jacob's despair was immediate. Was he too late? He knelt down beside Ben, shaking his shoulder, but Ben did not respond.

'He could be a German,' one of the soldiers said.

The corporal sighed. 'If he is, then we have captured a couple of the enemy. We need to get them back to the beach.'

★

'*Sprechen Sie Deutsch?*'

The question came from far away. Ben attempted to focus on the world around him. He knew he was sweating profusely and felt as if he was dying of thirst. His throat was dry and his head throbbed. He knew that he was lying on his back on a camp stretcher and through his blurred vision could see the canvas roof of some kind of lean-to tent.

'Water,' Ben eventually croaked, and a shadowy figure leaned over him, producing a water canteen which he put to Ben's lips. Ben reached out to grip the canteen, swallowing the brackish liquid of life.

'You speak English?' the blurred figure asked again.

'Bloody hell, yeah,' Ben finally answered when he'd drunk his fill. He attempted to sit up.

'The native who our men captured said your name is Benjamin Steele and that you are an Australian,' the young man said. 'It appears that he might be right.'

Hands helped Ben sit up and the world swirled into sharper focus. He could now see the uniform of an Australian army officer wearing the Tudor rose insignia of the Intelligence Corps on his cap. He could tell by the shadows outside that the sun was sinking.

'You need to take it easy, old chap,' the intelligence lieutenant said. 'You've been having the heebie-jeebies from a bout of fever for the last few hours.'

Ben could hear the distinctive sounds of the military all around him. Behind the officer he could see soldiers and sailors with rifles standing guard over supplies of wooden crates on the beach beyond the improvised canvas shelter.

'We couldn't transport you aboard any of our ships until we had clarification that you were not a German attempting to flee the island. But I also know from a briefing I received before we arrived that there was an Australian citizen trapped behind enemy lines who had been part of a covert mission before the outbreak of hostilities. From your photograph, and the way you responded to my question, I am satisfied you are Benjamin Steele, and I am sure that your family will be overjoyed to know that you are alive.'

Ben attempted to stand but almost fell when his feet met the floor. While he got his bearings again, the young intelligence officer told him the bout of malaria had almost killed him, and the quinine he had been administered had fought off the fever. Malaria was a recurring illness, he said. Ben would have to be repatriated to a hospital back in Australia.

'Where is Jacob?' Ben asked, taking another sip of water.

'Do you mean the native we took prisoner?' the officer countered. 'Now that we have a fair inkling of who you are, and you can vouch for the fact that he is not a German sympathiser, I will issue an order for him to be freed.'

'That I can,' Ben replied. 'It sounds like he saved my life.'

'The navy will organise transport for you back home when we wrap up our mission here. In the meantime, you will be taken out to the infirmary on one of the destroyers.'

Ben understood that the officer was giving him all the assistance he could. He sagged with relief, finally allowing himself to accept that he was safe in the military arms of his country. His mission was over, and all he could do now was recover fully to find Caroline.

FOURTEEN

The second column to advance towards Bita Paka were not aware of where Bowen's detachment was located so the commander, Elwell, sent scouts ahead. The long drought had caused a fine dust that rose in clouds, filling nostrils and increasing the men's thirst as they advanced. The men fighting their way through the dense jungle could not keep up with the small parties moving along the road ahead of the company in squads of six.

A sailor by the name of Mark Batterham approached a tree where he thought he'd seen a sniper, and was peering upwards when a native soldier hiding in the scrub nearby suddenly lunged at him, attempting to seize his rifle. The sailor was quick to react and fought off the man, retrieving his rifle, and as the native trooper turned to run away Batterham shot him dead. When he recovered his breath, Batterham noticed a wire at the foot of the large tree where he thought he had seen the sniper. It led towards the road about a hundred yards away, and Batterham realised it was connected to a mine buried in the road. The sailor also observed that the large tree was in fact a lookout with a view down the road. After a quick search of the area, Batterham and a fellow soldier found an electric battery and firing device, and quickly deactivated the device. Batterham had inadvertently forced the enemy to desert their post, and therefore they had been unable to detonate the landline under the advancing company on the road. It was just one of those lucky moments for the Australians.

Moments later they caught up with Bowen's detachment – now being led by a Lieutenant Hill – who were in a firefight with the Germans and native police entrenched ahead. The injured Bowen was still there, taking cover behind a tree trunk. He was able to talk and, under the impression that he was dying, begged that the Chinese man who had helped them earlier that day not be allowed to fall into German hands. He also asked that the Zeiss binoculars he had taken from a German officer who had been captured be returned to the man. The day drew on and so did the fighting.

★

A final assault was ordered within eighty yards of the German trench manned by native police.

Lieutenant Hill had wisely discarded all signs of his rank, as it appeared the enemy were deliberately targeting officers.

The order to fix bayonets was given and the men rose to charge the trenches.

The commander of the assault, Elwell, was immediately shot dead even as the German officers in command realised that reinforcements had arrived for the attacking force and that the Australians had outflanked their trench. When the German commander, Kempf, looked around him, he saw his troops cowering, none apparently prepared to fire over the parapet lest they be shot, and at about 1.30 pm a white flag was seen above the German trench. The order to cease fire was issued by Lieutenant Hill, and Kempf came forward to parley, but he refused to believe Lieutenant Hill was the senior officer as he wore no signs of his rank. Hill decided to take Kempf to meet with his senior officer, Commander Beresford, who was on his way from Kabakaul.

After a long and tedious discussion, Kempf agreed to surrender his remaining troops as well as the objective of the Australian mission, the radio station. It was agreed that they would continue along the road towards the radio station flying a flag of truce, with Kempf accompanying them to call on his troops to surrender as they advanced. The Australians were wary of landmines after the discovery of the first one earlier that day, and Kempf was forced to march ahead in case any other mines existed.

The truce party passed one trench uneventfully, but at the next, which was constructed on a steep cutting at the side of the road, the defenders opened fire on the advancing Australians and wounded three, with one of them later dying of his wounds.

The final objective lay ahead and the Australians continued to advance, capturing an unlucky armed German cyclist as they did so. On searching their prisoner, they discovered an order for the remaining defenders of the radio station to retire inland to a place called Toma. With only a thousand yards between them and the radio station, the small party of Australians encountered eight Germans and twenty native troops at a police barracks.

Kempf ordered his countrymen to surrender, but they refused. It was a tense situation until one of the Australians, Lieutenant Bond, having noticed the Germans were only armed with pistols, took the initiative to quickly snatch the weapons from the German officers' holsters, stunning them with his daring action. The native troops could not fire lest they hit their own German officers who were between them and the Australians.

The German prisoners were marched towards the radio station which was found to be abandoned, and by 7 pm, the station had been captured. Other than the radio mast being pulled down, all the radio equipment was undamaged.

It had been an eventful day, but it was still not over.

★

What the Australians did not know was that the Germans had intended to send a signal to their German Pacific fleet to steam to Rabaul, but a nervous German planter, thinking that he was helping the German defence, had cut the wires – thus preventing the message – or any message – being relayed.

As very little information was being transmitted to the Australian ships offshore, the decision was made to land four companies of infantry, a machine-gun section and a twelve-pounder artillery gun, with orders to make contact with the sailors advancing on the radio station.

Near the shore at Herbertshöhe, David climbed into a longboat from the *Berrima* to join the fight with his platoon. Watching the jungle and coconut palm–lined shore as the boat was being rowed in by the sailors of the troop ship, David experienced mixed emotions: the excitement of going into combat along with the shadow of fear for his life.

But, above all was the fear that he would not prove a competent leader of the men with him in the rowboat.

It took a long time to land the infantry and the artillery gun. Given that the battalion was now faced with almost impenetrable jungle and it was near dark, David ordered his men to bivouac at the beach.

After David had shared the evening meal with his men at their campsite, he went in search of a fellow officer he had befriended when they were barracked at Moore Park. Lieutenant Grahame White was an easygoing man, liked as well as respected by his men. He was a well-known rugby player whose powerful build made him a second rower in the forwards, but the reason David had struck up a conversation with him was that he had discovered White worked as a junior public servant in the Defence Department. David had asked him if he knew of any important persons located on Rabaul, particularly a Countess von Neumann. Grahame had replied that he did not, but that his boss, Mr Archibald Stokes, might. A week later, in the officers' mess at Moore Park, Grahame had leaned over to David and said quietly, 'You did not hear this from me, but Archie said there is a lady by that name and title living near Rabaul. Seems she is the daughter of a very influential aristocrat in Germany. That is about all I know, old chap.'

From their shared secret a friendship had developed.

The two men now sat on a log with hot mugs of tea as Grahame lit up his pipe. Around them they could hear the murmur of their troops settling in for the night.

'So, we bloody well finally got ashore,' Grahame said, sipping his tea. 'We should have been the first to land, but the bloody navy wanted the honour, to rub our noses in it.'

'Well, we are here now and will hopefully get the chance to show what we are made of,' David said.

'Indeed. And I suspect that your interest in the countess has been revived, now we are ashore?' Grahame said with a grin. 'I have also been informed that you met her when you were in Bavaria, and that the lady is unmarried and a real beauty.'

David blushed and was glad that the night hid his expression. 'We became friends when I was in Germany a few months ago. I am only concerned for her welfare as someone I know.'

The big infantry officer grinned. 'Pigs will fly,' he replied, swilling back the last of his tea. 'A reputed German aristocratic beauty you just happened to befriend. Pull the other one, Davy boy.'

David could see that he could not fool his friend and fellow platoon commander so he replied simply, 'You could be right.'

'Knew I was when you made your request back in Sydney,' Grahame said. 'But right now, all we have to do before chasing up old girlfriends is keep ourselves and our boys alive.'

David knew his friend was correct. For the moment the welfare of his men and his duty to his own leadership came first.

*

It was the nature of the tropics so close to the equator that the day and night were of equal measure: at 6 am the sun would rise, just as it set at 6 pm. Breakfast was early, before the sun crept over the hills. David made an inspection of his men, ensuring they had everything they would need to advance on the enemy. He showed a confident face, but inwardly his mind raced with doubts about whether he would lead them bravely and competently. He reflected on his grandfather, Captain Ian Steele, and his father, Josiah; how they might have felt before the coming battle. Had they, too, felt doubt and fear? He also remembered that his uncle Samuel had won a medal for bravery at the cost of his leg in South Africa. War demanded a price on men's minds and bodies. David wondered if he would have volunteered if he had not known that Caroline was at Rabaul.

Then word reached the battalion that their advance would not yet go ahead, as news had reached the fleet that the radio station at Bita Paka had been captured. David did not know if he was disappointed or relieved, but it meant he would live another day.

★

A message was delivered at dusk to Rear Admiral Sir George Patey from the acting governor of the island, Eduard Haber, who said that he did not have the authority to surrender. A reply was quickly dispatched. As the Australians' main objective of capturing the radio station had been achieved with the bonus of all German resistance in the Bita Paka region neutralised, the fighting would now be directed towards Toma, where the remainder of the German forces had consolidated and were giving no indication of surrendering.

David and his fellow battalion members were acutely aware that the battle would continue, and that they might be facing death – or worse, being severely wounded and maimed – if they had to take Toma by force of arms. But David also knew that he wore the uniform of an officer in the Australian army, and it was his sworn duty to fight for his King and country.

FIFTEEN

On the other side of the world in Bavaria, summer was dying; soon the leaves would start to turn red, orange and gold.

General Maximillian von Kellermann stood in the vast hunting room of his castle, surrounded by the heads and horns of deer and the tusked boar. He was not in the uniform of his high rank but dressed in a suit originally tailored for him in London.

His son entered the room in his elaborate officer's uniform and a servant hovering nearby offered him a glass of schnapps and then quietly departed.

The two men faced each other and raised their drinks in a silent toast to fallen comrades.

'When do you depart for the front?' the general asked his son.

'In a couple of days,' Hermann replied, taking a sip of

the fiery liquid. 'I will join my unit in Belgium and take up my command.'

'The British fought well at Mons, but their professional army did not have the numbers to hold us back.' Maximillian's voice held a touch of sadness for the losses on both sides.

'I have heard that captured Tommies said a vision of angels appeared over the battlefield and that they are calling them the Angels of Mons.'

'The supposed angels did not save them, and I suspect that the British have lost the core of their army, but one thing is clear: this war will *not* be over by Christmas.'

'You do not think we will capture Paris soon?' Hermann asked. His father was a high-ranking officer of the Kaiser and Hermann felt he would tell him the truth rather than merely echoing the sentiments of the German military hierarchy.

'Oh, we will eventually capture Paris, but it will be a hard-fought endeavour. The French have not forgotten their disgrace last century when we captured Paris in that campaign. There is also the fact that the British have a reserve of troops and navies belonging to their empire. They have the Canadians, Indian regiments, South Africans, New Zealanders and Australians. You and I have personal experience with the Australians and are aware of their prowess in the Boer War, along with the New Zealanders and Canadians. If the British are able to mobilise their imperial troops to reinforce them, we may be delayed.'

'Our intelligence has gleaned that the Australians are going to be deployed to South Africa to put down a Boer rebellion, so will be no threat to us in Belgium and France,' Hermann said. 'Nevertheless, I have a recurring nightmare that my dear friend David and I confront each other

143

on the battlefield and that it results in one of us having to kill the other.'

'I suspect that this war will see many die, but you will not be one of them, my son,' Maximillian said reassuringly. 'Your dreams are simply a reflection of the conflict you feel at having your best friend declared an enemy.'

Hermann looked at his father. 'Have you been reading that Austrian, Freud?' he asked with a chuckle. 'You are a soldier, and such psychological babble has no place in the realities we soldiers face.'

'Our conflict is nothing compared to my dear wife's pain of having her relatives among our enemies. She was born in Australia but reassures me her loyalty is now to Germany. I suspect that her disclosure of loyalty hides the pain of her memories of her life with her family of years past.'

Despite being wary of Rebecca in his early years, as she was considered a foreigner and followed the Jewish faith, Hermann had come to love his gentle stepmother, who had raised him and his siblings as if she had been their natural mother. Hermann knew that David was also a Jew, but his faith had never caused any differences in their friendship. As it was, Hermann knew there were many Jewish officers and soldiers fighting on the frontline and their proven loyalty was to Germany and not primarily to their religious beliefs.

'I have seen the reports that the Australians and New Zealanders have made a naval attack on our radio stations in the Pacific and wondered if you had heard anything about my cousin Caroline's fate? I know she was last known to be in Rabaul.'

The general poured himself another schnapps. 'I made enquires on behalf of her father,' he replied. 'It appears that she was shipped to Samoa before the invasion of Rabaul and that she is safe. It seems that the New Zealanders are considering allowing German civilians to be returned to Germany. A very civilised gesture by our enemy.'

'That is good,' Hermann said. 'I had a strong feeling that David was smitten by my cousin and might use his family resources to find an excuse to travel to Rabaul to make contact with her. But with the current situation, that does not appear possible. I know he was being groomed to head the family business.' Hermann finished his schnapps and placed his glass on the cabinet.

'I should go to the duchess,' he said. He had always called his stepmother by her title, although with genuine warmth. 'I suspect that she will be suffering.'

'She loves you, and much of her suffering is that she fears for your safety when you join your regiment, just as she fears for the welfare of her own family in Australia. Her position is not an easy one.'

Hermann bid his father farewell. Even as he did so, David was facing his first taste of armed conflict on the other side of the world.

★

Captured German officers admitted that they had under-estimated the Australian skill in fighting in the jungle, and so the toll stood at two Australian officers and four sailors killed with one officer and three sailors wounded. This was in contrast to the many German and native troops killed and wounded to date.

It was just before dawn when David once again readied his men to advance as part of two companies of infantry, a twelve-pounder artillery gun, machine-gun crew and sailors from the HMAS *Encounter,* which had begun a bombardment of six-inch shells of a stretch of jungle that lay between themselves and the village of Toma.

The sound of the exploding naval shells ahead made David and his men sense that this was going to be a real fight. David remembered the story of how his grandfather had always preferred arming himself with a rifle and not a sword to assist him to blend in rather than stand out as an officer for some enemy marksman. David had surprised the quartermaster when he requested a Lee Enfield rifle and bayonet, but he still retained his Webley revolver as a side-arm. When his men saw him armed with a rifle they gave him a little more respect for being armed like themselves.

When the *Encounter*'s six-inch naval guns fell silent, the force began its advance. They did not meet many enemy, and when they did, the artillery gun was wheeled up, and its shells dispersed any armed resistance.

David was almost disappointed when the advancing troops encountered a German carrying a white flag before they reached Toma. Discussions were held on the road regarding a four-hour armistice, but this was refused and the demand was made that the acting German governor should report to the Australians no later than 11 am the next day. The commander of the force advancing to Toma ordered that they return to Herbertshöhe for the night after conducting a reconnaissance of a nearby ridge.

That evening David joined his friend, Grahame, to grumble about the lack of action. This war was far from what they had expected. Months later, when David was surrounded by the gruesome reality of war, he would reflect fondly on nights spent under the starry constellations and wish he had never taken the relative peace for granted.

★

Ben had recovered enough to wander around the decks of the *Berrima*, where he was generally ignored by the khaki-uniformed soldiers. But he made friends with a couple of sailors after he explained that he had been crew on the *Ella*, and told them how he had been caught behind enemy lines when the sailing ship was forced to flee the imminent war in the Pacific.

As Ben's health improved, boredom set in, and he wondered how he could make himself useful. Eventually he was able to convince the captain of the ship that he was fit enough to go ashore, and was duly able to join a resupply rowboat to the growing camp of soldiers and sailors on the beach. There he mingled, chatting, and one man squatting by his billy of tea looked up and asked, 'Are you any relation to Lieutenant Steele from Sydney, by any chance?'

Ben froze. How many officers could there be with that name from Sydney? 'Is his first name David?' Ben asked eagerly. The soldier turned to his mate who was preparing the mugs of tea. 'Do you know Lieutenant Steele's first name?'

The soldier sat back and scratched his head before answering. 'I don' know his first name, but I know he comes from some posh Jew family. Had a cobber who worked for him out west on a cattle station. Said his boss's name was Josiah and he was a fair dinkum boss.'

That was enough to convince Ben that it must be David who was the officer on the island, and this surprised Ben. He'd thought his brother had little interest in continuing his military role, having chosen to take the reins of the family enterprises instead. So what had suddenly made David so patriotic? No matter the reason, Ben realised with excitement that his brother was close by.

'Do any of you blokes know where he is now?'

'Last I heard he was with his company heading for a place called Toma,' the soldier stirring the tea leaves answered.

Ben knew Toma. 'How do I get there from here?' he asked, and the second soldier laughed.

'You aren't in uniform, cobber,' he replied. 'I'd say your chances were as good as Buckley's. You will have to wait for them to return. Have a cuppa with us, if Mr Steele is your relation. He's a good officer.'

Thoughts swirled through Ben's brain; the soldier was right. It would be dangerous to set out for Toma as a civilian. Out of uniform he might be mistaken for a German and shot before questions were asked. All he could do was sit back on the beach and hope his brother returned in one piece.

★

David's platoon was part of the infantry company proceeding to meet with the German acting governor, Dr Haber. They met the German at a white bungalow with a view across Blanche Bay to the adjoining island. It was a pretty place, with flowering poinciana trees shading the wide, trellised verandas. Even as the terms of surrender were being discussed, a French cruiser flying the *Tricolore* came into view. It was the *Montcalm*, and the sight of it impressed the Germans present as she had joined the Australian fleet after her service assisting the New Zealanders in the capture of Samoa.

The negotiations, which Haber stated were neither 'pleasant nor easy', dragged on. By late afternoon Haber had still not signed the document, and said that he would have to discuss the matter with his superiors. He was aware that at Toma his still-considerable armed force was cut off from supplies, and that the Australian force had proved their skill in the bush. Added to this, Haber knew that the Australian ground force had naval gunfire support and that the Australians could bring up field artillery to bombard Toma.

Eventually, pressure from the island's German population and the obviously superior size of the invading force brought Haber to the opinion that any further armed resistance would be hopeless. Many of his German officers and experienced European senior men were suffering malaria and dysentery – they were fit neither to command nor fight.

Dr Haber signed the surrender. The resistance was over – almost.

One of Haber's officers chose not to surrender, and, taking around thirty native police with him, he slipped into the cover of the jungle.

Oberleutnant zur See Kurt Jäger knew his duty and would not bow to the command of a politician to accept capture.

★

It was the 21st of September, 1914, when David returned to the now-established garrison at Herbertshöhe. He was weary but elated that he had not lost any of his men, and yet also a little disappointed that he had not been given the opportunity to face the enemy in combat.

As he led his men into the camp, he thought he heard a familiar voice call to him.

'Davy!'

David glanced around to see a civilian standing a short distance away. He blinked to focus on the stranger waving to him.

'Bloody hell,' David exclaimed. 'Ben!' He stopped, turned to his platoon sergeant and quickly told him to settle the platoon into quarters before walking quickly to Ben who was also walking towards him. They met and hugged each other to the curiosity of soldiers scattered around.

'You're alive!' David said, holding Ben at arm's length

and looking him over. 'We will have to send a message to Sydney immediately to say that you are alive and well.'

'I tried, big brother, but the bastards denied me permission to send a non-military message,' Ben replied. 'But maybe you might have more luck now that you're a military type again. What the hell made you decide to give up your good and comfortable life to volunteer for this expedition?'

'What made you join the *Ella* for a covert spying operation?' David countered.

'Insanity and a desire to have a bit of an adventure,' Ben replied. 'It got a bit rough for me when we learned that war was imminent, and a lot rougher after it broke out. But in all this mess I was able to meet the woman I will spend the rest of my life with, the Countess Caroline von Neumann. She said that she met you while you were on your trip to Germany. When I last saw her she announced that she thought that she was carrying our child. Can you believe it?'

David stared at his brother, attempting to take in Ben's words and keep his expression from giving away the sudden turmoil of his thoughts. Could Ben really mean the woman David had actually come to Rabaul to find? Was it possible that his wild and reckless younger brother could have won her heart? Surely not, David tried to convince himself, but dread was already seeping through him.

As the silence strung out between them, Ben noticed his brother's sudden shift in mood.

'Is something wrong?' Ben asked in a concerned voice, but David simply turned his back on his brother and walked away.

SIXTEEN

The Australians of the expeditionary force sent to the German-occupied Pacific Islands had returned victorious to Sydney amid public acclaim and political satisfaction. But the Australian submarine *AE1* had not, and it was listed as missing, with the loss of over thirty submariners.

But the result of the northern operation was far from Josiah's thoughts.

Both his sons had returned safely from the island now being called New Britain, but Josiah was disturbed to see that neither was talking to the other. It was almost as if they were dead to each other. No matter how many times Josiah attempted to discreetly question them as to what had happened, he was met with a stony silence or a shrug. It tore Josiah's heart apart to see the terrible falling-out between two brothers who had once been so close.

Shortly after returning to Sydney, David informed his

father that he would be remaining with the army until the end of hostilities. Josiah knew that the war would not be over by Christmas as all had hoped, because the Russians had already suffered a strategic defeat on the Eastern Front at Tannenberg. At least the German onslaught had been stopped on the banks of the French river Marne, saving Paris, and the French had begun a counterattack only to face miles of barbed wire and German trenches. The days of rapid cavalry charges were long gone.

Even flimsy aircraft were finding a place in the static war of trenches. Manned by a pilot and an 'observer', who would deploy flechette darts (and later bombs), the aeroplanes brought death and wounding to vulnerable soldiers, the darts piercing helmets and soft bodies alike. Josiah suspected that these novel flying machines would play an even greater part in the future of warfare.

At home, thousands of men were enlisting on a voluntary basis. The federal government was now led by the Labor prime minister Mr Andrew Fisher, after the September elections when the previous prime minister, Mr Joseph Cook, resigned.

War profiteering had reared its head, with unscrupulous merchants using the war as an excuse to raise prices for goods purchased prior to hostilities. The government declared that they would be prosecuted if this was proven.

At least Australia had retained tennis's Davis Cup after defeating the Americans.

Josiah was pondering these events in the gardens of his harbourside estate on a balmy day towards the end of 1914 when saw his younger son, Ben, striding towards him in the uniform of a light horseman. On Ben's sleeve he wore the rank of sergeant. Josiah knew that Ben had enlisted almost immediately upon his return from Rabaul, choosing to ride to the battlefield rather than walk with the infantry, and he had also been influenced by the fact that his beloved uncle Samuel had been with the Mounted Infantry in South Africa.

'Good morning, Father,' Ben greeted Josiah as he slumped into a chair opposite him at the garden table.

'Good morning, Ben.' He looked curiously at his son. 'Why did you reject a commission when I was informed that you were eligible for officer training?'

'The war would have been over before I had a crack at the Kaiser,' Ben replied.

'Tea or coffee?' Josiah asked. 'I included coffee because I thought that you might have developed a taste for it when you were away in German territory.'

'Tea will be fine,' Ben replied, removing his slouch hat and placing it on the table. 'I was kind of hoping that you might have an idea of where the army will be shipping us off to. Most of the talk is that we will be going to France via England, now that the South Africans have put down the Boer revolt and don't need us.'

Josiah smiled. 'You of all people must appreciate that even if I knew, I could not tell you – or anyone else. Such is the importance of national security.'

'I still thought it worth a try.' Ben sighed. 'The boys and I are hoping that we will be going to France. David once told me it is a very pretty place with a good supply of excellent wines.'

'Speaking of your brother, have you spoken with him recently?' Josiah asked.

A dark cloud crossed Ben's face. 'The last I heard was that he was with an infantry battalion. That's about it.'

'I don't know why you two are not on speaking terms when you are probably about to face a truly terrible war in Europe. God forbid that one of you pays the ultimate price. I feel that the greatest regret you will have will be not resolving this mystifying antagonism between you.'

Ben shifted uncomfortably in his chair. 'It is not something that concerns you, Father,' he replied, almost apologetically. 'Just something David has to get over.'

Before Josiah could probe any further, Marian appeared from the house.

'Ben!' she called, and hurried to her beloved younger son. 'You must come up to the house. We have just taken hot scones from the oven, and I have not seen you in weeks.'

Ben turned to his father. 'Sorry, I will have to excuse myself, as scones trump the differences between my brother and myself.'

Josiah watched as his son strode away across the lawn. It hit home in that moment that his boys might not return to him, and he forced back a tear.

★

After the New Zealand government had generously allowed German civilians in Samoa to return to Germany, Caroline had spent weeks travelling by ship. Shortly before reaching Hamburg, she had sent a telegram announcing her return, and an expensive chauffeured automobile had picked her up from the port to drive her all the way to her home in Bavaria.

As the vehicle entered the streets of Munich, Caroline could see that the city, with its medieval buildings and streets, had not changed much – but the people had. The gaiety of peacetime had gone, and soldiers were often to be seen among the throngs of civilians. Other than that, the chill of winter hung over the avenues of leafless trees and a drizzle of rain made the day as grey as the German soldiers' uniforms. They passed one young soldier on the footpath leaning on crutches and Caroline could see that he had lost a leg. For a moment her thoughts were with Ben and she felt the pang of his absence from her life. She did not even know if he was dead or alive, as she had heard reports on the steamer travelling to Europe that there had been an armed resistance to the Australians fighting not far from her plantation.

Caroline was greeted at the door of her childhood home by the old housekeeper, who fussed over her as one would a child, but for Caroline the family mansion would always be haunted by the ghost of her mother. Even now, Caroline could still feel the spirit of her cold and aloof mother wandering the halls of the luxurious house. She had been six when her mother had passed away from the dreaded disease known as consumption. Caroline felt guilty that she did not miss her mother, but she could never remember her expressing any love to her only child.

Her mother's coldness had extended to Caroline's father who, in turn, poured all his affection onto his daughter. Count Manfred von Neumann had spoiled Caroline; it was his way of expressing how much he cherished and adored her, and she had returned his love.

Caroline had been disappointed that her father was not at the wharf to meet her, but also accepted that he was occupied in a ministry under the influence of the Kaiser himself.

After her meagre luggage had been taken upstairs by an old manservant, Caroline was standing in the hallway gazing at the portrait of herself as a girl of thirteen when voices at the front door alerted her that her father was home. Caroline experienced mixed emotions – she longed to see her beloved father, but was frightened of the secret she carried in her body.

'Oh, Father, I missed you so much,' Caroline said, tears welling in her eyes as her father entered the hallway and rushed towards her. The tall man's embrace was firm and loving.

'My little angel, I have feared for you ever since this damned war was declared against us by the French and now the English. You were so far away, and I felt helpless, unable to protect you.'

'I was always safe,' Caroline replied, trying to reassure him.

'Now you are at home with those who love you there is no reason to leave Munich again, at least while this war continues. But that will all change when we defeat the enemies of the Fatherland.'

Caroline shivered at the thought that the man she loved was officially classified as an 'enemy' by her country.

'You have blossomed since I last saw you those many months ago,' Manfred said, standing back to take in a complete picture of his daughter. 'That skinny waist of yours has finally filled out.'

Her heart sinking, Caroline knew she could not keep her secret from her father or the world.

'I am with child,' she blurted, and noted the stunned expression on her father's face. 'The father is a man I came to fall in love with while I was in Rabaul.'

'Not that naval officer, Jäger?' Manfred asked, taking a step back but holding his daughter at arm's length. 'I never liked him, nor is he worthy of your standing in society.'

'No, not Kurt,' Caroline replied. 'An Australian man.'

Her father's face went pale and for a moment he was speechless. 'The enemy,' he finally spluttered. 'The father of your child is one of the enemy? I do not know what to say.'

For a moment Caroline thought that her father might

faint as he swayed on his feet, but then he turned his back and walked slowly to the living room with its open fire-place and burning log. Caroline stood watching him, and the welling tears spilled and streamed down her face. She was at least glad she did not have to lie to the man she loved as much as the Australian she had left behind.

It was the elderly housekeeper who appeared in the hallway, holding out her arms in comfort. 'I overheard your conversation with the Count,' she said soothingly as she took Caroline to her bosom in a gentle embrace. 'You need to go upstairs, and I will prepare a hot bath for you. I am sure that your father will be a little more receptive to the news after he has time to consider that you are not a child but a woman. By the time you dine tonight I am certain he will have come to see that what has happened can't be changed and that he has to accept your condition.'

Caroline allowed the woman who had been like a mother to her to guide her gently up the stairs to her room.

*

Caroline was dreading sharing a meal with her father that evening, and her fears were realised when he ate without indulging in conversation. Only the clink of cutlery broke the silence, and the occasional *clip-clop* of horses' hooves on the cobbled street outside. Finally, after they had dined, her father said in a cold voice, 'I think you and I should go to the living room and discuss the situation you have got yourself into.'

'It's not a situation, Father. I am expecting a child, your grandchild,' Caroline retorted. 'But I will speak further on this matter with you.'

They entered the living room and Caroline sat in a comfortable leather chair opposite the fireplace. Her father walked to a cabinet where he retrieved a bottle of spirits, pouring himself a glass without offering one to his daughter. He took his drink and slumped down in his chair. 'You are not married, and you are with child.'

'I am engaged. I might have been married if this damned war had not intervened,' Caroline replied defensively. 'Benjamin and I did not start this war. When we first met, we were not enemies. If you had the opportunity to meet Ben, I think you would know why I fell in love with him.'

'That is all a moot point now,' Manfred said. 'The fact is that you are pregnant to a man we consider an enemy of the Fatherland – and you an unmarried woman. But there is a solution to our problem.'

'*Our* problem?' Caroline flared. 'I am the one who bears your half-enemy grandchild – not you.'

Manfred took a swig from the Scotch he had procured before hostilities broke out and raised his hand to still his daughter's obvious anger. 'You must be wed as soon as possible, and then the child will not be considered a bastard. As it happens, I have an eligible man in mind, a widower I know you will find acceptable. He has no children of his own and I am sure would be a wonderful father to the child you carry.'

Caroline could hardly take in what she was hearing and had a desire to storm out of the room, but this was her father and a man she had always admired and loved. 'I would need to think about your proposition,' she replied through gritted teeth.

'He is of great wealth and considered very eligible. He is only a few years your elder, and comes from an old and influential family in the Kaiser's court. I also know that you met him at a ball in Berlin only three years ago.'

'Who, Father?' Caroline asked.

'The Duke von Hauptmann,' her father answered.

'Karl!' Caroline gasped, remembering the impressive aristocrat she had once danced a waltz with at the ball organised to celebrate the Kaiser's birthday in Berlin. She had to admit that he was handsome and dashing, but he had a reputation in Berlin society for being a man with a wandering eye.

'Yes, it has been rumoured by friends that he was quite taken by you when you met him. I am sure that an arrangement can be made. Karl is in need of a wife to retain his reputation with the Kaiser and his court. And you are, after all, the daughter of a count, and have a dowry worthy of your heritage.'

Caroline could feel her heart beating fast.

'I will give you an answer tomorrow when I have had time to dwell on it,' she replied, rising on unsteady legs.

'Don't leave your answer too long, my love,' Manfred said, but with a gentleness in his caution that was the essence of the father Caroline had always known. She also knew that her answer would be critical, not just to her father but also to her current reality.

After a sleepless night weighing the options open to her, Caroline announced her decision over the breakfast table.

Part Three

1916

The Western Front and Palestine

SEVENTEEN

She heard him sobbing quietly in the early hours of the morning when the household was still asleep. He would be sitting on the stairs leading to the upper rooms of the old but comfortable stone country house owned by the Solomon family north of London.

Naomi knew that her distant relative was suffering a pain that no one truly understood. Sometimes she would hear his nightmares from the guestroom down the hallway. He would be yelling orders to soldiers she suspected were long dead at a place called Gallipoli. At those times she lay awake in her bed wishing that she could go to him and soothe his troubled spirit, but eventually he would fall silent. Naomi knew his troubled dreams awoke her parents sometimes, too, but in the morning, they made no comment at the breakfast table. After all, they had already lost their beloved son, Naomi's cherished brother, in the mud of France the previous year. And on his rare trips home on leave before his death, he had been in much the same state as Lieutenant David Steele.

Naomi had first met her distant relative on one of his visits before the war when she was a young lady of fifteen. Even then she had been smitten by him, but was too young to express her feelings in polite society, and in any case this would not have been encouraged by her traditional Jewish parents. Naomi was now twenty years old and considered a dark-haired beauty by the boys who had courted her before the terrible war took them away.

David had returned on extended leave after the disastrous Gallipoli campaign, scarred by a Turkish bayonet wound across his jaw that had now healed but had left him forever marked. His battalion had been evacuated to the Greek island of Lemnos and he had spent Christmas there, where the men had been able to purchase such delicacies as fresh mandarins, sardines and eggs, albeit at a high price. David's battalion had landed at Gallipoli with a strength of 1,300, but only 560 could be mustered on Lemnos.

Now, Naomi sat in the dark, tears running down her cheeks as she fought the desire to go to David and hold him in her arms, to assuage his pain with reassuring words and the warmth of her body. As far as she knew, David was not aware of her long-time attraction to him, and even if he was, he was being sent to France in a matter of days. It was she who was counting down the hours until that terrible time arrived when he would depart her parents' house to return to London and possibly vanish from her life forever.

Naomi raged against the absolute insanity of this war, which had emptied so many of the homes of her friends, who had lost a father, son or brother, as she had. Sometimes more than one. All she could do was listen secretly to a man crying in the dark for reasons only he truly knew.

★

The small, smoke-filled London pub was filled with uniformed soldiers from the British army as well as the occasional Canadian, New Zealand and Australian soldier. Sergeant Ben Steele of the Australian Light Horse was one of those soldiers, rubbing shoulders with the other patrons and gripping a large glass of English ale.

He was finally on his way to war. His regiment had sailed for Egypt without him after he'd broken his leg during a rough rugby game back in Australia. He had almost cried when he was told that he was classified as unfit for active service, and was still in hospital in Sydney when the troop ship steamed from the harbour with his regiment and their horses aboard.

The weeks had passed as the leg healed, and Ben knew that he was at risk of being discharged from the army if the broken leg failed him in the subsequent medical examination. But he was able to wrangle leave to convalesce at the family home – thanks to his father's influence with the army – which he felt gave him the best chance of recovery. There he fretted when he read about his regiment – less their horses – joining the army in the Gallipoli campaign. It was a ritual of his each morning to be the first to the newspaper over the breakfast table and to turn to the casualty lists. Sadly, he recognised the names of men he had trained with in Sydney in the long lists of killed or wounded, and cursed himself for not being by their side.

All the while, Ben prayed that he would not see the name of Lieutenant David Steele. His brother's letters were addressed to their father, but Ben listened intently when Josiah read them to the family. David's description of his days and nights on the Turkish peninsula were grim. David also expressed a few carefully worded views about the standard of leadership during the campaign, hinting at mismanagement from the British high command controlling the war on the Turkish peninsula. Ben would discuss the issues David raised with his father who, from military experience, commented that the British viewed their colonial troops with contempt. With every letter that arrived, Ben struggled more and more with his inability to join his regiment.

Then one day Ben read in the morning paper that an evacuation of the British forces at Gallipoli had been successful, removing the troops from the now bitterly cold trenches that had baked under a blazing sun when they originally landed in April 1915. Ben guessed that his brother would probably be shipped to England where he would await deployment to another front.

That had been back in August. Shortly afterwards, Ben had been medically cleared to steam for England with other reinforcements for the Australian Light Horse regiments, and despite his family's tears, he had been relieved to finally go. Now it was December and winter had fallen on the northern hemisphere. Ben knew that David was taking leave with their English relatives in a country cottage north of London, and already had a train ticket to use for his few days of leave before being posted to what most guessed was Egypt to rejoin the Light Horse detachments.

'Heard you order an ale,' a voice said beside him. Ben turned to see the uniform of a New Zealander with the chevrons of a sergeant, and also noticed the eye patch over the man's eye. 'Figure you must be an Aussie,' the sergeant said.

'You sound like a Kiwi,' Ben replied.

The man nodded. 'Noticed that you are with the Aussie Light Horse,' the Kiwi said. He was in his mid-twenties from what Ben could guess and taller than Ben. 'Were you with them fighting Johnny Turk on the peninsula?' he asked, taking a swig from his glass of ale.

'Sadly, no,' Ben replied. 'I was kept back home after I busted my leg, but am about to rejoin the lads.'

'You were bloody lucky to bust your leg. There's nothing sad about missing that lot,' the Kiwi replied. 'As for me, the loss of my eye gets me home – discharged as medically unfit for service. The best thing that could happen,' he added bitterly. 'I get to be with my wife and kids on the farm and let some other poor bugger cop it over here.'

'I read it was bad,' Ben said sympathetically. 'I can see that you have earned your leave of service, cobber.'

'If you get into any action, hope that you get a blighty,' the Kiwi sergeant said as he sculled the last of his beer. When he saw Ben's confusion, he added, 'That's a wound that is not fatal but gets you out of the hell of the trenches. Anyway, time to get back to the barracks for me, but I wish you all the luck you can get. That is all that you have over there.'

With this, the New Zealand sergeant left Ben to ponder this advice from a veteran of Gallipoli with just a little confusion. He could not consider a man who had lost an eye in battle a shirker, but this was not the idea of modern warfare that Ben had been expecting.

He would soon understand.

★

David took a walk in the chilly morning to the small stream that ran through the estate. He was in his uniform with the collar of his thick woollen greatcoat pulled up around his face for added warmth. The brown army-issue gloves he wore did not keep out much of the cold, but at least he did not have to deal with the Turks taking the occasional sniper's shot at him in the wintry English countryside.

He stood by the stream among the weeping willows, staring at the water, which was beginning to freeze over, and reflecting on the fact that he was still alive after the terrible carnage of Lone Pine. He couldn't rid his mind of the images of the attacking Australian troops clawing at the overhead cover to reach the Turkish soldiers in the trenches below, or flashes of being in those confined dark trenches. For a moment David closed his eyes, shuddering with both cold and fear as he remembered the screams of men calling for their mothers in two languages as they died from rifle bullets, bayonets and an assortment of vicious home-made close-quarter weapons. He hardly remembered the Turkish bayonet that had seared his face, its sharp edge like a surgeon's scalpel. He could not recollect killing the man who had inflicted the wound. All he could remember was that he had lost more than half the platoon he commanded in the hellish conditions of close-quarter combat. He hardly remembered surviving and wondered how it had been possible. His closest friend, Lieutenant Grahame White, had died. When they retrieved his body, they found the young officer entangled with a dead Turkish soldier. It appeared they had stabbed each other and had become brothers in death. Death did not differentiate between uniforms.

'David.'

David knew the voice behind him. It was Naomi. He turned, gripping his hands together to disguise their shaking.

'Naomi, you shouldn't be out here, it is too cold,' he said as she approached through the frost-frozen grass.

'Nor should you,' she said when she was within a pace of him. 'It is better that you return to the house where I can make us a pot of tea. I have some sweet cakes, too.'

David nodded and followed Naomi back to the comfortable stone house. When they entered the kitchen, the immediate heat from the wood-burning stove began to take away the chill from their bodies, and the aromatic scent of herbs and spices replaced the stench David felt would never leave the back of his throat: of rotting bodies, human waste – and blood.

Naomi helped David remove his greatcoat and hung it on a wooden peg near the door before preparing the tea things. When that was done, she sat in a chair across the table from him.

He thanked her when she poured the tea and produced a small tray of jam tarts. He took one and slowly ate it.

'They are very good,' he said after the last mouthful.

'I made them,' Naomi said. 'I am very pleased that you like them.'

'You are a very talented young lady,' David said. 'I believe that you were dux of your school in your last year and are now a rising star in the Solomon enterprises? Back home most men consider women ill-suited to being involved in the running of commercial concerns.'

'In my family we have had many strong women who have proved themselves the equal of any man,' Naomi replied defiantly, and David realised that his comment must have been misconstrued. He felt ashamed for appearing to question this young woman who he had developed a strange liking for. She was so different from any other woman he had met in his travels – with the exception of Caroline

169

von Neumann. But Caroline's memory had faded from his mind since he'd been at war, and he now bitterly regretted falling out with his beloved brother, Ben, over her. He had realised the difference between infatuation and love with the distance of time.

'I am sorry,' David said, reaching across the table to take Naomi's hands in his own. 'I did not mean to infer that you are not capable of equalling any man in the world of finance. It is just I have not encountered any other woman like you before. I am proud to know you.'

Naomi felt his hands grip her own and felt something almost like an electric shock. Did the man sitting opposite her realise the intimacy of this moment? 'I wish that you did not have to leave us,' she said, gazing into his eyes, and for a fleeting moment she could see her reflection there.

'It is my sworn duty,' David sighed, still holding her hands. 'I wish that I could remain here and see the flowers of spring arrive.' He lifted her hand and kissed it gently.

Naomi rose from her chair and walked to David, then, leaning over and taking his face in her hands, kissing him passionately on the lips.

At first David was stunned by the gesture but he quickly gave in to it, rising from the chair to hold her in his arms in an embrace that continued until Naomi broke away.

'I am sorry,' she gasped. 'That was impetuous. I hope that I have not caused you any embarrassment, but I must let you know that I have wanted to do that since you first arrived under our roof, David Steele.'

David smiled, gazing into her dark eyes. 'Did you ever consider that I was attracted to you from the moment we met?' Naomi's eyes widened. 'But I felt that you were so beautiful that you would meet a young man and wed him.'

'I frighten the young men who come to court me,'

Naomi said with a smile. 'They consider me a little unnatural because I am outspoken, and not the model of a pliant, obedient wife.'

'My scarred face is not pleasant to view,' David said gently. 'I am aware that people stare at it with curiosity. How is it that you do not?'

'I can see your scars, but I also know they go deeper than people can see,' Naomi said quietly. 'So often I had to force myself not to go to you when I heard you crying out in the night, or weeping on the stairs, knowing that you were in pain. I so much wanted to hold you so that you had someone to share the pain with. You are the man I have always imagined I would meet one day and share the rest of my life with, and I know that you may find my thoughts impulsive, but they are not. My feelings for you only strengthened when you made me laugh, or took time to listen and learn about my life when other men would not do so. I do not know what can be called love, but I feel that I have felt strongly about you from when we first met.'

David held Naomi at arm's length, as if examining her for the first time. Then he smiled and touched her face with his hand.

'I am not sure that I truly know what love is either, but this has to be very close,' he said, and as he kissed Naomi again, Caroline faded entirely from his life.

EIGHTEEN

The British naval blockade of German ports was having its desired effect. Like the British Isles, Germany relied very much on the import of raw materials and food to serve its strategic needs. Rationing was now part of life for ordinary Germans.

Duchess Caroline von Hauptmann née von Neumann did not have to concern herself with such matters, living in her husband's comfortable country estate in Bavaria. The best of the available food still flowed into the larders of the Duke Karl von Hauptmann, and the great house was kept warm in the bitter winter by a substantial supply of fuel.

Caroline's marriage to the duke had not been widely publicised, as the newspapers were more concerned with covering the bloody war raging across Europe and on the Eastern Front against the Russians. Perhaps that was for the best, she thought, because she had come to accept that her husband's interest lay not in an emotional partnership with her but in the simple fact that she had a son. Although he would not admit he was unable to cause any woman to become pregnant, the rumours of his infertility had quietly circulated in German society – until his marriage. Now he had a wife and a son to carry on his name – and only he need know that Caroline's son was not of his blood.

Caroline had named her son Sebastian, a name she had always liked. Now he lay in her arms as she sat before the fire in the room that was designated as the nursery, and she gazed down on a face that so much reminded her of the man she had once thought she loved. For a moment, she experienced a feeling of deep sadness. Oh, it could have been so different had the war not come to the world. She and Ben could have wed and lived forever in their tropical paradise on the other side of the earth. But Caroline was a realist and accepted that the situation had dramatically changed for her and Ben. She suspected that if he had survived, Ben was the kind of man who would do his duty and enlist to fight against her Fatherland, and she knew too that young men on both sides were being killed at a rate never before seen in warfare, thanks to the advancement of modern weapons.

Looking down at her baby, she knew she had at least the living memory of the man she had loved in her arms, and she forced back the memories and tears. She had to look forward now: she had her son and the security of a life with her esteemed husband. She just hoped her country would win the war against France, England and Russia, and then reestablish the proud German empire in the Pacific and Africa.

★

Sergeant Ben Steele stepped from the railway carriage onto the platform at the station located near the Solomon country estate. His visit was expected; he had sent a telegram from London. Ben knew that he would soon see his brother at the Solomon residence and was nervous about the reception he would receive. He desperately hoped that enough time had passed for his older brother to accept Ben's situation with Caroline.

The day was bitterly cold with sleeting rain and Ben hunched against a freezing wind, pulling up the collar of his thick greatcoat and slinging his kitbag over his shoulder as he looked around. A smallish man in his late forties wearing a bowler hat waved to him.

'Benjamin, my boy,' the man said as he hurried towards Ben. 'I am Israel Solomon.' He extended his gloved hand.

'How did you know it was me?' Ben asked, accepting his relative's hand.

Israel grinned. 'You could be no other from the description that your brother David gave us. Come, my automobile is just outside the station, and we must get you out of this weather. My family are very excited about meeting you. Your brother has told us so much about your adventures among the savage natives of the Pacific Islands.'

Ben was stunned by the older man's words; he had not expected David to say much about him, considering the animosity that had existed between them. What had changed?

As if knowing David was in Ben's thoughts, Israel went on, 'I must apologise, your brother was to meet you off the train but was needed to assist my daughter, Naomi, in our stables. One of our mares is delivering a foal.'

They arrived a short time later and Ben was ushered into the warmth of the cottage, where he was met by Israel's wife, Deborah.

'Please come in, Ben, and make yourself at home,' said Deborah kindly. 'Naomi and David should be here soon, and in the meantime I can show you to your room. It is sad that you will only have today and tonight to be with your brother, as David is to return tomorrow morning to his battalion in London.'

'It has been over a year since I last saw him,' Ben said, removing his greatcoat with relief. 'Any time together is worth it. In any case, I must return to London tomorrow too.'

'Ah, here is Naomi now,' Israel said as the door opened and a blast of cold air heralded the young woman's entry to the house. Ben could see a very pretty, dark-haired young woman, her clothes covered in the detritus of the new foal's delivery.

'How was it?' Israel asked as Naomi glanced at Ben. 'It went well, thanks to David's help,' Naomi said. 'You must be Benjamin,' she continued with a smile. 'David has told me so much about you and what it was like growing up in Australia. He calls you the wild colonial boy.'

Ben gave a short laugh. 'I have never heard him call me that before,' he replied. 'Is he coming up to the house?'

'Not yet; he wishes to remain for a while with our new arrival, a colt in good health. But he said he could meet with you in the stables if you wanted to walk down?' Naomi said. 'In the meantime, I must wash. If you will all excuse me.'

Ben put his greatcoat back on and, after Israel pointed out the stables, made his way there, trying to master the anxiety he felt over facing his brother. He pulled open the great wooden door and entered the semi-darkness to see David leaning against the railing of an enclosure in which rested the mare with her baby colt. David looked up.

'Ben,' he said simply, and Ben nodded in recognition.

'David.' Ben walked over to his brother.

'I would give you a hug, old chap,' said David quietly, 'but as you can see, I am a bit messy at the moment.'

The greeting was warm and genuine, and Ben felt the tension leave him. His brother had changed, and as Ben's thoughts flashed back to Naomi, it dawned on him that perhaps he knew the reason why.

'I was told that you will be returning to London tomorrow,' Ben said, approaching his brother. 'That's too bad.'

'It seems that we are returning to Egypt,' David said, wiping his hands on a rag. 'And from what I have heard, your lot are being sent to Palestine soon to reinforce the Light Horse already over there.'

Ben could not restrain himself anymore and blurted, 'What has changed between us, David? Since Rabaul you have shunned me because of Caroline.'

David seemed to stare into a space beyond his brother. 'I was a fool,' he said softly. 'I was so infatuated that it took all sense from me. Over time I have come to accept that my resentment towards you was merely my broken pride. You knew nothing of what I felt for Caroline and were not deserving of my ire. Time has come to teach me that I only have one brother who I have always loved – despite his wild ways –' David shot Ben a crooked grin, 'and that Caroline would never have been for me. She met a better Steele man. I am sorry.'

'I am sorry too,' said Ben. 'And I strongly suspect that the young lady I just met at the house might have some- thing to do with your current thoughts,' he added. 'Am I right?'

David nodded his head, smiling. 'I knew Naomi from my earlier visits to England, but only now realise that I was always attracted to her. She has confessed that the feelings have always been mutual. And now I have to leave just when I would give anything to remain and learn so much more about her. This bloody war has messed up your life as well as mine.'

'I missed my big brother,' Ben said. 'If only I had known about your feelings for Caroline, I would never have become involved with her – but it happened.' He shook his head sadly. 'The last I knew, Caroline was carrying my child.'

'I hope that one day, when this damned war ends, you will be reunited,' David said. 'In the meantime, I pray you and I will survive when so many of our friends have not – including Naomi's brother. You and I have a lot of catching up to do before I leave tomorrow. I'm on the early train back to London – and the bastard war.'

A cold wind continued to beat against the stables and chilly sleet fell on the estate, but for the moment a great warmth cloaked the two reunited brothers in a blanket of resolution. 'I think this means I can open the bottle of whiskey I brought with me.' Ben grinned as David approached and embraced his brother despite the mess on his clothes. They were glad that there was no one to see the tears that ran down their cheeks before they trudged back to the comfort of Solomon's cottage.

★

Three figures stood on the platform of the little country railway station the following morning as snow swirled around them. Two of the figures wore the uniforms of the Australian army while the third, smaller figure was wrapped in a fur coat and clung to the arm of the Australian officer. It was a common scene across British railway stations as soldiers and sailors came and went on leave – joyous upon return and sad upon departure.

Ben had his hands thrust into the pockets of his great-coat despite the military rule that this was not to be done. But Ben was never one for inane military regulations and besides, they were the only three waiting for the steam train to London. He discreetly walked away from Naomi and David to give them an opportunity to share their parting in private.

Ben retrieved a small silver flask of rum from his great-coat and stepped inside the tiny waiting room to take shelter from the lightly falling snow. He took a swig from the flask and noticed that the stationmaster behind his ticket portal gave him a disapproving look over his spectacles.

'Prescribed army medicine,' Ben said with a grin, holding up the flask. 'Guaranteed to prevent winter chills.'

The stationmaster made a noise in his throat that sounded very much like 'Bloody colonials!' and returned to reading the newspaper.

For a moment Ben was glad that he was not in his brother's shoes. He knew from experience that saying goodbye to someone you loved was always laced with the possibility that it would be the last time you would see them. Ben fully accepted that only the nebulous concept of luck dictated his and his brother's destinies.

Ben shook his head to dispel the morbid thoughts of death. After all, it would not be he or David who would die – it would be the man next to them. This desperate thought was unspoken but harboured by all soldiers facing the prospect of combat, and Ben was glad to cling to that illusion of immortality.

He could hear the distant *puff-puff* of the train nearing the station and, slipping the flask back into his pocket, he stepped outside to see the engine arrive in a cloud of hissing steam. Glancing down the platform, Ben caught sight of his brother embracing and kissing Naomi passionately before steam swallowed them up. In the carriages, Ben could make out the pale faces of British soldiers.

Ben waited as Naomi and his brother broke their embrace and David strode towards him. Over his brother's shoulder Ben could see the tears streaming down Naomi's pretty face. David did not look back but stepped inside the carriage. With a sombre nod of farewell to Naomi, Ben followed him aboard.

On the stationmaster's signal, the steam engine lurched forwards and began to pick up speed, passing Naomi who was standing forlornly on the platform. Both men waved, and then she was gone.

★

Ben and David shared their compartment with a middle-aged, well-dressed couple who sat opposite them. Ben knew that his brother was suffering after the separation from Naomi and passed David the flask of rum, much to the disapproval of the English matron, who frowned. 'Prescribed medicine for depression,' Ben said with a cheeky grin, and the English matron looked away in disgust.

Passing through the tranquillity of the English country-side, with its low dry-stone walls, tiny streams covered in glass-like sheets of ice, and fields of trees stripped of leaves and now displaying a white frosting of snow, the war seemed so far away. The train puffed ever closer to London, where both men would join their units. Ben wanted to be with his brother as long as he could, because deep within his soul he knew it could be for the last time. Even though he had convinced himself that no harm would come to either of them, Ben was a pragmatist. The war did not seem to be showing any sign of a peaceful solution. It was almost as if both sides were vying to see who would have the very last soldier standing alive on the battlefield.

NINETEEN

Christmas 1915 had come and gone across the globe when the first letter arrived from David, posted in England before his departure to Egypt.

Times had changed in Australia; the mailman had once been a welcome sight at the front door, but in the terrible months of the Gallipoli campaign, the sight of a boy employed by the General Post Office to deliver telegrams on his pushbike was absolutely dreaded by families in every small town, farm or Australian city suburb. The simple post office boy had now become the harbinger of death or, if one was lucky, wounding.

But for the Steele family, the mail that arrived one hot and sunny Sydney day was not a telegram but a letter, and the neat copperplate handwriting on the front of the envelope identified it as being from David.

Marian called delightedly to Josiah who met her in the hallway, where his wife held the letter up to him.

'It is from David,' she said, with tears in her eyes. 'It must mean that he is still alive.'

Josiah took the letter, opened it, and began reading aloud without even noticing how his hands were trembling. The contents were businesslike, as was David's nature in his correspondence, describing how he and Ben had met briefly at the Solomon estate near London and shared a wonderful time together before he had departed for London. Josiah noted that David did not mention anything of his experiences on the Gallipoli peninsula, and could imagine his son's reasons for this. David did mention in a few words that he had been recommended for the decoration of the Military Cross for his service, but brushed it off by writing that so many others deserved it before he did. It was so much like David to be humble in the face of such an honour, Josiah mused, feeling fiercely proud of the way his eldest son had upheld the family tradition of military service to his country.

Josiah glanced up at his wife. 'Whatever issue the boys had between them seems to have been resolved,' he said. 'I am so glad to know that they have reconciled their differences – whatever they were.' Marian nodded, wiping away her tears.

The reconciliation between the two brothers was corroborated a couple of days later when another letter arrived. This time the scribbled handwriting on the envelope was clearly Ben's. Josiah's younger son repeated the statement that he and David had spent a grand but short time together on leave. Like his brother, Ben said little of his military experiences to date, except that he was looking forward to rejoining his regiment overseas after they had been withdrawn from the disastrous Dardanelles campaign. Josiah and Marian were greatly relieved that at least 1916 had dawned with the good news that both their sons were still alive.

★

Lieutenant David Steele surveyed the conical tents which had finally arrived at Tel el Kebir, very aware that the camp set up for his battalion was on the same battlefield that his father knew from his service in the Sudan campaign of 1885 – albeit a little further north.

Training had been instituted for the infantrymen of the battalion, who had to acclimatise themselves to the military discipline of the British, which was more formal and regimented than they had experienced in the trenches of Gallipoli. Reinforcements were arriving to join the few hardened veterans of the Dardanelles campaign, and meanwhile, David had been granted a short leave to Cairo which was three hours away by train. He was excited by the leave as he was aware from letters that he would have a very rare opportunity to be reunited with his brother and brother-in-law, Captain Maurice Cohen, now an army surgeon who had been transferred from Lemnos. Ben was awaiting his transfer to his Light Horse regiment. The meeting would be in an apartment in Cairo owned by a Jewish family Maurice had met on leave, and as guests they would be welcomed to share an evening together.

When David arrived in the bustling city, he was guided by British military police to the apartment that was on the banks of the Nile River, where he was met by Maurice's friend, the owner of the furniture shop below the living quarters who spoke good English. He introduced himself as Yosef Abdalla, and guided David upstairs into a small but comfortable room that led to a small patio with a view of the river below. There he saw Ben and Maurice in uniform, sitting at a small table sipping gin and tonics and smoking cigars.

Both men rose and stepped inside to embrace David while Yosef's wife, Esther, beamed a happy smile at the reunion of family as she prepared plates of dates, bread, olives and other exotic treats for the three soldiers.

'Bloody hell! Who would ever have thought that the three of us would be together so far from home?' Ben said, disengaging from the embrace with his brother. 'The gods of war have smiled kindly down upon us.' It was a heretical off-hand statement that only Ben would use in the company of his devoutly Jewish brother-in-law, but in this instance Maurice didn't seem to mind.

The three men linked by blood and marriage sat at the table overlooking the Nile as the moon rose in the evening sky, listening to the sounds of a vibrant city still awake thanks to the influx of soldiers and sailors from distant lands.

All three men were aware of the pungent and spicy smells wafting on the night air as a chilly breeze drifted across the muddy water. Everything was so alien, but the soldiers of the empire were growing used to environments that were so different from the villages, country towns or small city suburbs that they knew. Many found themselves in the ancient lands of the Old Testament they had read about at home or listened to in religious teachings.

There was so much to catch up on and much news exchanged, but Ben noticed that his brother and brother-in-law spoke little of their experiences in the Dardanelles campaign. Ben knew that Maurice had operated on the wounded sent to the hospital ship off the Gallipoli coast while David had led his platoon of men ashore and been wounded himself. But Ben could sense a special bond between the two veterans of war, and despite knowing why it existed he envied it, feeling almost an outsider in the trio.

It was enough, though, that they had a chance to be together for this evening, in the full knowledge that it might be the last time for the foreseeable future. Ben would soon be riding the Palestinian hills and deserts with the Light Horse while Maurice would be transferred to the battlefields of what was known as the Western Front, encompassing territory primarily in France and Belgium, and David would remain in Egypt, for now.

Midnight arrived far too quickly, and the three men knew it was time to depart before they might be listed as absent without leave – according to the conditions of their respective leave passes. They thanked their hosts for the wonderful hospitality that had afforded them this intimate reunion, and as they departed, they all noticed a very old menorah proudly displayed, reminding all three soldiers of the roots of their faith.

★

Life settled into a numbing monotony for Lieutenant David Steele in January 1916. The absence of combat only highlighted the horror of the terrible battles being fought on the Western Front that were described in the newspapers.

But for now, the Australians in Egypt settled into a regime of training, drill and fatigue duties.

At night a heavy dew would descend on the conical tents, but by midday a hot sun baked the men as they marched, carried out bayonet training and spent some time on the rifle range. New uniforms were gradually replacing the tattered ones worn at Gallipoli, and a good supply of parcels and mail from home arrived to break the tedium of camp life.

David's platoon was now up to full strength again with the arrival of reinforcements from Australia, and he had been allocated a new platoon sergeant to replace the man who had lost an arm at Pope's Hill and had eventually been repatriated back to Melbourne.

David welcomed the appointment of his new sergeant, as the man was a veteran of the Boer War and an experienced infantryman. Sergeant Brian Williams was also something of a mystery, as it was rumoured that he had served as an Australian militiaman in the small wars that had sprung up in Africa after his service in the Boer War. He was a big, broad-shouldered man who bore the physical scars of war – David saw these one day when the sergeant stripped off his shirt, including the relatively fresh scars from bullets and shrapnel from his recent combat at Gallipoli. Brian's military record showed that he had just turned forty but he appeared to have the physical strength and stamina of a man half his age.

The two men came from different social classes, but Sergeant Williams soon developed a grudging respect for his toffy platoon commander after hearing stories from the platoon corporal section commanders about their boss. It seemed Steele was not only respected but also liked by the men who had served at Gallipoli with him. For his part, David was pleased to see that the men trained well under the platoon sergeant's supervision, which eased the pressure on him of leading his men.

At night David had the opportunity to sit in his tent and write letters home to friends and family, reassuring them that he was in no danger in his current location. But his most important letters were written to Naomi, and she replied with warm and loving words. David treasured her letters and very carefully preserved them from the ravages of the desert in a small, metal biscuit tin. His greatest aspiration was to see the war out and return to this remarkable young woman in England.

The monotony was broken around mid-January with the separate visits of Brigadier General Murray and Brigadier General Holmes to review the two divisions of Australian troops. Both remarked that the men they inspected were in fine shape despite the mixture of old and new uniforms. The review was good for the morale of the old hands and new reinforcements alike.

Then February arrived, and David's platoon, along with the rest of the Australian troops, were relocated to a new camp with the title Katoomba at a defensive position just east of the strategically vital Suez Canal. Katoomba Camp was established in a barren, treeless desert of soft sand. It was a dismal region on the banks of the canal, but at least mail and parcels continued to follow the battalions. The move to their new location saw the mutiny of eight soldiers but, from what David could see, it was more of a case of insubordination. The men who were charged and eventually convicted had been veterans of the Gallipoli campaign and David read between the lines of the indictments that there was a possibility of poor leadership from their immediate officers in command. Fortunately, none of his men appeared to show any mutinous signs and the matter was passed off as just another aspect of the tough military discipline of an army at war.

Digging the defensive trenches against a possible attack from their old but respected foes, the Turkish army, was difficult, as the sand would simply slide back into the trenches. But the problem was eventually overcome with matting, and a defensive line stretching over ninety miles was constructed and manned, with a battalion covering a mile of their allocated front. The line was also held by New Zealanders, English and Indian troops. So far, the men who had served at Gallipoli had not seen any real action since, and that secretly satisfied David, who was slowly recovering from the nervous mental state that terrible campaign had wrought on him.

Leave was granted on a rotational basis and the troops were allowed a short time in Cairo. But reports trickled back that the Aussies were gaining a reputation for ignoring military protocol by refusing to salute British officers, instead stating that this was reserved for their own officers they respected. Not only that, there were stories of bars being wrecked, as well as brawling and general mayhem. Every time any of David's men went on leave, he would fight the desire to chew his nails in anticipation that he would be told they had ended up as prisoners of the British Military Police in Cairo. But to his relief, this did not happen, and if it did, he saved himself the trouble of hearing about it by never asking what they had got up to on leave in the notorious city of temptation and vice. However, he was disappointed to learn that some of his men had reported to the Regimental Aid Post to be diagnosed with the dreaded sexually transmitted disease of gonorrhoea, which was an illness that could reduce the ranks as effectively as any enemy bullet.

The routine of fortifying their sandbagged and corrugated tin–lined trenches continued until early March, when everything changed.

The division David was part of was given an early warning order that they were to be posted to the carnage of the Western Front, leaving the relative safety of Egypt behind them.

TWENTY

There was blood in the sand and some of it was that of Sergeant Benjamin Steele.

Since he had rejoined his regiment, Ben had faced a sullen animosity from the old hands who had fought through the disastrous and bloody Gallipoli campaign while he had not. And even though there was nothing he could have done to change this, he experienced the guilt of a man who had not truly earned his rank within the regiment. He had tried to simply ignore the snide comments made behind his back since leaving Cairo as they'd headed for the Sinai to join the Desert Column, but they rankled.

There was one section commander in particular by the name of Ken Ford, a hulking veteran of the Gallipoli campaign, who had aspirations to be promoted to Ben's own rank of troop sergeant and was known to spread derogatory comments. Eventually Ben confronted the corporal about these remarks and offered him a chance to prove himself, despite Ben's more senior rank. Word quickly spread that there was going to be an impromptu bare-knuckle fight away from the prying eyes of commissioned officers, which meant those not on regimental duties would have an opportunity to lay bets on the outcome, bolstered by Ben's sworn promise that regardless of what happened, he would not be reporting it.

So on a bleak afternoon in the desolate desert flanking the Suez Canal, Ben had gone toe to toe with the mouthy corporal and now stood naked to the waist and with a broken nose and blood running down his face from a cut over his eye. But he was still standing while the big corporal was lying at his feet in a daze of red stars. A cheer rose from the throats of those who had made good money laying bets on the underdog.

Ben sucked in deep breaths of the already chilling desert night air and reached down to help the much more battered Corporal Ken Ford to his feet.

'You bloody well put up a bastard of a fight, Corp,' Ben said when the defeated junior non-commissioned officer had righted himself. 'I don't want any rematch. I hope we can call our disagreements settled?'

The big corporal had two almost-closed eyes, but he attempted to blink at the slightly smaller man who had delivered devastating blows to his head and torso. For a moment he said nothing, shaking his head, but then he extended his hand in a gesture of sportsmanship so prided by Australians when the game was over.

'No chance of that, Sarge,' he said, spitting a broken tooth into the desert sand. 'It was a fair dinkum fight and you won.'

The small crowd gathered around the two contestants,

agreeing that the sergeant could fight, and that marked him as a man probably competent when the bullets and bombs were flying.

The sun was disappearing behind the distant horizon. Ben slid on his shirt as the crowd dispersed to their evening duties. He was aware that he had not truly proved himself in battle, but he had at least showed he could shape up to any challenger in a physical fight. But more importantly, as time would tell, what had been forged in the battle of fists was the beginning of a deep friendship between Ben and the corporal.

★

Arriving by troop ship in the French port of Marseille in late March 1916 was a vast contrast for the Australian troops of David's battalion. Gone was the endless sand that had made life miserable when it rose from the earth in dust storms; gone too the dreary panorama of seemingly endless sand dunes and arid plains.

It was cold in France, but spring was already producing flowers on the rows of fruit trees that David could see from the window of his railway carriage, and he was reminded that the season of new growth would also be coming to England. He smiled, picturing Naomi surrounded by wildflowers at the Solomon estate. With any luck he might even be able to wrangle some leave to visit her – or be posted to one of the may specialist courses conducted on English soil. How different it was to view the lush green fields compared to the dreary monotony of the desert, and experience the warmth of contact with the French civilians, who waved to them as they passed through villages. It was so hard to imagine that further north raged a war that had turned all this beauty into barren ground, pitted with craters, endless mud, broken barbed wire and miles of trenches zigzagging across a belt of French earth that was now as close to hell as could be imagined.

David was sharing his cabin with three other platoon commanders while their khaki-uniformed men in their recognisable slouch hats occupied the crowded, tobacco smoke–filled second-class carriages.

David was the only officer in the small cabin who had served at Gallipoli, and the other three, all younger officers, had spotted the colourful riband of the Military Cross worn on his uniform. None had asked how David had won the coveted decoration for bravery as they knew that was a very private matter. But David could tell that the three inexperienced platoon commanders travelled with their own fears of what lay ahead, preoccupied by what would happen when they led their men into an action that might lead to their deaths.

There was little talk in the cabin as they journeyed north to the war. David spent his time staring out the window at the beautiful countryside, which awaited the birth of lambs and calves and the blooming of wildflowers. His thoughts were on memories of Naomi, and he hoped that somewhere across the English Channel she was thinking about him, too.

★

'Father, I wish to become a nurse,' Naomi declared over the evening meal in the cottage north of London.

Israel Solomon paused with his table napkin at his lips. 'My girl, you have an important place in our London business,' he replied. 'Is it not enough that we have lost your brother and our only son to this terrible war? If I know you, I think what you are really saying is that you want to be a nurse over in France treating the wounded.'

That was exactly Naomi's ambition. She realised that her beloved father knew her better than she had expected. 'It is my desire to treat the wounded in a French hospital,' she admitted. 'I speak French fairly well, and I have been to France before, when I visited the family office in Paris. I feel that this would be my way of honouring my brother's memory.'

'And it is not because you have learned that David has been posted to France?' Israel asked with a raised eyebrow. Deborah had yet to comment so Naomi turned to her. 'Mother, do you think it is foolish to desire employment helping the brave, wounded men of England?'

Deborah Solomon was far from a quiet, obedient wife, and Naomi had inherited her desire to be viewed as an equal to men in a male-dominated world. For their part, the Solomon family had for generations turned to their female folk for wise counsel. Had Ella Solomon not been the captain of the financial ship that had steered a course towards social acceptance in the highest echelons of aristocratic society, from what some viewed as shady beginnings? Ella had established the Solomon family's credentials before marrying her colorful British army captain and retiring with him to Australia. And now it was obvious that the grandson of the legendary Captain Ian Steele was the secret love of Naomi's life.

'I am sure that now Naomi is of age, she should be allowed to decide on the course of her life, and if becoming a nurse is her greatest desire, then she should have our blessing,' Deborah calmly answered. 'I know my daughter would be an excellent nurse.'

Israel's expression was troubled. 'It could be dangerous,' he said. 'My beautiful daughter might be sent to a dangerous place near the frontlines, and exposed to gun and artillery fire.'

'Father,' Naomi said, reaching across the table to grasp Israel's hands. 'The Germans do not fire on the Red Cross, and that badge would protect me. They may be the enemy, but they are also civilised Europeans beneath the surface. Please do not fear for my safety.'

Israel knew that he was no match for wife and daughter if they were allied against him, so he nodded slightly. 'If it is your wish, I will support you,' he said finally, and Naomi rose from her chair to go to him and throw her arms around his neck.

That evening after supper, Naomi sat down to compose a letter to David, announcing her plan to train as a nurse for service overseas. It was only as she began that it occurred to her that she had not considered how David might receive the news; would he be proud of her or consider the gesture too dangerous to her safety?

★

Despite her enthusiasm, in London Naomi's aspirations to join Queen Alexandra's Imperial Military Nursing Service were quickly dashed when she was informed that she required a minimum of three years' experience as a trained nurse, and had to be between twenty-five and thirty-five years of age.

Despondent, she returned to the family offices where she managed the leases of shops and enterprises owned by her father in the heart of the city. With the death of her brother on the Western Front, her father had informed Naomi of his plans for her to one day take the reins of the family company. Feeling bound by duty, Naomi had reluctantly accepted her role, which she appreciated as being of great importance in the male-dominated world of big business. She recognised that her current role at a lower level of management was training for future higher appointments.

Naomi flipped open a thick ledger and stared at the long lists of figures and client names. She closed the ledger and sighed. Her thoughts were not on making a financial profit for the family but on a man she knew she had loved since she first met him before the outbreak of this terrible war. Naomi left her desk and went to the window, which overlooked a narrow lane. Below she could see a young British soldier kissing a girl of her own age. It was obvious that they had ducked into the alleyway to avoid prying eyes, not realising that they were being watched from above. It was a warm sight of love being snatched in a time of uncertainty.

A knock at her office door tore Naomi away and she felt a twinge of guilt for covertly sharing the tender moment between lovers.

'Ma'am, may I speak with you?' A woman stood in the doorway. She seemed familiar; Naomi thought she might be one of the new employees of their shoe factory that was located a short distance away. Many of the men who had worked for the Solomons had resigned to enlist, and their jobs were now being filled with female employees. After training, Israel had accepted that his new workforce was just as good as the men who once produced his shoes. Now the Solomons had a contract with the government to produce army boots in great quantities.

Then Naomi remembered who the woman was – they had spoken when Naomi had gone with her father to inspect the factory. Her name was Edith Crosby, and she had lost her husband only days before Naomi's brother was killed in action in the same battle. She had no children.

'Mrs Crosby, please enter,' Naomi said. 'How can I help you?'

The widowed woman stepped inside, and Naomi could

see the slight frown of concern in her expression. Her words came out in a rush.

'Mr Solomon has been very good to me and so I hate to let him down, but I need to ask permission to join the VADs. I feel I will be more useful to our cause in this war there than here. I know my dear departed husband would approve of my choice, so I am requesting that I be able to do so.'

'VADs?' Naomi asked. 'What is that?'

'I am sorry, ma'am,' Edith said. 'The Volunteer Aid Detachments. They are posted here and in France.'

'What do they do?' Naomi asked, her ears pricking up upon hearing the word 'France'.

'They do a lot of things to help out the army,' Edith replied. 'Everything from working with the Red Cross to cooking in the hospitals. They also work with the ambulances bringing back the wounded.'

'What is required to join the VADs?' Naomi asked.

'Not a lot,' Edith replied. 'I have saved to pay for my medical first aid training. I hope that I will eventually be sent to France to be closer to where my dear husband lies.'

Naomi guessed that Edith was still grieving, and when Naomi thought about David, she felt a deep empathy for the woman standing before her.

'Mrs Crosby, I fully support your desire to join the VADs,' Naomi said. 'I am sure that I can convince my father to allow your resignation from our factory and I also feel it is only patriotic for my father to pay for any expenses you incur in your pursuit to help the war effort.'

Tears were forming at the corners of Edith's eyes. 'Thank you, Miss Solomon,' she said with a sniffle, trying to hold back her tears. 'You are a saint.'

Naomi felt a strange warmth for the woman before her.

Not only was it touching that this woman wanted to help their soldiers in the place where her own husband had been killed in action, but she had also shown Naomi a way to leave England to be closer to David.

Edith left the office and Naomi immediately sought out her father. She had already told him that she was ineligible to become a nurse posted to France, and although he didn't show it, she suspected he had been quite relieved to hear it. She knew he would not welcome the idea of her joining the Voluntary Aid Detachment which might lead to service in France, and it was possible David would feel the same way. However, it took time for the mail to be sent to and from France, so by the time David learned of her becoming a VAD, she would already have commenced her training.

TWENTY-ONE

The men of David's battalion could hear the heavy artillery guns in the distance from their camp near the peaceful French village at Boëseghem. For early April the weather was warm and sunny, the fields green with new life, and the scattered farms with their old stone buildings dating back to medieval times were picturesque. The booming sounds did not feel real during the days when David and his platoon trained in gas warfare, conducted route marches that included bayonet and rifle drills, and sat through lectures on subjects such as hygiene in the trenches.

There was even time to arrange cricket matches, much to the bemusement of the French spectators who learned new English words such as 'Howzat!' – a war cry of some kind, they decided. Knowing this respite would likely be brief, David spent his time lolling in the spring sunshine writing letters to Naomi and his family, as well as sharing thoughts and views with his fellow platoon commanders who had not as yet seen battle. David had come to learn of their backgrounds as graduates of the exclusive Public Schools where the sons of the rich were educated, much as he had been. Only one of the newly arrived platoon commanders rubbed David the wrong way. Lieutenant Christian Holmes was a young man who considered himself superior even to his colleagues, and from what Holmes' platoon sergeant had divulged in conversation with David's sergeant, the men of Holmes' platoon disliked their commanding officer for his arrogance and patronising attitude towards his men.

David realised that he had become something of a mentor to the young platoon commanders of the company, who were charged with protecting the lives of the thirty or so men in their command while carrying out the missions assigned by their commanders. For now, there was a sense of peace in the rear echelon of the frontlines, but all that changed when the British decided that it was time for the newly arrived Australians and other former colonial troops to be moved to the front.

They conducted a three-day march east to the forward area south of Armentières, from where they would occupy a section of the front in the Bois-Grenier Sector. It was a stretch of frontline referred to as the 'nursery', as it saw less intense activity than other sections of the Western Front. It would be an opportunity for the fresh Australian soldiers to acclimatise to life at the frontlines before they engaged in full-scale warfare further along the line.

For David, guiding his platoon into the trenches was all too familiar. At first, they were positioned in the support line of trenches, then were gradually moved forward to the reserve and frontlines that faced the brunt of any attack by the Germans facing them.

It was around mid-April when the new members of the battalion experienced their first taste of war when the German artillery shelled their area. Shrapnel rained down upon them, but the shelling was intermittent and no casualties were reported – with the exception of nearby farmhouses and the battalion cookhouse roof.

Within days, however, the situation changed for the worse. A cold spell brought rain, making life in the trenches miserable. In addition, the artillery fire increased on both sides, along with the deadly sniping.

★

While the men on the Western Front shivered miserably in the cold and wet conditions of their trenches, it was hot and clear in the arid lands around the Kantara Camp in Egypt. Sergeant Ben Steele felt the sweat trickle down his back as he sat astride his tough Waler mount. The previous evening, they had been positioned with the British in their camp, and that morning a rumour had circulated in the regiment that the Turks were a short distance away. This was soon corroborated, and now Ben expected to face real action. He felt more excited than fearful about what lay ahead.

His mount snorted as if understanding his tense expectation, and he leaned forward to pat the gelding's neck.

Ben's squadron followed a tarred road for a short distance under a baking sun, the only sound the clattering of metal horseshoes on the hard surface until the paved road ended and nothing but the broad sandy desert lay ahead.

'Load rifles!' came the cry as they rode past barbed-wire entanglements and redoubts. Ben ordered his troop to spread out into a skirmish line for the advance into a world of sand and small dunes topped by prickly scrub. After a while, they reached a small hill noted on their maps and linked up with a British unit of two infantry companies of British Royal Fusiliers. Ben's squadron then rode to the flanks of the advancing British infantry to provide cover against any sudden Turkish attack.

An hour later, the distant sound of small arms fire drifted to the Australian mounted flank guard, and Ben knew they were getting closer to a clash with the Turkish army. When he glanced around him, he saw how tense and excited the new reinforcement arrivals appeared as they rode with rifles ready.

The squadron received the order to hurry forward, and Ben spurred his mount into a trot until he could see up ahead the backs of Turkish soldiers who were well armed but who wisely realised that they had been caught in the open and quickly surrendered.

Leaving the prisoners behind with an armed guard, Ben and his troop continued the advance at a trot until they could see white tents and camel lines at the top of a sandy rise. They rode into the camp to see scattered Turkish and Bedouin bodies, and Ben wondered if the British Yeomanry had attacked the camp, but as they approached a small oasis, they saw their British counterparts lying wrapped in bloodied bandages and badly sunburned under the scant shade of the palms. The British soldiers glanced up, smiling, as they rode past, pleased to see that reinforcements had arrived, and it was obvious to Ben that it had been the Yeomanry who had been attacked. All around the ground lay Turkish soldiers dressed in yellow uniforms with a bright sash; some were still alive and they were taken prisoner.

The order was given by the squadron commander to continue the advance in pursuit of the attacking Turkish soldiers, but it was discovered they had fled on camels. When Ben's squadron met up with their brother squadron, they learned that they had forced the Turks to retreat when they came to the aid of the British Yeomanry. Ben's troop returned to the oasis where Ben was told by a wounded British soldier that his brigade, vastly outnumbered, had been attacked by a force of approximately five thousand Turkish soldiers.

'This is the price we paid,' the British soldier said sadly, gesturing to the bodies of nineteen of his comrades laid out in a row under the palm trees alongside their dead horses.

As Ben listened to him, he felt a bitter disappointment that they had not been able to close with the attackers to wreak revenge for the deaths of the Yeomanry troopers. At least he had not lost any of his own soldiers in the near contact with the enemy. But he would have to wait for another opportunity to prove that he had earned his rank of sergeant.

★

Although Naomi's parents supported her application for service with the Volunteer Aid Detachment, Naomi knew it was with some reluctance. But Israel ensured she had the right references when she stood before the selection board, who were impressed with her grasp of the French language as well as the fact that she had already been vaccinated against enteric fevers such as typhoid. She also assured the panel that she would comply with all VAD regulations and provide her own nursing uniform.

In the hallway outside the London office where the interview had been conducted, Naomi was approached by the matron who had been on the panel.

'Miss Solomon, I just wanted to say how impressed the board was with your application,' she said. 'You will most probably be posted to our hospitals in France once you complete your training and compulsory residency in a hospital in London. I am sure that your family will be very proud of you and your choice to serve the King.'

'Thank you, ma'am,' Naomi replied, trying not to show how excited she was at this hint that she would soon get the opportunity to serve in France. All she had to do now was dedicate herself to her training, which she knew would include first aid, home nursing, cookery and hygiene, and comply with the other requirements to graduate as a member of the VAD. She decided not to mention to her family that she might be posted to France. As far as her father knew, his beloved princess would simply be nursing the men repatriated from the battlefields in the safety of an English hospital.

★

Life in the trenches at La Rolanderie alternated between mud and sun, heavy and light artillery bombardment, and occasional sniping by both sides. Plus there was always fatigue duty to strengthen the trench defences with sandbags and barbed wire. David's men would spend a ten-day shift in the forward trenches before rotating back to the reserve trenches, after which they would eventually be granted rest in the safer rear echelon of the battalion defence.

David noticed that his men grumbled about the lack of rest and monotonous diet of canned bully beef and rock-hard biscuits while occupying the forward defences, but once back in the rear echelon they were able to consume fresher rations of hot stews and indulge in tinned fruit. But the most important part of the life of a soldier was the mail parade, when precious letters and parcels arrived, as it was a tangible link with the lives they had left behind.

David savoured his supply of letters and parcels from

Naomi and home in the rear echelon, away from the concern that the odd artillery shell might burst close enough to rip a man apart or a sniper's round might find a target of some unwary soldier. The threat of sudden death had become a constant in the lives of the men of David's battalion, but so far they had not faced conditions as severe as those suffered by the French and British engaged in major battles along the line. The title of 'nursery' was an apt one, David thought, as his men became accustomed to a lesser version of the fury they knew lay ahead.

The battalion even had a rotation system of leave to England. When David realised that a year had passed since he first saw action on the beaches of Gallipoli, he was granted preference for a ten-day pass for England. He would leave the men of his platoon in the capable care of his platoon sergeant, Brian Williams.

When he heard his leave had been granted, David immediately wrote a short letter to Naomi to disclose when and where he could meet her in London. He packed a few items and made a point of touring the trenches his men occupied, where they greeted him with warmth and bid him a good leave. Most had witnessed how calm their commander was when the German shelling rained down on their heads, and respected him for it. Lieutenant Steele would light his pipe and calmly stand at the centre of the trench, humming a popular tune, cracking jokes between explosions and generally reassuring his men that the bombardment would pass. Once or twice shrapnel had ripped up the earth very close to their leader, but he simply ignored these close calls. His example of courage gave the men a good feeling that they would be safe while he was nearby and in command. The men appreciated David all the more when stories were swapped between their fellow platoons which did not cast their own platoon commanders in such a glowing light. It seemed that the most despised officer was one Lieutenant Christian Holmes. David remembered the man he had noticed as being unpopular when he had first arrived in France. As David farewelled his men, he learned that some had been speaking to Holmes' men, and that they had divulged that the officer had been complaining about the fact that a Jew was commanding troops in the battalion.

Returning to the rear echelon area just before his departure, David saw the arrogant officer berating one of his corporals for failing to salute him. David watched until Holmes was alone and then strolled over to him.

'Do you mind if we have a quiet chat, Mr Holmes?' David said.

Startled, Holmes turned to David. 'What about, old chap?' he countered.

'I would rather we go somewhere out of hearing of the lads,' David said quietly. 'Just over there near the cookhouse seems a relatively private place to discuss a matter that has been raised with me.'

Holmes looked nervous but followed David. 'It has come to my attention that you object to serving alongside a Jew,' David said in a cold but steady voice.

Holmes' eyes blazed. 'It's well known that Jews are only interested in making money and have no concern for good Christians. It is also well known that your family have a fortune back in Australia,' Holmes spat.

'Is that so?' David replied. 'Funny, perhaps I should not have volunteered to serve only to have some Johnny Turk try to rearrange my face at Lone Pine with his bayonet. I should have stayed at home, making money off you good Christians.'

David could see that his words were having an impact

when his fellow officer's face rapidly reddened. Holmes appeared to be about to explode. 'I should add that my brother is with the Light Horse somewhere in the deserts of the Holy Land, risking his life. Another Jew who should be busy making money off the backs of good Christians, according to you. Furthermore, the man who helped establish our family's financial legacy was a Christian by the name of Colonel Ian Steele, but probably not a good Christian if the tales about his military exploits fighting for the Queen are any guide. So, here I am, and I wonder if you have any other objection to me serving as an officer in the Australian army – or perhaps I have misjudged you, and you have an apology for your deluded views?'

David could see that Holmes was almost shaking with rage at being confronted by a Jew, but it was obvious he was not about to apologise. 'I think this conversation is over, old chap,' he replied icily, then turned his back and walked away, leaving David bemused by the man's lack of courage to challenge him to something like a duel of fists. Yet David felt a sense of calm at having confronted Holmes and grinned when he thought about his brother; Ben would have simply punched the man in the face, laying him on his back with a bloody nose. It was fortunate that Ben did not hold the King's commission, as such behaviour was not deemed to be that of an officer and a gentleman.

That afternoon David boarded a train for the French coast to embark on a ferry to London. Later, he would notice that Holmes avoided him at every opportunity, and the term 'Jew officer' was heard less and less in the battalion lines.

TWENTY-TWO

Ben always felt a thrill at seeing the fragile low-flying biplanes overhead, as the idea of a man aloft in the sky navigating across the vast arid lands appealed to him. He envied how the pilots of the flying machines could look down on humanity engaged in vicious close-quarter killing where the opponent was all too real in the exchange of blood for blood. From above, a man was a mere object to destroy with machine gun and bomb; the horrific intimacy of close-quarter fighting did not concern the man in the flying machine.

Overhead a British fighter plane circled and dived low to the ground before gracefully climbing back into the clear, blue sky. It then turned to fly away, leaving the mounted patrol of thirty men below to continue with their mission.

'Those buggers have it good,' a trooper riding beside Ben grunted. 'Home for a bang-up breakfast while the poor bloody mounted infantry slog it out under a blazing sun, sucking in dust and riding until they get saddle sores . . .'

The trooper paused in his reflections when they ascended a low dune to gaze down on the remains of a crashed biplane, wisps of smoke marking its last moments. Ben could see that it was a German twin-seater that they had been informed might have been downed the day before after a skirmish between German and British aircraft on reconnaissance patrols.

The patrol could see the remains of two aviators, one inside the German aircraft and one on the ground nearby. Both had been burned to a charred and blackened state, and the body outside the aircraft had an arm missing. The figure was lying on his back with his one remaining arm pointing at the sky with a clenched fist. It appeared that his body had been burning as the aircraft plummeted to the earth, and the man had crawled from the wreckage minus an arm to die an agonising death.

Ben had heard stories of Australian aviators who ensured that they had a pistol within easy reach in the event that their aircraft might be set alight in a dogfight and they faced the inevitable slow death of burning in the flames. The two choices were to bail out and die from a fall, or to put a bullet in their own head for a quick death. Parachutes were forbidden to military pilots and observers to discourage the aviators from deserting their aircraft through so-called cowardice in action.

The members of Ben's troop dismounted, and a nominated section examined the crash site for anything of value. They found very little in the crumpled and burnt wreckage. Even the machine guns had been destroyed due to the heat of the fire, so all that was left to do was bury the charred corpses nearby. They had no idea who the two dead German aviators were, so they marked the graves with a few stones as a small cairn in the vastness of the desert.

'Still think that flying in one of those aeroplanes is a cushy job?' Ben asked the trooper who had previously commented on the easy life of a pilot or observer.

'Kind of a different opinion after seeing those two poor buggers,' the trooper replied, wiping sweat from his forehead with the back of his shirtsleeve. 'If I have to go, I'd rather have a Mauser bullet between the eyes.'

With the location of the downed German aircraft confirmed and the burial of the two corpses, the mission was over, and it was time to resume their desert patrol in search of the Turkish enemy. As they rode, Ben reflected on the names of the places they travelled through, which he'd heard in lessons from the Torah from his youth. Despite his lack of adherence to his faith, many nights Ben had laid on his groundsheet under the myriad crystalline stars and wondered if his Jewish ancestors had looked up at the same night sky, had perhaps also wondered about the universe and their place in it under the may eyes of Yahweh. But there were also many times he gazed up at the night sky and thought about Caroline. By now she must have given birth to their son or daughter, and the pain of the separation was as real to him as a bullet wound. He thought constantly about where she was and if he would ever meet her again.

★

The train pulled into Kings Cross station with its mixed cargo of civilian and military passengers either in uniform or civilian dress.

Rain drizzled over London as David stepped into the street to hail down a taxicab to take him to his hotel, the Langham, in the London suburb of Marylebone. It was

an establishment that David knew well from his stop-
overs in England before the war, and a place where he felt
comfortable.

Despite the fact that London's hotels were mostly fully
booked because of the transit of so many people, military
and civil servants alike, on missions for the war effort, David
was welcomed by the familiar face of a former veteran of the
Queen's colonial wars. David had befriended him when he
learned he had served in the Sudan in the 1885 campaign.
They had often chatted about the past and the man was
impressed that David's father had also served in that same
small war.

'Mr Steele.' The old man in his smart civilian suit recognised David immediately. 'I can see that you are one of our
colonial officers serving the King, God bless him. It is grand
having you stay with us.'

'We are no longer colonials, Harry.' David grinned,
taking the old man's hand in a firm handshake. 'Did
someone forget to tell you Poms that we became a self-
governing nation sixteen years ago?'

'I didn't know that,' Harry said, returning David's grin.
'I will help you sign into our fine establishment and hope
that you have a restful stay.'

David thanked him and they stepped into the hotel's
plush but unpretentious foyer, where David removed his
greatcoat. Harry glanced at the single military riband on
David's uniform, recognising it immediately as a decoration
for bravery.

'You have been on active service, then,' Harry said
respectfully. 'In France?'

'I'm there now, but no, this was from the Dardanelles
at Gallipoli,' David answered, following Harry's gaze. 'It
didn't go too well for us, or your lot.'

'I read in the papers that our First Lord of the Admiralty, Mr Churchill, is in a bit of trouble over that. We lost a lot of good lads from my regiment over there,' the doorman reflected.

They let the subject drop as David approached the reception desk to sign in to the hotel's register. The woman there was older than the receptionist he remembered from before the war, and when David enquired as to the whereabouts of the previous receptionist, he was informed that she was now working in a munitions factory out of a desire to help the war effort as her fiancé was serving with an artillery unit in France.

David located his room and quickly settled in. He had already sent a telegram to Naomi telling her where he was residing, and hoped it had reached her. He had, in fact, not received any mail from Naomi in quite a long while, and those missives he had received had only been brief, but he blamed the vagaries of the postal service in such a chaotic time. Nonetheless he was relieved when within the hour a porter knocked on his door to inform him that a young lady was in the hotel foyer requesting to see him.

David quickly glanced in a mirror to ensure that his hair was combed and that some of the rawness had gone out of his old bayonet scar. His heart was pounding, and he realised that he was acting like a nervous schoolboy on his first meeting with a beautiful young lady. Perhaps it was because this time, there would be no chaperone.

He hurried downstairs to find Naomi standing in the foyer holding a folded umbrella. She turned to see David striding towards her and smiled.

'Hello, my precious,' David said, holding back from embracing her in public despite the fact that every fibre in his body cried out to do so.

'Hello, David,' Naomi responded, with what David thought looked like rather a sad smile. Naomi was as lovely as ever, but he thought there was something different about her. Perhaps just the passage of a year in difficult times.

'I know a wonderful teahouse around the corner where we can catch up,' David said, and Naomi nodded. He escorted her from the hotel into a bleak afternoon of drizzling rain but they did not have to walk very far to the relatively crowded café full of well-dressed civilians and military officers. David steered Naomi to a small table by the window that had a view onto the street.

He pulled out the chair for her to sit, then sat down opposite the woman he had dreamed of seeing in person for all the days and nights he'd spent in the lice- and rat-infested trenches on the frontlines.

'David, it is grand that we are finally together, but I must apologise, our time is rather limited. I am to be sent from London to a hospital outside the city as part of my training for the VADs. I only just found out about it, so there wasn't time to write.'

David frowned. This was a blow. He knew from her letters that Naomi had joined the VADs but had hoped they would have this period of leave together, at least. 'Can't you delay your service with the excuse that you have important family matters to attend to here? As it is, my leave is very short and I don't know when I will next get the opportunity to return to London. My battalion will be deployed to a more active section of the lines when I return.'

'I wish I could, but my service is important to me,' Naomi answered, rather vaguely, David thought. It was then that David sensed something was wrong. If he was honest with himself, he had felt there was something a little distant in Naomi's letters to him of late, which had been warm

212

although polite in expressing her feelings towards him, and of course he had noticed that she hadn't written as often as she used to. However, he had preferred to simply dismiss the troubled feelings he experienced as his imagination. 'I fear that you do not share my belief in the importance of my service to my country,' Naomi added.

'I do,' David responded. 'But I also know that you might find yourself in France near the frontlines, and if that happens, I will fear for your safety. The Huns often shell our rear echelon institutions either intentionally or by accident, and that includes our medical services. I could not continue living if I ever learned that something had happened to you.'

But David's expression of support did not seem to move Naomi, who glanced away. When she turned back to David, he could see tears in her eyes.

'I have dreaded this moment since I learned of your leave,' she said. 'I have attempted many times to find a way to tell you – the truth is . . . I have met someone else.'

The statement hit David, stunning him . . . *met someone else*. For a moment he did not respond, attempting to take in the words Naomi had spoken.

'Why did you continue writing to me?' he asked in a broken voice. 'If you were with someone else?'

'You were risking your life and I did not have the heart to tell you the truth. I will not be posted to France now, so you can rest assured I'll be as safe as possible.' She looked into his eyes. 'You can't know how sorry I am about this, but I have my own life to think about. I feel that my love for you was very much an infatuation born of these uncertain times, rather than a deep love. I am terribly sorry and ashamed that I did not tell you before now. The man I have met is not a soldier but a civilian, and I am comforted knowing that he will not be sent overseas to the world you live in.'

Now David felt anger rising in him. 'I presume that this man has opted to remain out of uniform,' he said in a cold tone.

'He has,' Naomi answered. 'He is a banker and feels that he can do more good remaining in his civilian occupation, furthering our cause to win this terrible war. I know that you will not understand that all men do not have to be in uniform to fight in this war.'

'Do I know him?' David asked, trying his best to keep a rein on his anger and sorrow. So many days overseas in the arid lands of Egypt and now in the trenches of the Western Front, living for the moment each letter arrived from the woman he'd thought would be his. Now this.

'You do not know him,' Naomi replied. 'But he is a fine gentleman with prospects of one day becoming a member of parliament.'

'I don't think that we have anything else to say to each other,' David said, rising from his chair. 'I will hail a taxi for you if you wish.'

'I am sorry, David,' Naomi pleaded. 'I cannot control my feelings. I just pray that you eventually return home to find someone who can love you the way you deserve.'

The waiter arrived at the table, hovering for their order, and David told him they would be leaving without ordering.

He and Naomi stepped onto the chilly street in the misty rain. For David it truly felt that his heart was broken as surely as if a bullet had pierced it. But he stood tall, not allowing Naomi to see his pain. He hailed a passing taxi and instructed the driver to take Naomi wherever she directed. Then he stepped back onto the pavement.

'Goodbye, Naomi, and good luck,' he muttered as the

taxi drove away, leaving him empty of any feelings except confusion and sorrow for what had been lost to him.

★

Three miles away from the regimental camp in the Sinai, Ben was manning a listening post with twelve other members of his squadron. It was a bitterly cold night and Ben wrapped his greatcoat around himself like a blanket. He was located just below the height of the ridge with three other men, surrounded by a sea of undulating sand dunes. All Ben could do was wait for the warmth of the rising sun to take the chill from the still, crystal-clear night sky.

Every man in his regiment appreciated the importance of their duties to keep the Turkish army away from the Suez Canal only ten miles to their rear. If the enemy were spotted, the message would be relayed back to the next echelon of the regiment by a heliograph when the sun rose, and in turn the regiment had a telephone connection to stronger units behind them that could send up reinforcements.

When the sun finally breached the horizon, there was the promise of a meal and respite from the night chill – indeed, the sun would be baking hot before long. Ben stretched his stiff bones from a night of remaining absolutely still.

'Sarge, over there!' a trooper called out. When Ben swung around to look where the light horseman was pointing, he could see a Turkish patrol, and quickly ascertained that it comprised about thirty Turkish soldiers mounted on camels. They did not seem to be aware of the rest of Ben's party, who were on the higher ground. Ben calculated that they were about a quarter of a mile away and advancing cautiously in a spread-out skirmish line.

'Everyone take cover!' Ben barked, and the soldiers

standing quickly hit the sand on their bellies with their rifles ready.

'What do we do?' a corporal lying beside Ben asked. 'Do we helio about Jacko?'

'No time, they will be on us in a few minutes,' Ben answered, calculating the layout of his LP. 'I think that we have the numbers to take them on.'

Ben swivelled his head to see that the eight remaining men manning the post, who were up on a crest in groups of two, were fully aware of the approaching enemy and were looking to him for orders. Ben quickly wriggled away to speak with each section of two men. 'We don't fire until I give the order,' he hissed, and they nodded, acknowledging his command.

Ben wished that they had a Lewis gun, but all they had were their rifles and bayonets. He returned to his original position beside the corporal where he could clearly observe the approaching mounted Turkish soldiers. They appeared to be a reconnaissance patrol.

He felt a tightness in his stomach as the men on the camels grew closer, and when he looked along his defensive line – now an ambush – he could see in his troopers' faces that they were worried.

When the approaching enemy were fifty yards out and descending a large dune, Ben decided the time was right. He guessed that it would be difficult for the enemy to scramble back up the loose sand for cover on the higher ground.

'Fire!' Ben screamed, and a rattle of rifle fire broke the early-morning quiet with well-aimed death. Turkish troopers fell from their saddles and camels were also hit, throwing their riders into the gully below. The fusillade of shots appeared to kill or wound approximately one-third of the Turkish patrol, and the trailing remainder quickly dismounted to engage Ben and his men. Returning rifle fire kicked up the sand around the Australians on their ridge; the skirmish had settled into a fight of sniping.

Ben wondered if it was time to signal their regiment for reinforcements when to his horror approximately ten Turkish soldiers came into view shockingly close – it appeared they had somehow outflanked them. Ben guessed fleetingly that the new arrivals had been following their forward patrol out of sight. From the disciplined manner in which they'd undertaken this manoeuvre, it was obvious these were seasoned Turkish army mounted soldiers. Right now, a very large Turkish soldier was charging Ben with his bayoneted rifle and screaming, 'Allah Akbar!'

Ben desperately raised his Lee Enfield to fire on the almost crazed man, but the soldier was upon Ben before he could pull the trigger. Ben was at least able to parry the thrust and use the butt of his own weapon to land a blow on the man's head, knocking him off balance. Without thinking, Ben swung his rifle around and thrust forward, catching the Turkish soldier in the chest with his long bayonet. Then the man's face appeared to explode as a rifle shot from somewhere finished the task of killing him. Ben could see the corporal quickly working the bolt to eject the empty .303 case and reload a fresh round. Using their initiative, the troopers on the LP had turned to face the threat from their flank and a couple more of the enemy fell to the rifle fire of the defenders. The surviving Turkish soldiers quickly realised that they were up against very professional soldiers and took cover among the surrounding dunes.

After a few minutes of strained listening, the Australians could hear the sounds of retreat, and it was then that Ben took stock of their situation.

'Anyone wounded?' he called, and experienced a wave of

relief when the word came back that they had not sustained any killed or wounded. Ben had the signaller in his troop send a message back on the heliograph. The flashes of light on the mirror informed their regimental HQ that they had engaged an enemy patrol, killing eleven and with two wounded prisoners at the LP. No casualties to themselves.

'Bloody beauty, Sarge,' was echoed by all the troopers at the LP, and Ben knew that he had finally earned his three stripes among the Gallipoli veterans for his sound and calm leadership against difficult odds.

TWENTY-THREE

The terrible toll being taken on the Western Front was reflected in Australia's daily newspapers, as the names of Australian killed, wounded and missing began to mount. The rate of the British and French armies' casualties was even worse.

Josiah Steele slept very little; he dreaded opening his morning paper to review the casualty lists. Every name on the lists was that of a volunteer, and now it had been suggested in federal parliament that compulsory military service be introduced to support Britain.

It was a cold, wet day in Sydney as winter began in the southern hemisphere just as summer arrived in Europe. Josiah knew that the warmer, drier weather meant that the war on the Western Front would likely intensify and the casualty lists would only increase. David had written that the German artillery was causing more killed and wounded than small-arms fire – including machine guns – in his section of the frontlines at La Rolanderie. At least in winter many of the German artillery shells would disappear under the mud before exploding and hence the scatter of shrapnel was hindered. But, as the ground dried and hardened, the incoming shells would detonate on impact, spraying lethal shards of metal in a greater quantity and range.

'I have read that the government is considering intro-ducing compulsory military service.' Josiah glanced up to find his wife, Marian, in the doorway. 'Is there any tea in the pot?' she asked, sitting down with him at the dining table.

'Yes, it's still hot,' Josiah replied, and poured Marian a cup, adding milk from the silver tea set.

'Do you think that the prime minister will succeed in that?' Marian asked, taking a sip of her tea.

Josiah leaned back in his chair, ruminating on the ques-tion. 'It is hard to say,' he said. 'First there would have to be a referendum put to the people, and they will decide on the issue.'

'I think it is only fair that many of these young laya-bouts currently shirking their patriotic duty to the King and British empire should be forced to serve,' Marian stated firmly. 'We only have to think of the sacrifice that our sons are making for their country and then look out on the streets, where so many young and fit men are going about their lives as if there was no war.'

Josiah frowned. 'I don't know if forcing men to go to war will help,' he said, and Marian looked at him with surprise. In the past, Josiah knew his wife would have vehe-mently decried the idea of sending men to war, but time changed people, he considered. Maybe Marian's support of extra troops for service on the battlefields of Europe was a selfish one, evidence of her deep-seated desire to help her two much-loved sons. The issue had already caused a rift in opinions in the Steele family, and Josiah considered asking David and Ben their opinions on the matter in his next letters to them.

'I strongly suspect that the Irish among us will oppose any compulsory service. They have no love for the English,' Josiah said. 'For centuries they have viewed the British as military occupiers of their country, and some even sympathise with the Kaiser.'

'Not all of Irish descent here are supporters of the Germans,' Marian retorted. 'I know of many Irish families whose sons have heeded the call to arms.'

'That's true,' Josiah conceded. 'But the majority of those with Irish blood in Australia are Catholic, and already their priests are protesting service to Britain from the pulpits. If a referendum is held it will prove to be a close-run thing. I read recently that a speech against the war by Vida Goldstein was disrupted by returned soldiers in Melbourne. That incident might reflect the feelings of the men at the front on the need for extra troops to support them.'

'Our prime minister, Mr Hughes, is a strong voice of the nation in support of our troops, too,' Marian said. 'He has pointed out that we could face the same fate as Belgium if we lose this war.'

'I think that is unlikely,' Josiah scoffed, but he knew that Hughes was not a native-born Australian and seemed to put England's needs before those of the country he currently led. Josiah had personally met William Hughes in his role as an advisor to the military and did not like him. 'We have already quashed the German territories in the Pacific, and the Japanese navy is a strong force in this region and should discourage any attempt by the Kaiser to return to our waters.'

A silence fell between husband and wife as they sat with their different views. Josiah realised the issue would probably divide the new nation of Australia as well, and likely along sectarian lines, with the Protestant community supporting conscription while the Catholic Church opposed the idea.

It was time to go to his office. Josiah finished his tea, stood and leaned down to kiss his wife on the forehead, and she reached up to touch his arm. Despite their differences of opinion, their love for each other always came first.

Josiah flicked open his umbrella and hurried to the car where his chauffeur, a young man from an Irish family, stood in the rain to open his door.

'Good morning, Paddy,' Josiah said as his driver climbed behind the wheel.

'A good mornin' to you, Mr Steele. Just a bit on the wet side,' Paddy replied cheerfully. 'The traffic will be a bit of a bugger today.'

'No matter,' Josiah said. 'It is a lot worse for our boys overseas.'

'Talkin' about that, Mr Steele,' Paddy said. 'I have to tell you, I've signed up. I hope you don't mind, but I'm going to have to leave me job. I hope to be in France soon.'

Josiah was surprised and intrigued, given he and Marian had just discussed this very subject. 'I thought that most Irish were generally against the war?'

'We are, Mr Steele, but this is different. Many of my cobbers are over there and it's only right I go and help them. My family is not happy, but my sisters understand why I signed up. I was born in Australia, and I will be fighting for Australia, not for England.'

'Well, you have my full support, Paddy, and that of my wife,' Josiah said, reflecting on how the split in views would play out in Australia when a referendum was held on the conscription issue.

He had plenty of time to contemplate it as the car inched through the heavy traffic in the pouring rain.

★

The shelling was heavier than usual on the frontlines of David's sector. Men huddled in the deepest parts of their trenches and crushed into the underground shelters built into each side. Not able to find a shelter, David pressed himself against the corrugated lining of the earthwork parapet and pressed his trembling hands over his ears to try to shut out the deafening noise. He was not aware that he had wet himself. He wanted to scream his fear, but could see a few yards away a young soldier from his platoon staring at him wide-eyed as if asking what he should do.

But there was nothing anyone could do about an unseen enemy miles away sending a barrage of explosive artillery shells raining down on them.

A cry of agonised pain penetrated David's consciousness and he realised that it had come from the young soldier, whose name he suddenly remembered. He was about to call out to the man when David realised the wetness he could feel on his face was not water but blood. When he focused, he could see that a large shard of the exploding shell had torn through the young soldier from shoulder to hip, exposing his inner organs. The soldier slumped sideways, screaming for his mother until he mercifully fell silent.

But the barrage continued, working its way along the stretch of earthwork defences. David tried to control his trembling that was now a fully visible shaking. Tears clouded his eyes and all sense of time disappeared from his consciousness – except for a countdown to his own death.

'Boss, you all right?'

David, huddled with his knees under his chin, slowly realised that the shelling had ceased and men were emerging from the bunker-like defences to evaluate the damage. He recognised the voice of Sergeant Brian Williams and, as he became aware of himself again, saw that he had wet himself in his fear.

'I'm okay,' David answered in a shaking voice, but he was unable to stand on his own. Sergeant Williams reached out to pull David to his feet.

'You were lucky,' his platoon sergeant said, turning to the mangled body of the young soldier a mere three yards away. 'Private Wales not so much,' he said sadly. 'Good young bloke and only with us for a few weeks. One of the reinforcements we got in the last batch.'

David knew it would be his duty to check the company records to search for the next of kin for the letter he would write to a mother/wife/fiancée or brother/sister.

'Looks like you copped Private Wales' blood on you,' Sergeant Williams said. 'I will do a check on the rest of the platoon and report to you at platoon HQ. It will give you a chance to clean up.'

David nodded his thanks. Already he could smell the pungent coppery blood that covered his face and clothes. He could also hear the cries of other soldiers further along their stretch of trench, sobbing and moaning in pain, and could see soldiers shaking at their posts with what had become known as 'shell shock'. David knew that these victims of shelling had survived the metal shards of explosive shells only to have their minds damaged in a way doctors did not understand. But they were a matter for someone else, as he had a duty to feign bravery and to continue to lead his men.

David was beginning to rue his decision to enlist as an

officer. He often thought it would have been better to be a simple private soldier without the responsibility required of leadership. The word inferred wisdom, courage and a sense of duty, and he felt that all he had left now was the sense of duty. Courage and wisdom had been blown away long ago in the artillery shelling.

As David was about to proceed down the trench, one of his soldiers passed him and stopped. 'Boss, you must have copped one. There is a bit of claret on your back,' he said, and David stopped, reaching around to feel the flow of blood. Somehow the shell that had killed Private Wales had also struck him, but he had not felt it at the time. Now he did, and pain speared through his body.

Sergeant Williams also turned and noticed the wound that had torn open the back of David's uniform. 'I think you should head to the Regimental Aid Post to have that looked at,' he said.

'It's nothing, Sarge,' David replied automatically.

'Just get it looked at,' Sergeant Williams insisted. 'Then come back and tell us it's nothing.'

David knew his platoon sergeant was right and that he would need medical attention to ascertain how bad the wound was.

'While I'm gone you have command, Sergeant Williams,' David said, and struggled away down the trench of dead and wounded Australian soldiers.

★

David patiently waited to be treated outside the RAP tent as more seriously wounded were brought in ahead of him. But around him lay men on stretchers awaiting death, as their injuries had been diagnosed as beyond medical help. Morphine carried them through their final hours. Here and there a medical orderly might hold a soldier's hand until eternal sleep came to him, then his body would be moved away to make space for other wounded soldiers being littered in by stretcher-bearers. David tried to block out the faces of these men even as he despised himself for doing so.

Finally, David was examined and told that the shrapnel had sliced through the skin of his back, but missed his spine. It was the second time that day he had been told he was lucky. The wound was stitched and the army doctor impressed upon him how important it was to keep the now-bandaged wound clean. In the trenches that was a big ask, but at least David had been cleared to return to his platoon, which had now withdrawn to the rear for a well-deserved break. They would be billeted in the local village before rotating back to the front.

David rejoined his men in a cleared area where Red Cross staff provided tea and cakes.

'Good to see you back with us,' Sergeant Williams said as the men of David's command lay back under a warm sun, smoking pipes, cigarettes and some rare cigars, and luxuriating in the peace of the green pasture now beginning to wilt under the summer sun. Flowers and buzzing bees made the tiny clearing almost an oasis away from the war, but the distant rumbling explosions of the big guns reminded them all of a place on earth devoid of nature. Now the craters, bare earth and barbed wire marked man's destruction of the natural world.

'I told you it was nothing worth writing home about,' David said, grimacing slightly as a spasm of pain shot through his back.

'Mr Steele, you are required at Battalion Headquarters,' said a supercilious voice behind him. David knew the voice to belong to the battalion adjutant, a captain who had always remained aloof from mere lieutenants because of his role working closely with the battalion's commanding officer.

'When does the CO wish to see me?' David asked without attaching 'sir' to his reply. After all, the adjutant was only one rank above him, and most company captains had a close relationship with their junior officers.

'Now, Mr Steele. If you will come with me.'

David glanced at his platoon sergeant, who returned a questioning look. It was not normal for mere junior officers to meet with the battalion commanding officer.

David accompanied the adjutant to a farmhouse now established as the battalion's HQ, where he could see a staff car parked outside and cleanly dressed soldiers with clean rifles on guard duty, in contrast to his own men who had returned from the frontlines.

'The CO is expecting you,' the adjutant said, and David stepped inside, passing soldiers manning telephone exchanges and busily filling in forms, who ignored him. David was led to a small room whose walls were adorned with maps and clipboards. The room was occupied by the CO and two majors. David knew one of them but the other was a stranger.

'Mr Steele, I believe you were wounded today,' the CO said, turning away from a map on the wall. 'It is good to see that you are still with us as I have some news for you which I hope you will accept as good news.'

Confused and a little apprehensive, David simply replied, 'Sir.'

The CO was a man in his forties, a school headmaster before the war. He stepped away from the map board.

'You have been gazetted as a substantive captain as from today, and you will be transferred to assist with a brother battalion sorely in need of experienced officers. You will gather your things together and will be driven to join your new unit within the hour, as they are expecting you. Do you have any questions?'

David had a lot of questions, foremost among them, *Why me?* But he knew better than to ask. In a sense he was being honoured, recognised as an experienced officer with a promotion, but at the same time his current battalion had become his family. He knew the lives of his men as well as those of his family back in Australia. Leaving the battalion was akin to leaving the army family he belonged to. It would be a wrench.

As if sensing this, the CO said quietly, 'You will have enough time before you depart to say your goodbyes to your men, Captain Steele.' Then the CO turned his back to return to the company of the two majors and the map board, leaving David to ponder the events that had just unfolded.

He immediately returned to the clearing where his men were still resting, wondering what he would say to them. Maybe Sergeant Williams could inform the men after he had gone, when a new platoon commander was installed.

'Got you a cuppa, boss,' Sergeant Williams said when David approached.

'Thanks, Sergeant Williams,' David said, accepting the enamel mug.

'What did the brass want to see you for?' Williams asked. 'Or is that all hush-hush?'

'They informed me that I am now a captain,' David replied.

'But that means you will no longer be our platoon commander,' the sergeant said with a frown.

'I am afraid so,' David answered. 'Worse than that, I am being transferred to another battalion within the hour.

I don't want to say anything to the lads. Could you give them my apologies when I have departed? It's just that I would not be able to find the words to say how much each and every soldier means to me. I will leave that up to you, Brian.'

The familiar use of Sergeant Williams' first name was telling of the special bond David had with his stalwart sergeant and second-in-command, and acknowledged him as a man beyond his rank.

'I understand,' Williams replied. 'I know that you will be sorely missed by the lads, but the army got something right in promoting you.'

'They will hardly remember I was here, Sergeant. I will just be one of the many ghosts of August 1914 in their memories when they return home,' David said quietly, and stretched out his hand to his sergeant. 'To the best bloody sergeant in the Australian army, thank you for watching my back.'

Brian Williams accepted the firm clasp. 'To the best bloody officer I ever had the pleasure to serve under. Good luck in your new posting and I promise I will look after the lads for you.'

David nodded, then turned and walked away, fighting back the tears forming in his eyes. He would miss each and every one of his men.

TWENTY-FOUR

The night chill bit at Ben's face as they rode in silence through the desert back towards Romani. They had been headed for Katia, where they were to support the New Zealand Mounted Infantry attacking a Turkish outpost at Bir-el-Abd, but with help from British and Australian fighter aircraft, the Kiwis had been victorious, and their support was no longer needed.

Ben and his troop arrived at Romani at dawn to find themselves the target of a German fighter bomber that appeared out of the rising sun. The first bomb smashed the wireless station and the second killed the signals officer. Other bombs killed eight men and wounded another fifteen, and there were thirty-four dead and dying horses.

Then the German aeroplane swung around and made a strafing run of the camp, causing around three hundred horses to stampede into the desert.

During the attack, Ben and his men quickly dismounted to fire their rifles at the attacking fighter, but they could not disable it as its incoming rounds kicked up spurts of sand around them, killing some and injuring others, who cried out for help.

Then the German aircraft was gone as quickly as it had arrived, returning to its airfield somewhere out in the vast desert and leaving the Romani camp in disarray.

For the next few days Ben and his men spent their time tracking the stampeded horses. They recovered most near Katia where they came across a dead British sergeant lying in the desert beside a saddle and bridle. Ben guessed that the Tommy sergeant had been too badly wounded to mount his horse, but his last thoughts were to free it before he died. Ben understood the British sergeant's act of mercy as, like so many others of the Light Horse, his horse was probably his best friend. As they searched for the stampeded horses, they found other dead soldiers, both friend and foe, marking last desperate fights to the death in isolated pockets. The search was hampered by average daily temperatures of fifty degrees Celsius, and heatstroke was just as deadly an enemy as a Turkish bullet. Ben and his men had come to accept that death was as common as breathing.

★

The new posting, to Port Said, was not popular with Ben and his regiment – except for the improved rations provided there: steak and bacon for breakfast and a hearty stew of beef and potatoes in the evening. Even rissoles appeared for breakfast one day, and one of the troopers commented that the war must be over! Although it was a break from the countless hours of patrolling in the desert, where their canteens of water had to be sterilised with chlorine tablets, the inactivity was not something that appealed to the light horsemen. After all, they had volunteered for the war to fight the enemy. There were even cases of some light horsemen stowing away on transports bound for France to fight. It was well known to the troopers of the Light Horse that their campaign in the Sinai was viewed as a mere side show to the real war being fought in the trenches of the Western Front.

At least being camped in the backwater of the war meant letters and parcels from home arrived regularly. Ben was very pleased to receive a parcel containing tins of fruit, which were accompanied by letters from immediate family as well as a couple from David in France. Ben did not hesitate to share this prized treat with his comrades, but he kept one tin of apricots for himself. Ben knew that his actions weeks earlier in defending the LP had gained him the respect of the men he commanded, and he had even been informed that he had been recommended for a Mention in Dispatches for that action.

He found the shade of a tent and eagerly opened each letter, reading every word slowly to better remember the life he had left behind. A letter from his mother set out the conscription issue raging at home while his father rambled on with advice he had garnered in his service in this part of the world so long ago. A shadow fell over the letter, and Ben looked up to see Corporal Ken Ford, who he had come to know, respect and even like – the same man he had fought to a standstill months earlier.

'What would you think of a bloke serving alongside you if you knew he had been forced to come over here to fight?' Ben asked him.

Ken squinted as he considered the issue. 'Couldn't care less as long as he knew how to look after his horse and mates,' the big trooper answered. 'I got a message that you are wanted at the squadron HQ for a briefing. Maybe it's good news, maybe we're leaving this bloody hole.'

'Thanks, Ken,' Ben replied, folding away the precious letters and stowing them in his kitbag. 'Hope you're right.'

Grabbing his now battered slouch hat, Ben made his way to the squadron HQ.

★

The war was so far from Duke von Hauptmann's almost medieval estate in Bavaria that when Caroline sat with her baby son, Sebastian, in a field of wildflowers, it was as if she was living a serene dream. The duke held a high position in the government's War Materials Department, and as such the rationing introduced at the beginning of the war did not touch the lives of Caroline and her son. Because of Karl's work he virtually lived in his apartment in Berlin, and Caroline was left alone with the staff and workers of the duke's Bavarian estate. Fresh meat, fruit and vegetables were always readily available for Caroline and Sebastian, and their lifestyle was further supported by the duke's many shares in the armaments industry of the Krupp family. The war was making astute German industrialists rich beyond any expectations and Caroline's husband shared in that bounty. Caroline was divorced from the biting hardships faced by the urban population, where inadequate food supply was becoming a daily reality as the British naval blockade was having the desired effect of cutting off the German population from prewar overseas supplies.

On the rare occasions when the duke returned to his estate, he showed little interest in Caroline or her son. He was not a cruel man and treated her with respect, but she knew he had not bonded with Sebastian, seeing him simply as a means of ensuring a lineage for his name. But he would remind Caroline how fortunate she was to be able to enjoy the fruits of his position in the government when so many women in the cities were assuming the roles of men, working in munitions factories and doing other heavy manual labour.

Sitting with her son in the warmth of the summer sun, Caroline watched a small group of women and an old man working around a hay-laden horse-drawn wagon. It struck Caroline that there were no young men with them, as they had been called up for military service on the Western Front. Even the rural civilian population was impacted by the distant war raging in the fields of Belgium and France.

'Good morning, Duchess.'

Caroline turned to see the daughter of the head game-keeper behind her. She was around Caroline's age and one of the few people Caroline regarded as a friend on the estate. She was pretty, with the sturdy body of a rural girl used to manual work, and the days under the sun had bleached her hair a titian colour. Today it was tucked under a scarf.

'Good morning, Helga.'

The farm girl smiled and reached down to lift Sebastian into her arms. 'He is growing so fast,' she said. 'Soon he will be big enough to be a soldier for the Kaiser.'

Helga's innocent remark caused Caroline to frown. 'I truly hope that we see peace before my son becomes a young man,' Caroline said, but without rancour. 'From what I have read it appears the fighting is almost at a stalemate.'

'No, the Kaiser has promised us victory because God is on our side and not on that of the British and French,' Helga said, bouncing Sebastian in her arms and causing him to giggle with delight. 'Our army is the best in the world, and I am proud to say my Hans is now being sent to the front.'

Caroline knew that Hans was a young man from a neighboring village who Helga was infatuated with. It was assumed by all on the estate that the pair would one day wed in the local church. Now it seemed he was a soldier in the Kaiser's army.

'Are you not afraid that your young man might not return to you?' Caroline asked as gently as she could, and a dark cloud crossed Helga's face. She handed the toddler back to Caroline.

'I do not even wish to think about that,' she replied, and Caroline could see tears forming in her eyes. 'You are fortunate that the duke has a government job that keeps him close to you, and away from the front.'

Caroline did not comment but gazed out at the fields of yellowing crops ripe for harvest. She thought of the man she truly loved, but it all seemed like a lifetime ago on the other side of the world. Caroline did not know if Ben was still alive, but knew full well that if he was, he would have enlisted to fight because it was in his nature. She forced back her own tears as she rocked Sebastian in her lap. Helga could not know that the only true love she had ever known was now considered an enemy combatant. Or that whenever Caroline looked into the eyes of her son, she saw Ben staring back at her.

Helga had wiped away her tears and was also staring off into the distance as both women silently reflected on the fate of the two men they loved, but only Caroline had to keep her secret from all those she knew in her loveless marriage to the duke.

★

Ben's regiment had been briefed that the Turkish army was on the move, advancing south. When he relayed the news back to his troop, it was met with enthusiasm – finally a chance to fight!

The grindstone was busy sharpening bayonets as Ben's troop went about the business of caring for their mounts as well as their weapons.

The time came when the order to *file out* was declared, and even the tough Waler horses sensed the excitement of their riders, whinnying and snorting. It was late July, and as he rode Ben wondered where David was, and whether he was still safe. It was impossible for anything bad to happen to his brother, as he was the chosen one to inherit their family's business empire. It was not a task Ben had ever wished for, as the dry, dull world of big business had never appealed to him. Ben shrugged as the long desert column entered the searing heat of the Sinai desert. Death only came to the man beside you, he reminded himself. Not to you or those you loved.

★

The distant sound of exploding artillery shells was a constant in David's life as he arrived at the sprawling rear echelon encampment of the Australian division. He stepped out of the staff car and the driver said, 'Good luck, Captain Steele.'

David walked to the HQ, a partially destroyed farm-house, to report to the battalion commanding officer. On the way here, he had not seen a single structure that had not sustained shelling. Now he stood before his new CO, a man in his forties with a solemn, scholarly air about him.

'Captain Steele, welcome to the battalion,' the man said from behind his makeshift desk, which was a kitchen table scattered with papers and a map. 'You are a welcome addition to our battalion, if the reports I have read about you are anything to go by. I know it is not easy leaving a battalion that you have served with since Gallipoli, but you will be pleased to learn that a great number of my men are veterans of that campaign too, so you will hopefully feel at home with them. As a matter of fact, your new company CO has informed me that he personally knows you from last year when you were at Gallipoli – Major Goldstein. I believe he is a Jew like you.'

David was pleasantly surprised to learn he would be second-in-command to a man he had known both in London and Gallipoli. They had become casual friends, as both had served as platoon commanders at Gallipoli, and now it seemed Saul Goldstein had been promoted to major.

'Sir, I do know Major Goldstein, and he is a fine soldier,' David replied.

'Good,' the CO said. 'I will have the adjutant escort you to your quarters so you can settle in. We have a briefing tonight at twenty-hundred hours here. I expect that when you attend with Major Goldstein you will be brought up to speed on our operations.'

'Thank you, sir,' David said dutifully, and the CO stood and reached out to shake David's hand.

'Good show, Captain Steele,' he said, and David was then escorted by the adjutant to another partially destroyed stone farmhouse where they stepped inside to be greeted by the rank odour of sweating, unwashed bodies and cigarette smoke. The room set aside for the battalion's junior officers was a crowded affair with a pot-belly stove and a haphazard arrangement of bunks. The adjutant gestured to a bunk with a ragged blanket. When David glanced at the two officers already in the room, he could see that he was the most senior. The young officers were lieutenants.

'Welcome to the Savoy of France,' one of the young lieutenants said, approaching David. He was wearing his khaki trousers with braces over a flannel singlet. 'I am Trevor Plymin and the fool over there on his bed is John Carroll.' He shook David's hand. 'So, I heard a rumour that you and our CO, Major Goldstein, knew each other at Gallipoli. He's a Jew, you know.'

'So am I,' David responded, causing a look of acute embarrassment to flash across Lieutenant Plymin's face. 'We are not a unique race in Australia.'

'I am sorry, sir, I did not mean to suggest that there is anything wrong with being of the Jewish faith,' Plymin spluttered. 'It's just that I did not know any Jews back home. The Steele name is not exactly Jewish like our CO, Major Goldstein's.'

'Well, you now have both a Jewish CO and company second-in-command, so you can say that you have met at least two Jews in your life.'

David could see that the young officer was deeply regretting his poorly chosen comment, off-hand though it was, and was chagrined that he might have irritated the officer senior to him. 'I take no offence at your comment, Mr Plymin. And you are correct in your assumption that my family name is not traditionally Jewish. My family were originally Christians.'

The lanky officer lounging on his bunk sat up to join the conversation. 'Trev, old boy, our RMO, Captain Cohen, is also a Jew,' he said, addressing his colleague. 'And he is a bloody good surgeon. I would trust him to fix any shattered limb.' The officer pushed himself away from his bunk and walked over to David with his hand extended. 'I apologise for Mr Plymin's gaffe, sir. He did not have a Greater Public Schools education back home. My father has the greatest respect for your father and his service to his country and community in business and charity. I suppose that we should call the batman to prepare a brew for us before we go any further.'

David smiled, accepting the extended hand. 'Is the RMO's first name Maurice?' he asked, almost holding his breath.

'I believe it is,' Carroll replied. 'He calls Sydney home. As a matter of fact, he is currently working at the Regimental Aid Post. Do you know him?'

'If it is the same man, he is my brother-in-law,' David said.

'Bloody hell!' Carroll swore. 'It is a small world if that is so.'

Feeling a little lighter, David knew where he was going. He went back out into the sunlight, leaving the two junior officers to savour their mugs of cocoa.

TWENTY-FIVE

Traversing the scattered wooden crates of munitions and other military supplies, then passing a line of diggers waiting patiently for a hot meal from the mobile cooking wagons, David located the field hospital – a large, relatively undamaged stone building that was a combination of farmhouse and adjoining barns. A couple of bandaged Australian soldiers with minor shrapnel wounds rested outside, smoking and reclining in the warmth of the summer sun. Inside, David was assailed by the scent of blood and antiseptic. He was pleased to see that the field hospital was not busy, and moved further in to see the rows of bunks, mostly empty, as well as the section cordoned off for surgery. Hospital orderlies went about their tasks, changing linen and stocking rolls of bandages.

A white-coated doctor stepped out from the makeshift surgery, peeling off blood-soaked surgical gloves, and

David immediately recognised his brother-in-law, Captain Maurice Cohen. He looked older and wearier than David remembered, but when Maurice glanced in David's direction and saw who he was, his face lit up with a broad smile.

'David, is that really you?' he asked, striding towards David. The men met and exchanged vigorous handshakes. 'You caught me at a good time,' Maurice said, leading David to the entrance of the hospital. 'Very few casualties are being brought to us today, so let's go outside and soak up some sunshine.'

The two men stepped outside into the summer's day and David spied a couple of empty ammunition cases which he drew up for them to sit on.

'I can't believe that we are now in the same battalion,' David said, pulling out a packet of cigarettes and offering one to Maurice, who accepted.

'It appears we are now both smokers,' Maurice said, drawing deeply on the lit cigarette. 'How things have changed since we left Sydney's shores. Here we are now, captains and in the same battalion.'

'I didn't ask for the transfer, but finding you and Saul Goldstein here has helped dampen my misgivings,' said David.

'Major Goldstein mentioned a few weeks back in the officers' mess that you and he were at Gallipoli. He said that you got the medal, and he got the promotion. At the time when I enquired as to your whereabouts, he said you were a platoon commander with a battalion at the La Rolanderie section of the front.'

'It was deemed a "nursery" section but proved anything but. Towards the end we were always under Hun artillery shelling and the battalion lost a few,' David replied. 'Nowhere is really safe at the front.'

Maurice's face darkened. 'I fear things are going to get even worse here,' he said. 'We are getting extra supplies of medical items we normally have to fight for in our requisitions. I suspect the division might be facing a big push soon as the Poms are taking terrible casualties on the Somme. I overheard a couple of staff officers discussing an attempt to cut off German reinforcements, and that will mean a bigger show than we have dealt with before now.'

'Do you have any idea where and when that might be?' David asked, watching the cigarette smoke drift lazily away on the summer breeze.

Maurice shook his head. 'I am a mere RMO and so I am not consulted on such matters. All we can do is save as many lives as we can and make the men fit for future service on the front. Sometimes it feels more like being an automobile mechanic than a surgeon. It breaks my heart to see the wounds we treat in the hospitals. Young men with smashed bodies who, if lucky enough to survive, will go home to uncertain futures. Then there are the ones we have to set aside to die because their wounds are beyond our medical care.' Maurice paused in his lament, realising that his brother-in-law was well aware of the damage caused to human bodies on the battlefield. 'To brighter news, have you had any mail lately from home?'

They lapsed into a conversation about matters far from France, of family affairs and life in Sydney, and for a good half-hour, they sat together as if the war did not exist. Then a medical orderly hurried towards them from the hospital.

'Sir, we need you immediately,' he said to Maurice. 'One of the lads has taken a turn.'

Maurice stubbed out his fourth cigarette and stood up, extending his hand to David. 'With any luck we might get the chance to have a drink together in the mess, old chap.'

David rose, tossing aside his own cigarette. 'It will be my shout,' he said. 'Good luck, Morrie, and I will immediately write home to say that we are together over here. I am sure it will be welcome news for them all.'

Maurice followed the medical orderly back into the hospital, leaving David to ponder with some trepidation the rumour his brother-in-law had passed on: that they had yet to face a battle possibly on a scale as terrible as that suffered by the British on the Somme and by the French at Verdun.

★

For Ben the desert war settled into a routine of scattering whenever a German aeroplane arrived to bomb and strafe them, and being put on *stand to* with the intelligence that the Turkish army, supported by Germans and Austrians, were moving south towards them in considerable numbers. So far there had been no real clashes with the enemy. The frustration of the command to *stand down* rankled Ben's squadron as they listened at night to the howls of the desert wild dogs punctuated by the distant booming sound of Turkish artillery, rifles and machine guns as sister regiments engaged the advancing Turkish soldiers mounted on camels and on foot.

Ben had heard that the enemy comprised the finest of the Turkish army: the big men of the Anatolian regiments who his regiment had also faced at Gallipoli. Jacko – as Ben and his men called the Turks – was almost a term of endearment for their old enemy as the Turkish soldiers' courage could not be questioned. They were also fine soldiers.

Ben was asleep when he felt his shoulder being shaken. He came awake to focus on the face of his troop officer leaning over him. Lieutenant George Martin-Smith was well liked and respected by the men in the squadron and had been granted the fond nickname of 'Bluey' because of his very red hair.

'Sergeant Steele, get your troop together if you want to see some action,' the lieutenant said quietly.

'Boss?' Ben asked, rubbing away the last remnants of his dream of being on Manly Beach in Sydney with a pretty girl.

'We have been given permission to ride out now and reconnoitre Turkish positions. I am only taking you and five of the lads from your section, and I have to confess that it is a risky mission. I will leave it to you to select which men we take.'

'No worries, boss,' Ben replied as he sat up in the crystal-clear chilly night air, lit only by the blaze of the endless panorama of stars. 'I know the boys who will jump at the opportunity to see some real action, and I would also like to include Corporal Ford.'

'If he is your choice then do so,' the officer replied. 'Half an hour before we mount up. Report to the squadron HQ when you are ready.'

The lieutenant slipped back into the inky night and Ben made his way to where his men were bunked down in the sands. Moving at night was now a very familiar practice for Ben and he soon located the men he wanted for the mission.

'Jeez, Sarge, when the others find out what we are up to, they are goin' to be pissed orf that they weren't included,' one of the selected light horsemen said. Ben didn't express his own thoughts that if they were to advance into enemy territory and were detected, cut off from any realistic help from the regiment, this could be a suicide mission. But at least it was the chance to see some action.

When Ben found Corporal Ken Ford snoring a short distance away from the sleeping section, he woke him with the news and thought for a terrified second that the big corporal might kiss him for the chance to participate in the mission.

Within the half-hour the section assembled at squadron HQ. Extra provisions of the detested hard biscuits and cans of bully beef were issued, as well as extra water canteens, and they prepared their horses.

Before first light the small section rode away from the regiment to travel deep into the vastness of the Sinai, where the Turkish army had assembled an impressive force to push the infidels into the Suez Canal.

★

Ben's patrol arrived at a low ridge of sand and stone before sunrise and quickly settled in to observe the arid plains to their front, while the horses were hobbled behind them with a supply of grain and water.

For the first day they took turns with the set of binoculars, straining to see through the shimmering haze that lay over the baking dunes and plain below. Three men would keep a lookout just at the edge of the ridge while the others rested on the reverse slope before rotating roles.

Ben had finished cleaning his rifle to remove excess sand and opened a tin of bully beef, which had turned into an almost soup-like state that was far more attractive to the flies that swarmed in dark clouds around the opened tin than it was to him. Ben was careful not to swallow any of the sticky flies and took a sip of water from his canteen to wash down the near-melted processed meat.

'Hey, Ben, look what I found!' It was Corporal Ford who approached, holding something. 'Saw it when I was out digging a hole for my constitutional.'

Ben sat up to see the big corporal holding what appeared to be a shard of ancient pottery.

'What you think?'

Ben accepted the shard and examined it. All he could surmise was that it was clay hardened in a fire.

'Probably one of my ancestors dropped it when they were on the Exodus from Egypt,' Ben said with a serious expression.

'Fair dinkum!' Ken Ford exclaimed, and then saw the grin on Ben's face.

'I don't know. It could be anything from Egyptian to Roman for all I know. This place has been tramped over by just about every Mediterranean army since the pyramids were built, as well as being the home of my Jewish ancestors. Since we can't drop it into the nearest museum, you may as well hoist it.'

'I'm keepin' it,' Ken said, taking back the pottery shard. 'It might be worth something when we get to Jerusalem.'

Jerusalem . . . the word held meaning to Ben. It featured so strongly in his religious learnings, and he realised that it was a place that they might eventually capture. Ben had never been particularly religious, but the mention of a place sacred to his Christian friends and Turkish enemy alike echoed in his thoughts. It would be as if the Christian Crusaders had returned after the many centuries since the city had fallen to the Islamic empire. What would that mean to history?

He watched as Corporal Ford made his way to the ridge, assuming his observer role on the high ground and leaving Ben to ponder the piece of pottery and Jerusalem. He had loved reading as a child, and had read a lot of stories written by authorities on the Biblical lands. He reflected that in this moment he belonged to yet another invading army up against the thousand-year-old Moslem Ottoman Empire in its decline. He was also aware of the Zionist organisation that hinted at this rugged land once again becoming the home of all scattered and displaced Jews from around the world, a place where they could escape the persecution they had suffered for centuries in European lands from England to Russia. He also remembered how even in Australia there was a distinct coldness by the upper echelons of European descent towards those of the Jewish faith. Ben had learned that his squadron knew of his faith, but none seemed to care. All that mattered to them was that he performed his duties as their troop sergeant competently.

'Sergeant Steele. Up here!'

The command had come from Lieutenant Martin-Smith, and Ben scrambled to his feet, recognising the urgency in the other man's voice. When Ben reached the edge of the ridge, he could already see the long line of dust on the horizon, indicating a very large force of mounted troops. The officer passed Ben the binoculars.

'Jacko,' Ben said. 'And a bloody lot of them, probably only a couple of miles away and coming in our direction.'

'I think it is time to head back to the regiment and report what we have observed,' the officer said, marking on a map the approximate location of the enemy force and direction of their advance.

'Boss!' The startled cry came from a trooper positioned further along the ridge. Lieutenant Martin-Smith looked where the trooper was pointing. The well-educated young officer, reared in a staunchly religious Christian family who partook of neither alcohol nor cigarettes, used an obscene word none of his troopers had ever heard him utter before.

To their left and right flanks, they could see Turkish scouting patrols mounted on camels. The Turkish army had wisely sent troops forward to either side of the advancing main body.

Ben scrambled to his feet, realising that the flanking Turkish scouts would investigate any high ground in the advance of the main body of their troops, and they would quickly be spotted and surrounded.

'We ride as if the devil is chasing us,' the lieutenant said to the small party of men who were already hefting saddles to fling on their horses' backs. Scrambling down the slope, Ben snatched his saddle and all the troopers quickly reached their mounts, saddled up and took off the hobbles.

Ben swung himself into the saddle, noticing that the flanking enemy patrols were already galloping in their direction. It was now horse against camel in a death race rearward across the arid plain. The crack of bullets in the air around them indicated they were within rifle range, but Ben hoped that the pursuing camels would be wearier than their rested mounts.

They galloped in an uneven line with the patrol commander riding only a few yards from Ben, bent low over his tough mount's neck, making him a smaller target for the pursuing Turkish cameleers who were now around four hundred yards behind them, but Ben had been correct in his estimation. The camels were falling behind and the sporadic rifle fire was also tapering off.

'Bloody hell! Bluey is down!' The cry came from Corporal Ford, and as he spoke Ben saw out of the corner of his eye that the patrol commander's horse had tumbled, flinging the lieutenant into the sand.

Ben immediately pulled hard to bring his mount around, yelling to the rest of the fleeing party to keep going.

Ben flung himself from his saddle, kneeling beside the officer who he could see was alive but severely winded from the heavy impact with the hard surface. A few yards away the officer's horse whinnied in pain, and Ben could see that it had a broken leg. Ben did not have to think but quickly aimed and fired his rifle at the critically wounded horse. The bullet brought almost instant merciful death to the doomed animal.

Quickly grabbing the officer by the shoulders, he dragged him to his feet just as sand spurted nearby. With a sick feeling in his stomach, Ben could see the rapidly approaching Turkish patrol of around ten mounted soldiers now only a couple of hundred yards away, their rifle fire now more accurate.

Suddenly a fusillade of shots came from the opposite direction and Ben saw that the fleeing Australians had stopped, dismounted, and from a kneeling position were providing covering fire to aid Ben's escape.

Ben hefted the lieutenant onto his own horse's rump and threw himself into the saddle. Ben's mount hardly needed an order to gallop forward towards the men already remounting their own horses for the escape, leaving the pursuing Turkish scouts in their wake.

★

Exhausted horses in desperate need of water – with weary men in the saddles – arrived at the regiment a couple of hours later, with no fatal casualties and one very grateful patrol officer. Ben knew that it had been Corporal Ken Ford who had ordered the rearguard action, and that he really owed his life to this action, but before thanking him Ben knew that his first duty was to his horse who had carried both him and the lieutenant to safety.

After looking after his mount, he was summoned to meet with Lieutenant Martin-Smith.

'Sergeant Steele, I am recommending you for a decoration for your courageous action of saving me today,' he said. 'Had you not stopped to assist me I strongly suspect we would not be having this conversation.'

Ben was impressed by the offer but quickly countered, 'Boss, if it had not been for the quick actions of Corporal Ford, neither of us would be around to have this conversation, so I think Corporal Ford is the one you should be recommending for any gongs. It would mean a lot to his family.'

George Martin-Smith was taken aback by Ben's counter-offer but could see in the light horseman's expression that it was a conviction he held strongly.

'Very well, Sergeant Steele,' George Martin-Smith replied. 'Your recommendation is a selfless act deserving of consideration when I write up my report on today's action. It is possible I can compensate you for that in the future.' The officer held out his hand to Ben. 'My word on that.'

Ben took his commander's hand firmly. 'Thanks, boss,' he said. 'One never knows when one might have to call in a favour from friends.'

Ben did not realise that one day this promise would change his life forever.

TWENTY-SIX

The time had arrived for the Australian divisions to engage in a major military operation on the French battlefields of the Western Front.

Maurice had been right in his instinct that something big was being planned, and David found himself attending briefings and working closely with the company sergeant major to ensure that supplies were delivered to the men of the company, which left his friend and commander, Major Saul Goldstein, free to plan the tasks of each of his platoons in the upcoming attack on the German front lines – and beyond.

From what David had been told in the battalion briefings, the attack on the German lines was meant as a feint to prevent German reinforcements from reaching the British army on the Somme. An Australian division alongside a British division were to seize around 4,000 yards of

German frontlines centred around a feature known as the 'Sugar Loaf'. It would be the usual tactic of their artillery shelling the German lines prior to advancing infantry across no-man's-land, with the infantry using rifle, bayonet, grenades and the Lewis guns in support. All was scheduled for 19 July, using the long daylight hours of midsummer to assist in seeing their enemy.

On the afternoon of the day of the planned assault, David moved among the platoons, occasionally discussing issues with the young platoon commanders, and felt just a little despondent that he would not be leading a section of men as he had done as a platoon commander with his old battalion.

For a brief moment on this fateful day, David had a rare opportunity to be alone, and decided to scribble a letter to his parents before reassuming his role as company second-in-command. With his back to an ammunition crate he sat, pencil poised over a sheet of paper resting on his map board, his hands trembling uncontrollably and his stomach fluttering. David knew that the old fear had returned, but tried to reassure himself that the British artillery landing their deadly explosive shells on the German lines would help their attack. He had grown used to the constant *crump crump* of artillery in the background, and made an attempt to write, but his trembling hand prevented him from doing so. He sighed, folded the blank sheet and sat back to light a cigarette, which helped soothe his shattered nerves. *How much more can I take?* David asked himself. *Just get through this stunt*, he thought, and for a moment remembered Naomi. What would she be doing right now in London? He knew that despite everything, he still loved her, and the memories of those peaceful moments in the countryside flooded back in a warm wave, temporarily taking him out of the war.

'Sir, Major Goldstein requests your presence.'

It was the voice of the company sergeant major, a professional soldier in his mid-forties.

'Coming, Sarn't Major,' David said, rising to his feet and following the senior non-commissioned officer until they found Saul surrounded by his platoon commanders, providing last-minute briefings on their allocated tasks in the assault. When he had finished, he dismissed them and turned to David.

'Do you realise that a century and one year ago, Wellington fought Napoleon just north of here in Belgium, defeating him and bringing a hundred years of relative peace to Europe, with the help of the Germans? I can't get over the irony that here we are today, facing the Hun who were once instrumental in bringing that long peace, and fighting alongside the one-time enemy of all Europe, the French.' Saul stared off into the distance in the direction of the German lines.

'A bit philosophical for this moment in history, old chap,' David said with a slight smile. 'A century is a long time.'

Saul turned to David, retrieving a silver flask from his trouser pocket. 'We've had little chance to catch up since you arrived, so I feel it is time to share a drink.' He passed the flask to David, who held it up. 'Chin chin,' he said, taking a long swig and recognising the taste of gin, then he handed it back to Saul who responded with, 'Good luck to us today, because it is only luck that keeps us alive.' He drank too, then returned the flask to his pocket.

'Now, I need you to move with Mr Plymin's platoon when we hop the bags, and that will put you on the left flank of our formation in the assault. It seems that we are almost ready to step off, so keep your head down and we will get together again over there in the German trenches.'

253

Saul held out his hand and the two men shook before David made his way to his assigned position in the assembly area.

Unfortunately, the Australians were unaware that the Germans had been warned of the coming attack on their trenches by the pre-assault artillery bombardments, and their artillery observers were in a position to bring down their own artillery on the Australian and British assembly areas. All hell spewed down from the deadly German artillery on the helpless troops crouching in their formations ready to attack.

David was blown off his feet by the concussive shock wave of a nearby exploding shell, and could hear ringing in his ears just as he reached Lieutenant Plymin's platoon. The world around him was a nightmare of ear-shattering sound punctuated by the screams and cries of soldiers whose bodies had been torn apart by red-hot shrapnel, which ripped off limbs, disembowelled some and beheaded others.

David rose shakily to his feet to see that the platoon he was to join had taken a direct hit. Already comrades of the fallen were attempting to bandage the less severely wounded and David could see Trevor Plymin lying on his back, blood gushing from his shattered leg.

'Bloody hell!' The young officer grimaced, gripping his leg. 'The bastard hurts.'

Already courageous medical stretcher-bearers were moving among the wounded, taking away those they could help under heavy fire. Their red cross armbands meant little to blind artillery shells. David signalled to a couple of stretcher-bearers to attend to the wounded Australian officer.

'Sir, look after my boys,' Trevor said before he was taken away, and David promised that he would. Normally the platoon sergeant would take command, but David could see that he was dead.

Realising that the assembly area had become a slaughterhouse, the order was sent down the line to advance, but just as David turned to the survivors of Plymin's platoon, he heard his name called. It was the CSM.

'Sir, Major Goldstein has been killed. You are now acting company commander.'

David reeled, but the rational part of his mind knew the plan of attack, as the contingency of a company commander being taken out of action automatically made him the acting company commander.

'I'll look after the boys, sir,' a corporal called to David, overhearing the CSM's message. 'We'll be all right.'

'Good man, you are now acting platoon commander,' David responded hollowly, and followed the CSM to the centre of the company formation already moving forward.

It was 6 pm and David knew they only had three hours of daylight to achieve their mission of taking the German trenches with bullet, bayonet and grenades.

Under heavy small-arms and machine-gun fire, coupled with exploding German artillery rounds now adjusted to break up the attacking force, David's company advanced, dashing forward, ignoring those who fell in a desperate attempt to reach the enemy line of trenches.

David was accompanied by the CSM and one other soldier as they crossed no-man's-land. Although David carried a rifle, he did not fire a shot as he was more concerned with the advance of the platoons either side of him in the ragged extended line. Their advance had been fast enough that they could actually see the enemy, and before he had even registered that he was still alive, the men of his company were spilling into the zigzagging earthworks, tossing hand grenades and following up with hand-to-hand fighting in the narrow forward trenches.

This was now a primitive personal war of man against man using any object available, from rifle and bayonet to entrenching shovels and homemade clubs. Men on both sides screamed in fear and pain as death came to one or the other.

David's rank meant nothing when he was confronted by a German soldier who had appeared from an underground bunker with his rifle. The German soldier's rifle did not have a bayonet fitted when he appeared, white-faced and with terror in his eyes. Instinctively David lunged at the soldier with his bayonet-fitted Lee Enfield and the long bayonet pieced the German's chest. The German dropped his own rifle, clutching at the Australian bayonet in his chest, looking up at David as if pleading for mercy, but it was too late as David twisted the bayonet. Blood spattered David's face as the enemy soldier fell dead at his feet. David was vaguely aware that the CSM was clubbing to death an enemy soldier in the bottom of the trench with the metal-plated butt of his rifle. A soldier attached to company HQ was tossing a grenade around the corner of the trench, which had right angles built in to prevent anyone from firing a direct line down the length of the defences.

'We have cleared the Hun out along here,' the CSM said, stepping over the dead German soldier at his feet, and David sagged against the trench wall, relieved that their attack had been successful in overpowering the first line of German defences. The CSM was already working his way along the line, quickly recording the names of dead and wounded from the company. David was aware that the taking of the first line of defences was just the first objective in the overall battle plan, and waited until the CSM returned to make a report on their status. There were so many missing and so many dead and dying men of the company that it hardly registered with David. He focused on the next step.

'We have to push on and take their next line of defences,' David said. 'Get the boys ready and on my signal, I will blow the whistle for us to jump the bags.'

The CSM acknowledged David's order and moved away to brief surviving platoon commanders – and acting platoon commanders – of their next objective. When it was reported that the men were ready, David blew the whistle to begin the assault on what they had been told was another line of German defensive trenches.

Climbing over the rear of the captured line, they advanced under more artillery fire, but there were no German trenches to capture, and David realised that they were in the open being cut down. He gave the order to fall back to the captured trenches they had just left, knowing from instinct they were now so badly mauled that the concept of battalions and companies no longer existed. Their grand plan had been reduced to simply a small outpost of survivors clumped together.

It was time for David to formulate an escape plan back to their original start line in the learned knowledge that the enemy would almost certainly mount a counterattack which he knew would overwhelm them. Ammunition was just about spent and resupply a forlorn hope. It was obvious to every soldier and surviving officer that the attack had failed miserably. Now it was a case of getting out of the captured trenches before the Germans fell on them in their greater numbers.

Exhausted, drained of all feelings except despair and fear, the darkness of the summer night crept upon them.

★

Acting Company Commander David Steele was hardly aware of the stench of rotting flesh anymore. He had first seen action in Rabaul, a mere few weeks after the declaration of war, where Australians saw their first casualties fighting the German colonial troops, and then in the Dardanelles as a lieutenant commanding a platoon of infantry, where he had also been exposed to the sickly sweet smell of death.

Now David lay in a shell crater with five surviving men from the savagely depleted company he now commanded. David was aware that there were others from his company sheltering in the moonscape of craters who were also alive after the disastrous attack on the German-held ridge that was basically a manmade fortress of enemy trenches and machine-gun posts.

The echoes of the men he had lost rang in David's ears and haunted his mind when he closed his eyes. Men screaming curses in two languages, the awful sounds of others dying, and the strong smell of blood and ruptured bodies. David knew that his hands trembled uncontrollably. As night descended on that July day, he also knew that the Bavarian regiment they had faced would mount a counterattack, as this was the tactic the enemy always used when they lost ground. The order had trickled down to David's level of command that they must hold their captured ground to cover the withdrawal of other Australian troops after the disaster of what was the Battle of Fleurbaix. Later it was given another name – Fromelles.

David knew that he had to muster as many of the company still left alive as possible for their defence against the inevitable counterattack. But that meant leaving the relative safety of the shell crater to locate them across the bloody battlefield. The wounded had to be recovered, but the constant artillery fire made that almost impossible.

For a moment, David wished they were still back at Gallipoli, as bad as that had been. When redeployed to France and Belgium, the veterans had learned the meaning of industrial-scale mass slaughter with the artillery shells killing more than the bullets from machine guns or small arms. A soldier was helpless under an artillery barrage as the exploding shells tore bodies apart with deadly red-hot shards of jagged metal and caused trenches to collapse and bury men alive. With an unlucky direct hit, they virtually smashed a body to atoms.

David was aware that his men were looking at him with questioning expressions and he took a deep breath and tried to hide his trembling hands.

'What is our ammo state, Sergeant?' David asked, the question his way of displaying normalcy in this insane man-made butcher's shop. The company sergeant major had been killed hours earlier from a shell burst and now the sergeant with him was the acting CSM.

'Each of the lads has two bombs and around twenty rounds left, sir,' the sergeant answered. He had blood running down his sleeve from a shrapnel wound to his arm. 'Private Woods has been gut shot.'

David glanced over at the young private. He knew the gut wound was most probably fatal and that the soldier was in extreme agony, although he refused to admit it. One look at his ashen face twisted into a permanent grimace gave him away. David wished now that he had enlisted in the mounted infantry with his younger brother, Ben; then he might have been posted to Palestine with the Light Horse. Ben's letters to David complained of the long days of boredom on desert patrols, continual lack of water and searing heat. Well, right now David would have swapped places gladly.

'I will need to go out after dark and attempt to find the

other fellows of the company,' David said. 'When we have enough men gathered, we will organise a defence.'

The sergeant, a man around the same age as David, frowned. 'It's bloody suicide,' he said. 'I reckon we should wait for the brass to send up reinforcements to relieve us.'

'I wish we could,' David replied. 'But if I know the Hun, they will mount a counterattack before that occurs.'

The sergeant nodded. The man he knew who had come from the wealthy Steele family in Sydney was a volunteer like himself and had proved an officer men gladly followed for his leadership – and to an extent, his great luck keeping his men alive. But luck was a rare and fleeting concept. 'I will come with you, boss,' the sergeant said.

★

A mere three hundred yards away in the German trenches, deep in a heavily protected bunker, *Oberst* Hermann von Kellermann was holding a briefing with his junior officers by lantern light. He informed them that they were to lead their companies in a counterattack to sweep the battlefield clean of any remaining troops from the earlier assault on the ridge. Hermann was acting *Oberst*, which made him the equivalent of a British colonel. When his orders had been delivered to his officers, they withdrew to brief their own soldiers, leaving Hermann with his orderly, an old private soldier who had once been a gamekeeper for Hermann's father's duchy.

'The Tommies put up a spirited attack today,' the old man said, preparing a mug of coffee for his commander.

'Those on our section of the front were not British troops,' Hermann said. 'They were Australians. A different kind of soldier altogether.'

'I remember when you had a young Australian friend

who would stay with us when his family visited the duchy,' the old man said, stirring a rare ration of sugar into the coffee. 'You and he were as close as brothers, if I remember. You would go on hunts with him in our forests.'

'Yes, David Steele, nephew to my stepmother,' Hermann said with a note of sadness in his voice. 'I will always miss his friendship. Possibly one day when this war is over, we will meet under different circumstances and go hunting again. But right now, I must prepare to lead the sweep.' Hermann took a swig of the sweet black coffee from the enamel mug. It was always Hermann's way to personally lead his men and they respected him for sharing their dangers. He slipped on his cap – rather than a metal helmet – so his men could distinguish him in the sweep across what was now no-man's-land.

★

David did not have the chance to leave the shell crater before a flare went up to illuminate the lunar-like land-scape. There had been no preliminary bombardment by the German artillery, and as the small parachute flare descended David could see ominous shadows moving towards him and his few survivors. He could surrender – or die with his remaining men in their forlorn defence.

A Lewis machine gun opened up on David's left flank, indicating that it must be from one of his own surviving company members who had made the decision to fight.

'C'mon, lads, let's give 'em hell!' David yelled, and those who still could scrambled to the lip of the bomb crater, opening small-arms fire into the dark as another flare lit the sky, illuminating the sea of German soldiers advancing across no-man's-land.

On that summer night two close friends from opposing

armies would meet for the first time in two years, and only one would live to see the sun rise on the following day.

★

Hermann was pleased that his men had cleaned out any resistance to his counterattack, but grudgingly admired how the Australians had refused to surrender against his seasoned professional troops. He stood at the edge of a shell crater, and in the glare of a star shell could see the bodies twisted in death at the bottom. He also noted the rank of one of the Australian defenders – this was an officer, lying facedown in the blackened earth. He felt a twinge of sympathy for his opponent. Whoever he was, he could have surrendered, but instead chose to die for his country. It was time to move on.

Hermann had not recognised the body of his best friend.

TWENTY-SEVEN

. . . Regret to inform you Captain D. Steele MC, killed in action France July 1916

The key words of the telegram delivered to the door of the Steele residence by a General Post Office boy on a bicycle were burned into Josiah's mind and body.

He had not answered the door and the telegram had been walked upstairs by the young maid who, with trembling hands, passed it to Josiah in his library where he sat examining company reports.

As soon as Josiah heard the gentle tap on his office door and saw the expression on the maid's face, he immediately experienced the cold fear of what she held in her hand. *Is it David or Ben?*

As soon as she had given the telegram to her employer, the maid stumbled from the room, sobbing.

Josiah stared at the critical words . . . *killed in action* . . .

'Josiah, did you say something to upset Mary?' Marian asked from the doorway. 'I just passed her on the stairs, and she was in tears. What has the –' Marian ceased speaking when she saw the devastated, ashen expression on her husband's face. She immediately went to him.

'It's David,' Josiah said, staring down at the slip of official paper on the desk, and Marian needed no further explanation.

'Oh, no, not my dear David!' she wailed, sinking to her knees beside her husband.

It had been two weeks since Josiah had read about the terrible cost of a battle that Josiah knew his son would have been involved in. It was at a place called Fromelles. Josiah had read about the horrific casualties the Australian division had suffered within a mere twelve-hour period of the battle: five and a half thousand killed or wounded. For the last two weeks none of the family had received any correspondence from David. Needless to say, Josiah had awoken every day to reassure himself the sudden dearth of mail from his eldest son was due to the fact that he was too busy to write, as he could not bring himself to admit the silence could mean anything sinister. But now he was confronted with the harsh reality that his eldest son, this child he loved more than his own life and who would have been heir to his financial empire, was dead.

'I will have to write to Ben and tell him,' Josiah said in an almost monotone voice. Death on the battlefield was something he had personally experienced in his days as an army officer in Afghanistan and South Africa. He tried to hold back his tears of grief and function as if he had been David's commanding officer, simply relaying military information to another member of his military family.

★

They lay on their bellies with rifles pointed forward in the valley, observing hundreds of Turkish troops waiting for the Australian Light Horse to enter the ambush site.

Ben was on a sand ridge scanning the formation below through a pair of binoculars. Beside him was Corporal Ford and another trooper while a fourth trooper held their horses below the ridge on the reverse slope.

'Jacko was expecting us to come galloping into his trap,' Ben muttered, relieved that the squadron commander had not chosen to follow the easy route on their march northwards but instead had taken the long way behind the ridges of the valley.

'Over there,' Corporal Ford said quietly. 'Bunch of Bedouins hiding in that low scrub.'

Ben swivelled the binoculars to where Ken Ford was pointing and could see the Arab tribesmen loyal to the Ottoman Empire positioned to provide covering fire to the waiting Turkish soldiers.

'It's bloody hilarious.' Corporal Ford laughed softly. 'A whole Turkish regiment waiting to ambush our tiny patrol.' Just as he made this comment Ben could see a Turkish officer mounted on a fine steed riding down the far slope from the observation post that had been set up by the Turks. At that moment Ben and his patrol were joined by two artillery officers and their troop commander, Lieutenant Stanfield, from behind their sand ridge. He quickly assessed the situation.

'The game is up, boys, but I'd like one glance down behind the hill. There may be a movement of troops. Sergeant Steele, you take your patrol off the ridge and back to our old observation post behind us. Keep an eye out for any roaming Turkish camel troops. I will remain with the arty,' the troop commander said.

Ben scrambled down to where the horses were being held by the fourth trooper, mounted up and rode away, accompanied by Corporal Ford and the remaining men of the patrol. They quickly reached the hilltop and dismounted, leading the horses towards the observation post on top of the hill. But when they peered over the sharp ridge, they were met with a terrifying sight that took Ben's breath away. The post was occupied by Turkish infantry only a few yards away, with more Bedouin tribesmen reinforcements. Ben was instantly aware that they had been spotted when he saw three big Arabs suddenly stand up in the scrub to get a shot at them.

The situation was desperate, and for a fleeting moment Ben felt real panic, but he quickly swung his rifle at the three men he could see ahead of him. Then, about twenty paces away, a more direct threat appeared. An Arab militiaman was levelling his rifle on him. Instinctively Ben engaged the nearest threat just as the enemy's head appeared. Ben fired, slamming back the bolt to chamber another round, and fired again. The head disappeared and Ben saw the man roll from his ambush position, his face a bloody mess from the impact of the high-velocity .303 projectile.

'On your horses, boys, quick!' he shouted. Ben swung himself into the saddle. 'Come on, we will give these bastards a go for it! Ride like the hammers of hell!'

Ben's mount seemed to leap away under him as if it sensed the dire situation; the enemy were mere yards away, and Ben and his men were very exposed on the hillside in their retreat. Already Ben could see that the artillery officers now halfway down the hill were under heavy small-arms fire as sand spouted around them.

Suddenly Ben realised that his horse had stumbled on the slope, and he was flung from the saddle, experiencing the crushing weight of the warhorse on him before it rolled away.

'Whose horse is down?' a voice yelled.

Ben caught his breath as the horse floundered, crazed by the fall, but he was able to snatch the ringed bit to soothe the struggling horse now lying on its side. The tough mount quickly shook off its fear as Corporal Ford galloped back to Ben. 'Steady, Ben, there's plenty of time. Mount him again.'

Plenty of time! . . . Dazed, Ben could hear the cracking of passing Mauser rounds and thought how absurd the statement was, but, as he gripped the reins, Ben's horse rose up and Ben flung himself back into the saddle. As he galloped away, Ben dared not look over his shoulder lest he see the enemy on his tail.

The situation was once again coming into clear focus as he galloped down the hillside, hoping his mount would not fall again as the small patrol caught up with the rest of the light horsemen already making a rapid retreat from the overwhelming enemy numbers. Ben realised that he was laughing as if he had heard the world's funniest joke, and beside him Corporal Ford was doing the same.

In their dash for safety, they were for a short while dangerously exposed to the Turkish soldiers, and Ben could once again feel the air around him filled with bullets. By some miracle none found a mark before the troop was able to join up with the squadron waiting for them away from immediate danger.

As they reined in, their horses snorting from the hard ride, a trooper from the squadron said, 'Yer safe now, cobbers, well out of range.' Hardly had the words left his mouth when his slouch hat was ripped from his head by a Mauser round which Ben calculated had been fired from at least fourteen hundred yards away. There had been no loud sound indicating the rifle had been fired because of the distance, only the zipping sound the bullet made when it arrived, seeking a target.

The startled trooper who had lost his hat ended his sentence with an obscene exclamation, bringing on a howl of laughter from the rest of the light horsemen nearby.

It was then that Ben realised just how close he had come to being the cause of a telegram to his family back home. He was not aware that they had already received one for his brother's death in France.

★

The duke, Karl von Hauptmann, was on a rare visit home to his estate, but Caroline felt just as alone when he was in the room with her as when he was away. On this occasion, all he could do was pace the floor, a glass of cognac in his hand, ranting about the treachery of the German workers.

'That damned socialist union leader Liebknecht has called a strike protesting about our role in this war just when we are on the verge of defeating the French at Verdun, and our farmers are complaining about the government reassigning their fertiliser for the nitrogen we need for explosives. Don't they understand it is vital for us to win this war and restore our overseas empire?'

Caroline sat on a couch listening patiently. Secretly, she agreed with Liebknecht and the farmers.

'We are facing food shortages because of the British naval blockade and the people are facing severe hunger,' she said quietly. 'The gamekeeper's daughter, Helga, has learned that the young man she was in love with has been killed at Verdun. I doubt that she feels our glorious attack on the French at Verdun is worth the loss of her future with her love.'

Karl ceased pacing the room to glare at his wife. 'The Kaiser expects his subjects to be glad to sacrifice themselves for the Fatherland. It is their duty. You are a woman and I do not expect you to understand the meaning of real sacrifice.'

Caroline sighed. She knew nothing she said would influence the duke's opinions, but his last words echoed in her mind. *You do not understand the meaning of real sacrifice.*

Oh, but Caroline did understand sacrifice; she felt it every time she looked into the eyes of her son. His birth had meant marrying a man who did not really love her – and nor did she love him. She had at least hoped the marriage might provide some warmth, but had long ago realised that for him, it was simply a legal process which would provide him with an heir of the correct pedigree. Although her position as his wife had given her a sumptuous life in comparison with the rest of the German population, her loneliness was a terrible malady.

'I will retire for the night,' Karl said, swallowing the last of his cognac. 'I have to travel back to Berlin tomorrow.' He placed the crystal glass on a sideboard and stormed from the room, leaving Caroline with only the heads of deer and wild boar on the cold stone walls for company. She went to the cabinet and poured herself one of the fine French cognacs her husband had been drinking, then sat down to reflect on the past and future.

Her thoughts were focused on just one man – Benjamin Steele – the father of her son. In this great meat grinder of a war, she felt the odds that he was still alive were very slim – if he had indeed enlisted as she expected he had. Caroline had sought out any reference to the Australian involvement in the war and had learned how the German press had gloated over the British defeat in the Dardanelles at the hands of their Turkish allies. There had also been a recent mention of an Australian division supporting their British masters suffering appalling losses at a place called Fromelles. Had Ben been a part of that battle? Caroline wondered. She had come to learn that her cousin Hermann had fought there and vaguely remembered how Hermann's best friend had been David Steele, Ben's brother, and a man she suspected had once had a crush on her before the war.

Caroline took a long sip of the fiery liquor and stared at a portrait of the Kaiser that had been gifted to her husband. Kaiser Wilhelm II stared back at her, dressed in an elaborate military uniform. It was ironic to think that the Kaiser was a cousin of the British King and Russian Czar. This was truly a war between royal European families that was dragging millions of men to their deaths, she mused.

But there was only one man she truly cared about, and Caroline knew it was time to seek him out, if he was still alive. Caroline decided that she must contact her father, who she knew travelled to neutral Switzerland on a regular basis to do business. From there a letter could be sent to Sydney enquiring about Ben's welfare. Caroline knew about his family and even knew where to send the letter. But should she inform his father, Josiah Steele, that she and Ben had a son? Caroline agonised over this dilemma.

Caroline swallowed the rest of her cognac and let it cloak her in its warmth. She had once read how the Germans in Roman times would make a decision when they were drunk, and then when they became sober they would address the same issue and see if their drunken decision had merit. Caroline smiled; she was the descendant of those same warriors. She made her decision.

TWENTY-EIGHT

The letter sat in a pile of correspondence on Josiah's office desk. Josiah frowned when he came to it; he didn't recognise the handwriting or know why it should be postmarked from Switzerland.

He picked up a bronze Chinese letter opener and used it to open the envelope, removing a single sheet of fine-quality paper embossed with the Gothic letterhead he recognised as German. The words were neatly written in English and the letter was addressed to him. Josiah read the contents, which were from a German woman who identified herself as Caroline von Neumann and requested to know if his son Benjamin was still alive. She further explained that she had met Josiah's son while he was in Rabaul before the war, and they had become very good friends in their time together when he had acted as her plantation manager.

Josiah considered it strange that the woman would

want to know about Ben, and then remembered that his brother, Sam, had mentioned the lady who was a countess and very beautiful. Sam had mentioned that he had strong thoughts that the two had been romantically involved, and had even heard from a friend in Samoa that the countess had been pregnant while waiting to be repatriated to Germany from Samoa as part of the surrender conditions to the New Zealanders.

'Pregnant,' Josiah said aloud, and began joining the dots to her unusual request to know if Ben was still alive.

He pushed his chair away from his desk and walked to the window overlooking the harbour, now crowded with naval warships. Was he now a grandfather to Ben's child?

The thought both chilled him and made him feel joyous at the same time, as it was probable or possible that Ben did not know of the lady's pregnancy, or he would have surely mentioned it . . . wouldn't he?

David was dead on a French battlefield, but the last letter from Ben in the Sinai had proved he was still alive three weeks ago. Josiah drew a deep breath then exhaled. Would he write to his youngest son informing him of his contact with the German countess? Or should he remain silent on the matter? The letter gave a return address in Switzerland. Josiah remembered how his sister had corresponded using a Swiss postal address. One of the very few applications of the death sentence under the military act produced after Federation was for anyone treasonably entering into correspondence with the enemy. Josiah did not consider contact with his sister as an act of treason, and likewise the countess's letter enquiring into Ben's situation was simply a family matter, with no impact on strategic affairs.

Josiah returned to his desk and read the letter again.

All other matters took second place that day – in any case, the family's many enterprises were now making good profits on supporting the war effort.

He picked up his fountain pen and held it poised over a sheet of blank paper, but before he could write a word, his personal secretary knocked on his door.

'Mr Steele, your daughter Mrs Cohen is here to see you,' he said in a hesitant voice, and Josiah sensed that his secretary was withholding news he did not want to share. 'She is very distressed.'

Josiah stood up and hurried to the door, where he saw his eldest daughter, Judith, with tears streaming down her face.

'Judith, come in,' he said, placing his hand on her back to guide her into his office. 'Thomas, please fetch a pot of tea for us.'

Judith slumped into a comfortable leather chair to the side of Josiah's desk and began dabbing at her cheeks with a handkerchief. Josiah knelt to hold her hands. The family had already suffered the grief of losing David, and from his daughter's stricken expression he dreaded that she had been informed of Captain Maurice Cohen's death.

'I have been informed that Maurice has been wounded,' Judith said shakily. 'But I do not know how severe the wounding is. Please, Father, could you use your position to find out? I know that you have influential contacts in the government.'

Wounded – not killed in action. Josiah felt the chill of the worst-case scenario leave his body and hoped that his favourite son-in-law had not suffered any critical, disabling wound.

'I will immediately make enquiries with people I know to learn of the extent of Maurice's wounds,' Josiah said.

'Depending on what they are, it is likely he will be shipped back to us, and you will be reunited with him. As terrible as it is to be notified that he has been wounded, it might mean he will finally be out of the war and safe at home with his family.'

Judith looked into her father's eyes. He had always been the rock of the family, and his words could be trusted. 'Do you truly believe that Maurice will be returned to us soon?' she asked, and Josiah nodded, although he could not be sure in what physical condition. He had witnessed the casualties being taken off ships returning from Europe and had seen the many amputees being transported to Australian hospitals. He had also seen the terribly disfigured men whose faces were masks of horror, and the blind who groped their way ashore with their hand on the shoulder of a seeing soldier with lesser wounds. Just what kind of wounds had Maurice suffered?

The secretary arrived with a pot of tea on a tray and set it down on the small table. Josiah thanked him and Thomas quietly retreated.

'Who else have you told about Maurice?' Josiah asked.

'I telephoned Rose who said that she will visit today, and then I came here,' Judith replied as Josiah poured her a cup of tea. He felt reassured that his paternal role in his children's lives was not something of the past, and that they still came to him in times of trouble.

'I don't think that you should be alone for the moment. I will arrange for you and my grandchildren to stay with us until I find out more about Maurice's medical condition. I know Marian will be pleased to have you and the children with us until Maurice returns to home.'

Judith gratefully gripped her father's hand. 'Thank you, Father.' Impulsively she flung her arms around him, and

Josiah was suddenly reminded of the little girl who had grown up in his house on the harbour.

Caroline's letter was temporarily forgotten as he considered who he could contact to learn of the fate of Captain Maurice Cohen – WIA – Wounded in Action.

★

Moo Cow Farm was what the Aussie soldiers called the French location occupied by the Germans.

Its real name was Mouquet Farm, but the once bucolic beauty of the farmhouse and its surrounding countryside on the ridge north of Pozières was no more. It was where Captain Cohen had served as a surgeon during the terrible carnage of the battle for the destroyed French town.

As one of the many medical personnel in the Australian Army Medical Corps, he had lost count of the men on his surgical table who had lost limbs, eyes and faces. And they were the fortunate ones who had survived due to his extraordinary medical skills. But there had also been the men with chest, stomach and head wounds who had not.

The battle for Pozières was in the past now, fought and won as the Allied divisions pushed northwards in the ongoing contribution to the larger struggle to relieve pressure on the Somme.

The 'stunt' to capture the area of Mouquet Farm in August by combined British and Australian forces was repelled time and again, and it was Maurice and the other medical staff who dealt with the shattered bodies of young men each time the attacks on the German positions failed.

Maurice and his team were in a hastily erected tent laid out almost a mile from the frontlines. He was hardly aware of the sound of the incoming artillery shell as he operated on a very young, wounded German soldier who had been brought to him by a couple of compassionate Australian stretcher-bearers who did not discriminate on any wounded man they found on the battlefield.

The German artillery shell exploded only yards away. Maurice had no memory of the explosion, which partially flattened the tent, leaving under it dead and badly wounded medical staff. For a moment he was unconscious from the blast, and when he finally opened his eyes he saw his friend, a fellow army surgeon, bending over him. His patient and the table he had been lying on were gone. The stench of blood, cordite and dust overwhelmed Maurice's senses, and he was acutely aware that he could feel pain all over his body. As a surgeon he knew he'd been hit by shrapnel.

'Morrie, don't move,' the voice of his colleague drifted down to him. 'The stretcher-bearers are going to take you back down the line.'

Maurice attempted to sit up but the pain tore at him and he screamed.

'Cobber, your left leg is gone,' the army surgeon said, knowing that his friend would want a professional assessment of his major wound. 'But I have been able to stem the bleeding.'

Then two other faces bent over Maurice, and he recognised the stretcher-bearers of his unit. 'Got to take you now, sir,' one of them said as they carefully lifted Maurice into the stretcher. This time he couldn't help but let out a loud groan, although he wanted to scream. He did not remember the stretcher-bearers carrying him to better medical facilities further back from the frontlines, nor did he recall the treatment he received at each stage of his journey to a hospital beyond the reach of enemy weapons.

As the hours and days rolled by, Maurice accepted the loss of his leg and worried only about infection. He knew that if his wounds did not become infected he would be transported home to his family alive – if not in one piece. The battle for Mouquet Farm had cost the Australians over 11,000 casualties – the number akin to all men, women and children living in a large Australian town.

★

Caroline woke each day with the hope that her letter to Ben's father had reached him and that she would in turn receive a letter of reply concerning the fate of the man she had never stopped loving.

But the days became weeks, and the northern hemisphere was entering the months of autumn, with winter on the doorstep.

Caroline had come to accept that she could not spend any more time in a loveless marriage. She rued the decision her father had pushed her to make when she'd married the duke almost two years earlier. She had bent to the norms of German society in an attempt to avoid the scandal of being a single mother with a bastard son. Marriage had achieved this for her and given her son legitimacy, but Caroline had come to see that this was not enough.

Night after night she would return in her thoughts – and sometimes, her dreams – to a place she called paradise with a man she had truly fallen in love with. But in this third year of the war, she still had no idea if he was dead or alive. Everything depended on the arrival of a piece of paper in an envelope from faraway Australia – a country that was still Germany's enemy.

★

Josiah was finally able to ascertain Maurice's physical condition from a series of enquiries with friends in the Defence

Department. He learned that his son-in-law had lost his left leg below the knee and suffered several shrapnel wounds to his body that had been successfully treated. He was now in a hospital in England. A telegram was being prepared to send to his wife and family, assuring them that he was alive and that when he was deemed medically stable he would be returned to Sydney, where he would be officially discharged from the army on medical grounds.

They had also discovered via a letter from the government that Maurice would be commended for his service to King and Country. Over the period of his military service on the Western Front it had been noted that Captain Maurice Cohen had repeatedly volunteered to render his surgical services as close to the fighting as he was permitted, and that had been recognised as going above and beyond what was expected of a truly skilled surgeon.

Josiah hurried home from his office to deliver the good news to the family, and was pleased to be met by Judith at the front door.

'He's coming home! He is alive and is coming home soon!' Josiah said.

Judith burst into tears and flung her arms around her father's neck. Josiah did not have the heart to spoil the joyous moment by telling his daughter of the extent of her husband's injuries. That was a matter for a later time.

TWENTY-NINE

They were just north of Romani when Ben received mail posted from Sydney. He immediately recognised his father's handwriting.

Ben slit open the letter and began reading as the troopers around him went about their tasks of cleaning rifles, tending to their mounts and sharpening bayonets on the big grindstone. The words Josiah had written caused Ben to feel as if he had been stabbed in the stomach with a Turkish bayonet – *David had been killed in action in France!*

For a moment Ben sat in the sand, pale under his heavily suntanned face, stricken by the terrible news.

'You all right, Ben?'

Ben hardly heard the question asked by his friend, Corporal Ken Ford, who was standing nearby.

'Just got news that my brother David has gone west,' Ben replied in a hollow voice. 'He was an infantry captain who got it at some place called Fromelles a few weeks ago.'

'Sorry, cobber,' Ken said sympathetically. 'It's a bastard of a war.'

Ben nodded and slowly rose to his feet, folding the letter and slipping it into his shirt pocket. They stood still for a few moments in silent tribute.

'We are heading north,' Ken said eventually. 'The word is that Jacko is pushing south in force to take Romani. I heard that the Turks have captured Katia oasis.'

Ben knew the oasis was only a few miles from their current position. 'I reckon Chauvel will push us out to meet Jacko,' Ben said, striding towards his horse, who was eating from a nosebag.

Ben's guess was correct. The brilliant Australian tactician in desert warfare set up a defensive screen that night on the Allied southern flank.

That evening, as Ben lay on the cool sand facing the direction of the Turkish advance, his thoughts were on many things. He found himself considering the family's financial future; with David no longer able to head up their many and diverse enterprises when his father stepped down, would he, Ben, be expected to take that role – if he was lucky enough to survive this desert war? It was not a position he wanted, and the thought troubled him. Ben also found that he was thinking more and more about Caroline and the toddler she might now have. Where was she right at this moment? Was she thinking of him? Ben admitted that he loved Caroline as fiercely as he ever had, but their situation seemed hopeless when she was officially an enemy.

'Bloody hell!' The whispered urgent exclamation snapped Ben back to his present reality. 'There must be thousands of the bastards!'

Against the white sand of the dunes under the brilliance

of the starry night Ben could see the Turkish infantry clearly advancing towards them, and knew immediately that they were probably outnumbered by at least ten to one.

He could hear the war cry, *Allah Akbar*, drifting in the still night air, as well as the words '*Australian finish!*' in English, taunting them. The tough Turkish soldiers fearlessly advanced into a withering rifle fire from Ben's position atop the dune.

Beside Ben, Ken yelled back defiantly, 'Allah, you bastards? We will give you Allah!'

The greater number of Turkish infantry could not be stopped by the limited small-arms fire from Ben's regiment, and Ben rose to his feet as the enemy reached their defensive positions. Now came the vicious bayonet fighting of parry and thrust between the opposing forces. In the gloom, shadowy figures came together and killed each other with rifle butt, bayonet and even teeth in desperate hand–to–hand struggles. Ben would barely remember how many men he killed with his rifle and bayonet. Life had come down to a simple, desperate will to live. Ben's physical size worked to his advantage, and matched with the killing madness that came over him, he was able to best any man who attempted to take his life. He was vaguely aware that the same applied for his friend, Corporal Ford, who fought at his side. Curses and screams of agony rang out as the long bayonets plunged into torsos, along with pleas for mercy in both Turkish and English.

Using all his strength, Ben withdrew his bayonet from the lower chest of a big Turkish soldier who slid to the sand at his feet, and without hesitating Ben smashed the side of the man's head. Gasping for air he brought the rifle bayonet up again to face the next threat, but was vaguely aware that the desperate struggle to survive had abated. He heard a trooper call out defiantly, 'Try it again!' as the Turkish infantry withdrew, leaving bleeding dead and wounded behind.

'Sergeant Steele, get the troopers back to the horses.' Ben glanced across the field of bodies to see in the dimness of the night his troop commander calling to him.

'Yes, sir,' Ben replied, and turned to Ken. 'You heard the boss, Corporal, get the boys and any wounded we have back to the horses.'

Ben ensured that his wounded troopers were hoisted over shoulders and they staggered back to the horse line where the handlers waited. But there they discovered that as the Turkish soldiers had withdrawn in the dark, some had been able to penetrate the defensive screen and reach the Australian horse line, where they had bayoneted as many horses as possible.

Ben noticed a Turkish soldier only feet away and immediately shot him dead. Realising that riders now outnumbered their mounts, Ben yelled his instruction for troopers with mounts to also take any trooper who had lost his horse.

Immediately, mounted troopers reached out to snatch up their comrades who were on foot. Ken Ford looked around and saw in the half-light a man standing alone. He did not hesitate, reaching down to snatch the soldier's hand, pulling him behind his saddle only to realise that he had picked up a Turkish soldier in error. Ken twisted in the saddle to see the face of a young, very frightened Turkish soldier who was clinging to Ken in obvious fear. In the confusion of the close-quarter fighting, the Turkish infantryman must have thought he was being rescued by a Turkish cavalryman. Ken used his elbow to hit the man behind him in the head with enough force to stun him, and a second blow caused the Turk to tumble from his position behind Ken.

'Bloody hell!' Ken swore when he was free of his unwitting passenger. How would it have appeared to his mates if he had galloped back with an enemy in tow? Ken suspected he would not have lived down the situation.

But the Turkish army were already attempting to outflank the retreating Australian light horsemen, who were forced to dismount at any high sand dune and fight off any enemy closing in on them. The remainder of the squadron were able to withdraw to a huge sand dune dubbed Mount Meredith, which was already manned by Australian troopers fending off the Turkish infantry who were attempting to climb the sandy cliff face only to tumble back when met with the steel of an Australian bayonet.

Ben and his squadron could see that the defenders on the high ground were in a hopeless situation, and under orders they rode on as the defenders also made their way off the high ground to mount their horses and withdraw.

Dawn finally came to the harsh desert. Ben had swallowed the last of the water in his canteen. Through bleary eyes he could see that most of his troop could be accounted for although some of the horses carried two men, with one or two assisting troopers without mounts by allowing them to grip the stirrups as they retreated.

As the sun rose, worse than their thirst and exhaustion was the sight of the massive Turkish army attempting to envelop their right flank. But training and discipline allowed the remaining men of Ben's regiment to resume their squadron formations, falling back with each squadron and its troop sections alternating the cover fire by dismounting, firing on the advancing enemy, and then remounting to gallop away as the next section of troops from the squadron did the same. It was a fire-and-movement tactic that allowed continuous accurate small-arms fire on the attacking force, while also allowing the regiment to keep the enemy at bay.

Ben guessed that they might inflict heavy losses but would eventually be forced to withdraw before the Turkish soldiers reached them, knowing that it was only the fact that they had their mounts that kept the Australian Light Horse regiment one step ahead of the Turkish infantry.

Ben lost count of how many times he and his section dismounted to deliver a well-aimed volley into the ranks of the enemy advancing on them. Eventually, his squadron were guided to a slope that led to the high ground of a long ridge dubbed Wellington Ridge, where they dismounted into a long skirmish line to meet the threat of the advancing enemy.

Ben dismounted, handing the reins to the trooper assigned to hold at least four horses in the safest place they could find out of Turkish small-arms fire, and clambered into a firing position on the ridge. He checked his supply of cartridges and saw that it was low. He would be reduced to using only his bayonet if the Turkish infantry finally succeeded in taking the ridge. For a moment Ben despaired of surviving the major Turkish advance in the Sinai.

Then, as if in answer to some religious trooper's prayers, Ben caught sight of reinforcements galloping to the ridge he occupied through a heavy stream of machine-gun fire and artillery shrapnel. Ben's throat was so dry that he did not have the ability to raise a cheer as the men of Brigadier General Royston's relief force reached Ben's defensive positions.

An officer from the relief force took up a firing position only yards from Ben and Ben guessed that the newly arrived officer might have an idea of their current situation.

Ben rose and in a crouching run went to him.

'Sir, glad to see you and the boys,' he said, dropping down and lying beside the young officer. 'What's happening?'

The officer turned to Ben. 'Be prepared to get out of here, Sergeant,' he said grimly. 'Jacko will most probably bring his field arty to bear on the ridge as soon as he has enough daylight for his observers. We will be forced to fall back. It's a bloody dog's breakfast. From the little that I know, this is the biggest attack the Turks have mounted since we got here, and if we lose, the Turks will control the Suez Canal.'

Ben was already aware that in spite of the last seven hours of continuous fighting on their sector of the defensive mobile line they were losing, being beaten by the overwhelming numbers of the enemy who were advancing south slowly but surely.

Ben crawled back to his position and found Corporal Ken Ford. 'What news?' Ken asked, slamming back the bolt of his rifle to chamber another round from the magazine as he sought another target among the lines of Turkish infantry below the ridge.

'The officer said that a wagonload of cold bottled beer is currently being sent up to us,' Ben said with a crooked smile. 'The bad news is that we only get a half-dozen per trooper.'

Ken barked a laugh as he fired then quickly reloaded. 'I would kill for a cold beer,' Ken said. 'What other news?'

'Looks like we might have to get off the ridge and retire to another defensive position back near the railhead at Romani.'

By 7 am the order was given to withdraw while they still had the advantage. Ben had noticed that the Turkish infantry were slowing in their advance. Like the light horsemen they were physically exhausted, and the rising desert sun was already searing the earth below. No doubt Jacko was short of water too, Ben considered as he swung himself into his saddle. He also knew from a briefing before they'd left camp that the British Territorial Horse Artillery were somewhere in their sector of the battle. All going well, the batteries of the British mobile artillery would use the daylight to pour down explosive death on the enemy out in the open, and on the positions where Ben's regiment had been forced to cede ground.

The exhausted light horsemen retreated back to the supply dumps at the railhead, with its bountiful supply of water from a nearby oasis. But even there, Ben realised that they were not safe as their position would need to be defended. He overheard a squadron commander discussing with a staff officer how their brothers from the New Zealand equivalent of the Australian Light Horse had taken a terrible toll when they'd faced the brunt of the Turkish assault hours earlier. What Ben was not aware was that two Australian brigades and a New Zealand mounted rifles regiment had delayed the Turkish advance from the previous fortnight in running battles and skirmishes. Throughout that period of time Ben hardly remembered a day's silence in the vast desert as day and night the boom of distant artillery, chatter of machine guns and other small-arms fire drifted to Ben's squadron as observation posts flung out ahead of the Turkish advance came under fire, and in some cases were wiped out by the superior enemy forces.

And then the taubes – as the Allied troops referred to the German aircraft – filled the sky overhead with their bombs and strafing runs on all below. The defence of Romani came down to a last-ditch effort to wear down the attacking mix of Turkish, German and Austrian forces confronting them.

The roar of the eighteen-pounders of the Australian

Royal Horse Artillery nearby added to the cacophony of ear-shattering noise and Ben had a sick feeling that he would not live to see another sunrise over the desert lands of his ancestors.

THIRTY

For the first time, Ben felt truly close to his own death. He was gaunt, red-eyed from lack of sleep and covered in dry blood from the men he had fought at close quarter. In this exhausted state, Ben felt the overwhelming numbers of Turkish troops led by a German general would be almost impossible to resist on their way to capture the Suez Canal.

The order had come down to Ben's squadron that he and six troopers were to carry out a night patrol to a hill marked 383 on the maps. At midnight a telephone message arrived instructing the rest of the regiment to move out to delay the Turkish left flank advancing on a region called Nagid. A small New Zealand patrol had observed the enemy movements and reported that a great number of Turks were advancing from a place called Mageibra. After making their report, Ben watched the Kiwis ride away, and for the next few hours until sunrise he wondered about the fate of the courageous men from the other side of the Tasman Sea. The ANZAC relationship felt just as strong in the campaign waged in the biblical lands of Palestine as it had at Gallipoli, and the two nations continued to forge a bloody kinship.

Ben watched in the dark as the bulk of his regiment prepared to ride out while he took command of his patrol to ride to Hill 383. Ben and six of his troopers navigated their way to the hill and took up observation positions atop the rise. The distant sound of artillery guns and small arms drifted to him and his section as they lay in the cool desert sand. They were only in position for just under an hour when at 3 am the sound of gunfire became much louder and, especially worrying, they could hear the hammering of machine guns only a couple of miles to their front.

Ben felt his blood run cold. So often he and the men of his squadron had heard stories of observation posts being taken by the Turks in the night, the bayoneted bodies of the Australians left in their wake, and now, it was possible they were in the same situation.

'What do you think is going on?' Corporal Ford asked Ben.

'Don't know, Ken,' Ben answered, peering into the night where the occasional flash of gunfire lit the horizon. 'But our orders are to remain in place until relieved.'

Ken did not reply but took a sip from his water canteen while Ben worried about the welfare of the men under his command. Was it wise to use his initiative and withdraw from the high point, or should he wait for further orders? His question was answered when the trooper holding their horses called to Ben, 'Sarge, I got some Kiwis here who are relieving us.'

'I'll be down to see them,' Ben called back and stood to stretch his legs before scrambling down the sandy slope, where he could make out the vague outlines of the relieving New Zealand troopers. A tall New Zealand Mounted Infantry sergeant stepped forward.

'Good to see you, cobber,' Ben said to his counterpart. 'How are things at Romani?'

'We had a massive bayonet attack there only a few hours ago by Jacko, but it was stopped in its tracks. It was bad news for your posts out front of the lines, though – now our lads are going to reinforce your lot on the left flank. I have orders for you to return to Romani. It looks like you were lucky not to be with your regiment heading out to that left flank.'

Ben thanked the New Zealander and ordered his small section to prepare to return to their camp at Romani. As they rode away, a tiny worm of guilt ate into Ben's brain when he considered that being sent to the observation post might just have saved his life when he should have been with the regiment facing great numbers of enemy. But he and his small patrol also felt deeply frustrated that they were not with their regiment.

Just as they were dismounting back at the camp at Romani, a force of mounted British Yeomanry arrived only to gallop immediately from the camp to join the Australians and New Zealanders engaging the waves of Turkish fighters attempting to overwhelm the Romani railhead.

'Ben, the Poms are heading in the direction of where the regiment is,' Ken called. 'Maybe we could tag along.'

Despite their exhaustion, each and every trooper desperately wanted to find and help their regimental family.

'Good idea,' Ben replied, quickly readjusting his saddle and patting his mount on the nose with the tenderness all the men had for the creatures they considered more than mere animals. These horses had not volunteered for war but they gave their all for the men who rode them in this harsh land.

After quickly replenishing their water and preparing their mounts, Ben and his troopers were all in the saddle and waiting for the order to follow the British mounted soldiers when an irate Scottish major came striding towards them.

'You men there! What do you think you're doing?' he shouted.

'Just heading out to rejoin our regiment,' Ben replied.

'Get off your horses now. That's an order,' the Scottish major commanded. 'We need every man we can get here to meet Johnny Turk when he comes.'

Reluctantly, Ben and his troopers dismounted, chafing at the order, especially as it came from an officer not of the Australian army. Still, he was an officer, and therefore had to be obeyed.

The artillery guns continued to boom away from the camp while Ben organised his troop to be on standby if they were sent forward. It was a brief time to snatch some rest after they had ensured their mounts were watered and fed. The noble horses' heads drooped, and Ben was pleased that at least the horses would have a long-deserved rest from the near-constant activity of the past few days.

Ben sat in the sand under the shade of his broad-brimmed slouch hat, staring at the activity of the camp. Despite not having eaten for twenty-four hours he hardly had any appetite, but he sipped continuously from his canteen to relieve the eternal thirst of the desert. It was only now that he noticed the stench of the camp; the baking sun overhead was already causing the carcasses of so many dead horses to bloat, and the odour of rotting human and animal decomposition hung heavy in the air. Thick clouds of flies fed on the dead, and here and there the bodies of fallen comrades were being carried away on litters to be buried.

Ken joined him. 'I just heard that a Kiwi patrol at Nagid got themselves captured last night when they got caught between two Turk infantry columns. Poor bastards will probably be marched across the desert into captivity. Kind of think I would rather cop a clean shot through the skull than be a prisoner of Jacko.'

Ben silently agreed with his friend. A quick death was preferable to the hell of being a prisoner in the desert. 'How are the boys?' Ben asked.

'I think they are secretly pleased to get a break,' Ken replied. 'I made sure they scrounged extra ammo and a few more grenades.'

Ben nodded; he could see his troop resting under a sheet of canvas attached to a wagon, where some smoked tobacco pipes while others were already dozing with hats over their eyes. As a wave of exhaustion washed over him, he lay back too, put his hat over his face, and immediately fell asleep.

*

Josiah was surprised to receive a visit from his eldest daughter, Judith, at his office.

She was ushered into his presence and immediately he recognised the distressed expression on his beloved daughter's pinched face.

'My darling, I can see that you have much on your mind,' he said. 'Please take a seat and I will have tea delivered for us.' Josiah called to his secretary Thomas to bring the tea things and returned to his daughter, who had removed a small handkerchief to dab at her eyes. Josiah knelt beside Judith.

'It is Maurice,' Judith said. 'He is not the man I married.'

'What do you mean?' Josiah asked with a frown.

'He is simply not the same man he was when he left. Since his return from convalescent treatment for his missing leg Maurice has cut himself off from his family and the world. He was reassured that he could return to his practice by his partners, as they said the loss of his leg should not interfere with his duties as a surgeon. They were so nice about him returning to surgery, but he has rejected the offer. Now Maurice locks himself away and drinks until he passes out. It is as if we are strangers to him.' Judith was sobbing so hard she could say no more, and Josiah could only stroke her arm in an effort to reassure his daughter that he was there for her no matter the situation.

Already Josiah had an inkling of what afflicted his son-in-law. It was a malaise of the mind that he had seen in many who had returned to their homes – even those without physical injuries – and the medical fraternity were divided about what caused it. Some gave it the title of 'shell shock' while the military hierarchy considered it a form of cowardice. From his own experiences of war, Josiah leaned towards the idea that it was some kind of psychological disorder brought on by the stress of living so close to death. He remembered how he had suffered bouts of deep depression he could not explain after serving in active combat in Afghanistan and Africa. It had taken a long time for him to be able to control the trembling in his body and the shaking of his hands, coupled with nightmares of death and destruction. He had been able to keep his symptoms from his family and friends for many years, but it had been a hard road. Josiah had no doubt that his son-in-law was suffering the same mental illness.

'Judith, my love, I think that the war has changed Maurice. I experienced a similar condition when I came home from the army,' Josiah said. 'It seems to be a consequence of living in a world of terror and exposure to violent death. I was not the same man who had left my family, and was perhaps just fortunate that I was able to hide my irrational fears from those I loved. Eventually, helped by the fact that I met your mother and had you come into the world – along with your sister and brothers – I was able to focus on giving you all the best life that I could and my symptoms improved. It will take time and unconditional love and support from you and all of us in the family to help Maurice heal. Just reassure him that you are there for him despite not understanding the torment he is suffering. I pray with time he will eventually return to those who love him.'

Judith nodded slowly and looked into her father's face. 'I believe you are right, Father. I can only imagine the experiences of war are very damaging, both to body and soul,' she said softly.

After they'd taken a cup of tea, Josiah embraced his daughter before she departed his office looking a little more hopeful. Josiah felt for Maurice; felt for them both. How many young men had Maurice been forced to make life-or-death decisions about as they lay on his operating table? Josiah shook his head. So many people overlooked the vital role the men and women of the medical staff played in keeping the death toll down in war, and few would realise how traumatic the job could be. For a long time, Josiah stood at his window overlooking the tranquil harbour, pondering if his larrikin son Ben would return home physically or mentally scarred from this war – if he returned at all.

*

'Sergeant Steele, get your men ready to go out and repair a telephone line Jacko has cut.'

The order roused Ben's small patrol and they scrambled

to their feet. The squadron's sergeant major had delivered the command and quickly briefed Ben on the mission. Already his patrol had their mounts saddled and their ammunition restocked.

Ben and his men were pleased to get away from the camp, as the supercilious Scottish major had addressed them again earlier after he had received a complaint of rations being stolen by a small band of Aussie troopers. 'You are a damned nuisance. I cannot at the moment provide evidence that your men stole rations, Sergeant Steele, but I know it was your lot.'

At the time he had been dressed down by the pugnacious Scottish officer, Ben had glanced at his men lounging under the shadecloth and received a shrug from them.

'Sir, I am sure my men would not indulge in criminal activity of such a kind,' Ben replied. 'Stealing from the King's men is despicable.' Ben could hear strangled laughter and cursed his section, knowing full well they had taken the extra rations.

'What can a man expect of a country founded by convicts,' the major said angrily. 'You have not heard the last of this incident, Sergeant.'

Just as the senior commissioned officer was about to storm away, Ben threw him the smartest salute of his military career, hoping it would appease the British officer, who gave a half-hearted salute in return.

Now, though, it was time to depart on another dangerous mission, but Ben stifled his personal fear; above all, his concern was for his men who were his family of brothers.

THIRTY-ONE

Ben and his patrol were just mounting up when an orderly rushed from the CO's tent to warn him that the cut telephone wires were now in enemy territory, as the Turks were making such a rapid push towards the Suez Canal. Ben could indeed hear a rising crescendo in the stutter of machine guns and booming of the artillery.

Ben was astride his mount when an officer's groom he knew stood at the foot of his stirrup to inform him that their regiment had met thousands of enemy on the left flank that was still advancing under the cover of German aircraft. The groom also said that the regiment had been able to hold them off for a few hours before retiring at a gallop against the overwhelming force they faced.

'Bloody suicide job,' Ken grumbled after overhearing the report.

'But it beats sitting on our arses around here if we can't

join the boys of the regiment,' Ben replied. 'Time we moved out.'

Ben led his patrol into the desert as the sun rose into the crimson sky of a new dawn. They rode carefully, acutely aware that they might encounter a Turkish mounted patrol in the vanguard of the advancing enemy. The Turks could be on camel or horseback, which would mean a dangerous retreat for Ben and his patrol. If anything, Ben hoped any enemy they encountered would be Turkish infantry, which they would have a good chance of evading.

They reached the approximate position of the cut telephone wires, but try as they might, they could not locate them. At around 10.30 am, three German aircraft appeared in the blue sky. Ben looked up to see one of the fighter planes peel off to strafe them.

'Scatter!' he yelled, and immediately his troopers pulled back on their bridles to steer a course out into the dunes, making them a harder target. But already they could hear the chatter of the German machine guns, and suddenly sand flew up within a few feet of where Ben sat on his mount, which reared at the closeness of the bullets. Cursing, Ben wheeled his horse around to head at a right angle to the aircraft's line of attack as it swooped over him, chasing another of his troopers who was riding at breakneck speed towards a high dune. As it passed overhead, Ben could see the pilot clearly in his fragile biplane.

Ben quickly dismounted to seek cover in a natural ditch. Looking to the skies, he saw that the attacking aircraft had peeled away, and then he realised why. The German pilot had a greater problem than strafing a patrol of Australian light horsemen – two friendly fighter planes were now swooping on the predator, who had become the prey.

'Hooray!' The cheers of the scattered troopers echoed Ben's own relief.

'Get the bastards, boys!' Ken cried, shaking his fist at the sky a short distance away. Ben remounted as his patrol rode in to join him. For a short time, they all watched as the little planes droned into the distance, their machine guns clattering. Ben was disappointed when the two fighters from the Australian Flying Corps disappeared behind the horizon of sand dunes in their deadly pursuit of the lone German fighter plane.

Just after noon, Ben decided that they were not likely to locate the cut telephone lines and that it was time to return to the camp. When they did, they could see the British Yeomanry who had departed the camp in the early hours of that morning returning, with many wounded among them, as well as riderless horses.

'Poor bastards,' Ken muttered, watching the scene. 'They look like they copped a lot today.'

'I wonder how our cobbers are going?' Ben mused, dismounting to lead his horse to water. He knew it was not unusual for patrols to be separated from their regiments for specific missions but he and his men couldn't help feeling like orphans.

'The taubes are back!' someone yelled, and sure enough, when Ben looked skywards he could see a group of four German fighters flying from the north, low to the ground.

'Bloody hell!' Ben swore as a bomb fell close to where he stood, exploding and knocking him to the ground just as an Egyptian camel driver sprinted past him, only to be mown down by the shrapnel. Ben did not have to issue an order to take cover; already his men were aiming and firing their rifles at the enemy aircraft swooping on them like birds of prey. From somewhere Ben could hear the welcome sound of a Lewis machine gun returning the enemy fire, and as one of the German aircraft swooped overhead, Ben could see smoke streaming behind it from a hit to the engine. He struggled to his feet only to experience a searing pain in his shoulder, and it was then Ben was aware that he had been struck by shrapnel from the explosion.

The aircraft were already departing the campsite when one of the troopers looked over and noticed Ben's blood-soaked shirt.

'You all right, Sarge?' he asked. 'Looks like you copped one in the back.'

Ben attempted to feel around his shoulder for the wound, and winced when his hand came away covered in blood. His left arm was numb, and it was difficult to move his upper body.

'I'll live,' Ben grunted as Ken approached with a concerned expression on his face.

'Let me have a gander,' he said, slinging his rifle over his shoulder. Ben struggled to remove his shirt and when he had succeeded Ken peered at the bleeding wound. 'Looks like you have a bit of shrap still stuck in the wound,' he said. 'I reckon I can get it out.'

'Be my guest,' Ben replied as the others of the patrol gathered around. Ken gingerly gripped the edge of the exposed jagged metal in the wound, and with care he pulled the bomb fragment from Ben's shoulder. Ben bit his lip so as not to cry out in pain.

'Got it!' Ken said triumphantly. 'The RMO couldn't have done any better, I reckon. Now all we have to do is bandage it. You owe me a beer for my medical services.'

'I want to see your medical surgery authorisation first,' Ben said through a pain-racked grin. 'When was the last time we saw a cold beer – Cairo, if I remember rightly? That was a lifetime ago.'

'Good onya, Corp,' was echoed by the other troopers in the patrol as they slapped Ken on the back.

'Better get over to the RAP to get the shoulder bandaged properly,' Ken said. 'But don't tell the RMO I did a bit of home-grown surgery, eh? And here, keep the memento.' Ken passed the bit of jagged metal to Ben. It was a little larger than his thumb. Ben slipped it into his trouser pocket, aware that blood was streaming down his back.

The Regimental Medical Officer, an Englishman, finally saw Ben after treating badly wounded Yeomanry returning from the running battles with the Turkish advance force. He quickly assessed that Ben's wound would need packing and bandaging.

'It looks bad, but if you don't get an infection, all you will end up with is a scar, Sergeant,' he said, gesturing to one of the medical orderlies to bandage the wound as the surgeon moved on to the next patient.

'Looks like I can rejoin my boys,' Ben said when the bandaging had been completed.

'Just make sure you get the bandage redressed every day,' the orderly said. 'Best way to keep it clean. And I would suggest that you take it easy.'

Ken was waiting for Ben when he stepped outside the medical tent.

'How is it?' he asked.

'All right, but a bit stiff. It won't stop me from riding or using my rifle,' Ben replied.

It was nearing dusk when a column of horsemen entered the camp. The two men instantly recognised their regiment, and it was a joyous moment for the whole patrol to once again rejoin their family of brothers.

'Lucky I got this wound,' Ben said as they hurried to help the haggard, gaunt and exhausted troopers, whose mounts were in an equally bad state. 'Otherwise, the boys will accuse us of just sitting around the camp drinking tea while they were off fighting Jacko.'

Ken grinned. 'You could be right, because it looks like they have been given a leave pass from hell.'

The first item of news passed to Ben from a fellow sergeant of the regiment was that a brigade of their division had lost most of its officers and many troopers. Even as he wearily gave them this news, the horses of fallen British Yeomanry continued to trickle in alone with blood-stained saddles.

★

They came to Josiah's residence just after sunrise on a chilly late-autumn day: four grim-faced New South Wales policemen, two in uniform and two in plain clothes.

Josiah was always the first to rise, so he was already awake and sitting in his library when he heard the loud rapping on the front door below. It was the kind of knocking that raised a sense of urgency in Josiah's mind.

He walked quickly downstairs to open the door and saw the four men he recognised as police officers.

'Are you Mr Josiah Steele?' one of the plain-clothes officers asked in a formal tone.

'I am, and I wish to know why you are at my door at such an early hour of the morning?'

'Mr Steele, I have received orders from our federal government in Melbourne that you are to be questioned regarding a breach of the War Precautions Act which I am sure a learned man such as yourself would be aware of.'

'I know about the act of parliament, but I do not understand what your visit has to do with me,' Josiah retorted.

'I am sure you are aware that one of our roles is to inspect all domestic and international correspondence,' the officer replied. 'We have evidence that you are in breach of that section of the act, and require you to accompany us back to police headquarters.'

'Who has authorised your visit to my residence?' Josiah asked in a cold but calm voice.

'I believe the authority comes from Sir Horace Anderson,' the officer said. 'I am simply carrying out my job, Mr Steele, and so I would politely ask you to accompany us to the station where you can sort things out.'

Sir Horace Anderson . . . The name brought a savage anger to Josiah and he wished he had killed the man years earlier.

'Josiah, has something happened?' Marian came up behind Josiah, wearing a dressing-gown and an anxious expression.

'It is nothing for you to be concerned about,' Josiah replied gently. 'I am just going for a short time to speak with the police about a matter, so go inside and keep warm.'

His explanation did not seem to ease his wife's concern, but she trusted him and so she complied.

★

Josiah sat in a dank room of the Sydney police HQ with a lukewarm cup of tea before him. A uniformed officer sat on a chair in one corner and Josiah knew he was being guarded as if he were a criminal suspect. The air in the room was chilly and permeated by the smell of tobacco with a touch of vomit. It was a spartan room with a small window behind Josiah and just a wooden table and four rickety chairs.

Josiah's mind was racing. The senior officer who had formally requested his visit to the police station had said he was waiting for an important visitor before the interview began. Josiah suspected he knew who that was, and within the hour his suspicions were confirmed when the plain-clothes officer entered the room trailed by Sir Horace Anderson.

'We meet again, Mr Steele, but sadly under these unfortunate circumstances,' Anderson said by way of greeting, and took a chair opposite Josiah at the table while the plain-clothes officer stood to one side.

'What bloody unfortunate circumstances?' Josiah growled. 'And if there are any unfortunate circumstances, why am I not surprised to see you here?'

'These unfortunate circumstances,' Anderson said, placing two envelopes on the table between them. Josiah recognised them immediately as two letters he had written; one addressed to his sister and the other to his son's lover. 'I am sure you are aware of the war-time regulations clearly stating that correspondence with the enemy is a serious crime akin to treason.'

Josiah smile was grim. 'As you can see, these letters are addressed to a neutral country.'

'But the contents are addressed to women we both know are German, and both women are married to influential men in the enemy government. I believe your sister wed a German general, and this other woman is the wife of a high-ranking German official close to the Kaiser's war strategy planning. Our counter-security has clearly established both as potential threats after reading the contents of the letters.'

Josiah realised with chilling clarity that his enemy had made a technical legal point when he glanced up to see the smug expression on Anderson's face.

'It is only natural that I would wish to ascertain the wellbeing of my sister under the current circumstances, and as for the other woman, I have never met her – she is an acquaintance of my son Benjamin – and I was simply attempting to help him, since he is risking his life in the defence of his country and King. I have already lost my eldest son to this damned war. If I was able, I would also be back in uniform and standing beside them.'

'All that is well and good, but the facts are in those two letters,' Anderson persisted. 'However, because of your social position and influence within our government, you are fortunate that the matter was brought to my attention instead of being announced in the newspapers. They would have wasted no time in marking you as a Jewish traitor to this country.'

Josiah could feel his rage rising. His letters were clearly of a domestic nature and posed no threat to national security. He felt his body trembling with fury at the smugness of the man sitting opposite him, who he knew held the Steele family personally responsible for the death of his nephew, who had once faced a promising future in federal politics. 'Jewish traitor, is it? So that's it! Your contempt for my religion is well known in our social circles and I have no doubt it is supported by those who you call friends. I have never put my religious ideology before patriotism for this great nation.'

'You say so, but the devious nature of Jews is well accepted in this country,' Anderson replied. 'Everyone can see it in the prose of our great writers such as Paterson and Lawson, who reflect the feeling real Australians have for your kind.'

'So, you think that my religious beliefs will help secure a conviction against me?' Josiah said. 'We shall see about that. I have a strong feeling that in any court of law I can defeat this preposterous accusation of treachery. I demand legal representation immediately.'

Anderson leaned forward. 'You forget, Steele, we are

at war, and national security is a matter that trumps your desire for legal representation. You will remain in custody until formal charges are brought against you. Then the public will see your kind for what you are – devious traitors. I think we have reached the end of our discussion for now. Inspector, I am finished with this man, he is all yours to deal with.' With these parting words, Anderson pushed back his chair and left the room, leaving Josiah with the sick feeling that his old enemy had the prejudice of many Australians on his side. The walls suddenly felt as if they were closing in on him.

THIRTY-TWO

Josiah knew it was implied that he was not to leave the room, even though the police had not taken steps to charge him with any offence. When he asked, the plain-clothes officer finally introduced himself as Detective Sergeant Casey. Josiah sensed a reluctance by the police sergeant to be involved in the obvious political machinations of Horace Anderson, and guessed that the officer was of Irish descent and not inclined to those who considered themselves English aristocracy. The policeman ensured that Josiah had tea delivered to him and apologised gruffly that he had to await further instructions from Sir Horace Anderson.

'You must have knowledge of the letters' contents, Sergeant?' Josiah said. 'Would you consider anything in the correspondence to be of a treasonous nature?'

The detective sergeant looked away. 'It is not up to me to comment, Mr Steele,' he replied. He was a tough-looking man who might have been mistaken for a thug working the backstreets of Sydney's less salubrious suburbs. He even had a scar over one eye to enhance this impression.

'Do you have any idea how long I am to be detained?'

'Sorry, Mr Steele. No idea.'

Josiah sighed and sipped at the cup of tea, knowing that Marian would be telephoning people to support him.

It was midday when Detective Sergeant Casey returned with Josiah's son-in-law, Maurice. Josiah was surprised to see him, having expected a lawyer retained by his enterprises. Josiah rose from his chair as Maurice entered, walking with his crutches, the loss of his leg below the knee obvious.

'Dr Cohen informs me that you are his father-in-law, Mr Steele,' Casey said. 'We were able to have a good chat about you in the station.'

'Josiah, have you been mistreated?' Maurice asked.

'No, Detective Casey and his men have been very courteous towards me,' Josiah answered. 'I am hoping that I will be out of here before the rest of the family become concerned.'

Maurice turned to Casey. 'Mr Steele has already lost a son in France and has another serving with the Desert Column in Palestine, and as you can see, I have suffered a crippling injury on the Western Front, Sergeant. Do you really consider Mr Steele, a well-known philanthropist and leading businessman in the country, to be a traitor?'

The detective sergeant frowned. 'If it was up to me, I would not even have carried out our detention early this morning, Doctor. But Sir Horace said he had the authority of the government in Melbourne to take Mr Steele into custody. As a simple copper it's my duty to carry out orders given by those higher up than me. Sir Horace has yet to give me further instructions.'

'I would strongly suggest that you allow Mr Steele to return to his family and business affairs immediately. You may not be aware, but there is a history of enmity between Sir Horace and Mr Steele over the years. I suspect Anderson is indulging in a personal vendetta towards my father-in-law, who I might add held the Queen's commission in campaigns in Afghanistan and Africa. If Sir Horace has attempted to accuse Mr Steele of treachery, I am sure it will come back to bite him – and all those who have abetted him in this sham of a detention.'

Josiah could see that Maurice's words were having an effect on the policeman in charge. He did not have all the facts, but he had picked up on the simmering animosity between his man in custody and the English knighted civil servant.

'All right. I will release Mr Steele for the moment, since Sir Horace has not got back to me with his intentions,' Casey said. 'On the condition that Mr Steele is prepared to give his word as a gentleman that he will be readily available for any future interviews.'

'You have my word as a former holder of the Queen's commission that I have no intention of fleeing justice,' Josiah replied. 'I have important matters of war defence to attend to and will continue doing so. My thanks to you, Detective Sergeant Casey, for your understanding. Although I must warn you, by releasing me you may run afoul of Sir Horace.'

Casey smiled grimly. 'Do not concern yourself, Mr Steele,' he said. 'The enforcement of the law is still the domain of the police and not public servants. As no charges have been laid, I cannot see any reason to hold you any longer, and besides, I have read the letters in question and I feel that if my family were in an enemy territory, I would have tried to reach them by mail too. My family is in Ireland, God bless Her, and they are having their own problems with the English, so I am not overly inclined to bow to the whims of the high and mighty.'

Josiah sensed that the Irish-born police detective had an affinity with him as a member of another class of people looked down upon by the predominantly English-influenced hierarchy of society. But whatever motivated the police officer to make his decision to release Josiah, it did not matter, as he was now free to walk out of the dank office and return to his life.

Josiah and Maurice stepped onto the pavement outside under grey and threatening clouds. Josiah knew he was free for now, but how much power did Anderson have with the government? Josiah knew things would not end here.

★

Every soldier from the top generals to the lowliest trooper knew that the Suez Canal must not fall to the Ottoman Empire. If this occurred, it could mean the cutting off of vital supplies for the war effort in France, and thus disaster on the Western Front.

Ben rode along the Katia track as dawn broke, the crimson sky a precursor to the scorching heat of the daytime desert. They rode up a ridge to see the magnificent sight of Australian and New Zealand mounted desert columns below, the tinges of pink, grey and khaki winding all the way back to the redoubts of a place called Dueidar.

'Bloody beautiful sight,' Ken said. 'Jacko appears to be on the run.'

Ben did not answer. Although the Turkish army had suffered terrible losses in its attempts to storm Romani and seize the railhead, Ben was aware that there were also many missing faces of men he knew from the regiment. Now those who remained were assembled to advance northwards. Maybe they would reach the sacred city of Jerusalem? Ben hoped he would live to experience that monumental day.

They reached an oasis at Bir el Nuss, where the horses were watered and Ben's regiment waited for another two hours in any shade they could find. At that point they were joined by their other Australian, New Zealand and finally British counterparts – the helmeted Yeomanry. After them came the British artillery units, spoiling to get into the fight, and Ben also noted the long line of ambulance wagons, reminding him and his troop that these would be filled with casualties after their next encounter with the tough and brave Turkish troops.

Ben was now hardly aware of the haggard faces and staring eyes of the men riding in to join them, and guessed that if he could see himself in a mirror, it would reflect the same picture. The lack of sleep – or even rest – from fighting day and night was taking its toll. The horses' heads were drooping as they experienced the same exhaustion. The brief respite at the oasis was very welcome.

'Mount up!'

The order was shouted down the lines and the regiment of light horsemen obeyed, then rode out whistling, singing and laughing. Morale had been given a vital boost with the arrival of the badly needed fire support from British artillery trains and the rest of their logistic support.

As they rode north, stories of the events of the past twenty-four hours were passed along the files of mounted troopers. There had been the massacre of their forward observation posts; the courage under fire of other troopers rescuing mates who had lost their horses; grim stories of men without mounts desperately attempting to retreat but finding their leggings and boots full of sand, which slowed them down long enough to be bayoneted by pursuing Turkish troops.

Seeing this, the attacking Turkish troops had thrown away their boots so that they could run more easily, when eight thousand Turkish bayonets had glinted under the starlight as they attacked Mount Meredith while the British horse artillery unlimbered their guns time and time again to provide supporting fire. There were further stories of unimaginable ferocity in the close-quarter night fighting, as well as of supreme acts of individual courage that would never be recorded. But always the men would acknowledge their enemy by jest, curse or outright praise for the Turkish soldiers' courage and tenacity in their attacks.

The ride continued but gradually the singing, joking and whistling fell away as adrenaline drained from the troopers' bodies. Ben could see the drooping heads of men and horses as they rode. The grimy faces and tired, fever-bright eyes of Ben's section told the story of the previous days of life under fire, of the ever-present sound of artillery guns as they rode through the heavy sand in the hot sun, chewing their rock-hard biscuits for sustenance.

Ben glanced down to see a dead Turkish soldier bloated by decomposition lying beside wooden crates of shiny ammunition and, further on, a dozen empty but blood-soaked stretchers. Eventually they came across another small oasis littered with empty bottles left by the German and Turkish officers in their retreat.

'Must have had a bloody good piss-up,' Ken remarked, and Ben nodded, too weary to reply. Here, too, they saw many bloody stretchers, some occupied by dead Turkish soldiers bloating under the blazing sun. The stench of death pervaded the air, but Ben had grown used to it.

Then, without warning, a loud explosion of rifle fire

from somewhere nearby warned Ben and his section that as ever, death lurked close.

'*Halt! Taube! Taub-e! Taub-e!*'

The troops came to a stop as an armed German reconnaissance biplane droned overhead, mercifully leaving the advancing horsemen unscathed by its bombs and bullets before disappearing over the horizon.

'So much for seeing a bunch of troopers from the air,' Ken commented, swigging from his water canteen.

'Bloody happy they missed us,' Ben replied. 'We were a sitting target.'

Within the hour they could hear the rapid firing of machine guns ahead and suddenly the blue sky was filled with friendly aircraft swooping on their targets beyond a ridge line. The ridge obscured Ben's view of the enemy, but the air was filled with puffs of smoke from Turkish anti-aircraft guns attempting to destroy the Allied eagles of war.

The column was brought to a halt while the regimental commanders gathered. Ben and the rest of the regiment, around five hundred men, dismounted to water their horses and prepare themselves. They waited patiently – as is the tradition of all soldiers of all armies – until the word came that they were to mount up and ride to the top of the ridge.

When he got there, Ben could see a palm-fringed oasis under clouds of British air-burst shrapnel shells. It was situated on a plain of hard-packed sand about a mile away. The regimental commander stepped forward to address the assembled regiment as the infantry behind them caught up. He pointed at the enemy-occupied oasis to their front.

'A battery of heavy Austrian guns has been located in that oasis,' he said quietly but clearly. 'We have to charge and take the guns.'

The order was clear and simple, and Ben felt an electric feeling surge through his body.

The colonel swung himself into the saddle and called out in a loud parade-ground voice, '*Regiment fix bayonets!*'

The hot air was filled with the clicking sound of five hundred bayonets being attached to the ends of the troopers' rifles.

'Cobbers, this is it,' Ben said to the men closest to him. 'We are no longer mounted infantry. We are now to be cavalry.'

The commanding officer and his adjutant rode ahead as the squadrons fell into their formations for the charge across the plain. Then the regiment broke into a trot to conserve their strength for the last stretch, where they would let the horses have their heads in a full gallop.

Ben could feel the excitement of the moment, and all fear was gone. He kept his head down and held his rifle low in one hand as if it were a lance. He was knee to knee with the man who had become his closest friend, Corporal Ken Ford, and could feel the body heat of the close-packed formation of horses as they broke into a canter and then a mad gallop. The thunder of hooves on the hard sand sounded like war drums, urging them on to what tacticians would advise was a suicidal charge against entrenched enemy with machine guns, artillery and small arms.

All Ben experienced was the insane desire to contact the enemy and kill him. Nothing else mattered in his current life.

THIRTY-THREE

Josiah knew that his money could hire the best lawyers in the country, and as such he now sat in the office of his barrister, William Gooding, son of the renowned barrister Humphrey Gooding, KC, whose legal skills had saved the life of former Sergeant Major Conan Curry VC from the hangman's noose at Darlinghurst Gaol years earlier.

Josiah was struck by the likeness of young William Gooding to his esteemed father, both in his mannerisms and outward appearance, and hoped that similarity extended to his skills as a barrister.

'I will seek to have copies made of the letters that you wrote to your sister and this other person, Caroline von Neumann,' he said, peering through his spectacles at Josiah's formal statement of the events that had transpired. 'I have heard of Sir Horace Anderson, and I note that you make mention of his antagonism towards members of your family. How did that come about?'

'Anderson and I were at school together, and he was a bully I put in his place,' Josiah replied. 'About fifteen years ago he was behind his nephew, Cecil Anderson's, push for a seat in the new federal government. His nephew had served in the South African campaign as an officer who witnesses were prepared to say was a coward who disgraced the Queen's commission. He was also strongly implicated in the attempted murder of my brother and the murder of my brother's friend, former Captain Steve Walton. I was able to pass on the statements of men who served under him during the Boer War concerning his cowardice, and there was great interest in publishing the story. It appears that Cecil Anderson was not prepared to face the scandal arising from such revelations and chose to end his life with his service revolver. Horace Anderson blames me for his nephew's death and, it seems, will go to any lengths to disgrace me.'

'Hmm, I see,' William said, looking over his spectacles at Josiah. 'But any case against you will come down to the intent of your words in the letters that have been inter-cepted. I believe all mail is now steamed open to inspect the contents; this war has certainly curtailed our private freedoms. At any rate, leave the matter with me and I will contact you when I have reviewed all the material to plan a defence. In the meantime, I doubt that the police will be back to detain you, Mr Steele, as I know of your esteemed prominence in Sydney and beyond.'

Josiah rose from his chair and held out his hand. 'Thank you, Mr Gooding. I hope to hear from you very soon to have this ridiculous accusation of treachery set aside. I think we can make a compelling case for the truth: that it is a malicious complaint by a man who disgraces the bestowal of a knighthood.'

Despite these words, Josiah stepped onto the pavement below the lawyer's office still uncertain of his fate. Anderson was a dangerous and unpredictable man. And in the end, it had all been for naught: neither his sister nor the mysterious German woman would receive any news from him.

★

Ben's regiment crashed through the defences at the oasis without the terrible chatter of machine guns opposing them, as officers waved revolvers and the men shouted, bolstering their courage. To his right, Ben could see a sandbagged trench but no sign of the enemy, and he immediately hoped that the enemy flank had collapsed – or the defenders were either too terrified to rise or had already deserted.

The troopers urged their horses through the oasis and onto the plain beyond, where they were surrounded by a mile of palm trees.

'*Halt!*' The order was shouted by the colonel as he raised his arm, and his regiment pulled up and milled around him. It appeared that the Austrian artillery was not at the oasis after all. But the men's relief was short-lived. At that moment horses started to fall as bullets thudded into them from the oasis they had just charged through. The horrible realisation dawned that the Turkish defenders had laid low until they could pour their fire into the rear of the regiment. Wheeling around, the men of the regiment doubled back, straight into intense small-arms and machine-gun fire.

The order to dismount ran down the line and the horse handlers quickly gathered as many of the horses as they could. Ben felt his stomach churn as he flung himself from the saddle. Dates rained down on him and his comrades as they sought shelter among the palms. Out of the corner of his eye, he could see the pitiful sight of many of their mounts covered in blood, whinnying in pain as they collapsed in the sand. It appeared to Ben that the Turkish defenders were firing too high – or deliberately targeting their mounts.

Even the colonel's horse was down, but the men under his command had been trained well and Ben joined Ken Ford as they formed a defensive line among the palm groves.

'Didn't see that coming,' Ken muttered. 'The bastards are smarter than we give them credit for.'

The regiment pushed forward as an encircling formation to their right, moving in small groups between the palms and clumps of stunted scrub. It was then that the earth erupted as the Turkish artillery poured their explosive shells into the troopers' ranks.

Ben dropped, hugging the ground as bullets squirted up small fountains of sand, while the smaller guns of the British artillery returned a counter bombardment. But their guns were no match for the numerous and larger artillery pieces of the Turkish army.

'Bloody hell!' Ben swore when he noticed a New Zealand squadron of mounted infantry charge into the oasis, only to be quickly cut down by machine-gun fire. Ben watched the gruesome scene of the courageous Kiwis being flung from their mounts, their horses thrashing on the ground in their death throes. The murderous situation was compounded when Ben glimpsed to his left, out on the plain, dismounted men wearing pith helmets running towards the oasis. The British mounted soldiers advanced in small groups, firing, hitting the sand, then rising again to advance, only to flounder under the withering enemy small-arms fire and exploding artillery. Ben groaned at the courage of the British troopers, knowing that their action was akin to suicide, and he was right. None made it to the oasis.

The heat was overwhelming. After around twenty shots Ben's rifle became almost too hot to hold, while Ben experienced a terrible thirst. With his focus entirely on the terrain ahead, he dared not reach for his canteen. The enemy seemed to be invisible; it was only the never-ending incoming fire of artillery, machine guns and rifles that made their presence known to Ben and his regiment.

Then came the welcome sound of British artillery whispering overhead, targeting a larger oasis a distance away to Ben's front and dampening the incoming Turkish artillery under control of the Austrians. The noise of the guns and artillery was deafening, and Ben could hear his ears ringing.

'Kiwis!' Ken shouted. Ben swivelled his head to see their brothers from across the Tasman join them. They were panting and advancing on foot in small groups using fire and movement, and taking cover behind any scrub-covered mound they could find. Kneeling, they fired as sweat streamed down faces already reddened by exertion and the heat.

Then Ben noticed that their Kiwi brothers had located a nest of Turkish snipers, much hated by all who confronted them. Ben could see a man's head only fifty yards away, so he took careful aim and fired, noting that his aim had been true as the head dropped from view in a fine mist of red.

The New Zealand soldiers immediately launched an outright attack on the sniper post, firing as they ran forward, when suddenly, a white flag appeared from the bushes. A dozen Turkish soldiers with their hands raised stood up to surrender. Ben felt rage for the men surrendering, but also told himself that the snipers were brave men to remain behind when other among their comrades had withdrawn.

The Turkish soldiers were taken as prisoners of war after being searched by Kiwi and Aussie alike for souvenirs. As they did so, Ben noticed with relief other friendly brigades galloping in to bolster their numbers in the smaller oasis area. It was then that a Turkish prisoner informed them that the Austrian guns had been pulled back to the larger oasis Ben had spied earlier and were surrounded by machine-gun pits. Ben shuddered, realising that had they initially attacked the larger oasis, he doubted that he would still be alive.

Out on their left they could see the fighting continuing as the Turks refused to yield ground. Ben could see that a couple of Australian brigades were engaged in the savage fighting and knew that those troopers had not slept in three days or nights.

But the day was not over. Despite being at the limits of his endurance, Ben found himself advancing on foot with his squadron. He had an opportunity to swig the last of the water in his canteen, which he felt was near boiling point. But they were still fighting from the cover of palm to palm and mound to mound, where Ben felt the sand stick to his face and body as it mingled with his sweat.

Suddenly, five yards away a Turkish soldier with a bushy moustache rose from behind a mound, aiming down his rifle sights at Ben, who instinctively fired off a wild shot that narrowly missed. Without thinking, Ben leapt forward, thrusting the long bayonet affixed to his rifle into the Turkish soldier's throat before he could reload. The man dropped his rifle and Ben withdrew the bayonet, then swung the butt of his Lee Enfield as a club into the already dying man's head. Ben did not reflect on the berserk fighting; he knew only that he was desperate to live. Covered in warm blood that had gushed from the Turkish soldier's neck, he continued forward. But the situation worsened.

Ben and his men reached a strip of sand running like a road through the oasis, where they met another Light Horse squadron. Together they charged across the open road, only to be met by a wall of intense small-arms and machine-gun fire. Men fell around Ben, and as he flung himself down behind a scrubby mound, he could see just off to his right Ken dashing forward to join him. But to Ben's horror he saw Ken spin around, hit by a machine-gun bullet in the stomach just as he reached him. Ben immediately reached out and dragged the big corporal out of the line of invisible death in the hot air.

Ken was gasping for air as he gripped Ben's sleeve, his diaphragm torn by the bullet and his eyes racked with pain. The rain of enemy rifle fire intensified as Ken attempted to speak, but no words came. Ben felt the grip on his sleeve weaken and knew there was nothing he could do – he did not even have water to offer his friend in his final moments. There was only one option – the squadron survivors would have to move forward, continuing to clear the enemy – because if Ben stayed by his best friend, he would die with him.

Wretchedly, with a silent farewell to Ken, Ben crawled forward, with nothing in his mind but loading, aiming and firing at anything that might be a target as they advanced on the larger, Katia oasis. The firing from the enemy became even more intense, and for a fleeting second Ben reflected on the miracle that he was still alive amid this field of death, baked by a desert sun that sucked every last drop of moisture from their bodies. His thirst had become almost unbearable. As he crawled forward, he came across a dead Turkish soldier and quickly rummaged for the dead man's water canteen. When he found it empty, his disappointment threatened to overwhelm him.

'*A well, boys. Here's water!*' someone yelled above the deafening noise of battle, and Ben wondered if he was dreaming. Almost driven mad by thirst, Ben and the other men who had heard the call leapt up, ignoring the incoming fire, and rushed towards the well, where they saw half-filled Turkish water bottles strewn about. Ben snatched one and discovered, incredibly, that the water was ice cold. He gulped it down and filled his own water canteen as bullets spurted up sand around him. A trooper next to Ben was hit in the chest, slumping to the ground dead, while another nearby was hit in the head, spraying blood into the cold waters of the well they had captured. His body was pushed aside so the other troopers joining the crowd around the well could fill their water canteens. Ben wondered at the insanity that was this tiny piece of heaven in a hell on earth.

As soon as Ben had quenched his thirst, he and the others near the well rushed to the scrubby bushes in an attempt to push back and defend the precious water supply, allowing other survivors of the regiment to partake of the liquid gold. At least they had captured a vital water point, and had time to briefly rest after clearing the area of enemy. Ben considered returning to Ken's body, but knew that would be futile. For his own sanity, he would have to put his friend's death aside for now. He would mourn Ken's loss in time – if he survived the war and the desert himself.

'C'mon, boys, time to clear out Jacko!'

The order came from the squadron commander and once again, Ben checked his rifle and ammunition supply, and that his long bloody bayonet was still affixed, knowing that he would be using it again before the sun set over the harsh lands.

They advanced on a series of sandy bush-covered mounds, each of which concealed Turkish soldiers who fired through the scrub. The squadron split into small sections and attacked each mound, firing into them and following up with their long bayonets.

Ben and two troopers attacked one of the mounds, running crouched down, and when they reached it a couple of Turkish soldiers stood up as if to flee. A big Anatolian Turk snarled as he lunged at Ben with his long bayonet, but Ben parried the blow with his own and stepped forward to quickly thrust his bayonet into the big man's chest, twisting the blade to cause maximum damage. Ben slid his bayonet out, and a fountain of blood sprayed from the soldier's ruptured heart. The mound was cleared and it was time to move on to the next one.

The day wore on as the British, New Zealanders and Australians fought against an unyielding enemy for the vital ground of the oases. Ben no longer wondered whether he would live another day. His mind was numb and he felt like a dead man walking. He knew there was only one word that would decide his fate – *luck*. Nothing else.

THIRTY-FOUR

It was a magnificent late spring day when Josiah arranged to meet his brother, Sam, for a stroll along the Manly Corso. Sam had purchased a property on the North Shore of Sydney to get away from the now overcrowded inner suburbs of the southern side of the great harbour, and Josiah had taken a ferry to meet his brother in the suburb that had access to both the harbour and the sea.

Seagulls swirled and dived overhead as tourists took in the views in their Sunday best: gentlemen in straw boaters and colourfully striped sportscoat jackets, and ladies with long skirts and parasols for protection against the strong southern sun. Josiah wore a long-sleeved shirt and dark trousers as well as an expensive hat.

After disembarking from the ferry he walked over to Manly Beach, where he stood watching young couples strolling on the sand, some with bare feet.

'Good morning, big brother,' Sam greeted him. 'I received your message to meet with you. What's this mysterious rendezvous about?'

Josiah turned to his brother, who was also in casual clothing and leaning on his walking stick. 'Is the leg giving you a bit of trouble?' Josiah asked with a note of concern.

'Just a little bit lately,' Sam answered. 'Nothing that will slow me down as the captain of the *Ella,* though.'

Josiah nodded. 'There's a delicate matter I wish to discuss with you, and I thought it best to do so well away from the places we are familiar with,' he said, retrieving his pipe and plugging it with tobacco from a leather pouch. 'Our old friend Horace Anderson is back in the picture.'

'Anderson! I read that he was knighted for his services to the public service,' Sam replied bitterly. 'That bastard should have been strung up as a conspirator for the murder of my dear friend, Steve, many years ago.'

'Well, it seems that he has been harbouring a desire for revenge against us for the death of his nephew, and is now conspiring to have me charged with treason under that new war section act for entering into correspondence with the enemy.'

'How in hell could he do that?' Sam asked.

'I wrote a couple of letters to be posted to an address in Switzerland,' Josiah said.

'But the Swiss are a neutral mob,' Sam commented.

'The letters were to our sister Becky and a young lady it seems Ben knew in Rabaul. She wrote to me and I owed her a reply.'

'Caroline von Neumann,' Sam said. 'It could only be her.'

'Anderson has implied that I have been communicating information that can be used by the Germans,' Josiah said, puffing on the now lit pipe. 'I can assure you that there was nothing incriminating in either letter – they were of a purely domestic nature – but knowing Anderson he will use his influence to convince his government pals that I am a traitor.'

'Bloody ridiculous!' Sam exploded. 'You have served this country with great honour, even to the point of almost losing your life in the service of our late Queen.'

'That will not count when you consider the bias some have against those they identify to be Jews,' Josiah replied grimly.

'What if Anderson were to finally pay for his role in Steve's death?' Sam asked quietly. 'He will be no loss to the world if he suddenly and permanently departs this earth.'

Josiah smiled thinly. 'It is not like the old days when our father settled scores with natural justice for the guilty,' he said. 'Times have changed and the violent death of a knight of the realm will bring all the forces of the law down on the matter. It would be me who would swing.'

'Leave it with me,' Sam said, gazing out at a sea of rolling white-tipped waves.

'Remember, brother, you have a family to think of,' Josiah cautioned. 'If you can find a way to discredit Anderson, that is all I ask.'

Sam turned to his brother. 'I'll do whatever it takes to find justice for my best friend. He was as close to me as another brother. I have never forgotten his murder, and all because an arrogant and incompetent Cecil Anderson gave a suicidal order all those years ago. And now another member of that treacherous family threatens my one and only brother? Well, I will do what I have to do to rectify the situation.'

Sam's tone was chilling, and for a moment Josiah

regretted mentioning the dire situation. He was fully aware that Sam had always had a wild nature – it was what kept him on the seas like some sort of modern-day pirate.

With a simple nod, Josiah changed the subject and the brothers chatted about matters closer to home. The loss of David had left an unfillable hole in the family – and, from a pragmatic position, the loss of the heir to the Steele enterprises. Both men recognised that Ben was not someone who would be happy taking the reins, and both Josiah's daughters were already well established in their lives with their own families. Josiah had asked Sam if he would consider taking over, but he had politely declined. He loved his life on the open seas of the South Pacific.

'I guess I will try to convince Ben to take more responsibility when he returns from the war,' Josiah said with a sigh. 'I know he would, albeit reluctantly.'

'We are fortunate that Ben is in Palestine,' Sam commented. 'He is lucky not to be on the Western Front. I feel he is in less danger with the Light Horse.'

Josiah agreed with his brother, and they continued to secretly hope they were right.

★

Ben and those around him knew they were fighting for their very lives.

They had fought with bayonet and bullet from one mound to the next until finally they reached a point where they could view through the tall palms a circular, flat area of sand. Among the bushes surrounding the open area Ben could see Turkish soldiers scurrying away from the advancing troopers as white smoke, the remnants of bursting artillery shells, rose over the oasis. When he looked back the way they'd come, Ben saw the same white smoke and terrified riderless horses galloping through the clusters of palms. He prayed that his section of mounts had not been hit.

Suddenly a machine gun opened a devastating fire on them, spraying the area of Ben's immediate section of troopers. With his keen tactician's eye, Ben knew that staying in place meant eventual death. It was time to move forward and neutralise the now-located Austrian artillery batteries, but as they did so more troopers fell against the determined enemy resistance. Where possible the wounded were evacuated to the relative safety of the rear by their comrades, who would always return, panting and sweating, to resume the fighting. It was obvious to everyone from the newest trooper to the most battle-hardened colonel that the guns were too heavily defended and that their regiment had been decimated by the attack on the two oases.

Ben was impressed by the compassion of the Turkish soldiers, who could see the evacuation of the Australian wounded across open stretches of sand and refused to fire on them. Only when the troopers had attempted to return to the fight did they once again come under Turkish fire.

The sun was low on the horizon when Ben realised that they had been in continuous battle since the early morning, and there had not been a moment when they had not been under intense artillery and small-arms fire, not even an hour when they had not been engaging their enemy in close-quarter fighting in a form of warfare more familiar to warriors of the past.

Yard by yard, Ben and the surviving men of his regiment drove back the enemy until they were defending from the heart of the larger oasis, where the squadrons were fighting in isolation from one another and lacked the numbers to force the Turkish soldiers and their German auxiliaries into surrender or annihilation.

As night approached, Ben's squadron commander decided to return to the rear to receive orders on what their mission was under the current circumstances, and the men watched him go. When he crossed an open space, he was targeted by a machine gun and he flung himself into the sand, then rose again and crawled forward. The men watching him laughed at the comical figure he cut, and he turned and winked over his shoulder when he heard them. Then he rose to his knees but immediately fell flat again as the machine gun bullets flew overhead. Eventually he continued his perilous trek back to the mobile regimental HQ on his stomach.

A trooper Ben knew crawled up to take a position close to him.

'A bit bloody hot here, Sarge,' Lance Corporal Paul Shepherd said, referring to the exposed mound they huddled behind.

'Time to dig a scrape,' Ben said, and both men used their hands and bayonets to scrape away the sand to make a very shallow hollow. Bullets continued to rip into their mound, which only gave enough cover for two men. The body of a dead trooper just a yard away was a concern. They could not push the body away, nor could they use him as a kind of sandbag shield as his body would attract enemy attention. Instead, Ben reached out to drag the body behind the mound and pushed it into the shallow trench they had dug. Then they shovelled sand onto him and the two men were forced to lie across the body in its shallow grave and resume firing at anything that was exposed out to their front.

Finally, the squadron CO was able to return with orders from regimental HQ that they were to retire. But as soon as Ben and the rest of the physically exhausted survivors of the squadron began to pull back, the Turkish defenders went on a counterattack, swarming behind the withdrawing troopers. To hinder the rain of bullets following them, the Allied troopers fell back in an orderly and disciplined manner, using the tactic of fire and movement in small groups, with one section stopping to wheel around and fire at the pursuing Turkish soldiers while another sprinted for cover further back.

Ben could see that the pursuing enemy had become overenthusiastic in their victory and were standing to fire at his small section, which made them easier targets. Three of the Turkish soldiers fell to Ben's deadly accuracy with a rifle. But it was getting harder to gather the strength to even rise from one position to seek another. Only the thought of falling to a Turkish bayonet kept Ben and the rest of the troopers going. Ben and his men had one other terrible disadvantage: the setting sun silhouetted them to the pursuing Turkish troops.

It seemed almost impossible, but Ben and his squadron survivors staggered back towards a sand rise where their own machine guns were able to fire over their heads at the enemy following them, stopping the Turkish infantry momentarily. Bullets still fell dangerously close around them, every so often finding an occasional unlucky trooper.

Ben glanced at Lance Corporal Shepherd, who had been at his side for some hours now. 'We have to run,' Ben said hoarsely. His lungs felt like they were on fire and might collapse, but the lance corporal had spent the last of his strength. He simply shook his head in despair and staggered on towards the rise. Not far away was the squadron commander, who was also clawing his way up towards the rise, his rifle slung across his back. Just as Ben reached the top, he saw the squadron CO hit by a bullet and collapse into the firing line.

Ben was hardly aware that he was still alive but he saw that the men on the ridge were in a good position to put covering fire down on the advancing Turkish soldiers. There was a plentiful supply of ammunition here, and as weary as he was, Ben filled his bandolier and took up a position on the ridge, continuing the fight to break the counterattack. He smiled when he saw Lance Corporal Shepherd plod over the rise unscathed to collapse with exhaustion in the relative safety of the rest of the regiment. He was followed by other scattered groups of regimental survivors who, like Ben, then rejoined the fight. Behind the firing line the regimental doctor and padre tended to the wounded, and ambulance carts were evacuating as many as they could.

Despite the withering fire from the ridge the Turkish soldiers pressed their attack to the point that a few actually reached the Australian defensive line.

A New Zealand regimental doctor and his medical sergeant dashed partway down the slope to retrieve the wounded still on the forward edge, but they were cut down by the fire from the Turkish attackers. Both men were killed in their courageous attempt to bring the wounded men in.

'The horses are coming up!' Paul Shepherd exclaimed beside Ben on the ridge. 'Time to get out of here before Jacko forces his way up the ridge.'

Ben agreed. Troopers were already streaming down the rear slope, calling for their mates and their own mounts. The horses were rearing in panic and plunging wildly. Ben was exhilarated to recognise his troop horse handler and his mount, somehow still alive, and he seized the reins and struggled with great effort into the saddle.

'Mine's gone!' Paul Shepherd called to Ben, who held out his hand to swing the lance corporal up behind him. As he did so he heard the cry of 'Allah! Allah! Allah!' being shouted behind him as the Turkish soldiers finally took the ridge, now deserted by the defenders, who galloped away among the palms to put some distance between them and the enemy on foot.

★

The attack on the oases had been a failure.

Through the night, Ben rode with his passenger behind him. They were too exhausted even to exchange words as they made their way towards the relative safety of the camp at Romani. Occasionally they would have to halt to help the gunners of the small battery of horse-drawn artillery guns travelling with them to extricate themselves from the soft sand.

Throughout the night ride they would be challenged by infantry outposts with the command to *halt*. It was then that they would tumble from their mounts to snatch a couple of minutes' sleep before the command to *mount* woke them again, and then they would rise and continue. It was nearly dawn when they saw the defensive redoubts of Romani camp. They rode in and rolled out of their saddles to fall instantly into a dreamless sleep.

The men of Ben's regiment had spent the last sixty hours in constant action.

THIRTY-FIVE

Sam Steele stood on the wharf gazing at his schooner, the *Ella*.

Memories flooded through him of the exciting days he'd spent sailing the South Pacific, trading with the islanders and ensuring that his personal enterprise always showed a profit in the larger family businesses, but the war had changed things. German commercial raiders now roamed the seven seas. Sam spent more time at home with his children these days, much to the delight of Georgette and Saul.

The *Ella* looked so forlorn in a harbour filled with big warships, like an orphan waiting for someone to adopt her.

'I got your message, Sam,' said a voice beside him. It was Sam's second-in-command, Nate Welsh, the former New Zealander who had served with Sam during the Boer War. Nate looked older now, with his thick, dark hair greying and his dark complexion even more pronounced from years aboard the schooner under a tropical sun. 'How are the kids?'

'They're good,' Sam sighed. 'Pleased to have me at home.'

'Yeah, same with my family,' Nate commented. 'Any word on whether we will be taking the old girl out to sea again?' he asked.

'I talked to my brother, and he agrees that we should continue trading in the islands,' Sam replied. 'It seems we could make a good profit on copra again as it is in short supply, but before we do that, I need to finish something I should have done fifteen years ago.'

Nate frowned. 'What would that be?' he asked.

'Get rid of Cecil Anderson's uncle, Sir Horace Anderson.'

'Bloody hell!' Nate responded. 'What do you mean "get rid of" Anderson?'

'Just that,' Sam said. 'Kill the bastard before he is able to destroy Josiah and the family.' Sam went on to explain the circumstances of the trumped-up charge of treason against Josiah while Nate listened patiently.

'You are talking about murder,' Nate said quietly. 'How do we get rid of a well-known person?'

'That's why I need any ideas that you might have,' Sam replied. 'It's not like we haven't done this before, but I figure it is time we went for a cold beer.'

'Good idea,' Nate said, and the two men turned to walk towards a harbourside pub a short distance away.

★

It was another dawn, and Ben and the remainder of his section watered and fed their horses, and opened tins of bully beef and packets of the rock-hard biscuits. They had hardly finished tending to their mounts and themselves when the order came down the line, '*Moun-nt!*'

Ben continued to chew his biscuit as he swung himself into the saddle and the regiment formed up to ride out once again to the oasis at Katia. All were aware of how the new formation was missing many of their old comrades.

Ben experienced a dead feeling in his soul when he glanced at the place beside him where Ken had always ridden. At least Lance Corporal Paul Shepherd was a familiar face. The column moved on under a blazing sun, passing small groups of British infantry stumbling towards Katia, crazed with thirst.

'Look at those poor bloody Tommies,' Paul said, drawing Ben's attention to a couple of British infantrymen desperately scratching at a salt pan in an effort to find water. Beyond them Ben could see around a dozen British soldiers who had thrown off their gear and were running, laughing and screaming like maniacs.

Both Ben and Paul dismounted to offer sips of water from their canteens to the two young British soldiers, who gulped it down greedily.

'Sorry, cobber,' Ben said. 'We need to keep the rest for ourselves.' They swung themselves back into the saddle to rejoin the advancing column, noting that other troopers were also providing the thirst-crazed British infantry with water they could ill afford to spare.

And then they were at the silent oasis that had known deafening noise and death only a day before, riding past the bodies of Turkish soldiers and one or two New Zealanders, the stench of decomposition heavy in the still, hot air.

It was obvious that the Turkish army had abandoned the oasis the previous night.

Ben immediately cast about, trying to identify where he had been in the gradual, organised fighting withdrawal, and finally located the body of Corporal Ken Ford lying on his back, his body covered in a cloud of flies.

Ben dismounted and knelt beside the body of his big friend. 'Sorry that I had to leave you, cobber.'

Ben took a shovel he had found at the oasis and dug a shallow grave, rolling Ken's body into it. When this was done, he knelt beside the sandy grave, wiping away his tears for the man who would forever lie in the holy lands of Christian, Jew and Moslem alike.

'C'mon, Sarge,' Paul called. 'Looks like a couple of our brigades are already chasing Jacko.'

Ben mounted his horse and followed Paul back to the rest of his section. They could see fellow troopers in a long screen a mile ahead engaging the retreating enemy, while Ben was pleased to see that the men of the British infantry who they had left in their wake were now straggling into the oasis to find the icy-cold, life-giving water in the well.

At least I was able to give Ken a burial, Ben thought.

When Ben watched the dust rising on the horizon from the retreating Turkish army, he sensed that for the moment the battle for Romani was over. The next battle would lie beyond the horizon in the direction of Jerusalem, and Ben hoped that he would be alive to experience that historic moment when the modern-day crusaders arrived in the sacred city.

★

Sam sat in the backyard of his modest home at Manly, pondering how it was possible to neutralise the last real enemy of the Steele family. For a moment his thoughts turned to his beloved departed wife, Rosemary. Not a day passed when Sam did not think of her. He knew that Rosemary would have approved of his plot to kill Anderson, who had most certainly been complicit in the death of her brother years earlier.

Then he heard a motor car engine driving along a road outside his residence, and it came to him. Many people had been hit and killed by motor vehicles. The situation had become so common that a special act had been passed in the parliament less than a decade earlier to regulate driving practices. Very few drivers at fault had been convicted of the deaths of pedestrians when they had claimed the accident was unavoidable.

Sam now had his weapon, but he needed intelligence of where and when the 'accident' could occur. That was a matter of collecting information on Anderson's movements while he was in Sydney, and Sam had an idea how that could be achieved. It was an operation requiring subtle surveillance and planning while keeping his brother at arm's length. Sam also had a dark network that he could call on to assist him in the mission, and his most trusted assistant was his lifelong friend, Nate Welsh.

★

A harsh winter was creeping over the northern hemisphere, and it felt even harsher for Caroline as the days passed with no response to the letter she'd sent to Josiah Steele in Sydney.

Was it that Ben was no longer alive, and his father did not have the heart to inform her? Caroline asked herself as she sat by the library hearth in the sprawling old mansion of her husband's estate in the mountains of Bavaria. No, that could not be the answer. She resigned herself to the fact that she would not learn of the fate of the man she truly loved until the terrible war ended. But from the reports she'd gleaned from her husband, things appeared grimmer for Germany as 1916 waned. The United States of America still remained neutral in the conflict, but if for any reason the Americans entered the war on the British and French side, their wealth and powerful industrial base would be formidable.

Two nights later, at a sumptuous dinner the duke was hosting for top German officials, Caroline was privy to an informal discussion. The influential men were discussing the idea of proposing to the Mexican government a plan to invade the south of the USA, allowing them to reclaim old territories which had once belonged to Mexico. Such a venture would draw away any considerations of the United States joining the German enemy allies on the Western Front, where the war would be decided.

In fact, Caroline cared little for all their talk of grand strategy and was, in any case, hardly noticed in their company. Her thoughts concerning Ben's fate had become almost an obsession, and as such she wasn't aware that someone was trying to get her attention.

'Duchess von Hauptmann, can I be so bold as to ask if you are feeling unwell?'

Caroline turned to the army colonel who'd spoken. He was a shortish man in his forties sporting a black eye patch, and he walked with a limp. Caroline had noticed the army officer on a couple of previous visits and knew he was an attaché with one of her husband's high-ranking general staff officers. From the array of his medal decorations, Caroline could see that he was a brave man.

'Thank you for your concern, *Oberst*, but I am well,' Caroline replied.

'I should introduce myself. I am Friedrich Abrahams,' he said with a nod. 'I have noticed from my previous visits that this war might have cost you someone that you love.'

Caroline was impressed by the military man's perceptiveness and warmth. He was not like the other Prussian officers she had met, with their rigid personalities devoted to war. He exuded a genuine warmth which put her at ease. 'I can see that you have been recognised for your courage, *Oberst* Abrahams. I feel your consideration for the feelings of others is not common for a Prussian officer.'

'I am not Prussian, Duchess. I was born in Alsace on the Franco-German border. My mother was French and my father German. Unfortunately, I was born in the wrong place, and it has been a struggle to reach my rank. It has only been this damned war and my luck to survive some dangerous situations that have brought me any real recognition, but some in the army and government still look upon me with suspicion.'

'Because you are Alsatian?' Caroline asked.

'That – and because both my parents were Jews,' Friedrich replied. 'There is a strong anti-Jewish feeling across Europe.'

'I am not one of those who has any animosity towards those of the Jewish faith,' Caroline said.

'I know,' Friedreich said. 'The father of your son is Jewish.'

Caroline almost reeled in stunned surprise before spluttering, 'How could you know that?'

The German colonel glanced around to ensure that their conversation was not being overheard. 'I know your father has a contact in Switzerland who is able to send correspondence to those we consider the enemy.'

'Who are you really?' Caroline asked, this time with a note of suspicion.

'I am a man who loves my country and has given much to protect it,' Friedrich replied. 'But I am aware of the suffering of our people on the home front. I see the gaunt and starving children in the streets and the long lines of ambulances bringing back the shattered bodies of our young men in this never-ending war. There are many in Germany who would like to see the Kaiser call an armistice, but he is being guided by Ludendorff and the military. It is time for a change. I know that by even telling you this I could be endangering myself, and that could lead to a prison cell – or worse. I trust that my knowledge of your past and present situation will protect me from you informing your husband of our conversation. My final goal is to see peace return to Germany.'

Caroline felt her emotions swirling. She loved her country too, and knew that what this decorated soldier was telling her was akin to treason, but the mere fact that he knew so much about her connection to Benjamin Steele was enough to interest her in how he might be able to help her.

'I assure you, Colonel, that I love Germany, but I promise on the life of my son that what you have spoken about with me will remain our secret. I think that you may be in a position to help me with a situation I have concerning the father of my son, and in return I will assist you in any way that I can.' Just as Caroline had finished speaking, she noticed her husband approaching with a glass of champagne in one hand and a cigar in the other.

'Ah, *Oberst* Abrahams, I see that you have met my wife,' he said. 'I hope that Caroline has been an entertaining hostess.'

'Your wife is charming. We were discussing how cold this winter may be based on what we are now experiencing,' Friedrich replied blandly. 'But I must excuse myself as the general appears to be ready to depart for our journey back to Berlin.'

'I hope that we have the opportunity to speak again,

Oberst Abrahams,' Caroline said sweetly, offering her hand in the continental fashion favoured by German aristocracy.

He clicked his heels and bent his head to accept her extended hand. 'God willing, I might have the pleasure of a future invitation to your grand home,' he said. 'Thank you, sir, for the hospitality you have granted to the German army,' he added, addressing Caroline's husband.

He strode away, his limp distinctive. 'If we had more officers like the colonel we would win this war,' Karl remarked. 'He is one of the few who has worked his way up through the ranks to the position he now holds in the intelligence service, despite his Jewish and Alsatian background.'

'A remarkable and brave man,' Caroline answered. 'I hope that he is a guest of ours again.'

Karl sipped from his champagne and, hearing his name called, excused himself. Caroline took a moment to reflect on the short but stunning conversation she had just had with the German intelligence officer. Somehow, she felt that he was the key to finding out what had become of Ben.

★

Josiah rubbed his forehead and sighed. The police were at his door, but not for him. Between two burly uniformed constables stood Marian, her hat askew.

'Mr Steele,' one of the police greeted Josiah. 'We decided that it might be wise to escort your wife home rather than lock her up, in deference to you and your family.'

'Thank you, Constable,' Josiah said. 'I truly appreciate your kind gesture.'

'Very well, Mr Steele, your wife is free to go with you.'

Marian stepped into the residence and stood forlornly, like a school child fronting up to the principal's office, but when Josiah closed the door behind her, her fiery nature soon resurfaced. 'It was not my fault,' she said defiantly. 'It should be all those people supporting the referendum to conscript young men to this brutal and senseless war for Britain – they should be the ones being arrested.'

Josiah ordered a pot of tea and guided his wife into the living room. The complete reversal of Marian's support for conscription had been a surprise, and it had cut her off from many among her circle of friends and in her church. There were still many who supported the concept of compulsory military service to assist the Mother Country in her war against the enemy. One of her close friends had even asked Marian if she was a closet Roman Catholic, as it was well known that the Catholics were against forcing men to be called up. Josiah knew that there were politics at play here; many of those who belonged to the Catholic church in Australia were of Irish descent and hated the British for their brutal occupation of their old country. There had been an uprising the previous Easter, and it had failed as it was not generally supported by the Irish populace. But the summary execution of the leaders of the uprising had changed the minds of many who previously did not support the movement to have the British leave Ireland and let it have its independence. This sentiment had spread to all places where the Irish had emigrated. At the same time, many Irish Catholics had volunteered to fight for Britain in the war and proved to be brave soldiers.

The tea arrived and Josiah poured some for his wife. She took the cup in two hands, and Josiah could see that her hands were trembling. After taking a sip, she explained to Josiah what had happened.

Marian had attended a meeting in a small hall to hear the speakers outline why military service should be voluntary. It was not that they were against opposing the Germans and

Austrians on the battlefield, but that they felt men should be given the choice whether to fight or not. '*Shirkers!*' had been shouted from the back of the hall by a mix of men in army uniform and civilian men and women. Then scuffles broke out and the police were summoned. Marian had been grabbed by a soldier and flung to the floor, but then she had been helped to her feet by another man attending the meeting. She had noticed his scarred face.

'Where?' she had gasped, recognising the still healing wounds.

'Pozières,' he had replied. 'I don't want my brother going over there to fight for the bloody King.'

Josiah had not openly declared whether he was for or against the yes vote as he was in a difficult position with his government contracts. But he had lost a son for the King and fretted that he could lose another in the arid lands of Palestine. He personally did not believe it was right to force men to fight. As he sat with his wife, he realised that the new nation of Australia was bitterly divided on the issue, and blamed the English-loving, Welsh-born prime minister, Billy Hughes, for creating the situation for the upcoming vote in October.

Josiah was furious at the way Marian had been treated by the strangers who had manhandled her at the meeting, and gratitude for the soldier who had helped her. He was angry that she had been put in that situation in the first place. Was it not enough that their two sons had volunteered to fight, with David already killed in action?

THIRTY-SIX

Eight weeks had passed since Sam first formulated his plot to kill Anderson, and now time was running out. A rumour was circulating in his brother's political circles that Sir Horace Anderson was lobbying to have a charge of treason levied against Josiah, despite some reluctance by those in the judiciary to do so. Undaunted, Anderson was slowly but surely gathering support among his anti–Semitic cronies in the federal government in Melbourne.

When Anderson was in Sydney, informants hired by Nate on Sam's behalf had been surveilling his daily routine. Nate then called a meeting to report back to Sam at a pub in The Rocks region of Sydney, an establishment that was frequented by sailors and shady characters linked to the black market, prostitution, extortion and illegal gambling. Any attempt by undercover police to infiltrate the area was easily detected by these shady citizens, so the police were resigned to leaving the area alone, relying instead on their own informants from within the ranks of the city's criminal underworld. Sam and Nate were accepted as patrons of the pub because they were well known as sailors, and rumours that they were dangerous men were enough to garner the respect of the regular clientele.

Nonetheless, both men were aware that police informants might be lingering within the walls of the smoke-filled public bar, so they sat in a corner at a battered and wobbly table with their heads together, pretending a casual ease they did not feel.

'The bastard likes little girls,' Nate spat. 'One of our boys has tracked him to a tenement house in the city known for housing kids who work as prostitutes, where he goes whenever he is in Sydney. On top of that, it seems that Anderson is the landlord of a block of tenements in a slum area who is known to kick out the families of diggers killed overseas. He's a real bastard.'

Sam's blood ran cold. He knew of the practice of child prostitution of both sexes driven by poverty and desperation, and remembered how he felt about protecting his own more fortunate children.

'That alone is enough reason to kill the low bastard,' Sam snarled.

'The place he visits is in an area where people don't talk to the coppers,' Nate said, taking a swig from the beer in front of him. 'We could run him down and it would look like an accident.'

'Bloody perfect!' Sam exclaimed. 'One less piece of human waste gone from this world. We know he is back in Sydney, so it is now or never. I have good news for you, too – when we complete our mission, the *Ella* sails again.'

Nate grinned. 'I'm a pretty bad driver. I think that I should be behind the wheel for the job.'

'I know where we can get our hands on a lorry,' Sam said. 'And while I appreciate your offer, I will be with you for this one.'

It escaped neither man that they were planning to commit murder but, in their eyes, this was natural justice for a man the law could not touch. The fact that the so-called respected knight of the realm had been involved in the death of Sam's brother-in-law and best friend years earlier, coupled with the man's desire to destroy Josiah, was reason enough for Sam. But the fact that Anderson was also a man who preyed on innocent children justified the killing beyond any doubt in Sam's eyes.

Before they had finished their second round of beers the time, date and place for the death of Sir Horace Anderson had been decided. His death sentence was now a reality.

★

The letter addressed to Caroline was hand-delivered by a partially crippled former soldier who did not remain to talk with her. The contents explained that it was important that Caroline travel with her husband to Berlin within the week, where she would be approached by a man she knew.

It was all very mysterious, and for a moment the duchess considered that maybe she was being drawn into an action that would be considered treason by her government. But if it meant learning the fate of the man she continued to love, then Caroline decided it was worth the risk. She knew she could not go on living a lie for the sake of her son. She felt as if she was dying a little each day and yearned to be free to share the future with Ben and Sebastian.

Karl was pleased to have his wife accompany him to

Berlin as she had proved her role as an intelligent and entertaining partner in his dealings with his military and civil service colleagues. Leaving Sebastian at home in the care of a maidservant, they reached the city within the day in their chauffeured limousine, and Caroline was shocked to observe how much life in the capital had changed from the prewar days of colour and gaiety. Now everywhere she looked she saw crippled uniformed soldiers on the streets, and the pinched faces of women and children in rags suffering from hunger and shivering as they huddled together in the cold sleet, begging for food or money.

'Damned beggars!' Karl snarled. 'The police should arrest them. They give the impression that Germany is suffering from the war.'

Caroline turned away from the sights of despair and bit down her contempt for her husband's comment. He was of military age but used his aristocratic connections to ensure he was protected from serving on the battlefields. In addition, he was thriving on war profits. Caroline assumed the same situation applied to their enemies, where the rich got richer living decadent lives away from the death of war while the nation's working classes were fed into the carnage to die, come home crippled or simply lose their minds from what they had experienced. Sadly, she suspected it was in Ben's nature to put his life on the line as a patriot of his country. Was he on the Western Front? Caroline did not consider it could be anywhere else but was vaguely aware Germany was also sending troops to Africa and Palestine.

They arrived at one of the grand hotels in the city, which was mostly occupied by high-ranking army staff and naval officers, a few accompanied by their families.

After being escorted to their room, Caroline excused

herself from going to that evening's engagement with Karl, saying she was not feeling well after the long journey. He was annoyed but left shortly afterwards, leaving Caroline to ponder what would happen next.

She did not have to wait long before a hotel employee knocked on the door with a note on a silver platter. Caroline thanked the old man and closed the door before opening the small envelope. The note contained only a place to meet and a time. The address was vaguely familiar, heightening her curiosity.

*

Caroline arrived at the address on the outskirts of the city centre in a taxi and stepped out into the bitter cold. She now recognised the address as that of one of her father's offices.

No sooner had she entered the building than she saw her father and her heart skipped a beat.

'Caroline, my little princess,' he said with a warm smile. 'It is so good to see you. How is my little prince, Sebastian?'

Caroline was confused. How had this intrigue led her to her own father?

She stammered a greeting in return and then asked quietly, 'Why are we meeting? What do you have to do with *Oberst* Abrahams?'

'I will answer all your questions in my office,' Manfred von Neumann answered, then lowered his voice. 'When I do, you will know why we have chosen you to help us in our mission to secure an armistice.'

Caroline allowed herself to be steered into her father's office, where he closed the door behind them and they took a seat on either side of the large desk.

'What mission?' Caroline asked when she was sure no one else was in earshot. 'I have only agreed to assist *Oberst*

Abrahams if he is able to ascertain whether the real father of your grandson is alive or dead.'

'We have contacts who can help you with that question,' her father replied. 'But first, I need your agreement to help us.'

'Help you do what?'

'Help bring peace to our beloved Fatherland before it is destroyed by the Prussian dictators who hold sway over our Kaiser. Already there are rumblings on the streets from workers seeking a truce with the British and French, and if we do not do that now there is a very strong possibility the Americans might enter the war on the British and French side. If they do so, it would tip the balance against us and lead to a total defeat which will demand unconditional surrender. I am not a military man who understands grand strategy, but I am a businessman who understands the industrial power of the Americans to out-produce us in war. Better an armistice than an unconditional surrender.'

'How can I help do that?' Caroline asked. 'I am hardly in control of my own life, let alone anything else.'

'You are married to a very influential man in the Kaiser's court, and you may be able to persuade your husband with sound logic of the benefits of ceasing this needless bloodshed. In our family alone we have lost our plantations in the Pacific, and our other business interests are being strangled by blockades and lack of trade. I will have nothing left to leave you and my grandson if this senseless war continues. It is not treason for you to work with us but true patriotism towards the masses of German citizens who you know are suffering. All we ask is that you attempt to sway your husband's thoughts on seeking an armistice.'

Caroline could see that her father was motivated more by financial aims to have the war end than humanitarian ones, but bringing about its end would improve the situation on both fronts. The war had raged for over two years and neither side had anything to show for it. For a moment Caroline knew why she had always loved her aloof father. Regardless of his motivations, he was a brave man to enter into a covert venture for peace which most would regard as treasonous.

'I will do what you ask, if you will agree to try to discover if your grandson's father is alive or dead,' she repeated, and her father nodded. The conversation was over, and he invited her to share rare real coffee with him and not a tasteless substitute.

★

It was a hot and humid summer's day in Sydney and Josiah was having a strong cup of tea and fresh buttered scones when the afternoon newspaper was delivered to him by his butler. Josiah unfolded it, expecting to see the daily updates of the war on the other side of the world covering the front page.

But he was wrong.

Sharing the front-page war news was the announcement that a well-known citizen, Sir Horace Anderson, had been callously run down in a motor vehicle accident in the early hours of the morning. It was written that the suburb where Anderson owned many properties had been the scene of the hit-and-run incident and so far, the investigating police had very little to go on as no witnesses had come forward – and nor was there any trace of the vehicle, although it was suspected to have been a motor lorry. It was said that the knight had not died immediately from his many injuries but succumbed a short while later in hospital. He had been unable to give any information about the incident.

Anderson dead!

Josiah felt a rush of blood to his head. He had no doubt that his brother was behind the 'accident'. He saw that Sam had picked his ground well for the killing – as any military man would an ambush – and had no doubt that the lorry would never be found, and no one would ever come forward with information.

With Anderson gone, the threat of Josiah's being charged with treason would now be dead in the water.

'Your brother is here, Mr Steele,' the butler said, entering the room.

'Show him in,' Josiah said, setting aside the newspaper.

Sam limped in, leaning on his walking cane.

'I can see from the happy expression on your ugly face that you have heard the terrible news of Sir Horace Anderson's unfortunate demise,' Sam said with a wide smile. 'May he rest in peace in hell.'

'You were merely continuing the family tradition of meting out justice to those who thought they were beyond it,' Josiah said. 'I suspect that a cold beer is more fitting for our afternoon tea today,' he added, looking down at his tea.

'Let's just say that it was one of those strange coincidences that a big lorry would come out of the dark on a rainy night,' Sam commented as Josiah retrieved a bottle of cold beer from the icebox in the dining room. Sam accepted it, dismissing any offer of a glass, and took a long swig.

'I am heading down to the pub to join Nate, and you are invited,' Sam said.

'I will have to decline your offer,' Josiah said. 'I have a meeting with a couple of our rabbis this evening.'

'Fair enough,' Sam said, wiping his mouth with the back of his sleeve. 'I will see you before the *Ella* sets sail tomorrow.'

'I will make sure I am at the wharf before you leave,' Josiah said. 'I am sure that we will not have any more visits from the local police.'

'Pretty sure we won't,' Sam said. 'Until tomorrow afternoon.' With a parting wave, Sam made his way to join Nate Welsh at a better class of public house in the city to celebrate.

Part Four

1917

Jerusalem and Beyond

THIRTY-SEVEN

Towards the end of 1917, the Allies were advancing inexorably towards Jerusalem. The Turkish rearguard fought for every yard of the Holy Land, but the British general Edmund Allenby had proved to be a master of desert warfare and ensured modern technology such as armoured cars and aircraft were allocated to his campaign to defeat the Ottoman Empire.

For Ben and his regiment, it was often a heart-rending sight to encounter the wounded and battle-dazed Turkish soldiers left in the wake of their retreat. He and his men would look down with pity on a foe who had proved brave and even respectful towards them – if not always towards the civilians under their rule.

'*Shalom! Shalom! Shalom!*' was often heard coming from the people of the villages they passed through, but there was also always the feeling that they were aliens in the land of the Torah, Bible and Koran.

Over the past year, after the victory at Romani and with the Suez Canal secured, the Allies had advanced into Turkish territory. They had pushed forward doggedly over the months, fighting desperate battles from their saddles and on foot among the dunes. Thirst, lack of sleep, the intense heat, continuous clashes with the retreating Turkish army supported by the Germans and Austrians and – almost the worst thing for some – the lack of tobacco, had plagued them. The copious supplies of captured Turkish cigarettes were much prized after the Turkish supply depots were finally overrun.

Eventually they had finally left the desert behind and entered the more bountiful lands of northern Palestine, where the men of the ANZAC mounted infantry rode through hill villages with red-roofed white houses among orchards of oranges, olives and almonds. The weather was bitterly cold, with the occasional scudding clouds promising badly needed rain. Many of the settlements were bordered with prickly pear cactus and even the occasional stand of gum trees. Ben and his men were amazed to see and smell the Australian eucalyptus trees so far from home, and interested to learn that those villages were mostly occupied by Jews under the protection of the Ottoman Empire. The Turkish government had long realised that by protecting the Jewish population from their Arab neighbours they were able to exhort much-needed taxes from the enterprising people.

Even though the land was completely different from the harshness of the Sinai desert, water was still in high demand. Ben had lost his last two mounts in action and now rode a horse who had decided that he did not like Ben much. But with time and a good supply of oats in his forage nosebag, he gradually changed his mind about his new master. And he wasn't a camel, for which Ben was thankful. Although his mates in the camel corps swore by the big, lumbering animals, Ben was quietly pleased that he had not been selected to join them.

Now, Ben virtually rode alone as Lance Corporal Paul Shepherd had been evacuated to Cairo after shrapnel wounds had shredded his body. All his mates had marvelled that he was still alive when he was snatched from the battlefield and were cheered to hear that he was slowly recovering in a hospital in Egypt.

As Ben rode with his regiment, he thought about how they would be in the streets and narrow alleyways of Jerusalem before Christmas. This was a place he had never expected to lay eyes on, and he wrote home to his family about how strange it would feel to be there. He would see and smell the ancient culture of his ancestors. He often reflected on the fact that the Christian crusaders were back to retake the city so often fought over during the countless centuries of its history.

One evening in November, Ben heard of how their Kiwi brothers had captured Jaffa after a couple of days of fierce fighting with bayonet and bullet. It was good news, but when they rose in the early hours to prepare for the advance, Ben experienced a strange dread. He tried to shake it off, but it would not leave him. It was irrational, he told himself as he swung into the saddle.

They rode through an Arab village where the bodies of Turkish troops were covered in dust and looked like logs. Ben wondered why the Arab inhabitants had not buried them, but did not ask as the villagers were openly hostile towards the Australians. The men of the regiment were glad to leave the village to continue their advance. Eventually in the early afternoon they rode onto a heavily cultivated plain where they could actually see the white-painted town of Jaffa off to their flank, and the tiny villages surrounded by fruit trees all around them.

Then Turkish artillery opened fire on the light horsemen exposed on the flat plain between the hills. Ben's mount reared just as an artillery shell exploded yards from him, and the shrapnel ripped into his body, flinging him from his horse which was also thrashing about on the earth from terrible wounds.

Ben would never reach Jerusalem.

★

A young postal delivery boy arrived on his bicycle at the front door of the Steele mansion the day before Christmas. He was sweating; the ride had been long and even at his young age he was aware of his role in delivering the unwelcome piece of paper informing a loved one of the death or wounding of a son/brother/husband or lover.

A maid answered his knock on the door and confirmed this was the Steele residence. He passed the telegram to her and was glad to depart.

The young maid knew what she held in her hand, and for a fleeting moment she thought about destroying the telegram, knowing the pain she would bring to the family she very much liked for their kindness and generosity towards her own struggling family.

'Was that the mailman?' Marian called from the dining room, and the maid turned to walk inside, her hands trembling as she burst into tears.

'The post boy just delivered this,' she said, handing the telegram in its envelope to Marian.

For a moment Marian stood still, staring at the dreaded

missive and trying to convince herself that it was simply a business communication for Josiah. Then she thanked the sobbing girl and gently told her to go to the kitchen and make herself a cup of tea.

After the maid had left, Marian continued to stare at the envelope in her hand. Maybe she could leave it in her husband's office for him to open, she considered. After all, it was addressed to him. But if it contained the news she most feared, it would not be right to have her beloved husband carry the burden of knowing first.

Marian opened the envelope and could hardly focus on the short sentence.

Her mind went completely blank.

Ben was listed as killed in action.

★

But Ben was not dead. The army had got it wrong in the confusion of casualty reporting.

At the time, Ben hardly remembered the explosion that killed his horse and left him riddled with fragments of shrapnel. He lay in the grass and vaguely recalled a trooper leaning over him, saying the words, 'The sarge isn't goin' to make it.'

The next thing Ben was aware of was the terrible agony inflicted by the ambulance sand cart he was being conveyed in. Every bump sent searing pain through his body until finally he was delivered to a dressing station at nightfall. Here Ben wavered between life and death, coming to only when a medic probed for and removed shards of artillery shell splinters in his body before rebandaging him. Now conscious, he was able to sit up and accept a satisfying meal. The pain was too great to allow him to sleep, so he simply gritted his teeth and tried to rest. Around him other men were fighting for their lives – and some lost the battle before the sun rose again over the Holy Land.

Medical orderlies then transported Ben to a motorised ambulance on a stretcher and it was a long, painful journey to the next stage of his treatment. Ben gripped the stretcher with every jolt and forced himself not to cry out. Blood sloshed around him and the trooper in the stretcher beside him muttered, 'It's been a bloody good ride. Bad women and grog. No regrets.' Minutes later he was dead.

The next stop was the newly established Australian Casualty Clearing Station in Jaffa, which had been captured only days earlier.

Surgeons examined the men on the stretchers when they were carried into a huge dome-shaped place with a glass chandelier hanging from the high ceiling. The floors were of marble and cold, and the vast room was dimly lit, with lighted corridors branching off it where Ben and many other patients on stretchers were left for the night. Ben reflected how strange it was to be in this great room with no sign of the stars overhead, as for so long he had slept under the night sky. But at least he was given a hot meal that evening by the medical orderlies.

The next day Ben's litter was carried once more to a convoy of motorised ambulances and, after another painful journey, they arrived at the town of Ramleh. He and the other patients were carried into an old stone building that Ben thought might have once been a castle, and brought up a spiral staircase that opened onto musty stone passageways with dimly lit cubicles. Ben was taken to one of the stone rooms, where he saw tables surrounded by white-coated doctors. He was surprised to see a captured Turkish doctor bending over wounded Turkish soldiers.

The stretcher-bearers laid Ben's litter on the stone floor,

and it was then that he saw a pretty young Assyrian girl barely in her teens on the litter beside him. For a moment their eyes locked, and Ben felt a surge of pity for the girl. He could clearly see that her back had been torn open by shrapnel. An old, grey bearded village doctor was crouched beside her, tending to her terrible wounds as she moaned in pain. But all he could do was wipe the blood away with water from an earthen clay jar. Tears filled the young girl's eyes as she continued to stare at Ben who, for a brief moment, forgot his own wounds as he was reminded that it was not only soldiers who suffered war but the totally innocent.

Two British doctors went to her side to examine her shattered body, and Ben could see just from their expressions that there was nothing they could do to save her life. They then approached Ben and carefully examined his wounds, ordering a change of bandages after cleansing his many lacerations.

The pattern of the next few days was the same: Ben would be taken in his litter to join a convoy headed for a distant dressing station, gritting his teeth and trying desperately to dissociate his mind from his body as pain racked his body with every bump in the road. When they reached their next medical point, sometimes a building, sometimes rows of tents, Ben would be given a hot meal and have his wounds tended to. On one memorable occasion, Ben was given a fresh orange by a padre. He was never so grateful to be able to eat an orange, despite the constant pain of his wounds.

Finally, the patients were told they would complete their journey by train. For Ben and the others around him the message was greeted with great relief, and they were loaded onto a Red Crescent train captured from the Turks.

Ben was laid in one of the wooden bunks set in rows along the inside of the carriage, and there he saw the young

Assyrian girl lying in the bunk across the aisle. She was still alive and continued to moan in pain and despair. Ben gazed into her fear-filled eyes, guessing that she was near the end of her life. He could hear the muttered words of sympathy for the young girl from the tough soldiers from Britain, New Zealand and Australia around her. She could have been a daughter or sister to every man there, Ben thought, and he pictured his own sisters.

That night, medical orderlies distributed hot cocoa, bread and butter to the wounded. The train sped south through the desert lands and Ben lay staring at the bunk above him, occasionally turning his head to stare into the darkness where the pretty young girl lay. He could not hear her moaning anymore, and sadly guessed why she was now silent.

The following morning the ambulance train reached Kantara on the Suez Canal, and in the morning light Ben could see that the girl had died during the night. He did not know why, but tears welled in his eyes as he was lifted into a litter to be carried from the train carriage. After that he was transported to a huge clearing station he remembered from many months past when they had been stationed on the Suez.

That night Ben was loaded onto another train that took them to Cairo.

It was Christmas Eve when they arrived in Cairo, and Ben was placed in a fresh and airy ward where doctors and nurses gently attended to him.

On Christmas Day a British army doctor with a clipboard returned to Ben's side.

'Sergeant Steele, you are being repatriated home to Australia. The war is over for you.'

Ben fell back against the pillows and wept. He was finally going home and out of the hell of war.

THIRTY-EIGHT

Ben's health improved and, thankfully, there was no sign of serious infection as the days passed on the ship back to Australia.

He knew that it was a waste of time writing a letter with details of his return home as it would probably arrive after he was back in Sydney, so instead he decided to let his arrival be a happy surprise. As he steamed across the Indian Ocean, Ben had no idea that his family were mourning his death.

Josiah was using all his influence with various government departments to try to find out more about his son's death in Palestine, but in the muddle of wartime bureaucracy he was disappointed to learn very little. If the family had received a message from the army that Sergeant Benjamin Steele had been killed in operations near Jaffa, then it must be true, they informed him.

Only his son-in-law Maurice could give Josiah a tiny ray of hope. He had heard of cases in which the report of a soldier's death had been proven to be incorrect as paperwork had a habit of getting lost or simply overlooked on the other side of the world. Josiah understood this to be unlikely but appreciated Maurice's attempt to keep his hopes alive. He decided privately he would refuse to believe Ben was dead until his body was recovered and buried.

However, Ben's sisters mourned, as did Marian, despite her husband's attempts to console her.

'Soon, we will receive a letter from Ben to say his regiment has finally reached Jerusalem,' he would say in a soothing voice as he held her to him. 'Ben is indestructible.'

Marian held no hope. Even the narrow defeat of the referendum calling for conscription, which had forced the Labor prime minister to resign from his party, brought her no consolation now that her own sons were gone.

Deep down Josiah knew that he was simply denying the reality of war – men died. And no letters had arrived at the Steele residence from Ben since the telegram weeks earlier.

★

The winter was bitter in Europe. It was at the end of January 1918 when Caroline finally received news that the man she loved was serving in Palestine with the Australian Light Horse. Her father had contacts in the Swiss Red Cross who had uncovered the information. As far as they knew, Ben was still alive. Caroline finally allowed herself to dream of divorcing her husband and using the family fortune she had secured from her father before the war to reunite with Ben. She dreamed of travelling back to Rabaul and contacting Ben to join her in the paradise they had shared, but Caroline was also pragmatic – the war was far from over.

There were ominous indicators on the German home front of a popular uprising by the Communist cells in the cities in an attempt to overthrow the Kaiser and establish a society influenced by the writings of Karl Marx. With Lenin withdrawing the Russian armed forces from the war in March, the German army command could now bring back a vast number of sorely needed troops to concentrate on the Western Front, prolonging the conflict.

Caroline had been privy to several high-level conversations at her husband's meetings with high-ranking German officers and civil servants at their mansion in Bavaria. There was optimistic talk that a massive operation could be mounted before the Americans arrived in enough force to be effective on the British and French side. The grand strategy would be to split the British from the French and drive the British army back to the coast, and when that happened the war would be over, and the victory would be on the side of Germany and the Austrians.

Caroline passed on all the information she had to her father, who was the conduit to those seeking an armistice. She had also carefully dropped the idea of an armistice into conversation with Karl, to try to gauge how he felt about it, but thus far he had been tight-lipped on the subject.

She had been able to travel to Berlin with Karl again, where she could see that the situation at home had become even more drastic. The British naval blockade of German ports was working, and German civilians were suffering terrible hardships.

On the latest trip, Caroline met her father at his Berlin apartment and they greeted each other warmly. In her loneliness, Caroline was grateful that their mutual mission had drawn them closer together. Manfred von Neumann guided his daughter into a small but comfortable living room where his cook had provided coffee and pastries. Manfred explained that he had given her the afternoon off, leaving Caroline and Manfred alone in the apartment.

'Before we talk of important developments in the current situation of Germany, I would dearly like to hear of my grandson,' Manfred said, pouring coffee for them both.

'Sebastian grows so fast; he is almost four now,' Caroline answered with a warm smile. 'You should visit us more often in Bavaria.'

'Ah, but I wish that I could find excuses to do so.' Manfred sighed, offering his daughter a sweet cake. 'But the situation here is deteriorating despite the reassurances of the Kaiser and his general staff, and the Communists are daring the government to take steps against them in the streets. They fly their red flag and foment trouble among the factory workers, declaring that we need to sweep away the evil capitalists. We agree on one thing, though, and that is that the Kaiser must abdicate and the generals consider an armistice, or the country will find itself in a civil war. I fear for the future of a Communist-ruled Germany. We must convince more people in the government to act towards ending this war, and curtail the Reds' push to rule.'

Caroline had long been fully devoted to seeing an end to the war, and the fact that she now knew for certain that Ben was caught up in it only strengthened her resolve. But she could see that her father was troubled and did not think it was because of his participation in the peace movement.

'Father, I sense that there is something troubling you,' she said, resting her coffee cup on her knee.

Manfred grimaced and sighed. 'There is something that I regret I must tell you,' he said. 'I have heard from my contacts at the Red Cross. Your young man, Benjamin Steele, is recorded as killed in action in Palestine.'

With a jerk of her hand, the cup spilled and fell to the floor, soaking Caroline's long and expensive dress. Caroline's hands flew to her face.

'Are you sure of this?' she gasped.

Manfred squirmed. 'I am afraid that it has been confirmed by the Red Cross in Vienna. His name appeared on the casualty lists.'

For a moment it felt as if a great hole had opened and that Caroline had fallen into a dark abyss. Tears streamed down her pale face. Manfred stood and stepped towards his daughter, enfolding her in his arms.

'I am sorry, my little princess,' he said. 'From what you have told me about him, he was a fine man who you truly loved. I now curse myself for pressuring you into a loveless marriage just to protect our reputations. All that has been swept away by this bloody war.'

Caroline felt numb. Her plan to pass on the latest intelligence she had gleaned through her unwitting husband and his friends did not seem important anymore.

A heavy knocking on the door snapped Caroline out of her grief. It was the kind of knock that spoke of authority.

Manfred broke his embrace of his daughter to go to the front door.

'Count von Neumann,' a loud and menacing voice said. 'You are to accompany us to Tegel Prison for questioning. We believe that your daughter, the Duchess von Hauptmann, is also in your company, and she is to be escorted with you.'

Grief was now replaced with shock and fear as Caroline rose from the couch to join her father. At the door were an army officer and three uniformed police.

'How dare you!' Caroline flared. 'Do you know who we are? Do you know that my husband is one of the Kaiser's most trusted acquaintances?'

Caroline could see that the German officer held the rank of major. He was a thin, balding man in his early thirties and wore spectacles, but it was the iron cruelty in his expression that frightened Caroline.

'I am fully acquainted with who you are, Duchess. Indeed, it is partly due to your husband's assistance that we are here to interrogate you both. We have cars waiting outside.'

Caroline knew that any attempt to flee was out of the question, and experienced a feeling of dread for the fate of her son.

★

The convoy of three automobiles drove through the gates of the Berlin prison as sleet and snow fell on the sombre city.

Caroline was seated beside a uniformed policeman while her father was in another car. In the front passenger seat, the army officer remained silent on the journey through the virtually deserted streets. Caroline still glimpsed a few poverty-stricken families clothed in rags huddling in doorways with pinched and pallid faces.

'I have a son in Bavaria at my husband's estate,' Caroline said, addressing the officer in the front seat of the car. 'I need to be with him.'

'Your husband has assured us your son will be taken care of by his servants,' the officer replied coldly. 'I am afraid he has expressed his shame at what he has perceived to be your treachery towards our Fatherland.'

'What treachery!' Caroline exploded, wondering if her conversations with Karl about a possible armistice had led to this. 'A desire to see this war end? Don't we all wish for that?'

'You have been conspiring with the Communists to

overthrow the Kaiser – and that is treason,' the officer retorted. 'But you will tell us of your contacts in due course. There is nothing else to speak about, Duchess von Hauptmann.'

The vehicles arrived at the entrance and Caroline and her father were ushered into the reception area which was cold and bleak. Caroline shivered, fearing the worst. Would she and her father be subjected to torture? What was to become of her son if she was imprisoned? Who could possibly come to their aid? So many questions and none with an answer.

After Caroline and her father had their details recorded, they were led to separate cells. When the heavy door was closed behind her, Caroline felt utter despair. She had just learned that the man she had always dreamed of being reunited with had been killed, and she had been separated from her son.

The prison was eerily silent, with the exception of the sound of heavy boots trudging the corridor outside her dismal cell. Looking around, Caroline saw the room was furnished only with a thin mattress on the floor, a flimsy, well-worn blanket and a bucket in the corner. The lack of a window meant Caroline had no idea what time it was. Feeling completely numb, all she could do was huddle in a corner, pulling her fur coat tightly around her.

★

On the journey across the Indian Ocean, Ben's wounds healed to the point that he was able to go up on deck and stroll, taking in the fresh sea air, and also chat with other soldiers returning home because of their disabling wounds. Although his own wounds still pained him, he felt thankful they had only left scars when he saw other men who had lost arms, legs or their sight. It was pitiful to see the blind and bandaged men groping their way along the ship's rail. Ben would always step in with, 'Here, cobber, let me give you a hand.'

The food was good on the ship and the nursing staff were angels. The further southwest they steamed, the warmer it became, and Ben recalled they were travelling into a southern summer.

One morning the excited word quickly spread through the steamer that the Australian coast had been sighted. Cheers rose from the throats of the wounded soldiers, and those who could poured onto the decks to see the first sight of a land many had not seen in years.

A fellow sergeant from another Light Horse regiment who Ben had befriended leaned on the rail beside him, but it was a little awkward for the sergeant as he had lost an arm to a Turkish bullet.

'I swear I can smell gum trees,' the sergeant said.

'It's in your bloody imagination, cobber.' Ben grinned, slapping his new friend on the back. 'I'd rather smell a cold beer at my favourite pub in Sydney.'

'We have some good pubs in Adelaide,' the sergeant said. 'And I hope my sheila is still happy to see me, even with one wing missing.'

Ben thought about his statement. How many young men had been so disabled as to have lost their means of earning a living? The country was going to be a different place with such a high percentage of Australia's fittest and bravest gone forever. How many young women would never marry because of the loss of a loved fiancé? How many widows would be forced to scrape a living or to support their children on a meagre army pension?

Coming home would not be easy.

THIRTY-NINE

It was the young maid at the Steele residence who fainted first.

The doorbell rang, and when she answered it she focused on the tall, broad-shouldered soldier standing before her in his slouch hat and she knew that it could only be a ghost. The blood drained from her face.

Ben quickly stepped forward to catch the girl before she hit the floor.

The second person to faint was Marian when she heard the commotion at the front door and hurried to see what had caused it. She saw a face look up to her with a worried smile she immediately recognised.

'Oh, my God!' she uttered before swooning, and Ben quickly stepped over the fallen maid to grasp his mother.

But the third person to appear in the hallway did not faint. 'Damn in hell! You're alive!' Dr Maurice Cohen uttered in a shocked voice, grinning broadly as he leaned on his walking cane now that he'd acquired an artificial leg to help support him. 'I always told your father you were too hard to kill.'

'I think we need your medical services, Captain Cohen,' Ben said, cradling Marian's head in his lap as both the maid and his mother stirred into consciousness.

Maurice stepped forward but was satisfied that as the two women regained their senses, they would not require his medical expertise. The maid was already getting unsteadily to her feet, blinking with disbelief at the familiar sight of Ben Steele, who she had never thought to see again.

Ben was helping Marian up. 'I think we should get you to a chair,' he said, and the maid came to assist him.

'Is it really you, Mr Steele?' the girl asked in awe.

'I hope so,' Ben replied. 'Or I must be at the wrong house.'

'I will have tea fetched to the living room,' the maid said.

'Thank you . . . Iris,' Ben said, quickly remembering the young woman's name.

Marian was not fully alert but allowed herself to be guided into the living room and seated on a couch.

'You could have contacted the family to say you were alive,' Maurice growled.

'Why would I need to tell you I was still alive?' Ben frowned.

'Because the family received a notification that you had been killed in action in Palestine,' Maurice answered. 'After the telegram arrived, we no longer had any letters from you.'

Ben blinked in confusion, and it was his brother-in-law who supplied an explanation. 'Knowing the system as I do, I am guessing the army got it wrong. It would not be the first time. I suggested as much to your father, but of course it was a long shot. I can see you have been injured.'

Ben remembered that he had a large scar above his eye which a former army surgeon would have noticed immediately. 'I was not aware that I had been listed as KIA,' Ben said slowly. 'I thought that I would be home before any letter that I might write would arrive, so naturally I thought a personal appearance would suffice.'

Maurice shook his head and extended his hand. Ben accepted the gesture with a firm grip and was surprised to see that his brother-in-law had tears in his eyes.

'I think my duty is now to telephone your father and the rest of the family to announce your arrival home safe and mostly well,' Maurice said. 'In the meantime, you can answer all your mother's questions – I think she will have many.'

'Thanks, Morrie,' Ben said as Maurice limped away to telephone Josiah at his office.

At the doorway he turned back. 'What was it?' he asked.

'A bloody big Austrian arty shell,' Ben replied. 'I have one or two other scars as well.'

'We were the lucky ones,' said Maurice sadly.

★

That night the house was crowded with Ben's sisters and their families welcoming him home from the ranks of the dead. There were so many questions and hugs, and tears shed for the brother who had not come home, but at the end of the evening it was a quiet conversation between three former soldiers sharing a bottle of Josiah's finest Scotch that mattered the most to Ben. He knew that his father and brother-in-law could relate to his experiences living on the edge of death on the battlefield.

'I almost made it to Jerusalem,' Ben sighed, and Maurice raised his tumbler of Scotch.

'Next year, Jerusalem.'

It was a toast echoed by so many Jewish people across the world.

*

How many days and nights passed in the cell, Caroline wasn't sure. Her only visitors were the guards who brought her meals, which consisted mostly of sauerkraut, sausage and stale bread. She attempted to hang on to the hope that one day this nightmare would end and she would be reunited with Sebastian, but it was hard, and she felt the pull of the inevitable descent into despair.

Eventually she was allowed to shower under the watchful eye of a female prison guard and issued a prison dress. It was always cold in the prison and silence was enforced, but occasionally on her escorted release from the cell she would pass by other cells, where she glimpsed gaunt prisoners being prepared for an interrogation. Caroline desperately sought out her father, but she never saw him.

The gradual change of seasons and increasing warmth let Caroline know that the months were passing, but how long had she been a prisoner? The guards kept their strict silence so she had no way of knowing for sure. Any hope she had clung to was now turning to despair that she would never see her father or son again in her lifetime.

However, Caroline began to notice that over time she was slowly being granted small privileges. There was also an older guard, an ex-soldier, who she sensed was sympathetic towards her, and she began to talk to him. Before long, he began to reply, and they formed a friendship of sorts. It was through this guard that she was able to discover that there was someone on the outside ensuring she was not mistreated. When one day Caroline commented that the weather had started to turn cool again, her guard friend told her it was November in the year 1918. These small interactions sustained Caroline, but she knew she could not keep any hope alive forever.

On one of the long nights, she was woken in her dimly lit cell by a couple of grim-faced guards and informed that she was to go with them. Fear coursing through her, Caroline was escorted between the two guards to a bleak, windowless room where she saw the major who had been with the arresting party sitting behind a table. There was an empty chair arranged opposite him, and she was commanded to sit.

The German army officer was immaculately dressed and for a moment Caroline felt the shame of her dishevelled and gaunt appearance.

'It is not important that you know my name or unit,' the major finally said. 'What is important is that you provide a list of all those among the traitors to the war effort you have been in contact with. Your father has already cooperated and his assistance to us has been noted. Now I require you to assist us so that you may avoid the death sentence for treason.'

The words hardly impacted Caroline. Was this a ruse by the man sitting opposite her to pressure her to reveal all she knew, which was not much anyway?

'If my father has provided names then you do not need my cooperation,' Caroline replied defiantly. 'I do not know why I am even here.'

The officer sighed and stood up from the table. It was an intimidating gesture that worked, sending a shock of fear through Caroline.

'I regret that you are here, Duchess,' he said. 'But I have a duty to protect the Fatherland from people who would design to bring our nation to its knees from within when the sons of the Fatherland are sacrificing their lives to protect us from our enemies. I consider that you have been deluded by the fools who think that their attempts to force an armistice will bring an end to our war against the English and French, and now the Americans as well. We have a surge of social discontent in the streets of Berlin because of people like you and those you collaborate with. But your family has influential friends in the Kaiser's court and that is why we have only been able to detain you, even though I consider you a dangerous enemy to our Kaiser.'

'I am a daughter of the Fatherland and I only desire what is best for the people,' Caroline replied to the tirade, trying to stop her voice from shaking. 'I now only wish to be reunited with my son, and for the release of my father who has been falsely imprisoned somewhere within this prison's walls.'

Just before the officer could respond to this, a guard entered the room and the major glanced at him with an annoyed expression. The guard took the officer aside and said something that caused the interrogator to turn pale before returning his attention to Caroline.

'I am afraid our conversation must end there. Guards, have this traitor taken to her cell.'

As Caroline was being escorted back to her cell, she noticed that there was a different mood among her gaolers. The guards were agitated and whispered among themselves, but they said nothing to her. Just as she reached her cell, she was startled to see a face from the past standing with four army soldiers. *Oberst* Friedrich Abrahams nodded to her and turned his attention to the two escorting guards.

'The Duchess von Hauptmann is to be released into my custody under orders issued by the supreme military

command.' He held out a sheet of impressive stamped official papers. The guards glanced at them and then at each
other, then pushed Caroline towards Friedrich, whose stern
expression did not change as the sullen guards retreated.

'Come, Duchess,' Friedrich said quietly, taking her
elbow and guiding her down the corridor in the direction
from which Caroline had first entered almost a year earlier.
'The situation in Germany is in turmoil. The Kaiser has
fled the country for the Netherlands and the imperial navy
has mutinied in support of him.' They reached the front
entrance, where the guards did not attempt to interfere.

'My father?' Caroline asked when they had cleared the
main building and she saw the staff car waiting.

'I am sorry, Caroline,' Friedrich replied. 'But it appears
from the official report that your father died of pneumonia a
month ago. It does not surprise me that they did not inform
you of his death.'

Caroline wanted to weep in her grief, but her tears had
dried up long ago. She was helped into the vehicle and
Friedrich sat beside her, but her thoughts were now totally
focused on finding her son, Sebastian.

★

Ben's return to Australian shores was not what he expected.

His physical health returned, leaving observable scars on
his body including the one where a shard of shrapnel had
gouged a furrow over his eye. But it was the mental injuries
that could not be seen that Ben fought to heal.

When he closed his eyes at night, terrible dreams would
haunt him and Josiah and Marian would hear him call out
in his sleep. Josiah understood the nightmares as he had
suffered the same thing after returning from Afghanistan
and Africa.

During the day, Ben experienced mental shifts between depression and guilt. He was still alive when so many good men he knew had been killed. He began drinking heavily to assuage the pain, and only visited the doctors employed by the Repatriation Department for his physical assessments.

Ben could not rationally explain why he had a desire to return to his regiment, which was still overseas on active service, but he wanted a medical clearance to do so and only had six months to prove that he was fit for active service again before he might be permanently discharged from the army. Eventually he was granted a medical clearance, and by the end of June he found himself once again back on duty, with a promotion to the rank of Squadron Sergeant Major. He declined an offer to attend officer training and be granted a commission, fearing that the training would take too long and he would not be back in the saddle with his regiment in the dying months of the war.

By November he was pleased to see that he would rejoin his regiment overseas to ride with them in battle again.

And then it happened.

The war was over.

There was no longer a need for the soldiers and sailors to remain in service, and the demobilisation of the Australian armed forces began. This time Ben looked forward to his discharge from army service, as with no war to fight he could not envisage continuing with the restrictive, disciplined life of a soldier in the army.

But what next?

The answer was obvious. He would use his family's money to go in search of the woman he loved and their child, no matter what obstacles he might encounter.

It was summer in Australia when 1919 dawned across the world and, as if four years of war was not enough, a terrible and invisible new enemy had arrived to wreak an even greater death toll than all the years of the Great War on the battlefields.

The deadly touch of the so-called Spanish Influenza reached every man, woman and child on earth, and Ben feared that it would threaten the lives of Caroline and his child before he could find them. He began to despair that fate was cruelly against him in his quest to be with the only woman he had ever loved. She might even now be dead from the pandemic of influenza sweeping the world, he thought.

Ben had reached the lowest ebb of his life, and had no ambition to continue living.

FORTY

By the end of 1919, although the terrible influenza outbreak continued to ravage the world's population, it was now being controlled by strict quarantine rules in Australia.

So far Ben's family had been spared – with the exception of his youngest sister, Rose, who had lost her husband to the fatal virus.

Josiah was able to continue his enterprises from his office in Sydney, and on a hot summer's day leading up to Christmas, Ben stood beside his father's desk for a conversation both men knew they needed to have.

'I know that you would like to see me take a seat at the board and eventually take over from you, Father,' Ben said to Josiah. 'But we both know that I am not really cut out to be a leader in your world of finance. David was the man to continue the family business.'

Josiah sighed. He knew that his youngest son was right. There was no longer a male heir to take the reins after him, and neither of his daughters had any desire to step forward. Josiah faced the reality that his busy enterprises would have to be sold when he eventually passed away. Then, faceless people would take over the many companies across the numerous fields of business endeavour that had made the Steele family so well known and Josiah a leading philanthropist in society.

'I know from friends that you are still attempting to discover the fate of your countess,' Josiah said gently. 'I also know that Germany is in turmoil and the British naval blockade continues to starve the German population. Germany is crushed, and this insidious disease is killing so many over there. As sad as the situation is, I think that you should consider moving on in life.'

Ben frowned. 'Would you move on if there was a woman you have always loved somewhere out there, and possibly a child too?' he replied.

'I do understand,' Josiah replied gently. 'It is not in the family tradition to give up despite the odds. The last correspondence I have had from the Red Cross is that they do not have any knowledge of a Caroline von Neumann, but you have my full support to keep looking.'

'Thank you, Father,' Ben said, feeling a surge of love for this remarkable man. He turned to look out the window. 'I should go down to the wharf to meet Uncle Sam. I heard that the *Ella* is back from her tour of the Pacific,' he said.

'It will be good to have him home for a while,' Josiah said, returning to his big desk scattered with files and papers. 'His children miss him.'

Ben took a lift downstairs to the foyer and stepped out onto the street. There were fewer pedestrians these days and a combination of horse-drawn wagons and private motor vehicles. All those Ben passed wore white surgical masks. As it was only a ten-minute walk to the wharf where the *Ella* was usually located, Ben set out on foot, enjoying the balmy summer's day, but as he strolled to meet his uncle and Nate, Ben's mind was a swirl of plans to find Caroline and his child. He still did not even know if it was a boy or a girl, or if they had survived, let alone their name. How old would the child be now? About four? Five?

Finding them was the only thing that gave Ben's life any meaning.

★

That evening the family gathered at Josiah and Marian's house to welcome Sam home. All attended, including his children, Georgette and Saul, Ben, Judith and Maurice, and even Rose, despite still being in mourning for her late husband. They dined together and Josiah gazed down the table at his family, reflecting on how the descendants of Ian Steele had multiplied, enjoying the comfortable life he had established from the looting of a Russian baggage train during the Crimean War three-quarters of a century ago.

Josiah thought that his father would have been fiercely proud of the descendants he had provided the world. Maybe Ben still carried the spirit of Ian Steele, Josiah thought as he turned his attention to his youngest son. Or Josiah's brother, Sam, did. Maybe even Josiah himself.

After dinner the women gathered to share family news while Josiah, Sam, Maurice and Ben retired to the garden to enjoy the slightly cooler evening air and share a cold beer. They gazed down on the harbour which was dotted with small boats and larger watercraft. Josiah produced cigars and the four men sat on garden benches enjoying the serenity.

Josiah was aware that they all shared the common bond of having served as soldiers in a war zone at one time or another in their lives.

'To my much loved and brave brother, David,' Ben said solemnly, raising his glass of beer. 'I wish you could have been with us tonight.'

The sombre toast was echoed by the others, and then they settled into discussing current affairs. Maurice had returned to practising medicine but still struggled to cope with his experiences on the battlefields of the Western Front, while Ben kept his experiences to himself. Neither mentioned the war very often.

'I think it's time I gave up my berth on the *Ella* and remained home with my kids,' Sam said unexpectedly. 'I hardly know them, and I know that they want me to be with them. Now that Keith has retired and Nate has accepted the job as captain, I know our *Ella* is in good hands, but I'd feel even better if one of the family still had a hand in the business. Besides, the *Ella* is getting old and needs a gentle hand sailing the Pacific.' He glanced at Ben, whose interest he knew his statement would pique. 'You have any thoughts about your future, Ben?'

Josiah looked at his son's thoughtful expression. 'I think Ben would be just the man to skipper the schooner,' Josiah said, despite knowing that his youngest son was still obsessed with searching for Caroline and their child. Was this a possible way of distracting Ben's aspirations in a hopeless quest?

Ben stood and walked a short distance away, with his back to his father, uncle and brother-in-law.

'It might be a good idea to give it a go,' Maurice prompted him. 'Your father has told me about your search for Caroline and your child, but a short break at sea might be what the doctor ordered . . . at least this doctor.'

383

Ben turned, a pained expression on his face. 'Perhaps just for one trip,' he answered. 'But when this bloody flu has abated, I will continue with my search.'

'Do you have any objections to taking the *Ella* back to Rabaul?' Sam asked. 'We have a contract to take supplies to our government administration in New Britain. I know the place holds memories for you, both good and bad.'

'Why not?' Ben replied, shrugging his shoulders. 'It's just another port in the Pacific Islands.'

'Good,' Sam said. 'In that case, you have twenty-four hours to pack and be down at the wharf. Nate will run over matters with you, and you will be the overall boss of the mission, but the command of the schooner will be in Nate's hands.' Sam looked very satisfied. 'Now I can reassure my kids that their old man is home to stay for good. I am sure that my big brother will find me a job ashore.'

Ben had agonised over his decision to return to the sea, but after so many years of only seeing a sea of sand, the idea of being in a world of water had its appeal. Besides, until the epidemic afflicting the world was over, he had little chance of travelling to Europe in his search for Caroline and their child. The break might be good for the soul, away from the memories of the blood-soaked desert and his lost mates.

With the matter settled, Josiah, Maurice and Sam finished their beers and went inside to rejoin the rest of the Steele clan, leaving Ben to sit alone and stare at the harbour below, his thoughts on the future.

*

In an office with a view over an avenue of coconut palms sat former light horseman officer George Martin-Smith, who was working for the Australian administration of New

Britain, an island formerly ruled over by the now non-existent German empire.

Martin-Smith was pleased that he had been posted to the tropical island. He had resumed his position in the public service with a promotion after returning from the Great War, and was enjoying living in Rabaul, which showed little sign of the campaign waged there in September 1914.

A few German expatriates had returned in an attempt to pick up where they had left off before the war, and were pleased to find that the Australian government held some sympathy for their plight. They accepted that these former enemy civilians were experienced in managing copra production and would be an asset to revenue raising.

But George had not completed his task of processing a German plantation owner when one of his aides entered and announced a most unexpected visitor. He showed in a former German naval officer who, it appeared, had come out of the rugged hinterland to finally surrender himself after years of living with natives sympathetic to the Kaiser. *Oberleutnant zur See* Kurt Jäger stood before George unbowed, his head held high, and wearing what was left of his tattered uniform. He was barely a skeleton, gaunt from bouts of malaria, George assumed, but his blue eyes shone with defiance behind his deep suntan. The only clean item he carried was his Mauser rifle, which he ceremoniously handed to George's aide.

'Well, Herr Jäger, your adventure of holding out on an island occupied by my government for the last few years is an extraordinary one,' George said, staring at the man in front of him. There had been rumours, mostly dismissed as tall tales by the local natives around Rabaul, of a German soldier attempting to organise a resistance against the invaders. But here he was now, in the flesh, surrendering after the news had finally reached him that Germany had signed an armistice and the western European powers were now at peace.

'I must say I salute your courage and perseverance considering the hopeless situation that you found yourself in,' George continued. 'We will send telegraphic news of your survival to Berlin, but in the meantime, you are a free man.'

'I thank you for your courtesy, Herr Martin-Smith, but I am keen to journey back to Hamburg and rejoin my navy, as I have never left it.'

'I am sure that we can expect an answer in due course. I know of a German family who could can take you in until we receive word from your naval superiors. I will speak to my aide about making the arrangements. You are free to go, *Oberleutnant.*'

Kurt clicked his heels, bowed slightly to George and marched smartly out of the office. George leaned back in his chair, the fan swirling lazily above him, and considered the formal surrender he had just taken from the German. He wondered if he would have made the same choice back in 1914, if the shoe was on the other foot: to withdraw to the rugged hills of the island, leading a life of great hardship in the jungle, motivated only by the burning ambition to lead a native counterattack against the occupying forces.

'Deserves a bloody medal from his government,' George muttered as he looked down at the papers on his desk. He sighed when he saw the file of applications that concerned returning property to former German owners who had lived on the island they once knew as Neu-Pommern. He started to go through the applications, and raised his eyebrows when he saw one that was slightly different from the others he had processed.

'Mr Martin-Smith,' a junior public servant wearing the traditional white tropical suit said as he entered the office. 'Just a reminder that your friend, a Mr Benjamin Steele, should be arriving in Rabaul in the next forty-eight hours, according to the telegram we received from Townsville.'

'That's right,' George said. 'I am looking forward to catching up with him. He saved my life back in Egypt, you know.'

The young public service clerk feigned interest, but he had been too young to serve in the war and the comment by his superior meant little to him.

George returned his attention to the paperwork on his desk and frowned. There was something unusual about this applicant, but he would still arrange a meeting.

★

Ben stood at the bow of the schooner as it entered the deepwater harbour of Rabaul under the shadow of the surrounding active volcanoes. It was a beautiful, balmy tropical day and the sun shone warmly.

The wharf was within sight as Nate skilfully kept the schooner under full sail until the last moment, when the crew of Pacific Islanders commenced altering the tack to glide towards the wharf under part sail.

Ben felt a strange mix of emotions. He was pleased to see the place that had marked the beginning of his journey during the war years, and yet deeply saddened to know that this was where he had lost the most precious person in his life: the woman who had borne him a child.

As the schooner approached, three figures stood out on the wharf watching the *Ella* manoeuvring towards the pier. Ben shaded his eyes with his hand and could make out that they were a man, a woman and a child, possibly a young boy. The man he recognised as his former commanding officer, Lieutenant George Martin-Smith, who Ben had learned before leaving Sydney was now a public servant stationed at Rabaul.

The woman had fair skin and streaks of grey in her long hair which was piled in a bun. She was holding the boy's hand.

A shock ran through Ben and then utter disbelief swept over him as realisation dawned. He stood transfixed, afraid to allow himself to believe his eyes as the schooner drew ever closer to the wharf and the three figures came more clearly into view. It could not be possible. Surely the woman just reminded him of the past he'd once known at Rabaul?

'Ben!' His name on the woman's lips drifted faintly towards him on a gentle breeze.

Ben began to shake, and fought to keep himself from fainting. Then, as the side of the schooner slapped the wharf, he did not hesitate. He leapt from the deck to walk unsteadily towards the three people waiting for him, never taking his eyes off the woman with her child.

'Caroline,' he struggled to say, and then no words were needed. When he was within an arm's length he embraced Caroline with all his strength.

'Ben, it is you!'

'Pleased to see that I could repay an old debt, Sergeant Steele,' said George with a delighted grin, not daring to interrupt the reunion. 'I believe that you know the duchess, but not her son.'

The little boy was looking up at Ben, a slight frown on his face, obviously confused by the situation.

'Ben, my sweet darling, meet your son, Sebastian,' Caroline said, tears of joy running down her cheeks. Then she knelt and spoke in German to the boy, who looked up at Ben in wonder.

Ben could only stare at the child, whose small face was both achingly familiar and totally new to him. He knelt down and smiled at the boy. 'Hello, Sebastian. I am looking forward to getting to know you.'

The boy might not have understood Ben's words, but he rewarded him with a grin.

'We are back in our paradise, as it was always meant to be,' Caroline said, not attempting to wipe away her tears as Ben stood once more and took her hands in his. 'Mr Martin-Smith is going to arrange the return of my family's plantation and I will need a competent manager and husband to help me run it.'

The long years of separation were exorcised instantly as the ghosts of August vanished for Ben. Joy bubbled up inside him as he realised he had finally come to learn the true meaning of paradise: it was not simply a place on earth but a condition of the human spirit.

EPILOGUE

When released from Tegel Prison, Caroline had been able to reunite with her son with the assistance of *Oberst* Friedrich Abrahams. Caroline discovered her husband Karl had become a casualty of the epidemic and thus she was a widow. Sebastian was in the care of her husband's staff when Caroline found him.

Most of her father's fortune was gone, confiscated by the government before the end of the war, but Caroline was able to sell enough hidden family jewellery to pay her passage out of a Germany racked by civil disruption as Communists fought bands of returned soldiers on the streets. The British naval blockade continued starving thousands of women and children to death while the victorious Allied forces plotted the gutting of the German economy in revenge for the war that had in turn crippled them.

In the turmoil, Friedrich helped Caroline take tortuous

passage on cargo ships with the view of returning to one of the last family-held properties that remained in the renamed New Britain. She had heard that the Australian government was sympathetic to previous owners reclaiming plantations, but also that this was not guaranteed and there would be many bureaucratic obstacles.

She had only been on the island for a week when Ben arrived, but with the help of his former light horse officer they were able to send a flurry of telegrams to Sydney to request that the plantation be purchased by the Steele enterprises portfolio of properties. Permission was granted, and the couple prepared to move back to the place where they had been happiest so that Ben could become acquainted with his young son.

★

Kurt Jäger finally reached Germany and immediately reported for duty. He was received as a hero for his resistance in the jungles of New Britain and was promoted to *Kapitänleutnant* in recognition of his refusal to surrender. Kurt did not hesitate to volunteer for service with the German navy when its surrendered ships of war were forced to steam to Scapa Flow in the Scottish northern islands.

There the grand fleet was anchored, awaiting the decisions of the committees of the Versailles Treaty in Paris to decide their fate. The Allied countries pushed for the fleet to be handed over to their respective navies, while Britain demanded that all the German naval ships should be forfeited to them.

Aboard his flagship in Scapa Flow, the German admiral Ludwig von Reuter sat in his cabin, morosely reflecting on the dishonour he felt at seeing his ships become the spoils of war. He was a proud man who loved his country above all, and the thought that he would be remembered for passively leaving his beloved ships in the hands of former enemies was unbearable. For the months they had been forced to anchor in Scapa Flow, none of the German crew had been allowed ashore, and the rations sent to them by lighters were minimal. Already the crew were split, with many raising the red flag of Communism.

The German admiral knew that he had another option. A knock on his door roused him from his dark thoughts. He bade his trusted officer to enter, and Kurt stood to attention before him.

'Tomorrow, we put my plan into action,' the admiral said in a tired voice. 'I trust that you will pass on my command to every ship's captain?'

Kurt felt a surge of pride. He might have missed the war at sea and the battle of Jutland, but now they would show the British and their allies that the German navy could defy their shameful surrender with one last desperate act. When Kurt left the admiral's office, he hurried to have the message passed on to all German ships at anchor.

The next day the crews of the few remaining British warships were stunned to see the big German battleships slowly sinking. All means of allowing water in were employed; from the opening of sea cocks to torpedo tubes and portholes.

Panic gripped the remaining British naval crews as they watched the great warships slowly sinking.

The main British fleet had steamed out earlier to engage in torpedo practice, leaving only a handful of warships to guard the anchored German fleet. What ships the British naval command could muster set out to intercept the German sailors rowing away from their sinking ships towards the shore, and orders were bellowed for the

German sailors to return to their sinking ships, but they were ignored.

Kurt was in charge of his lifeboat as a small warship cut across his bow, with an officer using a megaphone ordering him to turn about. But Kurt was defiant and refused to do so and then his lifeboat was raked with machine-gun fire, which ripped through the densely packed sailors in the exposed open boat.

Three bullets tore into Kurt's body, and he tasted the blood in his mouth. Someone was holding him and cursing the British as Kurt died.

He was one among the last nineteen Germans to die seven months after the war had ended. It was a final defiant gesture of German naval pride.

AUTHOR'S NOTE

I have always found an interest in those long overlooked or virtually forgotten aspects of our history. On ANZAC Day we remember the landings at Gallipoli, but most are ignorant that a mere matter of weeks after war was declared in August 1914, we also undertook a coastal landing to our north. It was not a campaign on behalf of the British empire but a preemptive strike to defend our own eastern shores against the possibility of a German naval bombardment, as outlined in a prewar operational plan by the German Imperial Navy. A copy of that plan can be found in an internet search with translation.

I have attempted to briefly describe what might be considered a skirmish, but it did cost the lives of Australian soldiers and sailors and the loss of an Australian submarine, the *AE1*, which was only recently discovered with its crew still entombed. The scenes described are from eyewitness accounts. To commemorate our first Great War casualties, I have mixed fictional characters with real historical heroes.

It is recorded that one German officer refused to surrender and only emerged from the jungles of New Britain at the end of the war. I have used author's licence to make this the fictional character of *Oberleutnant zur See* Kurt Jäger.

The events of the war on the Western Front fought by Captain David Steele are lifted from the pages of a book written by a truly great commander I had the honour of serving with in my Army Reserve unit, the 1/19 Royal New South Wales Regiment – the Bushmen's Regiment. The author is Lieutenant Colonel Peter McGuiness MBE, RFD, ED, and the title of the book is *Boldly and Faithfully: The Official History of the 19th Australian Battalion, March 1915 – October 1918.*

An overlooked campaign fought in the deserts of Egypt and Palestine by the Australian Light Horse in company with the New Zealand Mounted Infantry and the British Yeomanry mounted troopers was critical to the eventual victory by the Allied forces, and yet most Australians only know about a charge at Beersheba.

To illustrate the harsh conditions of our light horsemen I have directly used the personal experiences of one of our greatest authors, Trooper Ion Idriess, as recorded in his greatest story, *The Desert Column.* Wounded twice, once at Gallipoli and again in Palestine, he was discharged after the Great War to live a life of total adventure, and he continued to record colourful and exotic stories of our frontiers.

As a young person growing up on a soldier settler block, I devoured as many of his books as I could, and I now realise that we had a bit in common. We were both born on 20 September in Sydney, albeit a few years apart, and we both enlisted in the army in Queensland during a time of military conflict. I often think that the ghost of the great Aussie author guides my stories.

All the events written in these pages reflect the direct experiences of Ion Idriess, lifted from his book recording his experiences in Gallipoli and Palestine as told through my fictional character of Sergeant Ben Steele. Whereas the taking of the wells at Beersheba was a tactical victory, the defence of the Suez Canal was a strategic victory ensuring that the vital waterway did not fall into the hands of the Ottoman Empire. Had the combined force of British and ANZACs not stopped the massive attack, then the cutting off of essential supplies to Britain might have had a disastrous outcome for the Allied forces in the Great War.

Idriess was eventually recognised for his contribution to Australian storytelling with an Order of the British Empire. Idriess expresses his great respect for the Turkish soldiers the ANZACs fought against and held little animosity towards their enemy.

I should note that we have an equivalent of *The Desert Column* in a recent work concerning the Vietnam War, in the form of a day-to-day record of life of an Australian battalion that fought the battle of Long Tan. That book is *Mentions in Dispatches* by former National Service officer, Dave Sabben, MG – Medal of Gallantry. An internet search provides information on Dave's historical record.

LEST WE FORGET

ACKNOWLEDGEMENTS

A special thank you to my publisher, Alex Lloyd, and editor, Brianne Collins. Also a thank you to editor Grace Carter, proofreader Annika Tague, designer Deborah Parry, publicity and marketing director Tracey Cheetham, publicist Dave Cain, marketer Tom Evans, marketing designer Isabel Moon, and the tireless sales team at Pan Macmillan for their work on this project. A particular thank you to Laurie Whiddon at Map Illustrations for the maps in this book, which were created from a range of historical sources.

In addition, my thanks to Rod and Brett Hardy for their continuing support in advancing the *Dark Frontier* TV project.

For Kristie Hildebrand, who established my Facebook page so many years ago, *Fans of Peter Watt Books*.

A thank you to the members of the Volunteer Emergency

Services Legacy project: Nick Clark, John Riggall, Tania Peene, Geoff Simmons, Steve Walton and Mark Carr. Our legacy is an attempt to provide support for the families of all Australian volunteer first responders who have made the ultimate sacrifice. It is similar to military/police legacies. VESL can be found on the internet at www.veslltd.org.au as a registered charity for tax deductions. A thank you to Rea Francis and Michael for their support in this project.

Without the support of my cobber, Pete Campbell, my computer would not work. A special thank you to Pete and Pat Campbell.

Significant people I would like to acknowledge are as follows: Mick and Andrea Prowse, John Wong, Larry Gilles, John and June Riggall, Perry Peary, Megan Todd, Chuck and Jan Digney, Ken Martin.

For Rod Henshaw and Anna, a special thank you for your support and in the memory of a very special and wonderful lady, Sandy, taken from us too young.

To my family and extended family: my brother Tom and sister-in-law Colleen, and my nieces Shannon, Jess, Charlotte and Sophie.

My sister, Lindy, and her husband, Jock, as well as Jules and Anna down in Tassie. For Ty and Kaz McKee. The Duffy boys, Tony, Greg, Rob and John, and their families. Virginia Wolfe, Madison and Mitch, Tim Payne, Daniel Payne and family. Monique, Nate, Mila and Reah, and never forgotten over the many years, Robbie and Tony Hill.

Not to forget my Rural Fire Service Family and a tribute to all other first responder volunteers who give so much without asking in the face of danger.

My writer family of Dave Sabben MG, Tony Park, Simon Higgins, Greg Barron and Paul MacNamara.

Finally, but not least my love and thank you for my wife, Naomi, who reviews any romantic aspects of the original manuscripts.

MORE BESTSELLING FICTION FROM PAN MACMILLAN

The Queen's Colonial
Peter Watt

Sometimes the fate for which you are destined is not your own . . .

1845, a village outside Sydney Town. Humble blacksmith Ian Steele struggles to support his widowed mother.
All the while he dreams of a life in uniform, serving in Queen Victoria's army.

1845, Puketutu, New Zealand. Second Lieutenant Samuel Forbes, a young poet from an aristocratic English family, wants nothing more than to discard the officer's uniform he never sought.

When the two men cross paths in the colony of New South Wales, they are struck by their brotherly resemblance and quickly hatch a plan for Ian to take Samuel's place in the British army.

Ian must travel to England, fool the treacherous Forbes family and accept a commission into their regiment as a company commander in the bloody Crimean war . . . but he will soon learn that there are even deadlier enemies close to home.

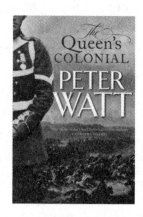

'One of Australia's best historical fiction authors' *Canberra Weekly*

The Queen's Tiger
Peter Watt

Peter Watt brings to the fore all the passion, adventure and white-knuckle battle scenes that made his beloved Duffy and Macintosh novels so popular.

It is 1857. Colonial India is a simmering volcano of nationalism about to erupt. Army surgeon Peter Campbell and his wife Alice, in India on their honeymoon, have no idea that they are about to be swept up in the chaos.

Ian Steele, known to all as Captain Samuel Forbes, is fighting for Queen and country in Persia. A world away, the real Samuel Forbes is planning to return to London – with potentially disastrous consequences for Samuel and Ian both.

Then Ian is posted to India, but not before a brief return to England and a reunion with the woman he loves. In India he renews his friendship with Peter Campbell, and discovers that Alice has taken on a most unlikely role. Together they face the enemy and the terrible deprivations and savagery of war – and then Ian receives news from London that crushes all his hopes . . .

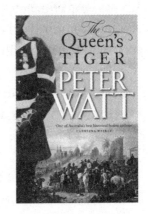

'Watt has a true knack for producing captivating historical adventures filled with action, intrigue and family drama'
Canberra Weekly

The Queen's Captain
Peter Watt

From India to America and New Zealand, action, intrigue and family drama.

In October 1863, Ian Steele, having taken on the identity of Captain Samuel Forbes, is fighting the Pashtun on the north-west frontier in India. Half a world away, the real Samuel Forbes is a lieutenant in the 3rd New York Volunteers and is facing the Confederates at the Battle of Mission Ridge in Tennessee. Neither is aware their lives will change beyond recognition in the year to come.

In London, Ella, the love of Ian's life, is unhappily married to Count Nikolai Kasatkin. As their relationship sours further, she tries to reclaim the son she and Ian share, but Nikolai makes a move that sees the boy sent far from Ella's reach.

As 1864 dawns, Ian is posted to the battlefields of the Waikato in New Zealand, where he comes face to face with an old nemesis. As the ten-year agreement between Steele and Forbes nears its end, their foe is desperate to catch them out and cruel all their hopes for the future . . .

'Australia's master of the historical fiction novel' *Canberra Weekly*

The Colonial's Son
Peter Watt

Danger, passion and bravery in nineteenth-century Australia, Europe and onto the battlefield of Kandahar.

As the son of 'the Colonial', legendary Queen's Captain Ian Steele, Josiah Steele has big shoes to fill. Although his home in the colony of New South Wales is a world away, he dreams of one day travelling to England so he can study to be a commissioned officer in the Scottish Regiment.

After cutting his teeth in business on the rough and ready goldfields of Far North Queensland's Palmer River, he finally realises his dream and travels to England, where he is accepted into the Sandhurst military academy. While in London he makes surprising new acquaintances – and runs into a few old ones he'd rather have left behind.

From the Australian bush to the glittering palaces of London, from the arid lands of Afghanistan to the newly established Germany dominated by Prussian ideas of militarism, Josiah Steele must now forge his own path.

'an adventure reader's delight . . . I was breathless as I read'
Central Western Daily

Call of Empire
Peter Watt

From the sands of Sudan to the veldt of South Africa in the Boer War, the Steele family face epic adventures and dangerous odds . . .

It is 1885. After a decade spent fighting for Queen and Country across the globe, Colonel Ian Steele is enjoying the quiet life in the colony of New South Wales, reunited with his friend Conan Curry and watching over his children and numerous business enterprises.

But the British Empire's pursuits are ceaseless, and when the colony's soldiers are required to assist a campaign in Sudan, North Africa, Ian's son Lieutenant Josiah Steele heeds the call, despite an ultimatum from the love of his life, Marian.

Meanwhile, Ian's younger son Samuel is learning the family business in the Pacific islands with his friend and colleague Ling Lee. However, Lee has become embroiled in a scheme to smuggle guns for the Chinese, which sees the pair sailing directly into danger in Singapore.

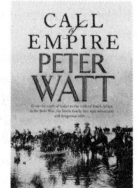

As the reign of Queen Victoria draws to a close and new battles loom on several frontiers, the Steele family must face loss and heartbreak like never before.

'An adventure reader's delight'
Central Western Daily